THE CAT WHO STOLE THE CREAM

THE CAT WHO STOLE THE CREAM

NICK SMITH

4 Horsemen
Publications, Inc.

Published By: 4 Horsemen Publications, Inc.

4 Horsemen Publications, Inc.
PO Box 417
Sylva, NC 28779
4horsemenpublications.com
info@4horsemenpublications.com

Cover Illustration by Oxford
Cover Typography and Typesetting by Autumn Skye
Edited by Kris Cotter

Library of Congress Control Number: 2024948141

Paperback ISBN-13: 979-8-8232-0720-1
Hardcover ISBN-13: 979-8-8232-0721-8
Audiobook ISBN-13: 979-8-8232-0723-2
Ebook ISBN-13: 979-8-8232-0722-5

Table of Contents

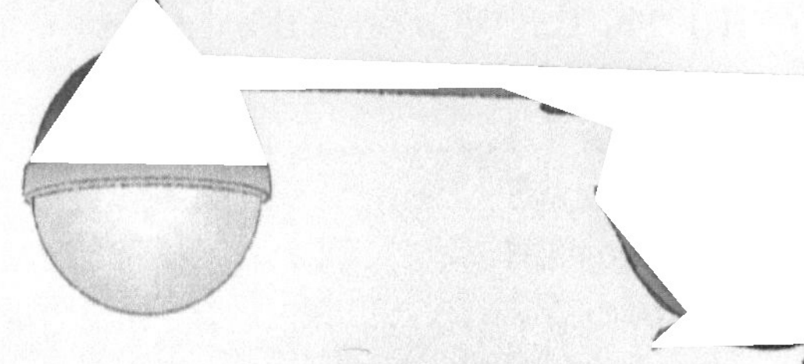

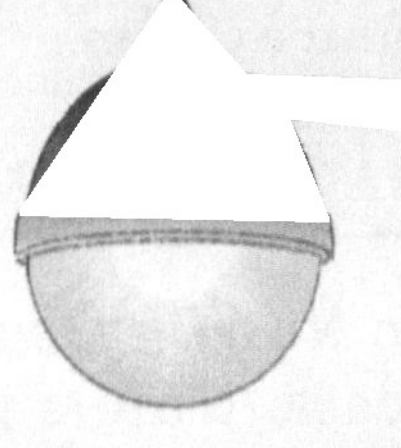

EVIDENCE:

PI Tiger Straight's reports on
surveillance of Trixie Bates

NUB CITY SHERIFF'S DEPARTMENT

Investigating Officer(s): Det. R. Murphy. Det. T.
Lamassu *Incident No.*: 000624-99A-2018

Case Description: Dawon Statuette Theft

Report from Private Investigator Tiger Straight
submitted to the Nub City Sheriff's Department in
response to a subpoena for same.

CASE DETAIL REPORT

Case Number: Bates23457

Hired Y/N: Y

Filed Y/N: Y

BACKGROUND:

Kept a low profile in Nub City, a crowded urban area ruled by civilized cats. Nub is progressive enough for mice to be tolerated before they are eaten.

Much of the food for the populace either comes from nearby dairies (where the cows, in this detective's opinion, talk too much) or from fishing villages on the coast. The valuable Dawon Statuette was smuggled via one such village to the home of private collector Trixie Bates, who took ownership of the *objet d'art*. Ms. Bates reported the statuette stolen last Tuesday night and has filed a sizeable insurance claim.

ACTIVITY REPORT:

Kept the subject, Trixie Bates, under surveillance for two days.

Wednesday: Subject left her upscale hillside apartment alone on foot. The cat wore a lemon-colored dress and a practical hat.

Subject visited her mother at the Silver Hairs retirement home for approx. one hour, then shopped at the neighboring strip mall. Subject spent at least an hour at the Horton Arts & crafts Supply Store before returning to her apartment. Large windows, so visual confirmation confirmed subject slept for approx. 15 hours.

Thursday: At approx. 7:30 a.m. subject went outside to sniff at a cardboard box in the alley behind her apartment block. She wore a faded blue housecoat and a polka-dot scarf tucked behind her ears. Subject curled up in the box and slept for another 6 hours. Posing as a stray, I checked box while subject was sleeping and noted paw prints sticky with an adhesive substance. Subject subsequently woke up, got bored, and went indoors, presumably to eat her supper. At approx. 2 p.m. monitored subject through window and saw what appeared to be pottery fragments. I conclude based on visual examination, that these were shards of the vase reported stolen. Subject drew curtains curtailing any further observation.

Photographic evidence available in Supplement A. Supplement A is not available to the public pending legal clearance.

FOLLOW-UP INFORMATION:

Posed as a Horton Arts & Crafts customer and friend of subject to ascertain from the supply store cashier that subject bought ceramic glue on Wednesday.

Questioned neighbor who heard a smashing sound on Tuesday. Coming from subject's apartment. Neighbor posited that it was "like pushing something off a table with your paw."

CONCLUSION:

Subject evidently broke vase and is in the process of repairing it with the glue. Insurance claim is fraudulent as theft never occurred.

Subject is guilty of making a false report to prowlers and pussyfooting around. Case closed. On to the next one!

Prologue

Nub City needed rain. The tangled streets were dark with grime, the buildings ugly with thick, persistent algae. Those cats fortunate enough to live in high-rise havens preferred to look up at the birds in the sky rather than down at the filth below. Down there, they'd see skinny houses crammed together like broken teeth, large, gray municipal buildings, the city hospital and zoo, and trams sparking their way along the main thoroughfares. On a clear day, they'd see cats padding about their business, crowding the food stores, fish markets, and office blocks. Beyond the city, the bayou stretched into the distance, wild and verdant, daring the citizens to venture into its soggy landscape. The cats preferred to stay on dry land, dreaming of catching brightly colored moths and fat swamp rats, watching the slow-moving creeks from their concrete haven. On a clear day.

Clear days were rare in Nub.

Tuna canning factories belched smoke and oil into the air, forming a salt-smelling fog that settled over the city. At night, incandescent lamps gave the fog an eerie sepia glow.

The glow was a siren sight for many. Sunshine was for sleeping; after dusk, Nub's citizens were wide awake. Night was when the litter-strewn city came to life. The darkness hid the danger or encouraged cats to seek it out. It was the time to prowl and explore.

For one detective, it was the best time to solve a mystery that placed his life, his loved ones, and his city in jeopardy. A mystery that would change him forever and threaten to wreck the world around him. It was the mystery of the cat who stole the cream.

1

They were killers, all four of them. Cammy was the worst—one jab of his claws and he'd spear his prey. What his brothers lacked in dexterity, they made up for in size and strength. They were complacent in their efficiency, looking professional as they stood upright, their thick ragdoll fur spooling from their matching overalls. None of them enjoyed death as much as Cammy.

He'd had a wicked glint in his eye since birth. Part of a litter of five, he'd practiced murder on ticks and ants before he could see. After suckling at his mother's belly, he'd cock an ear and listen for the scuttling—slap down a paw and flatten his catch. Not because he was hungry; it was in his blood. Killer instinct.

His brothers were made of kinder stuff. Beast, Grass, and Skead had never been malicious. They'd always been poor, and the Depression had made them poorer, so when Cammy had suggested going into the execution business, they'd agreed fast enough. They'd plowed every penny into the tools of the trade—traps, spray, electrified grids, powder—and set up shop. It hadn't taken them long to become the best bug bashers on the block.

Pest control was a dirty, thankless task. Cammy kept them motivated with his zeal. He loved to squash little critters, slice them, impale them, munch them up for supper. He'd remind his brothers they had a mortgage to cover, bills to pay, and a sister to support.

Beast never let his squeamish side get in the way of a commission. Some cats get excited when they see a termite, smack their lips, and dream of eating the little peckers. They know how good they taste. Beast would get a quiver in his belly, a queasy tremor as he watched the shiny bodies and spindled legs. He was no fan of bugs. If he unearthed a colony, he didn't hesitate to destroy it.

Grass was the crew's philosopher. Like Beast, he was quick enough to give his prey the chop. Maybe even take some home for supper. Once they were dead, his conscience would pay him a call. He'd start moralizing, wondering what right he had to snuff out so many lives—no matter how tiny. Eating them wasn't so bad, that was nature. So Grass was the crew's fat philosopher.

He'd share his worries with Skead, the most money-eager of the pack. Skead would tell his twin to stop blethering and buy something nice with his paycheck. Skead had tall hopes for himself; he was going to buy his way out of Skid Row, spend money in the right places, impress the bigwigs, and stake a place in the city. He hadn't shared his dreams with his brothers, but he did admonish them for spending so much of their earnings on paint and wallpaper for their sister's place. Keeping her happy seemed to make them happy.

The cats often worked late into the night—the critters they caught thrived in darkness. By the time they got home, all they wanted to do was collapse in their beds, looking forward to breakfast. They all knew what Grass was having.

One particular evening was spent knocking off rats. A cadre of the little terrors had run riot in a chip shop. The cats had stormed Arnie's Emporium, famous for its fishcakes; they'd battered the rats and carried them out by their tails, a crate-load of slick, filthy vermin carried to the local butchers. There the rats had been sold for a small amount, which Skead split into four pittances. He already had plans for his share.

At home, they found a package waiting for them. Marlax, a poison in powder form, and lots of it. None of the brothers could remember ordering the stock. Grass shrugged, promising he'd deal with it in the morning.

Exhausted, they hit the sack. Beast and Grass slept in one room; Cammy and Skead shared another. Come midnight, Beast thought he heard a stifled moan. He was about to get up and investigate when a paw clamped over his nose. He opened his mouth to warn his brothers, but no sound came.

Sinking into oblivion, he wondered if his victims felt the same fear, the same sense of disappointment. Of course not. The pests he killed weren't cats. They were plain dumb animals.

2

Doctor Selwyn Mopp was worried, a feeling with which he was unfamiliar. A proud Persian and veteran veterinarian, he enjoyed the respect of his peers and the general public. Even the gutter press treated him kindly, relying on him for comments on wide-ranging medical matters. He hadn't worried in his younger days, pioneering radical forms of medicine. He hadn't panicked while treating his patients as they lay on his operating table, fondly referred to by staff as the slab of doom. Cats clamored to be carved by him; if they lived, they'd be able to tell jealous friends they'd been saved by a surgeon named in all the history books.

Now Mopp was getting long in the claw, elderly pushing on for decrepit. In his late teens, his waning years, his paws had started to tremble. His eyes were muddy with myopia, his hearing shot. He was sure that some of his colleagues at the hospital suspected. The administrator for one: a quiet soul with the power to send him packing, get him struck off. Admiration and a place in history would mean nothing if he lost his monthly paycheck. He had a habit to support.

Mopp left the hospital as the sun reached its zenith. Lunch hour.

Most cats stretched the time as far as they could, filling their faces and taking a nap, ready to cope with an afternoon's drudge. For the doctor, it provided an opportunity for him to sate his urges.

Two minutes' trot from the ER was the high street, a Mecca of cash and carries, jewelry stores, and covered markets. He aimed for the large arcade at the far end of the street. His eyes swiveled in different directions, checking out the bargains in shop windows.

It had always amazed him that anyone would let him loose in an operating theater—if he couldn't control his eyes, how could he be expected to handle a scalpel? Of course, he could do his job, but his pupils liked to roll of their own accord. He didn't like to meet patients before operating on them; the eye thing had the potential to scare them off. He saw them (if he had the time) when the general anesthetic wore off instead. *Surgery successful. Thank you, Doc, you are a god. Is there something wrong with your eyes?*

They didn't work all that well anymore, sight wise. He had good days and bad, often having to press his face against the store windows to see displays. That wasn't what worried him so much as the atmosphere at his place of work.

Friends had stopped talking to him, giving him funny looks. He felt self-conscious where he would once have felt important. Certain doctors and nurses made sure not to work with him, especially where delicate transplants were involved. He'd dropped a few fresh organs—a heart, maybe a liver or two—but that was no reason for them to snub him. Once the flecks of dirt were brushed off, the organs still did their job. He had rivals, frontstabbers who majored in the mongering of rumors. His reputation was too strong to be eroded by gossip no matter how many boobs he made.

The first shop in the arcade sold dangly things. Mopp was well into these, although he quickly tired of each new purchase. They hung in a closet at home or ended up gift-wrapped for a relation. It was the act of buying the items that gave him the hots—and would get him into scalding water if he lost his position as Chief Surgeon at Nub City Infirmary. The lecture circuit would be fine for the occasional spree, but he needed a regular pay packet to feed his consumer habit.

Good afternoon, my name is Selwyn Mopp. I'm a shopaholic.

By the time he'd bought a dangly piece of merchandise and moved on to the second store, he was running out of time. He didn't need to buy anything; he had all the useful gizmos, clothes, and knickknacks he could ever want. There was no room left in his four-story house, chock full of trinkets. And there was something obscene about spending money frivolously while so many cats were out of work, their savings kaput after the austerity era of the Cod Wars. Banks foreclosed themselves, small cities went bankrupt; Nub itself was in a deep Depression, up to the tip of its tail in economic woe. Since no cat really wanted to work, unemployment was rampant, and the only stock of any value was the kind that came in beef cubes.

Nevertheless, a purchase made Mopp feel better; beat the waiting room blues. Every acquisition gave him a sprightly lift ... until he reached his credit limit. Then it was cold turkey until payday. The salary went into his account on a monthly basis; those thirty days could seem like nine lifetimes.

The second store, Feline Groovy, sold hippie fare—bead necklaces, incense burners, and environmentally friendly kitty litter. The owner raised his forepaws in dismay as Mopp bumped into a lava lamp.

"Watch out, dude! You break it, you pay for it."

The owner was Sonny, a shorthair Singapura with pink shades covering its big eyes, and a tie-dye sweatshirt over his ticked fur coat. He was a tiny, tan-colored dude, half the size of a regular cat, and he smelled crusty, like he hadn't washed himself in weeks.

There was no way any of the goods in the store could appeal to the doctor. A confirmed meatatarian, he'd never attended a give-peas-a-chance demo, never touched catnip like this hippie Singapura obviously had. He saw enough of the ill effects that drug could cause in the casualty ward. By the smell of things, the owner was burned out on the substance.

"What can I get for this?" Mopp asked, scattering his remaining change on the counter.

"Not a lot, effendi. Maybe one o' these." The hippie produced a sachet filled with gray powder.

"I don't partake of *nepeta cataria*," said Mopp, holding up his paws in protest.

"Hey, neither do I, effendi. Not on the record, anyway. This ain't that."

"It ain't? I mean, it isn't?"

"No siree Bobby Junior. This here," the hippie leaned in close enough for Mopp to gag at his breath, "is hard to find as a turtle's tuchus. It's finely ground mouse."

"Powdered mouse? Are you nuts? That's totally illegal!"

"Who's to know what you've got unless you tell 'em?"

Mopp barely hesitated. Ground mouse had a reputation. Its uncommon properties got some cats so excited that it sent them to the heights of ecstasy; it was frowned on in polite society.

"I'll throw in some Yummy Chunks, too, with extra yeast..."

"I'll take it." The sachet joined the dangly thing in a flashy shopping bag. It was time for Mopp to go back to work before someone spotted him. The operating theater was booked solid for the next six hours, with invalids already prepped. Although Mopp would have plenty of support, it was still his shift, the lives of the patients his responsibility. He would have to maintain his wits and stay away from the high street until the next opportunity presented itself. Late-night shopping on Thursday, maybe.

First on the slab of doom was a lardy fellow called Churchouse. Arteries hardened, heart in trouble, ugly as seven shades of silt. Mopp split him open with an intern's fervor, a tape playing the latest hit from hip-hop DJ Doctor Phat. The heart still beat, taking its time to pump its cargo around Mr. Churchouse's system. Mopp poked at it, jiggled it about a bit, then sewed the guy back together.

"I've done my best with this one," he explained to the nurse who licked his brow. "Next!"

Case number two was a lad who'd sewn his ears shut, an extreme protest against Prohibition, which banned the storage, transportation, and consumption of mice. The authorities saw Prohibition as a necessity; cats loved chasing and eating mice so much that the rodents had grown scarce. Rats were still plentiful, but mice were a no-no. Since no one had listened to the protester's initial, peaceful objections, he'd resorted to this stunt. Usually a case for the ER, this cloth-eared youth had left his wounds to fester. Delicate skin had grown around the infected areas, making the doctor's task a tricky one. He repaired the damage and neatened up the lobes without causing any loss of hearing. With luck and the chance to heal, the patient's aural faculties would be better than they'd been before the self-abusive act.

Miracle number three involved a punctured lung. Some careless tabby on a crowded tram had stabbed the patient with a long, filthy claw. Fortunately, the sheath had remained embedded in the chest, preventing any flooding of the lung. As Mopp fixed the mess, he grew tired. His paws quaked, and he forgot the names of important surgical instruments. Instead of forceps, he asked for chopsticks.

"Getting hungry, Doctor?" asked the anesthetist. He didn't mean anything by it, yet Mopp took it the wrong way, returning the comment with a glower.

What if I make a mistake? It was what he'd been dreading for months. *My paw could slip; I could forget what I'm doing, where I am. What if I have some terrible brain disease? I'll be scuppered for sure then. Ironic. I'd be the only one qualified to operate on myself around here. The only cat I trust.* Some days, he couldn't remember his own name. Knew it sounded like a household object, but that left the field wide open. The cleaners would know.

Mopp saved the patient, patching up the lung with help from an intern. By the time the fourth case was wheeled in, the doctor's sight was blurred. A John Doe had been attacked from behind; some ne'er-do-well had bitten a chunk out of his back. Mopp wanted to rest. He thought about the unnecessary items he'd purchased that day.

I'm a silly old cat. Got no business here, threatening innocent people's lives. Got to quit. He would write a letter as soon as he got home and hand in his notice in the morning. The administrator would enjoy that. First, he had to finish what he'd started.

Ensuring that the back and caudal bones were straight and secured on the operating table, Mopp removed all infected tissue and checked the sacral bones. Everything seemed in order, nothing severed. Placing gauze over the bite, he protected the wound from further harm. He was flying blind now, relying on instinct rather than his fuzzy sight. He could do this in his sleep, had done it a hundred times before.

"This *felis domesticus* unconscious mustn't be moved for some time, nurse. Please see that the details go on his chart."

Mopp's final job was a cosmetic one; an actor called Hairy Bancroft in for routine liposuction. By the time the surgeon was done, sitting panting in a narrow corridor, the windows were mottled with rain again. Staff entered the hospital drenched to the skin and unhappy. The wind was too strong for an umbrella to withstand, ready to turn it outside in, and wreck it in seconds. Rainfall levels were at a record high; the autumn seemed to be lasting forever.

After taking forty winks, Mopp stumbled to his office, taking care not to slip on the wet puddles left by dripping visitors. It wouldn't do for them to find him flat on his keister, even if it happened by accident. Reaching his sanctum, he found the administrator.

"Attabi!" Mopp exclaimed. "I don't think I heard you knock. Maybe because I wasn't here when you snuck into my room."

"You know I have the authority to rifle through your things if I'm in a nosy mood," the administrator replied in a light tone. "You have something to tell me?"

Mopp felt the weight of the hospital on his shoulders. This was his chance to come clean, express his fears to a cat who could sympathize... or destroy him. It wasn't worth the risk. He bottled out. "I don't think there's anything I want to discuss."

Attabi pursed his lips, tail coiling. "I've let you get away with a lot in this hospital," he said. "Allowed your reputation to buoy you up, as it were."

Mopp nodded carefully.

"I've turned a blind eye to your eccentricities, your lengthy lunch breaks, your outmoded opinions." Attabi drew closer to the surgeon. "You know why?"

"Because I'm your elder and better?"

"You are venerated, Doctor. I admire what you've done, the discoveries you made while I was still clamped to my mother's bosom. That's what makes this so difficult. I can't ignore what's going on in my institution, in this office. I have an obligation, by gum. You see that, don't you?"

I don't see much these days, Mopp thought, his eyes rolling about a bit. "I do," he told Attabi. "Clearer than I've seen anything in a long time."

"How d'you mean?" Attabi asked.

"I mean... I'm too old. Too run down to carry out my obligations." The surgeon cleared his throat, trying to look his boss in the eye. It wasn't easy. "My sight, hearing, and balance are all impaired. It's time I retired."

The administrator sank into a chair, brow furrowed. He lifted a plastic bag from the floor and dumped the contents onto Mopp's desk. "And you thought this could help?"

The doctor's shoulders drooped. He'd given the game away, spilled the beans and every other vegetable in his metaphorical allotment. Attabi wasn't interested in his age. He was staring at the sachet. "It's tough enough treating junkies in this place. We can't have staff addicted as well. Plus, if what you're telling me about your physical state is true... perhaps mouse powder has affected your health."

"You're probably right," Mopp said softly. "I'll clear out my desk in the morning."

"You can do it now," said Attabi. "I have more competent staff to concern myself with."

Mopp nodded slowly as the administrator left the room. He fell to the floor, licking up the contents of the sachet until there was no evidence left. All his personal bits and bobs fit in the carrier. He was surprised to find some loose change in a pencil holder. Wrapping himself in a heavy overcoat, he left the hospital and found himself back on the high street, tingling from his fix.

By now, all the shops were closed and only a few windows were lit. The wind blew the heavy rain sideways into his face, penetrating his coats. His paws were horribly damp. Attabi would probably sell his story to the papers, making a fast buck at Mopp's expense. It didn't matter anymore. Unable to pay his credit card bills and loans, the surgeon would soon receive a visit from the tailbreakers.

The hippie was heading the other way, a bobbly hat protecting his ears, squinting against the downpour. Mopp stopped him mid-lope.

"There's nothing open this time of night?" the doctor asked in desperation.

"Nah." The hippie paused. "I know you! Wrecked anything lately?" The hippie's eyelids were heavy with nip.

"Only my career." Mopp smiled sadly. "Kind of on purpose. So my boss wouldn't feel bad about firing me."

"It's never too late to hit restart, my friend. My dad's gone back to college. Dropped out when I was born. He's starting a whole new life."

"What's he studying?"

"Uh... dunno. Something to do with consumerism in contemporary society."

"A new career, eh?"

"Listen, effendi, you'll catch pneumonia stopping people in the street and talkin' small. I got to go."

"Sure, sure." Mopp watched the retailer turn a corner, disappearing into the gloom of a dripping side street. He followed the soggy moggy, and at the other end of the passageway, he saw one small gleam of hope. A shop was still open, selling frilly undies. A quick spend would relieve his despair for at least an hour.

There was no storekeeper inside, any hard sell. He slunk past the lacy lingerie and perused the thongs and see-through boxer shorts. The register was empty, its drawer sticking free like a dry black tongue. No sale. It didn't matter, he had to buy something. Picking a pair of briefs with a hand-stitched flap at the back for his tail, he placed his loose change in the cash drawer and shoved the pants in his soggy coat pocket.

He was about to leave when he spied a sign pointing towards the rear of the store: MORE BARGAINS THIS WAY. He couldn't resist. He heard distant, high-pitched voices shouting, "Heave! Heave!" as he made his way back past the frillies.

A low timber beam bopped his noggin. He let out a low growl—he would have an unsightly lump on his head. This had to be the unluckiest day of his life.

There were no goods out back; whoever was out there had booby-trapped the area. A long-handled fire ax was suspended from the timber, and as Mopp passed through, it swung down to cleave his head in two.

He lay on his back, staring at the ceiling. For once, both pupils were aimed in the same direction, although they were separated by several inches.

It wasn't easy finding a place to live in the overpopulated city. Plenty of folk were moving to the green belt, commuting to work. It made sense: there was more room out there, plenty of field mice, no pollution, no noise. The only snag was the travel time, wearing workers out before they reached the office. They blamed their bleary heads on the fresh country air.

In the boroughs of Nub City, cats lived virtually on top of each other. House prices were high, food was scarce, with cats lining up and crying for food and a soup kitchen on every second block. One in four cubs was born with chronic asthma. Most urbanites had adapted to their tough environment—they were used to the noise, breathed in scum, and got on well with their neighbors. They found the countryside too clean or quiet. They needed the sounds of trams and rowdy goons to lull them to sleep every night.

They didn't care about what went on when they hit the hay. When the sun went down, the streets turned black, and nocturnal citizens came out to play, to hunt. Disco kids looked for love; barflies and insomniacs hogged the milk bars. Strip joints flared into life, peddling exhibitionists. Females on heat! See the fur fly! Guaranteed six naked, musky mammaries! If you hung around the seedy streets long enough, you'd find drag queens, frisky kittens, cattle with unnatural appetites.

A detective named Tiger Straight spent the night in a diner lapping sour milk from a dirty dish, trench coat cinched around his waist, fedora at a tipsy angle, a terse expression on his gray mackerel tabby face, unable to doze with his head full of crimes unsolved.

As dawn grayed into existence, the red lights ebbed. Floozies stopped patrolling the streets. Cops swapped shifts and vulgar stories. Steel shutters tucked adult wares out of sight on all school routes. The youngsters were the shiftiest cats in Nub, stealing anything not nailed down, from spicy magazines to kitten carriers.

Drove Loan had once been a country lane. Hedged with green foliage, winding parallel to a bonny brook, it had linked two villages. The city had swallowed up the villages and the quaint little lane had been widened, resurfaced, and repaved. Now it was littered with cigarette butts and scattered treats, the sidewalks polka-dotted with hairballs hawked from the mouths of jaywalkers. The lane was cleaned once a week by a council employee who wasn't famous for taking pride in his work. For the rest of the week Drove Loan, like the borough it traversed, was left to fester.

An occasional tram rattled past Tiger Straight's apartment, threatening to loosen the windows from their frames. He wasn't fussed. A vase perched on the edge of the sideboard, ready to fall and shatter next time the 2R zipped past. He didn't care about that either. The vase could bleed all over the floor as far as he was concerned. He hadn't been back from the diner for very long, and he wasn't allowed to stay—he was having a final clear-out.

The windowpanes were muggy with dirt. They hadn't been cleaned for three weeks. Tiger had paid the cleaner off on his last visit, explaining that he couldn't afford him anymore. Unless the cleaner was willing to work for free, the windows would have to go unbuffed.

Tiger had gone without fresh milk for a few days as well. He'd left a note for the dairy, which was quite content to deliver pints to his home as long as he paid off his tab on a monthly basis. The tab had got extremely long that year, and when a couple of heavies had arrived in a milk float to settle the bill, he'd had to explain his financial situation to them. Bottles were no longer delivered to his address. Not that he had one, officially speaking. He was being evicted.

Tiger's apartment was fully furnished. It came complete with a leather Chesterfield, an antique standard lamp, a king-size bed, and a scratching post. The walls were decorated with beautifully crafted streamline *moderne* artwork, as well as a painting of apes playing pool. The place had central heating, double-glazing, and a mirror-lid television. None of it belonged to Tiger.

One bounced rent check, that's all it had taken. It wasn't the fact that he hadn't had the money to pay his landlord. The returned check had got him evicted, and there was only one possession that he cared to keep. It sat in a long tan case, carefully cushioned to stop it rattling.

Losing your home is a stressful experience, so he aimed to get some relaxation. The best place for that had to be the communal sunbaths. As long as you had a chunk of raw meat for the leopard at the door, he'd give you a sleep rug and beckon you in. Tiger picked a spot where he'd have plenty of space to roll about, flopped his rug down, and lay on his back, gazing up at the multiple skylights. They let in rivers of sunlight, raying the cats around him with heat to soothe the most savage aches.

He flexed his paws, warmth suffusing his body. His tail went limp. He panted softly, keeping himself cool. Other cats blinked at him, broad smiles on their faces. Everyone in the baths seemed content.

Tiger was about to drift off when a fat voice aroused him. "I've been looking for you, Mr. Straight."

Tiger gazed up, eyes already beginning to gum with slumber. The voice belonged to a broad bobcat with a towel wrapped around his waist.

"If you're looking for a bathing buddy," Tiger drawled, "you picked the wrong cat."

"Too hot in here for me," said the bob, licking his paws. "If I wanted this kinda heat, I'd move to the jungle. I'm from the letting agency, Mr. Straight. Your office's rent's in arrears. You're hereby instructed to clear your stuff outta there and stay out."

Tiger closed his eyes, frowned a little. First his apartment, now the office. How was a detective supposed to pay the bills with no clients and no prayer of an overdraft? His brothers didn't have this kind of trouble. They were all engineers, soldiers, and civil servants. They were able to go for a bath without being harassed by creditors.

This particular debt collector was a zealot with a capital ZZZ. He waited for his charge to get up, wash the sweat from his fur, snatch up the tan case, and head out of the honey-lit building. Tiger stopped at the exit, handing his rug to a muscle-bound leopard.

"You want to watch that bob over there," Tiger whispered to the big cat. "He don't like your kind. Called you a spotty nose heel." The leopard growled and padded over to deal with the letting agent. Tiger headed for his office, situated in an old, condemned building near Totterdown.

The office was furnished with a walnut desk, a tattered seat cushion, and a goldfish bowl. Tiger dipped a paw into the bowl, scaring the finned inhabitant out of its meager wits. The detective wasn't hungry yet; he'd wait until teatime.

The desk was full of files, records of past glories, and recent bills. He placed his tan case on the desktop, then tore up late reminders and bank statements. One or two folders fell open, revealing their contents like fleet memories. The Case of the Monkey's Uncle, the Rodeo Pirates, the Married Martinet—that file could never see the light of day again. Into the trash, it flew.

A dirty mirror hung above the goldfish bowl. Tiger caught his reflection. The trench coat was disheveled, his whiskers out of place. His fur, gray with concentric black rings, was matted from the day's heat. He felt clapped out.

Back to the files, more rubbish for the tin bin: the Cartoon Conundrum, the Golden Dog, the Living Dustbins, the Goat Train. All mysteries solved by the detective in better, more lucrative times. The prowlers, Nub City's police force, had come to him for answers, and he'd sold them at a premium rate. Now the rigors of the Depression had drained the cops' coffers, all his income had dried up, and his brains were half daft with too many riddles. His reputation had dissipated with the last generation of quick-witted peelers. His partner had left to study entomology.

Once the last folder had been shoveled into the bucket, Tiger struck a match and dropped it in. The pyre crumbled into ash, releasing a satisfying sigh. A red glow was mirrored in his lime-green eyes. About time the office got some heating of its own.

"Bored, Mr. Straight?"

Tiger turned with a start. He hadn't heard the dame enter, despite keen hearing. The ragdoll was perched on the edge of the desk, her tail coiled tight, a thin red dress covering her ginger fur. Tiger stood up, offered her the cushion. She was happy on her perch.

"I'm closing up, ma'am," Tiger drawled. "No fire sale, no retirement due. I'm out of here."

"Just as soon as you've heard my piece." The detective tried to keep an eye on the smoldering paper. It was hard with the distraction on his desk. She talked fast, even for a broad—life or death fast, as if he was the only private investigator in the book. He settled back to listen, not that he had much choice.

"I know you've got a handle on the Totterdown district," said the dame. "You solved more cases than a hundred cops down that way." Maybe she was older than she looked. "My mother done told me. You know Argyle Street, the way it breaks off into so many tributaries—little arched alleys and crossroads where no good is happy to take place?" She gave Tiger time to nod, then went on. "I know it too, 'cause my four brothers lived there. Cammy, Beast, Grass, Skead. They ran a pest control business. They don't control anything anymore.

"These boys were respected; if they were short of dough and the tax was due, the neighbors would help 'em out. Totterdown's like that. My brothers always paid folk back and made an honest living, as honest as can be in this part of town. They had no enemies, as I can think of, apart from the wee critters they exterminated. All the same, I was visiting them last week (they were out of milk, and you know how sour a tomcat gets when he ain't got a saucer to sup). I picked up seven pints from the dairy. Came up to their house, a place with stained roof tiles and rot in the walls. I let out a halloo. No answer. Slunk inside—not a breath. I checked the kitchen, the dining room. Nothing.

"Upstairs they were. Upstairs laid in their beds, looking so peaceful. They were dead, Mr. Straight. Killed." The visitor pulled a silk handkerchief from who-knew-where and dabbed her eyes. "Some freak tied them down, forced them to eat their own poison. The prowlers don't give a hoot, which only leaves me. I heard you were closing down, came here quick. Wondered if you wanted to end your career in a blaze of glory. Find the murderer and mete out some Argyle-style justice."

The detective was enthralled by the story. So caught up that he'd allowed the flames to spread from the bucket up the side of the desk. Now it singed his tail and made him jump.

"Excuse me!" He raced down the corridor until he found a discarded litter tray. It was full of sand and well used. Barging back past his would-be client, he threw the contents onto the fire. They didn't set it back by much but created a terrible stench.

"Not mine. Honest." Tiger yanked the frail out of his office, and they made for the street. "The building was getting old anyway," he said. "I wish you'd turned up a week ago, honey. Coulda paid my insurance."

The broad looked bashful. "I don't have any dough. I was hoping that blazing end to your career stuff would be enough to—"

"To sucker me in," sighed Tiger. She nodded. "Close," said the detective. "Bed and board, that's all I need. A floor to sleep on and a bite to eat. No things attached."

Not every female trusted a tom enough to let him spend the night in her home. Connie Hant knew Tiger's honest rep, and she needed to find a killer. Stowing a PI in the spare room sounded like a great idea.

"You're hired," she said with a mischievous smile. Tiger liked that smile a lot.

3

Another day, another new hotel.
For the past few years, Cole had been sinking money into leisure. It was a growth industry, booming despite the collapsed economy, or so his financial advisors said. Cats needed a distraction from their financial troubles. So Cole's corporation had funded hotels, casinos, saunas, and sunbaths, all in the hope that tourists would take the bait.

They came. They weren't to know that Totterdown had once been the poorest part of the city. There were still some dodgy back streets if you cared to take a walk on the wild side. Cole aimed to keep his guests in the hotels and their surrounding compounds, eating and gambling there. That way, his investments would eventually pay off.

He liked to oversee the building work—the laying of the first keystone, the last roof tile, the final double-glazed window. The workers' morale received a boost, and he felt that he had done some work.

Truth to tell, his business ran itself. He was called upon to make a decision or two—invest here, sell a subsidiary there. He attended board meetings, business lunches (lots of business lunches), press gatherings, and functions. Not real work, nothing that stretched his mind. Only detection did that.

Cole Tiddle, an ebony Bombay with short hair soft as velvet, grand viveur, debonair cat-about-town, enjoyed nothing better than solving a mystery. He had fallen into the trade, helping clueless employees, tracking down debtors, and finding stolen diamonds as effortlessly as he would scratch a fleabite. The papers loved his successes, and he quickly buried his failures.

This week, he'd retrieved a lost mongoose, unmasked a flasher on a rollercoaster ride, and foiled a blood bank robbery. The hotels had still opened on time, and Tiddles Inc. made a constant profit. No sweat.

His hobby wasn't born of boredom or a desire to help the common moggy. He had a skill for intelligent detection, a rare gift that he would have been churlish to hide. It was a gift to be shared with the prowler department, the press, and a stranger in trouble. He could afford to devote a lot of time to aiding them. If he received praise and good PR in return, then fine. If a couple of professional dicks were put out of work as a result... tough kitty.

Although Cole had never known hunger, he kept himself lean and well-toned. He stuck to a tough fitness regime every morning in his private gym. He'd had his wine cellar converted in his youth, and although the equipment was now several years old, it was still in good working order—tail weights, a whisker stretcher, a tummy rubber. His routine was consistent and repetitive: he'd stretch his limbs, complete several circuits at a run, then climb a wooden column in the center of the gym. The column sported stubby branches that he would chew and scratch. His body was toughened daily, and he practiced martial arts with disciplined aplomb.

Today, his muscles ached for action. He'd rushed his dawn routine to get to the building site, offering the builders a superior nod, giving his new hotel a cursory inspection. The Duncan looked sturdy enough, shiny, welcoming. A room there would be costly, but the guests who could afford it would be pampered. The reception desk was already polished and primed. An envelope addressed to Cole sat next to the register book.

He opened the note and gave it a sniff. Room 203. One of his many lady belles, without a doubt. Hopping into a paternoster elevator, he hoped she was one of the young impulsive types, the kind who let loose at lunchtime.

No floozy in Room 203. All Cole found was a ball of wool, placed tantalizingly on the bed. He sat beside it, pawed it a little. It rolled away. Stilling it with his other paw, he watched the loose end of the yarn. It didn't move. He crushed it between both paws, losing his composure, twisting his hind legs around so that he could use all fours. In his excitement, he fell from the bed, rankling the carpet, panting in a tangled heap of wool.

Enough. He was a grown tom with responsibilities and a respectable family. Separating himself from the tempting web, he chanced a last anguished look before leaving the room.

So what, Cole thought as he left the hotel compound. *We all let our fur down sometimes. All males are kittens deep down. I was getting in touch with my inner cub.*

As he took his personal tram home, Cole knew he'd done wrong. He resolved to restrain himself in the future. The resolution made him feel safer, and he relaxed for a cross-city nap. His folly had tuckered him out.

4

C onnie Hant resided on Lavis Lane, in a one-bedroom apartment with no mod cons. Bead curtains were draped over the entranceway, offering her scant privacy from the other fifteen families living in her tenement.

In an attempt to brighten the gloomy apartment, she'd tried her paw at a spot of home improvement. Her brothers had pitched in, painting the lounge a sunflower yellow, the bedroom pink, everywhere else white. She'd stenciled bluebird silhouettes on the kitchen cupboards. The white showed every hair, and she felt embarrassed if friends visited while she was molting.

She felt strangely comfortable with her new guest—perhaps due to his role as confidant. She was the first to admit that she was a user. When she wasn't relying on her brothers, she was cared for by one of her jellybeans. She never planned on exploiting them, yet it had happened with the last two beaux. She wasn't much good at holding down a job, doing what the boss told her, acting obsequious. She was a free spirit, getting up when she wanted to, and working when she had to.

A regular salary was alien to her. The males in her life had always brought home the bacon, indulged her whims. She'd cultivated a helpless manner that turned the blokes to blancmange. Their wallets were hers.

Connie would have been quite happy to settle down with one of those partners, but they never stuck around long enough. Her brothers had been overprotective at times, making threats, and throwing garbage at passing suitors. She knew they were only kidding, testing the mettle of the prospective hubbies. The mates she'd dated obviously didn't have mettle heavy enough to withstand the Hant cats' taunts, as they'd soon given her the boot. Now the brothers were gone, perhaps her love-luck would change.

Tiger was the first male to spend the night in her apartment that year. She was pretty, and her assumed ditziness made her all the more desirable. The detective hadn't made a play for her yet, and she was beginning to wonder if he'd been neutered. His lack of interest was exasperating; his grizzled good looks certainly held her attention. There was no way she was going to make the first move, that was for sure. Besides, he had no money; unless he won the lottery, he was no good to her.

Tiger had dutifully slept on a pile of cushions in the lounge, woken by sunlight peeking through Venetian blinds. He grabbed himself a salmon for breakfast, prowling the streets before Connie was awake. A female of leisure. He liked that. Without her brothers to pay the rent, she'd soon be begging for work. He liked that less.

His main aim was to solve his final case before he wore out his welcome with Connie. To do that, he had to visit the zoo.

Nub City Zoological Park had once been a botanical garden. Visiting cats had stripped the trees clean of bark and chewed on plants until they withered, despite protesting signs. Although the gardens had long since been filled with exotic fauna, a few notices still remained:

NO ROLLING ON THE GRASS, DO NOT FEED THE VISITORS, CAT CHORUSES PROHIBITED.

Unfortunately, most of the animals were more edible than the plants they'd replaced. They were carefully separated from the public by a deep moat. The zoo animals could roam freely on their own little islands, their food funded by entrance fees. Only one group of inhabitants couldn't be contained this way.

The keeper who took care of these creatures was so dedicated that she took on some of their characteristics. That would have been fine if her charge had been a wombat or a walrus. Natasha Lindsay's wee ones were insects.

They lived in a vast conservatory, all tinted glass and humidity. They weren't cooped up for malicious reasons; many of them had been rescued from bogs or tram accidents, nursed back to health. For safety reasons, glass stood between the bugs and cats who would have dearly loved to eat them.

Although it was clear some arachnids were capable of intelligent thought, insects lived a link farther down the food chain. The conservatory contained ladybirds, locusts, beetles, midges, and many more species besides. Natasha ate none of them; her love of insects was too great. She'd even taken to wearing a Deely bobber on her head, two fluffy antennae attached to an Alice band by springs, so the insects wouldn't see her as a threat. A daft theory, but as far as she was concerned, she was there to experiment. She was the only entomologist in the city.

Natasha was obsessed enough to earn herself a nickname. Colleagues called her Bug. The name had stuck since her schooldays when she'd spent more time talking to the flies on her desk than listening to her teacher. She didn't care. She could think of worse monikers.

Her current study was an environmental one, encouraging grasshoppers and crickets to live together in a patch of long grass. It was a noisy experiment.

The only visitor to the zoo that morning was Tiger. He was pleased to find Natasha up so early, looking bright and bushy-eared. She was crawling past the long grass, examining a roll of dung left by an errant beetle.

"You get more like your bugs every day." Tiger unbuttoned his trench coat, enjoying the greenhouse heat.

"How would you know? You don't see me every day," Natasha replied, snatching off her Deely bobber.

"Only 'cause of the entrance fee. Times are stiff: you know that. I had to close the business."

"Shame." Natasha packed away a magnifying glass.

"There's one last crime to fight. I could do with some help."

Natasha looked at her old boss. He had to be winding her up.

She'd resigned from her investigative assistant role at the detective agency, and he knew she'd taken the zoo job to make some cash and revive her original career, where her passion truly lay. She'd never made a good PI sidekick. She was Bug.

"You make a great sidekick," Tiger offered with his most charming grin. "You see the little things, the delicate details that everyone misses. Look a place over with me today. That's all I want."

"Where?" She could have kicked herself. She knew what curiosity could do to a cat.

"Off Argyle Street. It ain't that bad," Tiger stressed before Natasha could protest. "In daylight. Five minutes. It'll do you good to take a break from these creepy crawlies."

Oh dear. It was never a fine idea to insult Bug's best friends. She scooted Tiger out of the conservatory and got on with her work.

5

There was no moonlight in this part of the city, only neon and flickering streetlamps and dreams of butter-smothered tuna. Those lights felt fainter every night. The streets were slicked with dirty rain puddles, the gutters clogged long ago by trash the garbage cats didn't care to pick up. Although Totterdown was part of their route, most Ithacats refused to venture into the district.

That was a pity. Usually, Ithacats were respected for their hard work and aptitude. Like all the feline inhabitants of Nub, they had four toes on each back paw to help with agility, running, and jumping. Instead of five digits on their forepaws, however, they had six, enabling them to pick up objects and manipulate them in ways a normal cat could not. This made Ithacats perfect mechanics, tailors, and jewelers. The most sought-after job among them, however, spoken of in hushed whispers by regular cats, lauded by parents as a model role for their kittens, feted in the papers, quickly filled when a position opened up, was the hallowed *métier* of garbage collector.

The polydactyl cats worthy of this trade could collect trash faster than anyone else in the city, but they didn't just use their paws. They used their tails to sweep the sidewalks, their tongues to scrub their trucks clean, and their keen eyes to look for litter and the prizes that lived within all that nasty trash. They found lost necklaces and bracelets, scrap to sell to the local junk dealer, medals and weapons from the Cod Wars, and best of all—rats!

The rats were prevalent, especially in the fancier parts of town, having escaped from stores and restaurants, hiding and breeding in alleys and basements, out to feed on garbage day. The Ithacats took care of them all, chasing and catching them, devouring as many as they could, saving the rest in Ziplocs for later. This was why the profession was so revered; none had better perks than this.

Only time was against them. It was tough for the Ithacats to keep moving, avoid toying with their food, and ignore the morsels squeaking in remote holes, letting them live to scurry for another day. Totterdown, with its partly gentrified mess of buildings and half-built new homes, was the perfect place for rats to play hard to get. The garbage cats tended to leave Totterdown off their schedule until the neighborhood complained. Then they'd come around for a cursory sweep, or better yet, send in their rookies to complete the meticulous task.

Tim Tierney was the unluckiest rookie in the Public Works Department. He was the smallest cat recruited in living memory, a dark-furred tabby with light brown paws and a cappuccino chest. Black fur around his eyes made him look permanently sad, accentuating his often-bemused state. He'd been smart enough to know when his neighbors made fun of his extra toes. When they weren't mocking his polydactyly, they picked on his diminutive stature; only his next-door kittenhood friend, a Savannah called Lona Dash, had stuck up for him as they roamed the Straylite Rest Trailer Park where they grew up, play-fighting together, pouncing and batting at each other—with his big paws, Tim was always the better batter.

"Not so rough!" Lona had told him with a smile.

"No fair," Tim had replied. "You're so tall, I can barely reach your face."

"Okay, Little Tim!"

Reaching maturity, the two cats had stuck together, playing outdoors as often as possible. It was Lona's mother who had discouraged her, pointing out that it was time for Lona to grow up and find someone her own size to hang with. Between pressure from her mother and the lure of the young male cats in the park, Lona had seen little choice but to turn on her friend.

"You still spending time with that munchkin?" one ruffian had asked.

"Who, you mean Little Tim?" Lona had replied. "I call him Little for short. Get it? Little, for short?"

The cruel nickname had spread all the way to Tim's new workplace, where his colleagues were more interested in his potential than his shortcomings. Since Tim didn't spend much time thinking about his size, he was surprised by his moniker's popularity. He accepted it. Little Tim.

Tim's forepaws splayed out when he used them, soft pads surrounded by fluff, making his paws look larger and more clumsy than they really were. Few places would have seen this as a plus except the Public Works recruiters who snapped him up as soon as he was old enough to carry a trash bag. In fact, Tim could carry a few at a time if he needed to. Neighbors be damned.

He had found somewhere he was wanted, and he was determined to please his employers. Working for local government meant decent paychecks, especially for a cat as young as he was, job security (the city would never run out of garbage), and those perks, perks with pointy faces, perks with tails. The tasty rats made any bad smells or cranky residents bearable. There was nothing Tim liked better than a juicy, little rat.

When Tim was sent into Totterdown, he didn't know what to expect, but he jumped at the chance to impress his new bosses. He was still on probation, after all; an unknown quantity, lumped in with all the lazy felines of his generation until he proved his worth. He would prove it that morning, cleaning up a crazy-paved, sloping neighborhood with a pushcart to fill and a deadline to meet. Four blocks by high noon. He was determined to finish early and be back at the city dump with a full cart and plenty of energy for the chores to come.

Tim lost a bit of his vigor when he reached Argyle Street. Black trash bags sat in the gutter, some split, all sagging. He imagined fumes rising from some of them. Flies buzzed around the litter that was piled against one wall, with stray clumps of grit scattered on the sidewalk.

I'm not putting my tail near that, Tim thought. He had plenty to work on, hefting the trash bags into his cart and snapping up a little brown insect that turned out to be a chunk of an old welcome mat. The fibers caught in his mouth, and he stuck his tongue out, shaking his head until the lump dropped into his cart.

So much trash. He was going to need a second cart at this rate. By the time he went to the dump and fetched another, an hour would be lost. He realized what an impossible task he'd been set.

Confusing.

He would do his best. He would keep working until his blocks were clean, and if that made him late, he was sure his boss would understand. No cat likes to keep a calendar or stick to a set schedule. Why expect Tim to do so?

Cats do not use packaging, as a rule. They don't want to waste time opening a container when they can start eating instantly. Beside the trash bags, Tim found fishbones, stripped ribs, cigarette ends, and empty milk bottles cluttering up the sidewalk. By the time he'd cleaned Argyle Street, the sun was high in the sky and he was exhausted. This had to be some kind of initiation.

The second block was worse. Tim scooped up rotten eggshells and corn husks, taking care not to get anything nasty on his fur. He dumped slimy banana peels and cantaloupe seeds in a bag and squeezed that into his cart, which already bulged with waste. He stopped for a breather, licking his paws and drawing them slowly over his head.

Two more blocks, he told himself. *Two more blocks, and it's not noon yet. The boss will understand.*

Like all cats, Tim's peripheral vision was excellent, with a 200-degree field of view. He'd always spotted the neighborhood bullies sneaking up on him, escaping before they overpowered him with their greater size and number. As he cleaned up, he noticed a blur of movement under a worn flap of cardboard resting up against the Totterdown Pavilion.

Tim went into predator mode, inching his way toward the cardboard, low to the ground, watching for further movement. Was that...? Had he imagined it, or was the cardboard moving slightly? He sprang forward, just as he'd practiced so many times with Lona. He batted the cardboard aside, revealing a plump rat gnawing on a ricotta rind. It was hard to tell how old the cheese was, covered in mauve-colored mold. The rat was enjoying it, no matter the age; so much so that it held the cheese in its teeth as it ran under the pavilion.

Tim followed.

The pavilion was an old theater with plenty of nooks for rats to shelter in. Tim was small enough to squat down and venture under the building, past a loose metal vent, through a rectangular hole into a wide crawlspace full of junk treasures like screws, springs, coils of wire, and wheels of stinky cheese. Tim wanted to cover his nose with his paw but there wasn't room or time; he needed both his paws free to catch his treat, and he had to get back to his job, pronto.

He stopped, listening for signs of life. He heard a scuffle in the far corner of the crawlspace. His pupils expanded, letting as much light in as possible so he could peer into the corner. The rat was there, hiding in the dark. Tim moved deeper into the space, drooling with excitement.

Knowing it was cornered, the rate shook, nerves jangling, body jolting a step forward. It would bite Tim if the cat came too close. Tim didn't care. He was hungry, and he couldn't understand why the rat was so anxious. This was the natural order of life, after all, with predator and prey dancing a nocturne. Better for this tidbit to accept the inevitable, cut the fuss, and allow itself to be eaten.

So confusing.

Tim didn't bother with the whole creeping-and-pouncing bit this time. He moved lightning-fast into the corner in seconds, sweeping the rat into his mouth and biting down, hard. His first meal of the day, but not his last; the rat was not alone. He heard more movement and saw a tail flit by. He was ecstatic. The crawlspace was a home for many rodents, and the rat Tim had hunted was the first course in a lengthy meal.

It took Tim a while to squeeze back out into daylight. Not only was his belly full of rat, but he also dragged a half-pack by the tail out of the building, slinging his catch on top of his cart. He would take these home to share with his family and even with Lona, if she would accept a gift from her bullying victim.

The sun was directly above him now. He hadn't hit his deadline. But he'd gained something far more precious—the knowledge that the rumors were true. The perks of being a garbage cat did include all the rats he could eat. Full of protein and bravado, he felt ready to face any complaint the boss could throw at him. He pushed his cart back to the dump, singing his favorite song, "Vicki Eating."

> "On the other side of the line,
> "All I hear is munching.
> "On the other end of the call,
> "No words, just crunching.
> "I can't get in a word.
> "She's chewing on a bird.
> "Our conversation's fleeting,

"'Cause Vicki's busy eating."

"She ignores the pips,
"With feathers on her lips.
"Puts more quarters in the slot,
"A quarter pounder's what she's got.
"A cat after my heart,
"A gourmet from the start.
"Now when I ring her bell,
"My mouth is full as well."

After Tim dumped his garbage, he went to the Public Works Director's office and explained that he needed a fresh cart to finish his run.

"You're going to have to work faster," said the boss, a white Aegean called Anatolios. "Pick up the pace, Little Tim, or find other work. We've got plenty of cats waiting to take your job if you can't handle it."

So even the boss knew him as Little Tim. Great. Anatolios didn't complain when Tim gave him a rat snack, but the rookie still had a lot to do to earn his stripes and keep his perks. He worked all afternoon to clean the third and fourth blocks on his list, finding plenty more trash and rats in the process.

Tim couldn't bring a cart home with him, but he was able to borrow a sack from work, fill it with the rats he'd caught but didn't have time to eat, and bring them home in triumph. Some of them were fresh, wriggling to escape and gnawing at their canvas prison, but Tim got them all back intact.

That evening, at least, the neighbors were impressed with him. He had enough rats to share with all the older cats in the trailer park, with a few left over for the bullies, who took more from their elders. Tim hoped his generosity would encourage them to see him in a new light and stop calling him names.

After passing out his booty, he sat alone in his trailer, eyes drooping. He'd missed his daily nap, and he was feeling weary. If he got to sleep right away, he'd be able to snatch 12 hours; not enough for a cat to fully recuperate, but enough to keep him going for another day.

A perky knock on the trailer shell made his eyes snap open. Lona wanted to come in.

"Got any more of those sweet treats?" she asked, ducking her head to enter the trailer.

Tim had been saving one last rat for a midnight feast. He gave it to Lona instead.

"This isn't your last one, is it, Little Tim?" Lona asked.

Yes, Tim thought. *And I'd appreciate it if you'd stop calling me Little Tim.*

"No," Tim lied.

"You're very kind, handing out all your goodies," said Lona, brushing a paw over the kitchen counter, remembering past playtimes. "Mother wouldn't have done that. She would have kept all the catches for herself."

"What about you?" Tim wanted to know. "What would you have done?"

"I'm still figuring that out." Lona sighed. "The differences between me and Mother. How much of her is in me, and how much I decide things for myself. You're lucky. You don't have that problem."

"No orphan is lucky," said Tim, puzzled. "You're tough on your mom. She might have shared these rats; you don't know for sure. You might too."

"She's always saying I'm too loud, that I'll wake Father. She even says I laugh too loud! I need space, Tim." Lona lowered her voice. "I want to run away."

Tim nodded. Cats needed freedom. "To do that, you need resources," he said. "Public Works is hiring."

Lona laughed loud enough for her mom to hear next door. "Me, work with trash?" she scoffed. "I don't know if I'm like my mother, but I'm definitely not like you." She bit into the rat, its tail waving in distress. "You don't know any better. That's why you'll always be Little."

Tim watched Lona leave. He sat alone, tail drooping, listening to the sounds of jollity outside. He had brought happiness to his neighborhood, surprise treats, and a reason to celebrate. For now, at least, he was known as Little by many and a hero to a few.

His stomach rumbled. Part of him wished he had kept the last rat for himself, but that wasn't in his nature. And he could get more—he would get more—rats in the morning.

Until then, he slept alone, lulled into dreams by nighttime laughter.

Cats aren't natural farmers. Plowing and planting goes against the grain. They're hunters, chasing prey, eating meat. The only thing they like better than hunting is sleeping. Farmers rise early, go to bed late. Not typical feline behavior.

The stores needed cereal, plants, and milk, and somebody had to produce them. Unemployment being high, Old Scrumpy Dean had been forced to take their pay and till some land. Grocery stores—pah! He had no time for them except on payday.

The work wasn't all bad. The shorthaired barn cat had salvaged an electric plow with a remote control. When the batteries died, he pulled the plow himself or got Nut to do it.

Scrumpy was a big tom. His muscles developed from sowing and reaping. Not many would trifle with him. He left deep paw marks in the soil as he crossed his largest field, heading for the cowshed. Scrumpy brooked no nonsense. A plain-speaking animal, he believed in the value of verbal agreements. Once he'd licked his paw and shaken on a deal, it couldn't be broken. He liked to get his farming over fast so that he could go home, spending most afternoons curled up in front of the fire. His hearthrug bore a bald patch where he lay. He had no phone and no television. He enjoyed the peace and solitude of the countryside; they were the only things that made his job bearable. Most of his cattle were well-behaved, if peevish, and only one cow needled him every single morning; a maverick named Nut.

Nut was a sassy cookie, always complaining. The only time she didn't moan was when she was being milked. That was because Scrumpy yanked real tight on her udders.

"Easy there darling," she'd giggle. "I'm starting to enjoy myself."

"Shut up, you dumb Friesian. I'd kick your keister, only it's so fat I'd probably lose my boot." Banter like this helped keep Scrumpy sane. He had a lot of milking to do—a herd of cows, complaining all the time. *Moo, when you going to get heating in this barn? Moo, the strip lights are hurting my eyes. Moo, I've got a cramp—can you massage my hooves a little?* Nut was the worst, always edging for a better deal.

"I see my insurance premiums have gone up again," Nut noted.

"Ain't nothing to do with me," hissed Scrumpy.

"We got a deal, darling. We all know how I'll end up. No use denying it." Some of the other cows clamped their ears down in annoyance. "Come winter, I'll be a crate load of Yummy Chunks. Only reason I'm going along with this is for the insurance. In the event of my slaughter, my calves will be well provided for." Nut batted her long eyelashes.

"So what's yer problem?" asked Scrumpy, loading pails of milk onto a pallet.

"These premiums don't level out. I'm paying loads more than I should for the same end amount."

"Blame the banks." Scrumpy spat in one of the buckets. "Blame the sunken stock market. Blame the darned superstores if you have to."

"There is an alternative. Double indemnity."

"The game show?"

"No, silly," the cow snorted. "It's a clause in my insurance. I get murdered, *my* family gets twice the money. You bludgeon me with a fence post... lay the blame on some passing hobo..."

Scrumpy's whiskers twitched. A cow angling for double indemnity. He'd never heard of such a thing.

"I couldn't kill nobody," the farmer replied. "Unless I was hungry." The herd cleared their throats anxiously. "That's me done," Scrumpy concluded. "I'll hear no more of murder."

Scrumpy heard nothing ever again. As he left his barn, a pitchfork swung up to impale his stomach. He bled to death slowly in the hay; penned in as they were, the cows were powerless to help him.

The zoo always got busier in the afternoon. Kittens were done with school, housewives or full-time fathers had finished their chores, and jobless cats had nowhere much to go. Bug was kept busy. She detailed the lives of her tiny crawly chums, outlined the rules of their mating games and their lifespans, and illustrated their alien habits.

The heat rose in the glass cage, and she washed herself constantly. She enjoyed the taste of her own fur; it reassured her, calmed her. So much so that she jumped when Tiger tapped on the glass. His claws scraped the steamed-up panes.

"What do you want this time?" she asked, loath to let him in.

"I brought a bribe," said Tiger. "I mean, a present."

Bug felt silly. Passers-by were cocking their ears in her direction. She let Tiger in, and he presented her with a matchbox.

"Not much of a bribe."

"Check inside." Something scuttled within—a four-winged *lapidicolous* pip coupler. Natasha's heart melted.

"It's what I've always wanted!" said Bug. The creature wriggled in a miniature puddle of poop. She picked it up. "So rare. Where did you find it?"

"I'm a detective." Tiger blinked at Bug. "I'm good at finding things."

"I'll have to put it somewhere safe." She placed it in a special air-conditioned tank. Once her back was turned, Tiger ate the pip coupler and clamped his teeth together.

"I'll get someone to hold the fort," said Bug as she whistled for another keeper. "You got something on your face."

Tiger shoved the last of the beetle's legs into his mouth.

6

S omeone had left the water running in the Hant brothers' kitchen. The plug wasn't in, but a cup sat over the hole. The room had flooded. The floor so wet that if you kicked it, water would spray from the carpet. The smell of dirty dishes lingered; the tea towels hadn't been washed in weeks. Mugs waited for the sud fairy to come along and spruce them up, scrape the fungus from their bottoms. The elements in the kettle squealed, not enough liquid in the vessel. Steam tried to raise the alarm; no one attended.

Four stools, rickety and worn at the seat, were cold without their owners' rumps. Moldy tea bags and ripped cartons lay in a sad pile on the draining board.

The detective had already visited the house once, taking care not to disturb anything. He crept slowly through the brothers' bedrooms, ensuring that his tail didn't drag in the dust. The lads had slept two to a room, and the impressions of their bodies remained in each mattress. A chemical scent informed the air— the poisonous powder they'd used to kill pests. The powder that had apparently been fed to them.

Continuing his snoop, the investigator checked through bottles and packets on bedside cabinets.

The prowlers would have taken away any obvious evidence, but Cole Tiddle had learned that the least obvious evidence could turn out to be the most important.

Cole had to hurry. He had a network brunch to attend at eleven. How had the killer managed to tie up any of the brothers before the others rushed to help?

One photograph had been pinned to the wall in the master bedroom. The four lads, back from a successful mission, holding a pack of dead rats by their tails. Cole felt hungry. The lads were accompanied by their sister, looking innocent and content, her fur cropped and curled. Her 'do and their clothes placed the photo a decade ago; feline fashion is ruthlessly fickle.

Cole felt little for the aggrieved sister. He hadn't climbed the corporate pyramid by being sentimental. His mind raced, developing theories, exploring possibilities. The brothers could have short-changed a client—hardly sufficient motive for something so brutal. He had to find out more about their past, their characters.

A visit to the sister was called for. Judging by her photo, the task would be a pleasant one.

Death was common in the cat city: traffic accidents, scraps over territory, gang wars, breed-related incidents. The prowlers rarely investigated a murder. Nevertheless, when a bizarre killing took place and there was a chance that the perp would strike again— the cops were on the case. For Inspector Bix Mortis, a dour ale guzzler with a dicky ticker—the only rodent on the force, a token gesture made by the mayor to soothe race relations—it was just another job to do.

The barn was a mess. Scrumpy's blood had streamed into a central channel that traversed the floor. Hay was strewn everywhere, and the place stank of fear and death.

"I never thought a fellow could make such a hash with a pitchfork!" Nut exclaimed.

The inspector made pertinent notes in a minuscule black book.

"I mean guts and straw..." Nut shook her head slowly.

"You saw him?" asked the rodent.

"Who, dear?"

"The killer," Bix twitched. "Your boss's murderer."

"Oh no. Couldn't look. We all closed our eyes, didn't we?" Nut's herd nodded slowly.

"You reckon a guy did this?" Bix continued to scribble.

"Beg pardon?"

"'I never thought a fellow could make such a mess.'"

"A mere assumption, Inspector. A rather sexist one at that. Chalk it down to cow chauvinism. I'll tell you—it was scary."

"You heard a cry, saw Scrumpy fall..."

"I was so frightened I almost milked myself."

"Speaking of milk, there is a significant quantity of cream missing from, ahem, Scrumpy's store."

"Never touch the stuff myself."

"So, you know nothing about this theft?"

"I know nothing, period."

"Thank you, Nut."

A forensics officer was busy taking measurements and snapshots. Large paw prints had been found with an unnatural number of toes.

Doctor Snow, the peterbald pathologist, had already been called to the scene. "He's been stabbed to death with a pitchfork," the doctor diagnosed in a breathless tone.

"Thank you." Bix craned his neck to look up at the cat. Like all mice, he despised the feline race for its single-mindedness. "Anything helpful you can tell us?"

"Entrance wound from a low angle. Very steep." Snow was a balding cat with rubbery jowls. "Whoever did this was either down on his haunches or your size, Inspector."

"Lovely." Bix made a sour face. "Let's wrap this up. This farmyard's got enough pigs without us trampling about."

The winter days were shrinking. Sensible souls hibernated, giving their hides a rest from the harsh frosts that were approaching fast. Hailstorms were frequent, warm spells less so. The wind was insidious, blowing rain up noses and into the most secure homes. Only citizens with an iron resolve ignored the weather, going about their business as though spring was ready to commence. Tiger wasn't the kind of cat who let a seasonal shift disrupt his work.

It had grown dark by the time he and Bug reached the Hant brothers' residence. Youngsters hung around outside, nothing better to do than drink sour milkshakes and whack each other with fake foam tails. The adults tried to ignore them. One of the youths coughed a hairball at Tiger as he passed.

"Cubs are so cheeky these days."

"And you were the essence of good manners when you were their age?" Bug smirked as she found an unlatched window. "Looks like someone's preceded us."

"They might still be here." Tiger clambered through the window after his friend.

"Nah. They're long gone, I reckon. No fresh paw prints."

"Could've been wearing mittens." Statisticians believed that 64% of cat burglars wore mittens while breaking and entering. The majority of arrests for the crime involved kittens who'd lost their mittens.

The cats' eyes became black pools as they adjusted to the gloom. For the most part, they used their whiskers to find their way upstairs and into the master bedroom.

"Some geezer's definitely been here today," sniffed Bug. "Left his scent. Strong. A big bad tom."

"Keep a hold on yourself, Natasha." Tiger nudged her with his forehead. "We're looking for clues, remember?"

"Yeah." Bug nodded. "Murder, deceit, the snuffing out of four innocent existences... Hey, wait! I've found something."

"Already?"

Bug showed Tiger her find. It was a long, slender sheath extension, coated with a blood-red varnish. Vain females wore them to give their claws an ornate look. Nail biters and factory workers were particularly fond of the accessory. It glinted in the dark room, reflected in Bug's bright green eyes. She flashed a toothy grin, twisting the extension around in her paw. Passing it to her friend, she stretched her back slowly.

"Was I worth two trips to the zoo? That expensive present?"

"You're worth your weight in kitty litter, doll." Tiger started to feel guilty about eating her present. It would give him indigestion. "You think these boys were transvestites?"

"Cross-dressing pest controllers?" Bug batted her eyelashes. "No." She dropped the possibility. "I don't approve of the life these guys led. If you'd told me what they did back at the zoo, I never woulda come here. But nobody should die like... like they died, even if they did get a taste of their own poison. I'll do what I can to help."

"Cheers." Tiger headed back downstairs. "I'm gonna have to find out who made this extension. Some good old legwork."

"I get mine from a fine lady named Jo," Bug mused as she followed Tiger out of the house. "You've got a hairball stuck to your coat."

He wiped the gooey mess from his sleeve. "I was always neat and good-natured when I was young," he mused. "Did as I was told, pulled my socks up. Didn't rock the Kasbah. Once folks realized that, they made my life a tragedy. Used me. It took me a long time to change."

"There was me thinking you were born a rebel." Bug handed him the sheath. It glimmered in the cloud-flecked moonlight. "I still admire you, Boss."

"You going back to the zoo?"

"Have to. Got an afternoon's work to catch up on. Can't think who's to blame." She gave Tiger a farewell wink.

"Natasha..."

"Yes?"

"I'll be in touch." He watched as his old partner slunk around a street corner. Today, he felt young and energized. Seeing her again had helped. Wondering if a vet could prescribe something similar, he headed off to report to Connie Hant.

7

Sometimes Connie wasn't sure whether she'd made the right choice. She was the one who had to live with her decision, day and night. It was the most serious selection she'd ever made—apart from hiring Tiger. Home decorating was an earnest business; she'd had the whole lounge painted bright yellow with furnishings to match. Now that she was alone without a job, she couldn't afford to change it. She felt daft as Cole settled himself on a buttercup cushion, gazing at his loud surroundings.

"My favorite color's yellow," he admitted.

"Really? We'll get along great, sure." She knew he was humoring her. Surely a cat as tough and masculine as her visitor would prefer a more virile color. Red or brown.

"You don't mind me asking about your brothers?"

"No."

Good. He was asking her anyway.

"They ran their business with money borrowed from the bank; their favorite eatery was the Golden Cage, and they doted on you?"

"So far, so right."

"Did they ever fight?"

"Not as far as I know, and I was always visiting them. Mainly to get away from this crazy color scheme." Connie smiled. "They bickered... in a siblingy sort of way. Winding each other up for a laugh. They were always laughing."

"Happy in their work."

"Exactly. There was a lot of love in our family. Mr. Tiddle, you're sure I can't offer you a saucer of milk? It's the least I can do."

"That's very generous of you. This isn't a social call. My client wants this case solved as much as you do."

"I need to know who your client is." She drew close to him.

"They wish to remain anonymous," said Cole. "I want to tell you, but a detective is like a priest. I don't fart in public, and I don't give out secrets."

"Maybe this will change things." Connie rubbed her nose gently against Cole's forehead. He let out a sigh.

"Mate of yours?" asked Tiger, loping into the apartment. The couple broke apart hurriedly. "You want me to leave?"

"I'm the one who's leaving," purred Cole, standing up and stretching. "I have an AGM at four." He raised his eyes to meet Connie's, smoldering full of intent. "You know the number. Call me if you think of anything that might ... help."

Connie had lost all power of speech. She could only watch the millionaire leave her home, his tail wiggling behind him.

"How many guys you putting up?" asked Tiger, replacing Cole on the buttercup cushion. He'd made a point of ignoring the large tom.

"I didn't hire him," replied his host in a huff. "Someone else did!"

"Who?"

"Dunno. One of my brothers' friends or neighbors. I don't see how they could afford him."

Whereas I come cheap, thought Tiger. "Any news on your clue?" Connie asked.

The detective shook his blunt gray head. "Not so far. I've seen about every beautician in town. A few more to try."

Connie settled back on her narcissus couch, her huff deflated. Tiger was making some headway, trying hard; she had faith in him. Next time she saw Cole, she'd tell that smug fellow what she really thought of him.

8

When he woke the next morning, Tim felt aches and pains that were brand new to him. He had never worked so hard in his life. During training, he had learned the Public Works route, memorized the rules, which recyclables to collect or discard, and who had the right of way while he pushed a cart, but the shorter days had made his instruction bearable. He liked cleaning high spots and looking for greasy problem areas; these challenges appealed to his completist nature. Following all his directives and noticing trash his fellow novices missed, he had completed his training with flying colors. His apprenticeship had not prepared him for the hard labor of cleaning streets alone, pushing a cart in the hot morning sun, chasing his lunch under an old theater.

No matter how overwhelmed he felt, Tim was determined to keep his word and get to work on time. Leaving his trailer, he stepped carefully around his sleeping neighbors, curled up outside in the dawnlight, sated from the previous night's food and conviviality.

They think I'm lucky with my plumb job, Tim thought. *They're the lucky ones, sleeping in, big and round and tough. Not a care in the world because they know I'll bring them more rats tonight, and the night after. Because I want them to stop their bullying and like me.*

For once, he wished his paws were normal, five toes, no extra dexterity, so he could stay home and bond with the cats. His abnormality made him a prime asset for Public Works, so he had to get to work.

He started with Argyle Street, again. Usually, trash day was a weekly affair, but some messy moggies had left a heap of burned kippers on their doorstep. Tim had to collect the fish and tolerate its stench all the way to his next port of call. Broughton Road had received a recent kibble delivery, and there were still broken pellets and crumbs on the road. This time, Tim used his tail—and his mouth—to clear the area. He looked forward to a time when he would be on a team, instead of stuck doing solitary rookie work. He had to earn his place on a crew, he supposed. The only other option was to quit, and he was too stubborn to give Anatolios the satisfaction.

Plus, quitting would mean losing his glorious perks, which included nibbling on kibble, a tasty combination of meat, vegetables, maize, and other mystery ingredients that Tim didn't want to think about. The quickest way to take care of the baked treats was to hoover them up in his half-pint mouth, and if he sucked up some dust and hair in the process, he didn't care. He was doing his job, cleaning up the town and saving a fortune on packed lunches.

Tim made his way uphill. Not every part of town had the same trash day, which meant that there was plenty of collecting to do. As the sun rose, he began to realize that his duties were never-ending. Here was job security. Price: one soul. Bonus: finding out what made cats tick via their detritus.

The uphill cats obviously had short attention spans and more wealth than they knew what to do with. Tim found empty cardboard boxes that hadn't even been sat in (he sat in them), kibble, intact and uneaten (he ate it), a tin fish with tooth marks, also uneaten, retractable wands with bright, dangly objects attached (he played with them), and a fabric tube that kittens could use as a play-tunnel, hardly used. He collapsed the tunnel, placed it neatly in his cart, and aimed to save it for the newborns at his trailer park. His grown neighbors would probably play with it too. For now, he focused on completing his daunting task, making the street look presentable, careful not to cut his paws on broken glass, or dawdle too long playing with insects.

At the top of the hill, he looked down at his work and smiled. There was still some dust and dirt, and a couple of empty trashcans made dark blots on the vista. But he wasn't a housepainter, and the home-owners were responsible for taking in their empty cans after he was done. He wondered why they didn't do it straight away. Cats could be so puzzling sometimes.

Tim's cart was almost full again, and he whizzed it back down the hill, making up precious time, trying to ignore the harsh fact that he'd have to work his way up the same route all over again next week. He had one more road to hit this rookie morning: Pinkham's Twist, a labyrinthine byway surely chosen to test his determination.

Despite its cutesy name, Pinkham's Twist was known for its bad cat inhabitants and scurvy kittens. The trash wasn't just on the sidewalk; it lived in the council houses too in the form of jobless toms and mollies. The Twist made Tim's trailer park look classy and woe betide any cat who got lost in this narrow maze after sundown.

With noon approaching, Tim wasn't concerned about his safety. Pushing his cart and wearing his bright yellow vest, he was obviously a garbage cat. In his sacrosanct position, he would not be attacked or teased. Only the bullies back home would dare to harass him, and he was working on them with his bribes.

He could only do so much before his cart was full, but Tim's training had included a lecture about not returning carts until they were brimming with waste. He looked at a long row of bags, tried to calculate how many he could fit in his wagon, then gave up in a dither. He would tackle one bag at a time, hot and uncomfortable in his uniform, eyes drowsy with lassitude.

His ears perked up when he heard a high-pitched cry from a brownstone alcove. Hoping it was a rat to catch for brunch, he trotted over to the recess, sniffing at a pile of boxes, wooden panels, and newspapers, which were bound with a length of twine. The tower of trash had fallen on its side, trapping a cat—the source of the cry. Tim could never resist helping someone in distress.

"How long have you been here?" Tim asked a bedraggled ginger Maine Coon, also wearing a yellow vest. The cat scowled at him.

"Forever," said the longhair. "Out of the hundreds of cats who live on this street, not one of them has spotted me or come out to help me."

Tim took the hint and pulled the pile of newspapers off the longhair, amazed by the amount of fur coating the cat.

"Thank you," the longhair coughed. Tim used a broom to lever the wood panels off the cat's back, helping him up and giving him a heavy nudge to make sure he could stand upright.

"I thought I was the only one on this route today," said Tim.

"Anatolios has everything regulated and planned out. He must have figured you'd fill up your cart, so he sent me to tidy half the street. But I got curious and got myself in a jam." The longhair stared at Tim. "I know you."

Tim hadn't seen this ginger mess at the Public Works depot; he certainly hadn't trained with him. "You do?"

"You're the little guy who makes all us other workers look like lazy bums, the over-achiever eager beaver, the fastest thumbs in the west."

"I'm not a beaver," Tim clarified.

"You're Little Tim, and I can see why." The longhair was tall and proud despite his recent predicament, looking down on Tim.

"My friends call me Tim," said Tim.

"Sure they do. My friends call me Lincoln, 'cause that's my name. Lincoln Purrview III." Lincoln rolled his Rs as he pronounced his last name.

"That's a fancy handle for a garbage cat," said Tim as they walked back to his cart.

"My dream all through finishing school was to take this job," Lincoln gushed. "The legacy, the camaraderie, the perks... you know about the perks, right?"

"Oh, yes." Tim hefted a trash bag into his cart while Lincoln watched. "I like the perks."

"Speaking of which, you need feeding up, Little Tim. Come with me." Lincoln led Tim to a breezeway between two old houses. He poked a paw at an overgrown patch of pampas grass, its white plumes resembling his fluffy tail.

"I'm on a tight schedule," Tim balked.

"I know," said Lincoln. "This won't take long."

As Lincoln ventured into the long grass, Tim realized how the longhair had got himself in a jam. Either he was brave, or he had no sense of self-preservation. Tim vowed to watch this cat's back and stop him from getting in too deep.

"You're getting in too deep," said Tim. Lincoln shushed him, drawing a curtain of pampas stalks and gesturing at a woven ball of leaves, twigs, and shredded paper. At first, Tim thought Lincoln was indicating some loose trash to be picked up and taken to the dump; that was until he saw small forms writhing in the nest, intertwined, miniature paws catching in the walls.

"*Bon appétit*," said Lincoln, whiskers twitching with hunger.

As if impatient, the grass shifted and sighed in the breeze. "This is going to sound strange coming from a cat," said Tim. "But I feel bad eating these rats. It's not like I'm getting them from a store shelf, ready to heat and serve. They're so free and alive and so helpless."

Lincoln withdrew his paws, letting the pampas stalks rise back into place. He looked at his new friend in disbelief.

"That makes them taste better!" Lincoln purred. "You're doing the city a service, Tim. These vermin spread disease, chew on wires, and get the old folks so excited when they see them; they're a major cause of heart attacks and apoplexy... they have to be dealt with, and we're the dealers. Now the eating of mice is prohibited 'cause they're an endangered breed, or species, or whatever, the rats have proliferated somehow, as if they've multiplied to take the meese's places. It's up to us to find the nests, control the swarm, keep it at manageable levels."

"We're garbage cats," Tim argued. "Not ecologists."

"We're do-what-we're-told-to-keep-our-jobs," Lincoln retorted. "A day you don't get fired is a good day. Do you know how many cats are ready and raring to take your place?"

"Yeah." Tim nodded sadly. "The boss keeps telling me."

"Listen to your boss. And follow my lead." Lincoln parted the grass again and, in less than an instant, went from casual cat to savage hunter, pouncing on the nest and gobbling at its contents with sharp, unforgiving teeth. He turned to Tim with blood on his chops, soaking into his cotton-soft ginger fur. A rat ran away from the chaos but was unlucky enough to head in Tim's direction; Tim stepped on the rat, wrapped a polydactyl paw around it, and lifted it to his mouth. He couldn't resist. *Just one snack, then back to work*, he told himself. *A harmless bite before noon.*

Seven rats later, Tim lay on his back, letting the sun tickle his burgeoning belly, listening to the whispers of the pampas.

"I should get back to work," Tim drawled.

"You're allowed a break," Lincoln assured him. He'd cleaned out the nest and sated his appetite, for now. "And I'll vouch for you. You're a hero, saving me from that embarrassing disaster back there."

"I'm very grateful," said Tim, rolling over and walking slowly back to his cart. "But I only know you. I mean, I didn't before this morning."

"I get it," Lincoln replied as Tim filled up his cart with more trash bags, not an easy feat with a full stomach. "A stranger offering to vouch for you ain't worth a hill of ants."

"You're a rookie like me, aren't you?" Why else would Lincoln be in Pinkham's Twist, messing with trash alone?

"Oh no," Lincoln chuckled. "I represent EGG."

Tim leaned on his cart, which was packed full. "You represent an egg?"

"The Egalitarian Group for Garbage cats. You didn't see the paperwork?"

Tim shook his head.

"Not even a pamphlet?" Lincoln spat on the ground. "What is the world coming to, I ask you?"

"I don't know."

"These division members promise me so much but deliver nothing. They were supposed to distribute literature to all new hires. That's you, Tim."

"I know," said Tim, glum. Lincoln helped him push the cart back toward the dump, giving him more EGG info.

"You remember that big wave of strikes after the Cod Wars? Cats with placards demanding more tuna. Fur flying across the picket lines. Garbage stinking up the streets 'cause no one was willing to pick it up."

"My nose remembers," said Tim. "Public Works raised salaries, introduced the perks program... the trash got picked up."

"Thanks to EGG, and unions like it." Lincoln and Tim reached the dump, where Lincoln was acknowledged by all his colleagues as a "right gee," decent and trustworthy. "We're well-funded, and pretty much all the workers here are brothers and sisters."

"They're related?" Tim was befuddled.

"They're brethren. Union members. I can't wait to sign you up."

Although Tim felt honored, he wasn't stupid. He needed to know more about any organization before he joined up. He went to see Anatolios, who purred when he heard Tim was interested.

"Oh yes," the boss chirped. "The sooner you join, the sooner you become eligible for benefits. Catch so much as a cat cold and your vet bills are covered. "

"Are you a member?"

Anatolios gave Tim a look of pity. "EGG is for laborers like yourself. Achievement through numbers and all that. Better for me to stay objective, supervising from a vantage point—"

"Like the top of the hill in Totterdown," said Tim.

"Exactly." Anatolios nodded. "Top of the trash heap."

"So I should join then, sir?"

"That's up to you to decide, son. If I was you, I'd sign up on the double."

"Okay, I will." Tim hoped his decision would impress Anatolios.

"I trust your new brothers will encourage you to work faster," the boss added. "You're still taking an hour too long. Remember, I'm setting you up for success. I'm not setting you up for failure. Work smarter, not slower."

"Yes, sir." Tim frowned. He had no idea what Anatolios meant, but the tone was so confident, it had to be good advice.

Tim left the office, found Lincoln, and joined the union. Tim felt revived, ready to sweep up the whole city with his new friend by his side. He touched Lincoln's arm affectionately.

Lincoln recoiled as if disgusted. "Be careful, I don't like to be touched," Lincoln scowled. "Try that again and I'll scratch you."

"I was just being—"

"Don't take it personally," said Lincoln, rolling an empty cart toward his colleague. "I was raised to protect my fine coat of fur at all costs."

Tim nodded. Lincoln's coat had to be hard to manage. All that ginger and fluff and white streaks begging for blemishing.

"Come on, lollipop." Lincoln smiled as if his knee-jerk reaction had never happened. "We've got trash to collect, a schedule to keep, and many, many rats to take care of before sunset."

Ten miles west of Nub City lay the coast, rocky and unkind. A small group of cats eked out a living there, supplying fresh fish to urban areas.

A regular train took the food from the fishing village, cod and tuna packed in briny crates, and returned empty. Today the water was choppy; white foam mingled with gray waves. Cole stepped from the train, licking his lips. He'd helped himself in the buffet car and no one had complained.

Sometimes the fishercats tolerated visits from wealthy executives looking for a respite from the office. For a fat fee, a boat could be hired and the vacationers could join a fishing expedition. Fishing was a tricky business for cats, wary of water. If they could overcome their fear of getting wet and prevent themselves from scoffing the catch, they had a secure job that would see them through all nine lives.

It took a certain kind of animal to work on the sea. There were no gender or age distinctions—the village couldn't afford to be selective. Those who took the job were rugged, wind-scarred, stank of stale salt. City folk called them mercats because they spent so much time at sea. Extra help was always welcomed, even when a pampered puss like Cole provided it.

Deep-sea fishing was an intricate art, usually involving two boats. Between them, a cat's cradle of rope was stretched, each length of hemp barbed with old claws and sticky with seaweed. Every so often, the mercats would trawl the net and raise it to grab as many fish as possible.

The net wasn't the only way to fish—they'd also scoop food from the water with their bare paws. The catch was dumped in a squared-off area in the middle of the boat. On a long run, the cats would eat some of the raw fish to keep their bellies satisfied.

The mercats usually sensed an impending weather change. They knew a gale was brewing. With Cole in attendance, they decided to ignore it, sure that a rough time would shake up the businessman and give them a giggle. Cole watched the waves rise as he helped lower the cat's cradle, feeling a bit sick.

The number of fish in this part of the sea was dwindling. Sewage from the city flowed through pipes into rivers and streams that leaked into the sea. The once clear water was now brown with pollution. Consumers were still eager to eat fresh fish, so the mercats continued their daily trawls. The mercats knew that the life of their village was nearing its end. Some of their stubborn colleagues would move up the coast, seeking an untainted area where they could continue to fish for a long time to come. Most of the villagers would go to the city, find work in a factory or office block. They'd miss the breeze, the lifestyle, the freedom of deep-sea fishing. Missing it wouldn't bring back what was lost for good.

For now, they were remorseless, increasing their catches against all likelihood, rising earlier, coming home later. The food would all be bad or dead soon. They would make the most of what they had.

Lona Dash was never going back. She'd had enough of her mother's nagging, telling her what to do, treating her like a newborn kitten. She was old enough to work now, ready to be responsible. Running away from home was the next stage in her development. She had to find her own way—with her mom's money, makeup, jewelry, and the petty amount of cash she'd saved from her short-lived job at the Blind Tiger. She'd tarted herself up to look as old as possible and stowed away in a boxcar to reach the thriving city of Lac Hong. She sat on a crate of herring, relaxed by the train's steady rattle. Her parents would be sorry. They'd start to miss her eventually, worrying about her. She'd show them.

Like most young cats, Lona was impatient. After ten minutes in the dull car, she stretched her legs and peeked outside. She had to be close to the city by now. The world rushed by outside, harsh sunlight hurting her eyes. Through sudden tears she glimpsed the sea.

The train was following the coastline—that couldn't be right. Could trains take a wrong turn? No. It was far more likely that *she'd* taken the wrong turn—heading away from the city instead of toward it. At home, she messed up all the time; it seemed as if she couldn't get things right in the real world either. Now she was lost. Trees and rocks were a blur, whistling past the dirty train.

Lona got hungry, sniffed at the crates, and tried to open one with her teeth and forepaws. The blurs became large smudges, solidifying into recognizable shapes as the boxcar clanged to a halt. She backed into a corner, waiting for someone to collect the crates. She'd appeal to their better nature, find out where she was, and ask them to help her find her way home. She was tired and angry with herself. There was still a lot of growing up to do.

Now that the train had stopped juddering, Lona tuned her keen hearing to another sound. A skritching, hesitant shuffle as if something was trying to keep quiet, hold its breath. It was coming from a shadowy corner of the boxcar. She was not alone. There was a creature in there with her, trying its best not to announce its presence.

When she was still in kitten britches, Lona's mom had warned her of the animals that ate naughty little cubs, of the dogs and rats and goats that couldn't wait to get their teeth into her if she misbehaved. She hadn't believed her cautionary tales; Lona was too practical for that. Now she had second thoughts.

Anything benign would have announced its presence when she embarked. There was no way a kindly traveler would make such a sinister sound. Whatever was making the noise couldn't see her in the darkness and couldn't guess that she'd detected its presence. So, she backed toward the corner, ready to spin around at the last moment and confront it.

As she moved carefully backward, her forepaws outstretched, she detected a smell as black as the skritching. The musty, wheat odor of an animal that hadn't had a bath for months. The fish had obscured the stink until now, but it scared Lona more than the noises.

A small, craggy paw grabbed her shoulder and over-balanced her. Five or six paws grabbed and scratched her, teeth snapping at her windpipe. Mewling, she fainted dead away.

Spray matted Cole's fur and dripped from his whiskers. He hardly noticed. He was distracted by the thought of a package that had appeared in his desk drawer earlier in the week. A sealed manila envelope, no address, no postmark. Twenty-four shots of a male caught in a clinch. Twenty-four frantic, crazed, blissful moments. He was the subject, and he had wool on his face.

As he'd lost his head in that hotel room—snared in a trap that shouldn't have caught a newborn cub—someone had watched. A concealed camera had captured evidence capable of destroying his empire. If the public—worse, his shareholders—saw him with his guard down, they would lose all faith in him. Investors would pull out, demanding money that had already been spent on failed projects. That couldn't be allowed to happen.

He trawled his net through the water once more. His serene features hid every trace of concern. His companions had no way of knowing that the envelope had also contained a note. The snapper wanted Cole to solve a crime. If the Hant murderer was not found he would soon be kissing Tiddles Inc. goodbye.

Lona's world was moving again. A different motion this time, an uncertain seesaw. She heard the swirl of waves, smelled the sea, and realized she was on a boat. She tried to stand up, but her head spun, and the vessel rocked. She squatted in the cargo hold where she'd been dumped, washing herself thoroughly. Although she was bedraggled, her mom's jacket and jewelry made her feel presentable. She found her sea legs, banged on the hatch above her, and discovered that it had been left unbolted.

She let out a querulous mew as she stepped onto the deck. The white-hot sun was high in the sky now, warming her face. Her confidence grew as she failed to spot anybody. She was out of sight of the coastline; there was nothing on the horizon. Large waves crashed against the boat's barnacled hull. In the cabin, the wheel had been strapped still. Padding to the bow, she looked down at the swirling water and recalled the scaly paws that had grabbed her.

Lona hissed as she was lifted bodily off the deck, hanging off the bow. Reaching behind her, she found that she was dangling from a boathook, the sharp point digging into her flesh. A thin chuckle reached her on a current of wind, then the boat hook dipped, and she entered the water. Lona missed her mother dreadfully. The sea was too cold to think anymore. It was easier to give in to the deep freeze and sleep for a while.

Warming himself by the fireplace, Cole paid a young female to clean his fur. She complied without a word, no doubt dreaming of how she'd spend the cash. The grooming relaxed him as he lapped a bowl of milk. He emptied the bowl—a day on the ocean had made him mighty thirsty.

As he felt his cockles warm, thoughts drifted back to the case he had to solve. Tomorrow he would meet with Bowyer, the chief of the prowlers. With the aid of the authorities, the murders would be solved in no time.

Dunbar Bay was not the prettiest part of Cambor. It smelled bad. Way back before trains and mass angling expeditions, a feeble sea wall had been built to save a huddle of houses from the water. The mercats had used the bay to moor their boats, swearing blind in the local tavern that they had discovered the most efficient mode of transport in the world.

As the fishing expeditions had grown into an industry, more homes had been built. Struggling for space, the area had become increasingly built up with low-level shacks with high prices. Territorial disputes were common with the loser giving up his property to the victor. The sea didn't care about mortgages or lease agreements. It battered the wall, and the stone began to crumble. The locals had been too busy scrapping and scraping a living to notice until one year when the water had risen, demolishing half the houses on the front. The cats took to their boats or moved inland. The sea was an unkind host; you didn't mess with it or take it for granted. You tried not to sink.

Now Dunbar Bay was cluttered with trash and dead fish. The water was still here, stuffed with scum. The remaining houses looked onto each other in a protective square, centering on a minuscule courtyard where clothes could be hung out to dry. The younger people spent their earnings on luxurious, waterproof furniture—in case their dwellings flooded. The older folk sat upstairs, gazing from their bedroom windows at the craggy coast west of the bay. They twitched their net curtains, assured everyone who cared to listen that the sea level had risen that week, and cultivated a condescending attitude toward the trains—a noisier and far less efficient form of travel than boats.

A couple of houses lay derelict, blinded with bricks through the windows, a haven for sex-hungry toms who left their scent for all to find. No one would buy the old red buildings, aged with salty rain. They were used as a toilet and a nookie parlor. Their front gardens were flowered with wood and plastic rubbish thrown from passing ships. Smells of sewage and stagnant pools of water dominated the air, but today there was another taint.

A young couple found its source. Their parents were strict, didn't like them necking. The female was on heat and her partner was excitable. They tripped along the seawall, the lass gazing at the moon, her partner examining the trash for trinkets.

"This is for you," said the tom tenderly, offering his mate a silver bracelet. Her eyes grew wide with wonder.

"You shouldn't have!" She gave the bracelet a close examination, finding silt and grit in the links. "You didn't, did you? Where did you find it?"

The tom pointed guiltily at a mound that had piled against the wall. He apologized for his lack of finesse.

"Don't worry about it; there might be more jewelry down there!"

The couple found more jewelry, modeled by the lifeless form of a kitten. The necklace and earrings made her look younger, not older; a slick-furred tailor's mannequin, long out of fashion.

9

Gerry Igoe had everything he could possibly want. He lived on his boat, moored in Cambor Harbor beside the mercats he considered to be good neighbors. In the summer afternoons when the sun was game, he'd lie stretched out on the deck and drink in the hot rays. They would make sparkled patterns on the water, surprising him with a different color for each day of the week. He needed the warmth and the rest—his mornings were spent gathering food from the bountiful sea. He caught enough to eat and passed a couple of fish to the authorities in lieu of mooring fees. He would have been content had he not possessed a miserable mien.

Gerry never shared a joke in the local tavern or bought anyone a drink. He wouldn't purr at a passing beauty or give his priest a courteous nod. He was grumpy to his sister and grumpy to the fish that circled his boat. He supposed that they were taunting him; in fact, they were curious.

Gerry's misery stemmed from his furless physical state. He smelled weird, and he'd been devoid of hair since birth, often cold as a result. His ancestors had come from a desert climate, and he still bore the trademarks of their exotic breed—a pointy head and a long, tapering tail. He'd never seen or heard anyone make fun of him, pointing him out as a freak. That was because they did it behind his back, round street corners, out of earshot. They made fun of him and over the years, because of his testy temper, he'd become the naked, furless butt of countless Cambor jokes.

Gerry had decided to spend as much time as possible at sea, a recluse in his boat. Once out of sight of the mainland, he could show off his kitelike ears, his skinny torso exposed to the brisk elements. It made him shiver, and he'd caught a chill a couple of times, yet it felt good to flaunt his bod without fear of derision. Unless he counted the pesky fish.

The monks hadn't laughed at him when they asked to hire the boat. They'd been extremely quiet as monks were wont to be. They carried no calling cards; their robes and their tranquil composures had provided proof enough of their identities. They obviously weren't seafarers, so Gerry hadn't been sure whether to trust them with his proudest possession.

He'd no idea why they wanted his boat in particular. It had the usual trimmings: stout masts, a deep hold for his catch, brown paint flaking from its hull. There were dozens of vessels like his in the harbor, many of them for hire. He wasn't in the habit of lending his boat to strangers. He had everything he could possibly want, so he'd refused the monks' generous offer with no good grace. He'd told them where to stick their payment, ready to send them away. They'd negotiated a better deal.

Gerry supposed that monks had a lot of time to practice their negotiation skills. Meditation and arbitration, that's what monks did. The offer had been so tempting that he'd lent them his boat for a day after all. To his relief, they'd returned it intact, nice and early, so he still had time to take the boat out, hoping to score some herring before the light failed. He stood upright in his cabin, not caring if anyone saw him. He had no reason to care now.

If the fishercat had taken a close look at his boat, he'd have noticed a couple of blood spots down in the hold. They belonged to Lona. He would also have spotted scratch marks on the hull, as if the kitten had tried to claw her way to safety before the current swept her away. The grooves were faint; after a few weeks at sea, they would be invisible.

Gusts of wind tickled Gerry's skin. For the first time he could remember, he was happy. He gave the fish around his boat a cheerful greeting, chuckled as he hauled them in, and bit a mackerel's head off. When he got back to the harbor, he would pay a friendly visit to his sister, spend an hour in the tavern, and tell a joke or two. He'd been saving them up. For now, he headed for the horizon, in full view of any mercats who were barmy enough to be fishing so late in the day. They wouldn't have recognized Gerry if they had passed him because his figure was obscured by baggy monk's robes, complete with cowl; they kept him warm and dry, and when he wore them he didn't feel ridiculous. No one would laugh at him again.

Cole stumbled into Connie's apartment, sharing a joke with her. Tiger was waiting for the couple, greeting them with a scowl.

"I'm trying to solve a mystery here, if you don't mind," Tiger huffed.

"You haven't cracked the case yet?" asked Cole with a sneer. "How far have you got?"

"Wouldn't you like to know."

"Any clues?" Cole removed his opera cloak. He'd taken Connie to see a performance of the Cats' Fugue at the Garden Wall open-air theater.

"One or two," Tiger assured him. He found himself hanging up his rival's cloak. Cole had a knack for making others feel inferior.

"Lads, lads," Connie interrupted. "Can you not work together?" Tiger wouldn't speak to her. He'd begged her not to go out with the tycoon, worried that an excursion could leave her open to an attack.

Connie was the kind of lady who always did the opposite of what she was told. If her actions made Tiger jealous, all the better.

"You gonna spend the night?" he asked, squinting at his rival. Cole scratched his chin with a manicured claw.

"That's up to Ms. Hant," he purred. She bade him goodnight and rubbed up against him on his way out.

"Don't say a word," she said to Tiger, strutting into the bathroom. The down-at-heel detective's head spun. He had to arrange new accommodation before Connie did something that he would regret.

10

Felines aren't the easiest folk to ana-
lyze. They're a solitary bunch, don't like to share
their feelings unless there's something in it for them.
Fortunately, Doctor Mildrew was adept at drawing
the most insular patients out of their shells. He would
listen to them carefully, help them to answer their own
questions, and make life choices. At the end of each
expensive session, he would remind them of the faults
that had been revealed. Patients often left the office
more depressed than when they went in, but Mildrew
believed the means justified the end: mental fitness.

The working classes wouldn't have dreamed of visiting Mildrew. His books were filled with professional
couples, upper-class nits and tits, members of the aris-
tocracy, and even a few cats with genuine emotional
problems. Most of his cases involved overeating dis-
orders, narcissism, young cubs who would chew grass
then throw up, nip addicts, males convinced that their
paws were too small demanding surgery (he tried to
dissuade them), vegans, compulsive washers, and suf-
ferers of cupboard love syndrome. He treated them

all with equal care and tact. He was their friend and helper. Almost all of them looked forward to coming.

However, some were forced to attend. The prowler department funded Inspector Mortis's sessions. They believed that his unique situation could cause emotional distress, and his thoughts and feelings should be monitored. They'd hired the best psychologist in Nub City to see him once a week. When the psychologist suffered a mental breakdown, refusing to see the inspector again, Mildrew had taken over. He considered the sessions a waste of time although a couple of childhood traumas had been unearthed during his time with Bix. Today he had better places to be.

"I was sure your secretary licked her lips on my way in," the mouse said as soon as he arrived. "Seems like everyone sees me as a starter course on their daily menu."

"Ms. Torrancu has just finished her lunch. Full as an egg, she can't possibly be after you."

"You've told me to look at every angle, Doc." Bix hopped onto a firm black couch.

"There's a fine line between being open-minded and being paranoid."

"If you were me, wouldn't you be paranoid? I'm small, edible, my legs're only little. I have to have my wits about me every second. My employers are as likely to gobble me up as they are to pay me."

"Perhaps this explains why you don't have a personal life."

"Then I'd let my guard down. At work, I deal with perverts, murderers, and pencil necks. I don't relax; that would be the worst thing to do."

"You've never spoken of your family."

"Nothing to speak. Don't know them. I've always fended for myself. I never sought them out, sent a postcard to anyone. Folks tolerate me, barely. They don't care for me." The inspector descended from the couch and brushed a crumb from his faun jacket. "I've got a case to solve."

"Our hour isn't up yet," the doctor protested.

"Credit me a few minutes. I'll return; don't you worry."

As Bix stomped out of the office, Mildrew gave a sage nod. The cop would be back with more whys and woes. He couldn't wait.

"A rum business all around," Bowyer admitted. His nose twitched with anticipation. "Bad for our rep. Bad for morale." The chief was tall, in galoshes and a matching green jacket. He stood on the vast lawn that stretched behind his country manor. The grass was kept daintily manicured by slave-wage sheep. Nobody asked where the money that funded his lifestyle came from; it was assumed that he'd inherited a healthy income from a dotty aunt. In fact, Bowyer was as corrupt as he was influential. Cole knew this but accompanied the chief anyway. He needed information, and he was getting it.

A hundred yards from the pair sat a catapult, set by a cub. On the stoop lay a small pigeon, its wings clipped. More birds queued beside the cub.

"We still don't understand who murdered those exterminators," Bowyer whined, his teeth chattering. "Or why."

"I didn't think you cared. Argyle Street isn't exactly a gentrified area."

"Quite. But whoever killed the Hant boys is obviously insane. We can't have loonies running about the place, can we? Pull!" The bird on the scoop was flung into the air and Bowyer opened his jaws wide. With a hop, he snatched the pigeon from the air and feathers fell from the side of his mouth.

"Next we lose a farmer in a nasty fashion," said the chief when he'd finished the bird. "More work for us."

"There's been another incident?" Cole asked.

"Pull!" Another bird sailed through the sky. The tycoon caught it and plucked it clean.

"Two. The farmer got forked. Something worse happened this morning in a fishing village not far from here."

"Cambor."

"Yes."

"I was just there."

"I know. You'll be familiar with a small bay there, a graveyard for flotsam and jetsam. It wasn't trash that washed up there today. It was a drowned kitten." Bowyer's eyes narrowed. "Someone impaled her on a boathook, judging by the wound and the grooves in her fur. I'd like to think she never felt the cold water filling her lungs, the helplessness, the chest pains... You're a suspect."

"I'm not a murderer," growled Cole. "I build things. I don't destroy them."

"I know you're innocent. No one else does. Not so easy to keep out the papers."

"You're looking for a donation to your retirement fund." Cole wasn't surprised.

"What do you take me for?" Bowyer hissed. "I'm the Chief of Prowlers, not some one-bit bent bobby. Your interest in this case has created waves. If your interest ebbs—to the level of, say, nothing—I won't have you hauled in."

"Got it." Cole stroked his chin.

"Pull!" Two birds shot from the catapult and Bowyer leaped, grabbing one with his forepaws and the other with his teeth. He snacked on both of them.

"One more question before I leave," said Cole. Bowyer looked up from his meal. "Who's on the case?"

"One of our most efficient and smallest officers." A stray feather tickled the chief's nose. "Inspector Bix Mortis."

11

"Wisest of dumb animals
"Runs from rats and cannibals
"Tatty ear and kinky tail
"Following the bad guys' trail."

"He's the squirt who puts out fires
"Catches miscreants 'n' liars
"Hides out in a rubbish dump
"Scary villains make him jump."

"Doesn't charge a grinding fee
"Offers services for free
"As long as he's home for tea
"With She-Cat and Wonder Flea."

"Teaches kittens wrong from right
"Saves his hide with hiss or bite
"Costume is a tad too tight
"Scared of mice, mad as a kite."

"Heroes are so scarce today
"He's the savior here to stay

"Whether we like it or not
"Wonder Cat's the best we've got."

Wonder Cat Theme
By Doctor Phat

The factory was always cold. The draught froze the crew despite their fur coats. Long since stripped of its machinery, the building was a dusty husk, with no insulation, no soul. Wind, rain, and pigeons flew in through holes in the roof. Windows were cracked and shutters warped. It made the perfect location for a TV show.

Each floor held a workspace the size of a football field, surrounded by smaller rooms that had once been offices. Now only spiders enjoyed the benefits of the air vents, spinning their traps in ducting and desk drawers. Metal pins jutted from the concrete, spiking in all directions like cave formations. The machines that they had once supported had produced Harman's Biscuits before some dietary boffin had suggested that the product might be bad for consumers.* The place duly closed, and hundreds of workers lost their jobs and their supply of crunchy perks.

Now the red husk was up for sale—four million to the first real estate developer that came along. Before that, there was an interim function for the factory to perform. Some of the rooms had been transformed into sets and several film crews had hired it out for a month or two.

Cats love going to the movies. They enjoy sitting in a dark, warm room with a like-minded audience and plenty of food and drink handy in cardboard maxi-cartons. Anyone whose cell phone rings in the middle of a film gets their eyes scratched out. Movie theaters make their money not from tickets but from marked-up popcorn, milk, and pieces of string. The audience has a very short attention span—anything longer than a one-reeler begs intolerance.[1]

Number one at the box office was a yarn starring Scratch and Sniff, a popular cat-and-mouse combo. They'd enjoyed many adventures together, chasing each other across locations around the globe.

The stories were always the same, but the film-makers took the opportunity to visit exotic locations and generally enjoy themselves. The audiences kept paying to see the movies, no matter how slipshod their quality.

Whatever scrapes they got into, the characters would always survive for another encounter. Scratch the Cat would be charged by his boss with the capture of the notorious rodent, Sniff. Either that or Scratch would be minding his own business and Sniff would come along and tease him until the chase began. Or vice versa. Scratch always won in the end, of course, but Sniff gained small victories in the course of the narrative. An adaptation for the theater (*The Cat Trap*) had recently completed the longest run in showbiz history, with patrons coming back repeatedly, even though they knew the ending.

Softly, Softly Catchee Mousy, the latest Sniff movie, was in the can. The factory was clear for a TV crew to

---

[1] The biscuits have been found to contain a gelatin substance that may be proved to be harmful when ingested, especially during pregnancy. While no firm evidence can be provided at this time—such proof would only appear after years of research—the negative effects cannot be satisfactorily disproved either. In the meantime, we cannot recommend the vending of said items. (MAYORAL SURGEON'S REPORT, CENTRAL CITY RECORDS)

set up, ready to shoot an equally successful series for the small screen.

Hairy Bancroft was hungry. He loved getting fan mail and adored the fact that he got more than any of his co-stars. There wasn't a TV personality as worshipped as he. Meowed at in the street, given preferential treatment in public lavatories, he only had one foe: his producer.

Joel Venet wasn't a mean or petulant guy. He was perpetually stressed and had no time to molly-coddle his star. He threatened to cut the actor's ample wages and shouted at him when a line was skipped; worst of all, he'd put Hairy on a diet.

A dirty word in the cat dictionary, dieting was the worst fate that could be forced upon them. Burning at the stake, being eaten alive by goats, a gherkin up the nose... all fates were preferable to the Big D. Hairy was powerless to complain; there was a clause in his contract. It was written in print so small that the typist had required a special set of midget keys to set it out. Those wee words, so unassuming in size, insisted that the star of *Wonder Cat* remain under a certain weight. But with the stresses of fame and wealth, Hairy continued to balloon.

He looked different in every episode, fat one week, starving the next. His costume had been taken in and let out more times than a hokey cokey dancer's leg. He ate boring food, walked from his Winnebago to each location, exercised his eyebrows every morning. None of this seemed to suffice; he was gross. Watching the crew stuff their faces at the craft table every five minutes made things tougher.

Even though he'd signed away his fun, Hairy was a trouper. For years he'd entertained the masses with his deeds of derring-do. He still remembered the audition with awful clarity, although he'd tried hard to erase it from his mind. It hadn't been his first kettle run, but he was still nervous. His agent had told him it was some kind of presenting job, and he'd turned up in a black velvet suit.

He'd soon learned that the producers were looking for something completely different, an athletic type. His background was in modeling; he was known as the Super Chunks Hunk. Their background was in double-dealing, brown-nosing, and grabbing as many freebies as possible. He'd read for them ("truth, justice and get out of my way!"), unable to glance up from the script, a video camera catching his every grimace.

Back then, he'd been shy, wiry, and handsome as a crooner. He lacked experience and talent. The producers saw past these deficiencies—never imperatives for a TV star—and saw a greenhorn they could mold, exploit. He would thank them for it. As the show became a success, ratings increased and Hairy's head swelled, he learned some big words: contractual dispute, moral copyright, repeat fees. With an efficient lawyer and a series of hypnotherapy sessions with Doctor Matt Mildrew to help him recall his lines, he'd established himself as a major pain-in-the-ass star.

Four wives, six children, twelve agents, and one salad later, he was knackered. He still provided entertainment for nationwide audiences, who tuned in every week to follow the adventures of a loveable, overweight superhero.

Wonder Cat lived in the fictional suburb of Pickles. He worked with other feisty champions (Wonder Dog and Captain Cow; Super Skunk worked alone) battling colorful villains and getting into scrapes. Critics lauded Hairy's portrayal of an ignorant naïf until everyone realized that he wasn't acting. He was ignorant and innocent. Now he was a national treasure, loved by grannies, admired for his candor in a world of deceit and solicitors.

Every year he asked for a raise; every year Joel begged him to lose ten pounds. Neither cat got quite what they wanted, but the friction helped to keep the set vibrant.

This week's vibrancy was provided by shivering crewmembers freezing their pads in the draughty factory. Grips and sound recordists stood around, shuffling their paws; Hairy was taking too long in make-up.

Jo Madrigal was a voluptuous Birman who specialized in deception. She rejuvenated the old, disguised the most notorious of stars, and even managed to give Hairy's sagging face some sparkle. He was the first to admit that he'd lost his good looks; his jowls drooped like unset jelly, the bags beneath his eyes had their own matching luggage, his chins flapped, and his fur had started to gray. No wonder he spent so much time in makeup. With all the magic of show business at his disposal, he was determined to use every single spell to fix his face.

Jo was his favorite makeup artist, best at disguising his furrow. She had a long silky coat and ruff, a round face, full body, her tail long but shaggy, her deft paws white as granulated sugar. She took time and care over each fold, adding foundation and concealer with the deft brushstrokes of an Old Master. She'd also fix the fur on top of his head, which was cursed with a wayward tuft that tickled his right ear.

"What you doing today, Hairy?" asked Jo, making conversation. She was a congenial hostess, warm and sympathetic to everyone's problems.

"No idea, sweetie." The actor glanced at his script, his chin nudged upright by Jo's firm paw. "They keep changing the shooting order all around the place. Have to wing it as usual."

"I wouldn't blame the director." Jo laughed. "He's doing the best he can. I think we're already over budget. This is my own makeup kit, you know. The production company ran out of blusher. If I hadn't used my initiative, She-Cat's cheeks would be sallow."

"Has it started raining again?" Hairy wasn't interested in Jo's woes. "I'm not leaving this trailer without a brolly."

The actor admired himself in the mirror while Jo popped her head outside. When it rained in Nub City, it rained darkly. Black clouds raged above the factory, unleashing a steady shower. She whistled for a runner, who sauntered up to the makeup trailer.

"Lord Muck insists on an umbrella," she explained to the lackey. Rolling his eyes, he disappeared to fetch an umbrella. The costume and continuity people would be pleased to see that Hairy's superhero outfit would stay dry, but Jo took exception to the star's insistence that someone hold the umbrella for him. A perk of the job, he called it. She saw it as a petty display of elitism, intended to make the rest of the cast jealous. It worked.

The factory was the least glamorous location the director could find. As Hairy was escorted from the makeup trailer, he passed scrap and junk piled up in the yard before entering a rear passage that was dank and leaking. There wasn't room for the umbrella, so the runner held a copy of the script over Hairy's head. Rain-sodden flags steam-dried beside hot halogens; dry ice was spread around the set by runners waving pieces of cardboard. Extras kipped in an anteroom, ready to spring into inaction in an instant. The director, a chubby old moggy, and veteran of a thousand cat food commercials, ignored whole pages of the script and made shots up as he went along; the continuity cat noted all mangled dialogue and miss-takes; grips leaned on a console, smoking and farting. The sound mixer and boom operator gossiped like spider monkeys. The PA ensured everyone was on their mark at the right time; the actors mumbled to themselves, sipping coffee and scoffing biscuits. The producer oversaw everything, the general, the grand magician, holding the purse strings. The producer was a nervous wreck.

The scene in production was a simple one. Wonder Cat would discuss a murder with his mate and partner in crime-busting, She-Cat. Joel had made sure that Hairy's lines would be few and simple.

SHE-CAT: The victim had no enemies.

WONDER CAT: He was bothered by a phone pest? We've a killer to catch.

The words didn't quite come out like that.

SHE-CAT: We've run a trace on the corpse, the family, close friends—they don't know how the killer got into... into... (actress looks for prompt, stifles a giggle, Take 2) the museum. All his col-leagues have alibis.

WONDER CAT: The victim had no enemas.

SHE-CAT: Except for the obscene calls.

WONDER CAT: He was bothered by a pone fest?

Cut.

The third attempt was an improvement, although Hairy still had trouble with the "pone fest" line. By the fourth take, the director settled for a dialogue change.

"Hairy," the director said in a quiet and supportive tone. "Let's do a take with a minor switch. How do you feel about saying, 'problem caller?'"

Hairy felt good about this and the next take was seamless—apart from recurring sound difficulties, the source of which was tracked to the lead actor's rumbling stomach.

"Could we break for lunch, please?" asked Hairy innocently. The director nodded ruefully, sure that his star acted up on purpose. The crew moved back to first positions, then raced to the chuck wagon for a quick cup of milk. The producer snuck off to satisfy his own view.

The only thing that kept Joel sane during production was veiled from the rest of the crew. Only once had a second AD caught him with a speck of white on his nose, and Joel had passed it off as spilled milk.

Sneaking into the gallery, a narrow booth filled with monitors displaying each camera's POV, he began to relax. Tranquility. No one to ask him daft questions, shout at him, or beg him to stretch the budget in their direction. Easing open a console drawer, he rummaged inside until he found a saucer. Pulling it out, he placed it on top of a DAT player. Joel didn't hate Hairy; he found him endearing. The actor was a creative type, a drama darling. Joel didn't appreciate the finite budgets, ballooning production costs, and the money it took to keep his saucer full.

Listening out for his colleagues, he leaned over his saucer and opened his mouth. Lowering his flat pink tongue, he curled it into a spoon shape and lapped up scoops of full-fat double cream from the saucer. As he swallowed the nectar, a cool, delightful feeling slid down his chest, into his stomach.

"Keeping busy, Joel?"

The producer looked up, hiding the saucer behind his back. He offered a relieved smile to his colleague, who whacked him in the face with an Apollo stand. Joel fell backward, banging his head on a console. Before he could pick himself up, his attacker was on top of him, a wire clutched in each forepaw. The producer struggled as the two bare ends of the wires were placed in his ears. The attacker backed off. From the corner of his eye, Joel could see a switch being flicked.

12

"You're coming with me, whether you like it or not." Tiger sweated in the hot-house, watching a school of greenfly settle on a plant.

Bug couldn't argue with her friend; he had already grasped her by the shoulder and was dragging her from her pedipalps. "Where's the fire?" she asked.

"In the old biscuit factory. They're filming a TV show there. Someone's copped it. Heard it on the prowler band."

"You want me to have a look?"

"I want us to examine the crime scene before the cops hop their clods all over the place. You know I wouldn't interrupt your important research if this weren't a matter—"

"Of life and death, I know. I could lose my job because of you, pal." They reached the zoo exit. "I'm supposed to let my supervisor know before I take a break. In writing. In triplicate. She's very strict."

"If she says anything, I'll have a word with her and explain the severity of the situation," Tiger soothed. "Whatever it takes to smooth things over."

Bug gave Tiger a smile. She'd enjoyed her visit to the Hant house and had been itching for a new adventure until her old boss had rushed in to grab her.

The 3C's upholstery design had been okayed by an official with no imagination. He or she had tried to please everyone with gray seats and cushions; no one enjoyed the result. Fine lines of blue, red, yellow, and green ran across the back of each tram seat. The floor and windows were trimmed with black rubber. Netting hung from above, ready to bear passengers' parcels and messages. Beside each seat was a Request Stop bell, which could be rung with a flick of a paw or tail. The windows were stickered: NO HISSING, NO DROOLING. The tram mucky enough as it was, covered in paw prints.

"What's in this for you, exactly? You fancy this Connie dame or something?" Bug curled up on a seat, tucking her tail around her belly.

"I have a mystery to solve. Why do you always think there's a romantic angle to these cases?" Tiger took a good look at his friend. She looked cozy.

"I never said anything about romance. These dames are bad for you. Always get you flustered, make you miss things. Sidetrack you. Why else would you wanna move in with dizzy Ms. Hant?"

"She needs looking after. She's in mourning."

"She's leading you on," sighed Bug. "Using you. Got you running around chasing after nothing. You gonna tell me where we're headed?"

"It ain't nothing. I'll tell you that much."

Reaching their destination, Tiger and Natasha hopped off the tram, sniffing at the thick-smogged air. The factory loomed, a stout red tower at the center. The detective strolled toward it, his assistant at his heels trying to look reluctant. Tiger stopped and pointed. A group of cats in baggy suits were marching purposefully up the street. At their head, bellowing orders and running to keep up, was a mouse.

"Prowlers," Tiger explained. "We've got to beat them to the body." He hurtled down a side alley, followed closely by Natasha. The pair scattered trashcans, garbage bags, and cardboard boxes in their wake. Drainpipes arched above them, a skyful of lead-lined tubing. The ground was icy, and Tiger skated on frozen puddles of rain and urine. Light at the other end of the alleyway led them to their destination.

Dashing under a security gate and into the monstrous building, they ascended three flights of stairs and reached the set. The prowlers were right behind them.

"I'm Detective Straight; this is my colleague," Tiger harangued the key grip. "Where's the body?" Marching paw steps echoed behind him. "There are some guys on their way, posing as prowlers. Fake ID. Stall 'em." The grip indicated the gallery; the investigators went in, scanning the room for clues.

"Cream fan." Tiger placed a paw in Joel's saucer, took a lick. "A drop of the rich stuff. Looks like he was interrupted mid-meal."

"This is no time for eating," Bug panted.

"There's *always* time for eating." Tiger savored an aftertaste. "Meaty," he said curiously.

"Meaty cream?"

Tiger shrugged. "Question: where did it all go?"

"Maybe he drank it?" Bug shrugged.

"He's glazed, not cream-filled. No excess cream, no container, just this saucer. Someone absconded with the goods after they offed him." Tiger pointed at a print left in the spilled cream, made by a big forepaw with an extra digit. That narrowed the suspect pool down a hair.

"It wasn't an accident, then."

"Bastet on a bicycle, no. The poor geezer's roasted." The wires still hung from Joel's ears. He was slumped against a swivel chair, a silly grin on his blackened face.

Natasha had already extracted her magnifying glass, giving the corpse a once-over, not the least bit squeamish. Tiger could hear voices arguing outside.

"Take a look at this," he said, drawing Natasha's attention to the wire trailing from Joel's left ear. Bringing her tool to bear, the assistant found a scrage of red on the insulation.

"Blood?"

"Polish. The same kind that coated that claw extension."

"Let me guess," interrupted Inspector Mortis. "You're two hams rehearsing the next episode. There's been a murder, and someone's got to pay?"

"Not bad, Inspector," said Tiger, towering over the rodent. "Are you a late lunch?"

"Don't test me, laddie. You're messing with due procedure." Natasha was ready to leave. She gave her partner a wary look. "If you've disturbed anything," the mouse continued, "I'll have your collars felt."

"We're not messing with anything," said Tiger. "We're leaving."

"Nobody's leaving until I say so."

"Nice one, Chief," Natasha glowered. Tiger gave her a shrug. He showed Mortis his card with an impressive flourish.

"You think this will get you special treatment?" piped the inspector. "I've heard of you, Tiger Straight. Thought you'd retired."

"I wish. My bones ache and my kidneys are kaput. But I've got incisors that are good and sharp." He proved it by chattering his teeth together. "My taste buds are tip-top ... little mousy."

The inspector clapped his paws together. The sound was barely audible in the factory, but his underlings hung on his every movement. Two constables pushed Tiger and Natasha onto canvas chairs beside the set. "How long you gonna be?" asked the detective.

"As long as I like." Tiger had never seen a mouse wield so much power. The implications were frightening.

With the slow sureness that only a prowler could have, Bix interviewed the crewmembers. The grips hated Joel because he was a grammar school toff, and he ignored them except when they made a mistake. They hadn't seen anything. No wires or cables were missing.

The sound mixer had always found the producer annoying because Joel would make mysterious slurping noises during a take. The director argued with him about shots and the script supervisor was sick of disputes over dialogue. They were all glad to see the back of him, though they didn't approve of the way he'd died.

Hairy's turn came.

"You can't interrogate me. I'm an icon. I represent something that television viewers nationwide aspire to. Heroism. Masculinity. Swift intelligence. Stoicism in the face of danger." He prostrated himself in front of Mortis. "I'm a lively soul. Magazine readers want to know what I eat, what I inhale. You don't want them reading about prowler harassment, their best-loved pin-up grilled by a rodent. They'll march on City Hall and demand the instant dissolution of your prowler force. If they don't get it (proving once and for all that our democracy is a sham) they'll gobble you up, notebook and pencil."

"A few questions, Mr. Bancroft. That's all." Mortis was the stoic one, with the panicked actor towering over him. "I don't watch TV, and I don't read magazines. I'm too busy earning my cheese although I do hear that glossy periodicals make good bedding when shredded. Don't look glum; I am familiar with your face. According to the other folks I've questioned, you're a liability to your channel. You're a party favor, a fop, a brute who can't remember a line of script. You're a numbskull, a fluff merchant, a blooper and a bloomer. I don't think in terms of repercussions, Hairy. I deal with the here and now. I ask simple questions; I expect them to be answered simply. In your case, I don't think that'll be trouble."

"My agent knows more solicitors than—"

"The longer you procrastinate, the more suspicious my colleagues become. Do *you* want your fans to read about your night in the nick? Your trial? Your sentence?"

Hairy shook his head.

"Did you kill Joel Venet?" Bix asked.

"No," Hairy sniffled.

"Thank you. Go on home."

"Is it our turn yet?" asked Tiger, feeling flippant.

"It's your turn when I say it is," Bix twittered, scratching in his dinky book. "It's your turn."

"Great. Where do we start? You want to hear about our day in general?" Bug gave the inspector a wink, but she felt worried. It's a bad idea to rile an official, even one who happens to be a rodent.

"Don't bother with all that nonsense," said Bix. "Stick to the plain truth."

"That's all you're interested in?" Tiger started playing with one of the cameras, positioning it so it faced another. Feedback screeched from a monitor; the sound mixer hurriedly turned the volume down. "No conjecture, or intelligent analysis of the situation, or jokes about frying tonight?"

"Tell me what happened."

"We heard this guy was dead. We came for a sniff. Held our noses. Ready to leave when you turned up and pooped our party." Tiger watched the howlaround on the monitor, as the two cameras bounced images off each other. Jigsaw shapes fluctuated, disappeared, reemerged, and swirled across the screen.

"What's your interest in this case?" Mortis asked wearily. He liked to look his suspects in the eye, even if it meant they had to stoop down to him. All the better, in fact—they were more likely to crack with a sore back.

"We solve murders." Tiger still refused to make eye contact with his interrogator.

"I know you've been out of work for a while, Mr. Straight. When a person loses their home, their office, their friends—they get desperate." That got the cat's attention. "You can't pin this on me, bub."

"Desperate enough to kill. Job creation?"

"I don't work that way. I've got a sound record. Always keep my whiskers clean."

"I'm fully conversant with your record." Aside to Bug he noted, "Not as spot-free as he makes out. I don't want to see you on the scenes of any more crimes. I've no time for private dicks."

"Can we go now?" asked Natasha.

"I suppose so," said Mortis with a dismissive wave of his paw. "But I'm sure I don't have to tell you—"

"Not to leave town. No. We've got lots to keep us busy round here." Tiger led his friend away from the set. "Detention's over," he muttered. "Let's go."

On his way out of the building, Tiger bumped into Jo, the beautiful Birman.

"Nice claws," said Tiger to the makeup artist. "Do them yourself?"

Jo's talons gleamed with ripe red varnish—the same shade he'd seen on the extension. Natasha's ears pricked up.

"I do everyone's claws. It's part of my job." The detectives introduced themselves.

"I'm Jo." She gave Tiger a faint curtsey. "You know who did this terrible thing? 'Cause I'd like to kick his back."

"You were a good friend of the producer?"

"Nah. The production will be suspended. Until they find another whiskerless wonder to finish the job, I'm out on my ear. No point taking another post in the meantime—this show's so popular, long-running, it's the closest they got to a secure contract in this industry."

"I don't suppose this accident'll hurt *Wonder Cat's* success any."

"That's a morbid thought." Jo's eyes narrowed.

"I might have to get in touch with you again, miss. Ask you a few questions."

"Sure." Jo gave him her card, watched the pair leave, and examined her claws carefully. The prowlers were interrogating the director. He wasn't getting home in time for tea.

"It's over," Bug purred. "The case is solved. We know who dunnit. The cops will do the dirty work for us. She'll be in jail by nightfall."

Tiger stayed silent, deep in thought.

"Whassamatter? I got your tongue?" Bug ran around until she was in front of her partner, slowing him down. He gave her a stern look. "You haven't!" Bug giggled.

Tiger broke his silence. "Haven't what?"

"Fallen for her."

"I don't believe this case is as simple as it seems. It has hidden depths. Jo's a suspect, sure, but she's not the only doll who wears red varnish."

"You're besotted with her. The cops'll put two and two together—"

"They won't make four." Tiger showed Bug his hankie; it was smeared blood red. "I tampered with the evidence."

"Why?"

"I need to do more investigating," said Tiger. "Can't have Inspector Mortis diluting the solution."

"You saw Jo's claws before you checked out the gallery?"

"I took a course in resourceful. Heck, I wrote the training manual."

"Pleased with yourself?" Bug asked.

"Enthused like you. Don't deny it. You know this is dangerous. Connie's in danger, so are we. Innocent lives."

"We're not innocent."

Tiger hesitated before answering. "We're on the right side."

"So, what do the good guys do next? From what you're saying, that varnish could be more of a red herring than a clue."

"Red herring?"

"Yes."

"We do what any self-respecting cat should do at this time of day," said Tiger. "We eat."

There was a cafe in the zoo. Natasha suggested they snack there; she could apologize for leaving her glasshouse post. When they got there, her employers didn't want to know.

"Leave this to me," said Natasha, storming toward the head zookeeper's office. "I'll meet you in the cafe."

The office sported an eclectic mix of wooden floorboards, columns pink as a newborn pup, a silver desk and chairs, and a heater shaped like a beach umbrella. The walls were yellow and gray, with small, circular lights beaming from discreet alcoves. The ceiling was turquoise; another set of inset lights spread star splashes of yellow overhead. Brent Motter, head of Nub City Zoo, was sniffing Bug's personal file.

"What's going on? Someone else running my area, caring for my subjects?"

"Your subjects are meant for public display," said Motter, calm but firm. "We've tolerated your experiments and secrecy up until now. Your papers and reports have been immaculate."

"Then what's your point?"

"My point is there is no point." There was a sadness in his eyes. "Folks are interested in bugs as a source of food, not of scientific research. You might as well study mince and tatties. We can't fund your work anymore."

"No one can look after the insects like I can," Bug insisted. "They're my friends."

"That's another reason why we have to let you go. You scare the cubs with your creepy crawling."

Natasha slammed a paw on the desk, which gave a hollow metallic ring. "This is entomological discrimination. I shall complain to the Board of Governors."

"Your methods are too unorthodox to interest any board of study. Putting different classes together, hoping they'll get along. What kind of research is that? We'll give you good references and a week's pay in lieu."

Natasha was already on her way out of the office.

"Hell mend you, Brent. For all your 'we' crap, you're the one who's firing me. I won't forget it."

The cafe was a vast, high-tech building with murals depicting edible fauna. Visitors took their mealtimes seriously. Tiger had ordered a chicken, a bowl of milk, beef on the bone, a lucky rabbit's foot, and a plate of marshmallows. The starter had arrived when Natasha collared the PI.

"We're leaving."

"I'm eating!"

"You can't patronize this establishment."

"The rabbit's foot is a nice touch."

"They've let me go. I seem to be a liability." A serving Lynx protested.

"Bill me," Natasha snorted as they hurried away.

13

Nut crossed her hooves. She needed the bathroom again.

Since the murder, the barn had become a spookier place to be. Dust rained from the rafters and carpeted the floor. The straw had a fetid taste. Strange echoes and ugly thuds interrupted her sleep. Shadows lost their form, oozed. She wasn't sure what cast them anymore.

There was something about a shadow, a half-glimpsed memory that refused to surface. She would have kicked herself, but that was impossible with crossed legs. She unfolded them and went to the bathroom.

The sun had set in spades. There was no light to see by. Walking on the tips of her hooves, taking care not to wake the neighbors, Nut maneuvered past stalls and hay bales. Her· eyes refused to adjust to the dark, so she kept walking until her nose bumped into something. It was warm and breathing heavily. She gave a shudder, clamping her eyes tightly shut.

A blunt object struck her under the chin, knocking her on the floor. Before she could utter a sound, a second blow to the head whacked her silly. She knew this was the end; as consciousness slipped away, she thought of her calves, and a fat check from the insurance company.

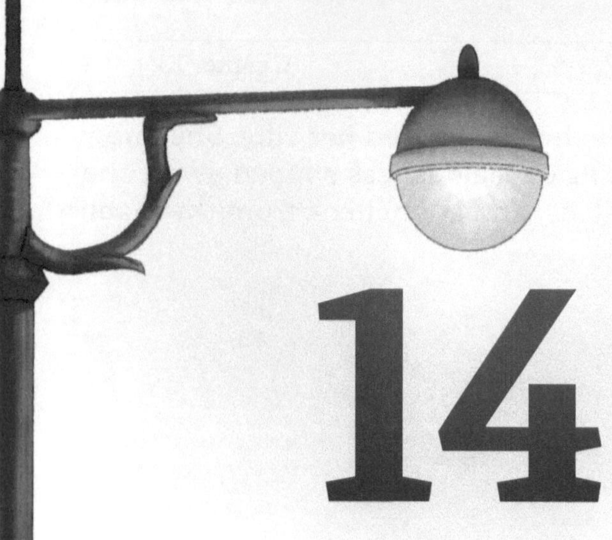

14

"Who needs exercise and runs?
"I'm a fan of toasted buns.
"Low-fat cheese, low-fat spread
"Never were my daily bread."

"Stop the presses, hold the phones
"I'm in love with herringbones.
"I'm cooler than ten ice cream cones
"Frozen in the snow."

"Hunger ain't my cup of tea.
"Starving doesn't set me free.
"Who wants to be skin and ribs,
"When we can be wearing bibs?"

"With your breath of Dover sole,
"You're my tuna casserole.
"Now I'm on a jelly roll
"I can see my belly loll."

"Watch your weight don't watch me wait.
"My fridge door is heaven's gate.

"Heading for pastures new
"So many cakes to get through."

"Veg and salad's not for me.
"Not all life can be fat-free.
"One chin ain't as good as four
"Ban diets—stay on the floor."

"Dover Soul"
By The Food Fighters

"Can you help me fix my fur? I can't do a thing with it," said Tiger. Jo hoped Tiger was joking. He proved her right when he cracked a grin. He'd visited her house with the express intention of grilling her for information. He hadn't got around to it so far; he was distracted.

"I'm a makeup artist, not a furdresser. You're all windblown." Jo obligingly stroked his head, the back of his neck, fussing over him maternally. He couldn't recall the last time he'd been stroked, and he had a damned good memory. He stood in her front hall, eyes closed, enjoying the moment. Then he collected his senses and reminded himself why he was there.

"I've got those questions for you if they're not too much to ask." Tiger cleared his throat.

Jo snatched her paw away and gave her visitor a strange look. He gave her his business card—she sniffed it, reading the scent that formed his credentials. Nodding slowly, she bade him sit on one of the swanky leather cushions.

"You know where you were when your producer copped it?"

"Reckon so." Jo shrugged. "I was on set. Hairy Bancroft—the lummox who plays Wonder Cat—gets precious about his laughter lines, the state of his whiskers. I'm always there to touch him up if necessary. The crew'll vouch for me."

"You always wear those claw extensions?" Jo was wearing her red-varnished claws again. Manual work would have been impossible with those talons attached; Tiger was surprised that she could make Hairy over without poking the actor's eyes out.

"Once they're adhered, it's hell getting them off again. They're my one vanity." Her fur was tousled, and she wore a faded white dress. Nothing fancy. Jo had nothing to accessorize, but she insisted on wearing her extensions.

"So you don't lose 'em very often?" Tiger asked.

"Impossible. I chuck 'em away when they're done, when the varnish starts flaking. Not every day. Why the big interest in my claws?"

"One more question," Tiger mumbled.

"Query away."

"Can you come dancing with me tonight? I'd like to spend the evening flattering you mercilessly."

"If every tom gave me a line like that, I'd spend my evenings at home. You're different. Call me a guppy, I'm hooked."

"Fine. Eight o'clock, the Wu Wu Club?"

"My favorite haybarn. See you there."

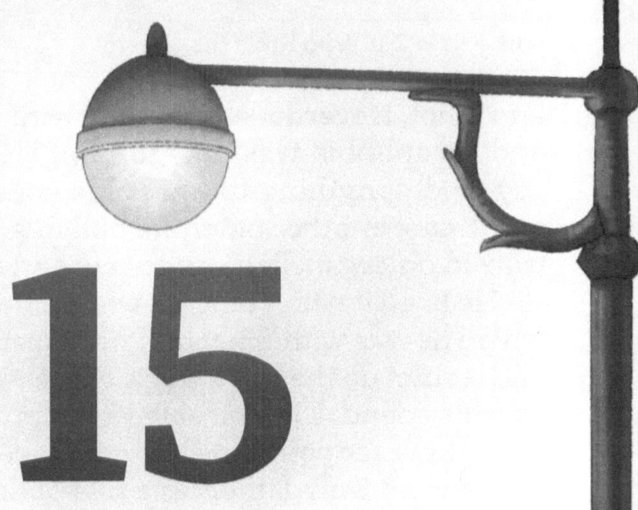

15

It only took a few days for Little Tim to finish his initiation and move on up to full garbage cat status. He suspected Lincoln helped to speed up the process, although his friend never admitted as much.

There was no fanfare or ticker tape parade; Anatolios did not dance a jig, and Tim did not get a golden broom. He was grateful to have help on the road, to be part of a crew, with two cats pushing a larger cart and two cats collecting trash and adding it to the movable heap. Still new, Tim was invariably one of the collectors; he preferred constant movement to pushing the heavy cart, then waiting and pushing and waiting. He needed the exercise.

His dozen-rats-a-day diet was filling him out. If he kept eating with such gusto, he'd soon lose his right to be called little. Maybe that wasn't a bad situation to be in. With four cats on the lookout for lunch, more rats were found and no cat ever starved. They needed sustenance to get through the day and unfortunately for their prey, the rats were it.

Tim missed the simplicity of working alone. As a rookie, he'd felt rushed and stressed and tired, daunted and inept. Nevertheless, dealing with lazy workmates and ergophobia was new to him. He didn't want to say or do anything to upset his colleagues' routine and create another potential bullying situation. So he walked on eggshells, figuratively and literally.

He liked it when Lincoln was on the crew; he knew where he was with Lincoln. The ginger cat nagged him and let him do the lion's share of the work, but Lincoln was his friend. Tim felt safe with him around.

"I didn't see you at the last meeting," said Lincoln as he watched Tim gather up a pile of damp corrugated cardboard.

"I couldn't make it," Tim replied, short of breath. "Had to get home. My neighbor went missing... then she was found. She had so much more to do with her life. It was terrible. Her mom needed support..."

"I'm sorry, brother." Lincoln bumped Tiger with his forehead, a little too rough. "But we're only as strong as our numbers. You have to attend meetings. If no one takes an interest, if we don't check each other's tails, EGG is as fragile as its namesake. Besides, how else will you know what's going on in the world of workers?"

"You'll tell me." Tim frowned.

"I may not always be around to tell you."

That sounded ominous to Tim. "Are you going somewhere?"

"Jeepers, no." Lincoln shook his impressively furry head. "However, I have many concerns that take me all around the city. You might not see me for weeks at a time."

"I can wait?"

It was Lincoln's turn to frown. "What did you say?"

"When you get back, you can tell me all about them. The meetings, I mean."

Lincoln shook his head. Tim could be such a simp. "Go to the gatherings," Lincoln said, taking the damp trash from Tim and throwing it in the cart. "For your own good health."

Back at the dump, Lincoln and Tim upended their cart onto a waste pile, made sure their trash was covered up, then went to a sunlit break area to clean themselves up.

"Have you ever wondered if there's something greater than yourself?" Lincoln asked, wiping his ears with his forepaws. Tim followed his lead.

"I'm Little Tim," said Tim, as if that was the perfect response.

"Greater than this place, your job, your fellow workers?" Lincoln washed his impressive whiskers.

"I don't attend church, if that's what you mean." Tim sat on his haunches, looking around. The two cats were alone. Tim wanted to make the most of his break from work. Lincoln was disturbing his rest, but Tim appreciated his company.

"I'm talking about other bodies," Lincoln explained slowly. "Other organizations larger and even more essential than EGG."

"Oh. I thought you meant church," said Tim. Organizations didn't come much larger.

Lincoln looked left and right fast, making sure they could talk undisturbed. "Have you ever heard of CREAM?" he asked. He pressed on before Tim's mind could wander down another path of misinterpretation. "It's a larger—"

"Organization," Tim caught on.

"Exactly! It does not focus on one specific job or workforce. Its purpose is greater, its methods more effective."

"More meetings," Tim sighed. While he wouldn't admit it to Lincoln, he found meetings rather boring. Especially union meetings.

"Meetings of minds." Lincoln cleaned his toes with his tongue. "Despite your lack of consistent participation, you are an asset to the Egalitarian Group for Garbage Cats. Your stature shows that the smallest cat can thrive with the right support. And your work ethic is an example to all. You must join CREAM."

"I don't know..." Tim stood up, ready to change the subject.

"Have I steered you wrong, brother?"

"No. Would Anatolios approve? I've already missed some work, handing out pamphlets and whatnot for the union."

"Approve?" Lincoln jumped upright. "Why, he's a founding member!"

"From the top of the hill," Tim mumbled to himself.

"You won't regret this," said Lincoln.

"Why do you want me to join so badly?" Tim squinted.

"Like I said, you're our smallest asset." As they left the break area, Lincoln rubbed his paws together, excited. "I can't wait to introduce you to the elite."

"What does it stand for, CREAM?"

Either Lincoln didn't hear Tim, or he ignored him, his blandishment complete.

The two cats got back to work, Lincoln supervising and helping when Tim got overloaded. Tim asked the two cart-pushers what they thought of CREAM. They considered it a naughty delicacy.

"I mean, the other kind," said Tim. He realized why cats got frustrated with him when he got the wrong end of the stick. "The big organization with a great purpose."

His workmates shook their heads. They had no idea what Tim was talking about, chalked it down to another tiresome example of his usual asinine rambling.

"Only very special cats know about CREAM," Lincoln shushed. "Don't mention it again, not to the likes of them."

Undeterred, Tim wanted to know more about the secretive society before he joined. He went to Anatolios for answers. To Tim's surprise, his boss seemed offended.

"This is very alarming," said the Aegean. "Lincoln brought you into the union, into his confidence. He trusts you to show solidarity, to add your unique talents to EGG."

Tim was confused. He didn't consider himself talented, and he didn't understand why Anatolios was upset. Tim stood in the boss's office, looking at him with his large, sad eyes.

Anatolios cooled down. He couldn't stay mad at this daft little factotum, and he had a leaning tower of paperwork on his desk. "By all means, think about CREAM."

"I do," Tim nodded.

"Consider the ramifications of your involvement. Weigh the pros and cons, although there are no cons." Anatolios popped out a claw and riffled through the documents in his in-tray, pulling Tim's personnel file from the pile.

Tim nodded again, brow wrinkled with concentration as he listened.

"But to go around asking about it..." Anatolios clicked his tongue. "CREAM is not for everyone."

"No, sir."

"Only the best of us are members of that organization. Only the brightest, the hardest working... and the highest paid." Anatolios opened Tim's file and checked the wage amount. He drew an extra fish beside it, cocked an eyebrow at Tim, whose eyes widened. "How can we help others if we are lower than them?" Anatolios asked. "Spreading gossip and asking questions that should not be asked?" Anatolios tapped his temple. "Keep it up here, Tim. Do not speak of it."

"What does it stand for?"

"It stands for success, not just for us but for the cats we take care of through our good works and maneuvers. It means a better world for all." Anatolios organized his documents on his desk but kept an eye on his employee, gauging his reaction.

Tim's shoulders drooped. The boss obviously knew what was best for him.

"Thank you ... for the opportunity," said Tim.

Papers laid out, Anatolios climbed onto his desk and curled up, ready for a midday nap. "I'm glad we understand each other."

"Oh, yes."

"Don't thank me, though," Anatolios said with his eyes closed. "Thank your friend Lincoln."

Nut was hanging upside down. Her hooves were numb, blood rushing to her head. Straining to look up, she found herself suspended from a steel wire, stirrups looped around her ankles. Her legs ached.

Inchmeal, she took in her surroundings. She could smell blood and dead flesh; on the far side of the icy room, she could see carcasses swinging from hooks.

Dozens of dead cows stripped of their hides, eyes frosted over. An obscene sight. She was next.

To her right, almost level with her head, was a metal box on runners. It automatically traveled across the floor, and every now and again, a thick bolt jutted from its side. There was a greasy pop whenever this happened. Nut dully realized that the box would soon reach her; the bolt would be in line with her skull. She began to struggle, flicking her tail, writhing in her bonds. They held firm.

I ain't going out like this. Straining her udder muscles, she summoned up every ounce of milk in her system and squooshed it upward. Warm white liquid jetted from her teats, lubricating the stirrups enough for her to wriggle her forehooves free. Now she dangled precariously, swinging close to the box. Gravity did the rest of the work, wrenching her free so she landed in a heap on the concrete floor. Inches from her head, the bolt popped. She offered it a derisory snort, stumbling from the slaughterhouse.

The Wu Wu Club had a strict dress code: no butterfly collars, no platform boots, no clip-on ties or studded leather. It was an up-to-date establishment with a young, hip clientele. It wasn't the most lavish club in the city. It was the best Tiger could afford, and the drinks were cheap.

So he took the plunge and lined up with his date. He'd managed to rescue some furniture from his apartment and hock it for a bagful of dough. He needed enough to bribe informants, pay off bad guys, impress Jo, and generally buy himself out of trouble.

The pawnshop provided a short-term solution. Tiger sold a few items he'd rescued from his old home: his favorite litter tray, used sax reeds, a knitted tail warmer that was a gift from a generous ex. He didn't want to think about the long term.

The pumas at the entrance looked uncomfortable in their tuxes. They were on orders to let only hep cats into the club and asked each oncomer to prove how cool they were. A couple of young cats in zoot suits performed a pathetic polka. They were sent packing, their heads hung low. Tiger and Jo watched as two females in front of them pogoed into the club.

"Let me handle this," said Jo softly, dancing a five-second ballet around the bouncers. She was fantastically graceful, a stranger to gravity, floating back to her date. They were allowed in no problem.

The foyer was decorated with soothing greens and blues. Enticing sounds and smells ushered the clubbers onward; a vast cloakroom was filled with the vain cats' garments. At the end of the foyer lay the club proper, flanked by bars offering live food and milk pitchers.

On a small stage stood a DJ with two turntables. A trio of jazz musicians, including a cat with a fiddle, joined him. Together they played repetitive music, easy to dance to, hard to forget. Skittish young clubbers capered on a checkered neon dance floor. More laid back, shy, or elderly felines sat on cushions, bopping their heads and shoulders to the tunes in ancient catdancing tradition.

Tiger made a beeline for the bar, where Jo offered to buy the first round. Lactose dependents lazed on stools, their weakness given away by their milk mustaches.

"What'll it be?" asked the bartender. The couple couldn't hear him, deafened by the music, each wall an amplifier.

"Two pints of milk," shouted Tiger, glancing at his date. "In the bottles." The drinks came fresh from the fridge. Jo paid the barkeep and bopped over to a mound of cushions. Tiger joined her as she supped her white stuff.

"Been here before?" she asked. He shrugged; the band had deafened him, and his paws were tapping involuntarily. He watched the DJ on stage, who'd clambered onto the turntables and was spinning at 45 rpm. Jo put down her bottle and dragged the detective onto the dance floor.

Together, they muscled their way past boogying couples and danced close to each other. Tiger nudged Jo's forehead tenderly with his nose, and they relaxed in each other's paws. His money worries faded as he gazed into her jade eyes. The club's resident rapper, Doctor Phat, appeared on stage and sang a ballad. His belly quivered with emotion.

A spotlight picked out various dancers, their hind paws kicking up purple dust, the faint smell of sour dairy products in their nostrils. They swanned or smooched or jiggled their way through Doctor Phat's set list, blissful smiles on their furry faces. The spotlight reached Tiger, tilting up to catch his eyes. The singer recognized him immediately.

No words were exchanged. Phat never spoke—he only sang. It was his trademark. He nodded at the saxophonist, who removed the black sling from around his neck and held out his instrument to Tiger. The detective exchanged a reluctant glance with his partner, then shimmied up to the stage. He shook his head, but the musicians were already hauling him up to join them. Tiger took the precious sax and wrapped his lips over the mouthpiece. Phat belted out a soulful song, and the crowd stopped mid-step to hear the saxophone's lilt.

Their ears clamped downward. Some of them went to the bar for a stiff pint; many left the club altogether. Tiger was oblivious, writhing to his own beat, while the band shook their heads and motioned to their engineer to switch off his PA.

Tiger didn't need a mike. He was in solo heaven, his paws gripping the sax, his eyes locked on Jo's. She wore a pained expression, so he finished his toneless tune and made an announcement to the dwindling audience.

"I'd like to dedicate this last piece to the prettiest lady in makeup." The patrons applauded, grateful that Tiger was finishing up.

If they'd known that the piece would consist of twenty minutes of noodling, they wouldn't have been so encouraging.

"You're lucky they're so polite in there," said Jo after the performance. "Any place else and you'd have been keel-hauled."

"It was a bit cheeky of me, taking to the stage like that." They took a moonlight prowl homeward. Tonight, Tiger felt invincible. "I hate to overshadow Doctor Phat. He didn't seem to mind. Recognizes talent when he hears it."

"He packed up and left halfway through your act."

"Yeah. Said—or sang—that he needed to get out of there fast. Know what he means, that place is stuffy. Lack of ventilation, I guess." The sax hung around his neck, spit dribbling from an open valve. Tiger tipped the spit onto his fur and rubbed it in, giving himself a good clean. "Maybe I should enter a new profession."

"You're a fine detective," replied Jo hurriedly. "Stick to what you're best at." Tiger gave her a funny look.

"What I'm best at is what I love. And what I love is music." Tiger placed the mouthpiece to his puffed pink lips, took a deep—

Jo yanked the instrument away. "I'll take that. It's not yours, anyway."

"But I..."

"There's a lot of families in this neighborhood; you'll wake the kittens. I'll return this to its rightful owner first thing in the morning."

"Sorry. I love you, Jo."

"I thought music was what you loved," said Jo with a raised eyebrow.

"I wasn't thinking when I said that. I didn't plan on ... telling you how I felt about us. It slipped out."

Tiger's timing was lousy as ever. He reached Jo's house, and without a further word, she went inside. He stood in the street for a long time, the night growing cold. Foolish. He was getting sidetracked. Jo reckoned he was a detective; it was time to live up to his reputation.

"Thank you, Lincoln," said Little Tim, following the union rep on a short walk to one of the largest buildings in Nub. Lincoln had led Tim away from the Public Works site after their shift, no words necessary; it was obvious from the longhair's insistent blinks and body movements that he wanted to show something to Tim.

In the wake of Lincoln's long, confident gait, Tim ran out of breath, fast. He had put on a few pounds, what with all the snacks he'd enjoyed. Apparently, no amount of manual labor could compete with a ratty treat.

They reached the city's hydroelectric station, harnessing the force of two fast-flowing rivers, providing the power to light thousands of homes. While cats weren't keen on large bodies of water, they knew how to use them to make their lives easier; they were masters of the workaround, finding ways to minimize labor. Garbage collection was a polydactyly's job, for now; one day that would be automated, just like lamp lighting, deep sea trawling, and fundamental factory work.

The station's huge, sandstone exterior was adorned with massive scratching post columns and bas-relief big cats carved into the cornices. Lincoln and Tim ascended a flight of steep steps into an empty portico. As Tim gazed at the cavernous entranceway, Lincoln produced a strip of black silk from his overalls. It was a blindfold, which Lincoln held up in front of Tim's eyes.

"Is this...?"

"Necessary? Oh yes."

Tim took a step back.

"Stay calm," said Lincoln, who to the contrary was shaking with excitement. "This initiation will be a lot easier than your first few days with the Public Works."

Tim took a breath and, as always, trusted his friend as the longhair blindfolded him and led him through the tall, dark entranceway. From the way his paw steps echoed, Tim could tell he was in a long stone hallway; Lincoln seemed to lead him for several minutes before they stopped. Tim could hear a clowder of cats slowly breathing, smell their spit-shined fur close to him. He wanted to run. Neither Lincoln nor Anatolios had warned him about this rite of passage.

Would he have come, though, if he had known what was going to happen? His fear of disappointing Lincoln and Anatolios far outweighed his fear of the unknown. But for a moment he realized what his rats felt like, trapped in the dark, cowering against strange and impossible odds.

Tim felt a soft material settle on his back and whirled around. Paws steadied him, kept him from panicking. Lincoln again, he was sure. He was lucky to have such a reliable friend.

"Are you ready to see with new eyes?" asked a deep, aged voice. Tim nodded, desperate to lose his blindfold. Once it was removed, candlelight spilled into his eyes, which adjusted to see six cats in red robes staring at him. He shivered at the sight, looking for Lincoln, but all faces were hooded and impenetrable. Tim had an identical robe draped on his shoulders; two cats helped him slip his forepaws into the sleeves, a slow and solemn movement.

"What now?" asked Tim, more confused than ever. "Who are you? Lincoln?"

With great formality, the largest cat drew back his hood, revealing a cruel-looking caracal.

"To join us, you must recite the litany," said the caracal in an ominous tone.

Tim faced him, looking dumbfounded.

"Repeat after me," the caracal scowled.

"After me," said Tim, nervous.

"I am one of many, yet I am unique in the way I can help others. I will tame my wild heart and fashion my words in kind, not harmful ways. The indigent will be my prey, and fairness will sustain me. All lives are important to me and essential to the future of my city.

Although his vocabulary was as small as his name, the litany made sense to Tim. Except for "indigent."

He didn't know what that meant. Otherwise, it all made sense, except the bit about sustenance. That puzzled him. Still, he didn't have any problem with taking the vow. It was only temporary, after all, a try-before-you-buy into the organization.

"Welcome to our family," said Anatolios.

That was why Tim was here, he realized. He had gained a family. He would have to get to know his new brothers and sisters, do his best to fit in. It would be difficult, but he would belong.

He was amazed by the cats' discipline. Usually, cats liked to do their own thing, quickly losing interest in prescribed activities. These philanthropists were different. He hadn't seen this kind of dedication in the trailer park or at the Public Works. It was a reassuring reminder that when they put their canny minds to it, cats could get things done.

Someone poked him in the back. Tim whirled around, felt an object swinging behind him. He looked over his shoulder and saw that a second tail was clipped to his waistband, right beside his real one. He didn't like it. He instinctively wanted to wash it.

A hooded cat got close to Tim. The eyes gave away Lincoln's identity. "I have one as well," Lincoln whispered. "We all do."

Tim caught a glimpse of other double tails.

"Why?" Tim asked his friend. "I don't feel ... balanced."

"You will," said Lincoln with a subtle bow of his head. "Here, we sport two tails to remind us that there are many, varied forms in our world. Cats are ever exploring, ever evolving, meeting new breeds and species, learning how to help and guide them."

"Growing extra tails?" When Tim let out a snort, the caracal stiffened.

"Expanding our minds," Lincoln explained patiently. "Becoming better cats in the process."

Little Tim still wasn't sure who all the cats were, or what Lincoln's "process" would be. But he was a fully-fledged member of CREAM and that fact warmed his belly. He would help the group in any way he could.

Nut was spending too much time in Bertie's Tavern. Her pals were present. She'd met her beau for the first time here. Yet it still was unnatural for a cow to prop up a bar. Since Scrumpy's demise, she'd been drowning her sorrows, getting over the fright, waiting for delayed shock. There was some niggling thought at the back of her brain, struggling for attention. Frustrating.

Work continued as if no one had died; the dairy had appointed a new boss, and the interim had seen various tabbies collecting the milk. They had cold pads and a brusque demeanor. So, after a shift, the cows would visit Bertie's—for a quick one—leaving Nut to spend the evening there. She'd wake up the next morning in a pool of drool; she was too heavy for the barkeep to carry home. Back to the daily grind, chewing the cud, lining up in a field for hours, giving on-demand milk. She hadn't seen her calves for days.

Every item of bar gossip was old news, every joke was as stale as last month's bread. The latest topics of conversation included poor work conditions, the draughty shed, the big ears on the cow in stall 3B, hoofache, and the latest bovine fashions (mostly outrageous headgear).

Nut had been an idiosyncratic cow since her college days. She'd spent precious little time learning how to chew cud in a refined manner. Most of her activities had centered on trying to catch a bull's eye. That bull had become her husband, loyal, full of tact, and flatulent. She was delicate and bright, with a big family. She was concerned about two large black spots on her forehead, teased about them since childhood. Apparently, all Friesians had the same trouble; she'd been affected worse than most, lying awake worrying about her appearance. Hubby chalked it down to vanity. He hadn't suffered catcalls from the local farmers. He couldn't understand.

After escaping from the abattoir, she'd reported her abduction to the prowlers. They hadn't sounded particularly interested; they assumed that this was just another example of cow hysteria.

A mouse walked into the bar. It was the cop who'd interrogated her before, Inspector Mortis. He was too small to mount a stool, and no one noticed him except for Nut. He scurried past one of the bar staff, who almost trampled the rodent. Unruffled, the inspector squeaked at Nut, "Come with me. You're not safe here."

"You're going to protect me?" asked the cow. "Where are we going?"

Bix led her out of the bar. "Prowler Headquarters. We need to know exactly what you saw."

"That might be difficult. I can't remember what my kidnapper looked like. My mind's a complete blank."

Bix's nose twitched in annoyance. He'd already decided that Nut was just a typical cow, and all she cared about was chewing the cud.

"We're going to have to unblank that mind of yours," he told her. "Whatever it takes."

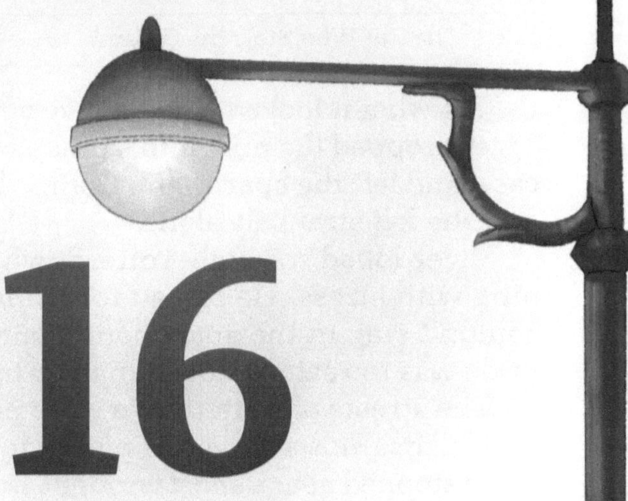

16

As soon as Tiger got back to Connie's place, he aimed for the fridge. It held one pint of milk, which he carried gingerly into the living room. Sinking his weary buttocks onto a cushion, he popped the cap off the bottle and took a leisurely swig.

"What the hell do you think you're doing?" hissed Connie, looming over the private eye.

"Whatever I can to solve your case. I don't wanna be here any longer than I have to." The cold drink whet his whistle, left him with a milky nose.

"Since when did sniffing for clues include dating your prime suspect?" Connie's left ear fluttered.

"I need to find out a lot of things about Ms. Madrigal. Things she might not tell a stranger."

"I think it's disgusting." Connie waggled a paw at the window. "If you're tired of this place, you can go."

"So, you'll have more room for Mr. Suave? Want plenty of space to roll around with him?"

"That's not what it's like." Connie shut up, wondering if Tiger was jealous. What tom wouldn't envy the buff Cole Tiddle?

"It's what it looked like. I'll give you some privacy." Tiger dropped the milk into a bin, picked up his worn case, and left the apartment. Connie had lost a friend, and she felt strangely alone.

Tiger lolled through Totterdown, his brain spinning with stress. He feared for Connie's life, yet he couldn't stay in the apartment against her will. His pride was too set to allow him to go back, apologize.

The streets of Totterdown were paved with green-gray slabs, mossed over in places for extra traction. Tiger stopped near a short wrought-iron gate, exhaling icy breath in primitive rings. A dirty plastic canopy jutted over the pavement, keeping some of the wind off. There was no way Jo could be involved in the murder. She wasn't the brutal type. In the unlikely event that she could have been responsible, she was far too canny to kill her producer. No alibi, a high level of risk, and electrical savvy, to boot. He'd been a detective for longer than he remembered to care. His guts told him she was clean.

Tiger wasn't going to give up the case, not after weeks of work. He certainly wasn't going to leave the job to his rival—he only trusted one guy, and that cat played the sax. Cole could be busy double-dealing or (worse) get so horny he'd trip up. Tiger wanted to be there, watch him fall. Right now, his only lead was a beautiful female desperate for companionship. Drop the case or pay her a visit? No contest!

Leafless trees jutted skyward like TV antennae. The setting sun silhouetted the branches, and staying out late wasn't the done thing in this quarter. The predators came out, seeking a feast. Even a cat who could take care of himself needed to find shelter. Tiger struck out for Jo's house.

Crime solving is a solitary occupation. You can't ask your missus to spend the night with you if you're on surveillance; she'll get bored, and you might miss something while you're necking. The role calls for love of detail, focus, clarity of thought—all the things a relationship can cloud. Tiger had been celibate for years, and he refused to believe that his music had anything to do with it. It'd been a conscious decision on his part to stay frosty.

Connie's original plea had appealed to his ego, his intellect, and his belly. Jo invoked baser instincts. He wondered if Connie was jealous, then discounted the fancy. She was focused on herself—on Cole's pecs.

Stone buildings gave way to wooden ones with lacy curtains and charming chrome drainpipes. Almost there. Two more blocks and he'd have somewhere warm to spend the night.

Twelve minutes later he reached her house, a hundred years old, crumbling at the cornices. The windows were dead dark and his distinctive howl prompted no response. Filming of *Wonder Cat* was suspended pending an inquest. Jo was probably out on the tiles with a butch beau.

Great. He was miles from home. The only friend he had in this part of town was a makeup artist he'd questioned in the course of the investigation ... and she didn't appear to be home. Tiger wanted to make sure before he made the journey back to Connie's and begged her to let him back in, so he entered Jo's house and sniffed around. The bedroom was his last port of call. He found Jo on an orthopedic mattress, her eyes wide open. Her breathing was shallow.

Tiger set down his case and tentatively nudged her, listened for a heartbeat. It was so faint he almost missed it. He breathed into her mouth and nose, his actions becoming more desperate as she refused to respond. Her body was cold, and she smelled clammy; he wrapped a sheet around her, staying close to warm her. Growing frustrated with his lack of success, he placed a paw on her exposed tummy and jabbed her with his claws.

Jo stirred, pain showing in her eyes. She looked at Tiger and moved away from him, surprised to find him in her bed.

"You're gonna live," he told her in relief. "Try and breathe. You hurt anywhere?"

"My chest," she replied, making sure the sheet covered her from neck to tail. She didn't let any old tom look at her stomach. "Feels tight. Hard to breathe."

"It'll pass. Relax. You've had a minor attack is all."

Jo soon improved, breathing carefully. The room still seemed to be spinning around her, but Tiger was a constant that she locked onto. He held her tight until she was well enough to talk.

"This minor attack... they wanted me dead."

"Who?" Tiger fumed. "Someone slip you a mickey?"

"Gas. Heard noises on the landing. Thought it was a burglar! When I went to investigate, I found a pipe leading up the stairs. It started pumping some foul-smelling smoke into my face. I made it to the bed..."

"I didn't see any burglars. No pipe, either."

"They must have cleared it away, scarpered before you got here. No evidence. It was the kitty killers. They want me dead. Same reason they wanted to kill Joel."

"And the reason is?"

"I'm trying to work it out. You're the detective. Maybe they don't like our show. Joel's death was in all the papers—maybe they're making a political statement."

"Nah. If these deaths are linked... the other deaths didn't make front-page news. They would have hit bigger targets, more prominent cats."

"You're right. I'm not important enough. They're crazy."

"Did you see anything? Apart from the disappearing pipe, I mean?" As he spoke, Tiger took a gander at the landing. There was a trail of rust leading down the stairs and a long groove had been left in the carpet.

"Nothing." Jo shook her head, still groggy. "I was looking out my bedroom window until I heard the—"

"Strange noises. Yeah. What did you see?"

"Outside? Some youths coming home from the workhouse. Three of the neighborhood toms on their way to the local sauna. Guys lining up for the bread line down the road. Nothing out of the usual."

"I should make some inquiries," Tiger mumbled.

"It's too late. Not right now. Stay with me, in case they come back—try to kill me again."

"We need to find out who 'they' are. I'm not going to do that curled up here on your oh-so-comfortable bed."

"It's a special mattress. I spend a lot of time hunched over people in my line of work, painting their faces, fixing their fur. This helps me straighten out my back and tail."

"Fancy."

Jo led her friend downstairs, and they cooked up several kippers. Her near-death experience had given her an appetite, and Tiger was permanently hungry. He picked daintily at the fish, using his tongue to extract the bones and dribbling them onto his plate. Jo picked her teeth with her claws, making eyes at Tiger.

"I was wondering how long it'd take you to pay me a proper visit. Not on some pretext, I mean."

"Interrogating you? I've run out of questions." Tiger felt suddenly bashful.

"You got a mother? A father?"

"You'd like my dad. He's a genuine original. If he was any more down to earth, he'd be dragging himself around on his belly. Mom died a long time ago."

"I lost touch with my parents. It was easier to stay away, I guess." Most cats had an independent streak knocked into them at an early age. The offspring would often go too far, shunning their family. Jo would close her eyes and imagine her folks looking down on her, blissful with pride. Every day, their faces became less distinct; soon she wouldn't be able to remember what they looked like.

"If I have kids, I'll stay close to them, let them know I love them. Even after they leave home, I'll be there for them."

"That's pretty much the way I feel." Tiger felt drowsy, cleaned his plate quick. After supper he returned to the bedroom, Jo offering him her bed. It looked mighty cozy: a thick duvet, pillows that were soft but not too soft, a hot water bottle buried deep within.

"It's your place. You take the bed." Tiger removed his trench coat. "I'm fine in the linen closet. It's warm and cozy, and I'm not proud,"

Jo protested. "You're the guest. Take the bed!" There was no point standing around arguing all night. Sleeping on a bed where she'd almost died obviously didn't appeal to Jo. Tiger gave his host a friendly sniff on the neck, then dived under the duvet. Bliss!

Nevertheless, the gumshoe found himself unable to sleep. Rolled onto his side, then his stomach, hind paws entwined in a clean green sheet. He poked his nose out from under the covers, sure it had become colder in the room. He was about to sacrifice his place when a paw slipped under the duvet beside him. Slowly and carefully, trying not to disturb Tiger, Jo climbed into bed and stretched herself out. Tiger breathed in her scent, didn't mind cold pads and sharp claws on his flanks.

"You shouldn't get me excited, not in your condition."

"You mean I'll be too weak to resist?"

"I'm the weak one," said Tiger, turning to embrace her. He didn't get much shuteye that night.

Connie entered the pub anxiously. She quickly caught sight of Cole sitting on a leather brass-studded seat cushion. His hind paws barely reached the carpet, patterned with red seashells, interspersed with patches of gray. He'd found a polished hardwood table close to the kitchen. On it sat a circular glass ashtray, with indents to rest cigarette butts. Two menus were lacquered and tarted up with a sprig of red ribbon on each spine. The items on the menu were garnished with dreadful gags and puns: "You'll lap up our soup!" "Milk our shakes for all they're worth," "*The Lost Keys—the place to meet for a plate of meat.*"

Viewtone televisions were stationed on either side of the bar, flashing bright pictures at the patrons, mesmerizing them, interrupting conversations with the sound of tinkling bells and squeaks. Posters on the walls were a reminder of past pub glories—epic quizzes, famous visitors.

The landlord's mustache was carefully trimmed and waxed, almost as long as the bar at full stretch. Punters traveled from near and far to see the face fungus. The milk was inexpensive; the pub made most of its money from fruit machines, cigarette dispensers, and bar snacks. Their *vole au vent* was a specialty.

"I was expecting somewhere more ... swanky," said Connie as she joined Cole at the small round table.

"I'll let you into a secret," whispered Cole, tapping his nose with a carefully extended claw. "Having more moolah than you could hope to spend in nine lifetimes is boring. Deadly dull. Sometimes I like to escape from the millionaire trappings, slum it a little. A relaxed setting like this makes for a fun date. No formalities." Connie opened her mouth to respond, but Cole didn't grant her the luxury. "The mutton with lamb dressing looks rather nice. Oh, don't take it personally." Cole continued, "I haven't invited you here because of your upbringing or anything like that. I'm not trying to bring myself down to your level—I don't think I could. I'm indulging myself. If you have any whims, I'd be happy to tolerate them for you."

Connie gave her date a mischievous smile. "Show me the trappings," she said.

Cole's house was in a far better neighborhood than Connie could ever aspire to. Each room was the size of her apartment, carefully furnished, ornately decorated. The minute she entered the dwelling, she got depressed, vowing to give up interior decorating for good. She'd worked hard to create a world in which she'd be comfortable; here was a place where her host would always be satisfied.

"Would you like a rubdown?"

"Ooh, we hardly know each other," Connie said coquettishly. "After we..."

"It's not a come-on," Cole assured her. "My personal masseur's in the west wing. He's excellent at unstiffening the joints. Fancy it?"

Connie nodded, embarrassed. She'd almost put her paw in her mouth there. She didn't want her host to know she planned to seduce him, work out who'd hired him. Not yet.

The cats visited a sauna room, languishing in the steamy heat. Connie tried to keep her towel on while Cole showed off his sexy body. It got too hot, so she let the towel drop, her modesty preserved by clouds of steam. Once they were ready to leave the room, the masseur was ready to work them over.

"You're a wonder, Snoke." Cole sighed as his back received a soothing massage. He told Connie, "Snoke's adept at acupuncture as well, aren't you Snoke?"

"That's right, sir," the masseur replied, digging a claw into Connie's gluteus maximus. She unleashed a happy yelp.

Once the pair had been rubbed up the right way, Cole gave his guest a tour. Labyrinthine hallways led to rooms that Cole seldom had the time to visit. They were kept free of dust by a horde of domestic staff, all provided by Purrtemps, an elite employment agency. The few areas that the millionaire *did* use included a games room where he could play Catch the Bright Shiny Thing and that most popular of pastimes, Chase the Dangly Thing. He showed Connie a lounge complete with leather cushions, a sunbed, and a movie screen. The kitchens were a part of the house he only visited when panged with the midnight munchies to grab himself a bowl of ratatouille or a packet of go-gos. He enjoyed cooking, though he had little time for it in his busy schedule; he saved his culinary conjuring tricks for special occasions and very special ladies.

A nursery waited for the children that Cole had never had. He hoped to fill the room one day; until then, he would look at the cots and toys occasionally, hoping they'd inspire him. The simplicity of a cub's building blocks, or the merchandising possibilities of a stuffed toy, could send ideas rocketing around his head.

"You could house a whole family in here," Connie mused, pressing the funnel on a scaled-down safari train. It emitted cheerful huffs and whistles.

Cole swatted Connie's paw away from the toy. "This is for my family," he rasped, ushering his date out of the room. He rapidly regained his composure. "I didn't mean to be lionesque."

"It's okay," said Connie.

"I was married once. Penny was barren. No, that's not true. I was the one who couldn't provide her with— couldn't make babies with her. We separated."

"That can't have been the only reason you married." This was more like it. Connie was getting under his skin, making him open up. At this rate, he'd give her the information she needed before the evening ended.

"It wasn't. We split for other reasons, too."

"She was a gold digger?"

"I should have seen her shovel coming. Gold, silver, and jade, my dear."

"Nothing like me, then," said Connie under her breath.

"No. Nothing like you. I still hope to have a progeny one day. I've been taking fertility drugs, you know."

"Any side effects?"

"They instill in me the urge to give my guests an exhaustive tour of my home and bore them to death with talk of past relationships."

"Don't get you frisky, then?" Connie giggled.

"No. Life's too short for lust, don't you agree?"

"Whatever you say."

Connie was particularly impressed with the personal gym and the hallway, which was dominated by a heavy tapestry. Ancient and beautiful, it depicted a group of cats shattering the bonds of slavery. An ancient race had once kept them as pets, cooped up, under control. No feline could put up with such treatment for long. Above the tableau was a heraldic symbol, Cole's family crest. His noble lineage was rooted in servitude.

Connie looked up at the sumptuous cloth, the woven tableau, thinking naughty thoughts.

"Go ahead," said Cole softly.

"What?"

"Go on. I know what you want to do. Do it."

"No, no, I couldn't." Connie became bashful. "What would you think of me?"

"I would think that you're not afraid to live out your fantasies. Get up there." She didn't need any more coaxing. Jumping as high as she could, she unleashed her claws and hooked them into the tapestry. Using them to hoist herself up, she made a scrambling ascent. Within seconds, the cloth was ruined, shredded strips floating to the floor.

From the top of the tapestry, Connie could see out the window across the front lawn. She paused for breath, her purchase shaky. Cole joined her on the tableau, breathing hard. Their makeshift ladder swayed from side to side; the hooks that supported it half out of the wall.

"I think we should get down from here, don't you?" she said.

"If we can..." Cole grabbed at Connie to support himself. "Help me," he said as they started to descend. She didn't want to let go of his paw. Within feet of the floor, the hooks gave way, and the cats landed, covered by the dusty cloth. Connie sneezed.

"You must think I'm awful clumsy," laughed Cole. Connie shook her head.

"Look what I've done to your tapestry!" she said in dismay. "I hope it isn't expensive to repair."

"It'll cost more than the house," Cole told her in a nonchalant manner. "Worth it." Connie would have felt nervous, but the tom hadn't relaxed his grip on her. If anything, it seemed to tighten.

"Take a look at this," said Jo cheerfully, waking Tiger from an exhausted doze. She was staring out the window, her naked form haloed by harsh sunlight.

"Don't you have a nightdress or something?" Tiger squinted. "Someone might see in."

"Only the birds." At Jo's behest, the detective climbed out, wrapping a sheet around his middle. Someone had left breadcrumbs out in the street, scattered along the sidewalk. Birds wheeled and swooped, excited at their find—sparrows, seagulls, and a couple of evil-looking crows. They flew past the bedroom window, mere inches from Tiger and Jo.

It was a wonderful and painful sight. The couple fought the urge to open the window and leap for the birds; the winged taunters could easily glide out of their reach, and there were a fair few feet for the cats to plummet. Instead, they stood watching the show together, tails locked in a soft embrace, chirruping softly. The cats' attempted squawks didn't draw any birds to the window ledge; once all the breadcrumbs were gobbled up, the feathered creatures returned to the trees, tantalizingly out of reach.

17

Tiger's day was spoiled by an invitation.

A couple of official-looking bruisers stopped him in the street and took him to Prowler Headquarters. Inspector Mortis was waiting for him there.

"What's up, Inspector?" Tiger asked blithely as the bruisers left him with Bix in the mouse's office. "You got a stirring in your breastie?"

"I'm not satisfied," Bix grumbled.

"I understand. Can't find a strumpet your size. You have my sympathy."

"You know more about Joel Venet's death than you're letting on. For all I know, you could be withholding evidence."

Tiger grimaced, turned away. Bix had an instinctive talent for reading every tiny twitch on a cat's face, one reason why he was Nub's best copper.

"Mr. Straight?" Bix insisted.

Tiger looked through the vertical blinds into the bullpen where most of the prowlers worked. His ears sprang upward. "There's a cow going bonkers in the office," he told Bix. "Got a pain in her udders or something. Probably bust up the joint."

Bix looked startled. "Excuse me." He scooted from the room. Tiger heard a moo, followed by a couple of squeaks. He used the diversion as an excuse to look around the inspector's office.

On the mouse's desk lay an unmarked folder. Between two sections of brown card were pieces of paper showing the bank account details of some familiar folk. Tiger neatly folded the papers and tucked them under his hat. He took the inspector's small black notebook, too.

Bix popped his head back into the office. "We're going to have to continue this conversation at a later date," he whined.

"I can see you have your paws full," the detective replied, bidding him farewell. He refrained from tipping his fedora to the cop, preferring to stroll from the building whistling a blues riff.

Doctor Mildrew had a headache. His ears were abuzz with other people's problems. As soon as they opened their mouths, he got a headache. He'd sit behind them so he didn't have to look interested and offer a few reassuring *hmms* to prove that he was awake. With his head full of their complaints, he couldn't find the time to sort himself out.

He had his own difficulties to deal with. The landlord kept raising his office rent, and he had to increase his fees accordingly. Fortunately, his patients believed that they'd get what they paid for, sure that the more they spent, the higher the quality of service would be.

In truth, they didn't receive a greater number of *hmms* than any low-rent quack could offer. One look at the doc's gorgeously decorated office reassured them.

Mildrew owned a leather-bound swivel chair with a high back and padded arms. He had not one desk but two on opposite sides of the room, with drawers full of case notes too dull to ever see daylight. A set of red scales sat on one desk, flanked by two fat phones and a mug that proclaimed: "You don't have to be mad to work here, but it helps if you have an Oedipal complex." A mouthful even for a learned professional like Doctor Mildrew, but he'd found the gag funny in the china shop.

Humor was an important part of the therapeutic process although some patients didn't like having their tails pulled and others didn't respect a therapist who clowned around. He was a father figure, an advocate, a smother superior. His office was a confession booth and his couch a talk show sofa. Patients dreamed about him and asked him to interpret. Nothing hidden there. Mildrew simply booked more sessions for them, keeping his bills at bay.

No one appreciated how the debts could pile up. His furniture was scratched to death by disaffected mogs. Vases or ornaments were jarred and smashed as panthers got in touch with their inner rage. Some of the worst cases underwent hypnotic regression; they were prone to pawing at Mildew's dangling pocket watch or eating it whole while under the influence. He didn't blame them in the least, but he did get through a lot of pocket watches.

The doctor had a scant social life; he had no idea how or where to pick up broads and they'd always found him too cerebral, anyway. He'd get off on thoughts or ideas rather than physical acts or visual stimuli. As a youth, he'd written frilly letters to his sweetheart; she'd lost love interest in him when he'd failed to back up his words with deeds. As a grown-up, most of his jollies were derived from *Puss Out of Boots*, the popular adult magazine.

His failings made him an excellent psychiatrist—he could truly sympathize with the lonely, wretched screwballs on his couch. The female patients swore by him. He always had a kind *mm* for them, even if he did ogle their tails every so often.

Courteous, understanding, lecherous. A male prepared to feel your feelings, something lacking in many husbands. Mildrew would listen intently, or appear to with his well-honed *hmm*ing.

His most difficult task was not to appear jaded. He'd seen it all and heard more besides—personal worries, marital fatalities, suicides (not all his fault). One cat had confided a desire to be swung around a small room, another had a fetish for rattraps, still another had spent all her time watching a goldfish revolving in a bowl in the corner of her living room. He'd reassured her there was nothing unnatural about that.

"Gotta sec, Doctor?" The screen slid back with a squeak. Inspector Mortis raised an eyebrow, making sure he had the therapist's attention. "I always have a second for you, Bix. Come on in." Mildrew nodded the cop toward the couch.

"I've brought a friend," Bix said. "I hope you don't mind."

"I'm amenable."

"You're not going to charge double?"

"We can discuss billing at the end of the session. Who's the cow?"

Nut glanced around the office, hooves unsteady. Bix introduced her in gentle tones. The doctor tried to get her to rest comfortably on the couch. It didn't work; Nut couldn't relax, her udders trapped between two seat cushions. Mildrew gave up and let her stand.

"I want you to hypnotize this cow," said Bix. Nut let out a low moo.

"A cow?" Mildrew asked, as if he had just noticed Nut's presence.

"She has important information to impart," said Bix. "I have reason to believe she witnessed a murder and has mentally blocked the details."

"I don't want to remember anything. Not that I saw diddly." Nut shook her head sadly. "I want to go home. My herd needs me. They look up to me."

"This is unorthodox," warned the doctor, leafing through a series of charts. "Cows are notoriously difficult to regress. Large cranium, small brain."

"Charming." Nut flicked her tail, trying to look intelligent. "I'll do it. I've got the chops."

"Okay, here we go." Mildrew pinned a monochrome chart to the wall. "Look at the center. Don't take your eyes off it. Relax." Nut began to grind her teeth automatically, although she was cudless. Soon her eyes drooped and the doc had her spellbound.

"It's all dark. I'm blind!"

"Open your eyes."

"Oh! Okay," said Nut.

Bix looked on, intent. His paw hovered over his hip pocket, ready to draw out his notebook if necessary.

"It's still dark."

"What can you hear?" asked Mildrew.

"A big thumping. Swishing noises, like a rumbling tummy. A botty burp."

"You're in the womb." Mildrew realized, explaining to Bix that Nut had regressed a little further than expected. "I want to take you forward, my dear. Picture the shed where you live. Can you see it?"

"Yes, my calves are there. Stop that! Stop biting Lizzie. Bob's always biting Lizzie. To get attention, you know. Farmer Scrumpy's there, too. *Moo-hoo!* He's ignoring me as usual."

"Something bad happened to Scrumpy," Bix interjected. "You were there. What did you see?"

Mildrew held up a paw to silence the rodent. "This is a delicate operation, Inspector. We must peel away layers of this lady's mind until she is free to share her memory. As yet... she won't tell us anything."

"Oh!" Nut perked up. "You won't *believe* what happened to me the other day. I asked for some sort of financial assistance from Scrumpy. I won't go into the details, deadly dull—when what should happen, but he falls down dead. We thought he'd tripped until the blood began to flow. That wasn't so nice."

Bix unholstered his spare notebook, flipped it open to a crisp blank page, pencil poised, and said, "Go on."

"I saw... I saw a shadow. Must have been the killer. Whoever it was, he had to be big. Tall, broad, with a tail like a hemp rope. Round ears. Glimpsed for an instant. Gone."

"What did he sound like, the attacker?"

"I don't know."

Bix repeated his question, but Nut shook her head. A tear teetered from one thick lash. The doc clapped his paws together and she jerked awake.

"What are you doing?" Bix exploded.

"We'd gone too deep. Too traumatic. Any more and her little mind would snap."

"You don't understand. There's a cat killer out there. I have to stop him—you could be next, for Bastet's sake! Put her back under!"

"More than my job's worth. I'd lose my license—"

"To print money. I know. How much do I owe you?"

"Six pigeons. Sort it with the secretary on your way out."

Nut stumbled along Lough Street, dazed and bemused. Bix kept pace, taking care not to get trodden under hoof.

"What happened back there?" asked Nut in a sing-song voice.

"You don't remember?" Bix asked, surprised. He related the afternoon's events.

Nut stopped in her tracks. "How could you do that to me?"

"I didn't do anything. I'm trying to prevent another murder, and you can help. You're sticking with me until we've rounded up some suspects."

"You and me?"

"Yep." Bix motioned Nut onward.

"Through thick and thin? Like two buddies in an unlikely partnership?"

"No. You're a witness. You didn't see much. The something you did see is better than nothing. So, you're going to help."

Nut looked pleased. "Do I get a baton?"

"Certainly not. I'm not deputizing you. I'm keeping an eye on you. No batons."

Nut shrugged, wondering whether the mouse had a smaller truncheon than his colleagues. Some avenues were best left unexplored, and this was one of them. "What now?"

"We visit an old pal of mine," Bix harrumphed. "Who's helped me on more than one occasion." Okay, the friend had tried to eat him on more than two occasions, but that was an accepted hazard for a mouse living in a cat's world. "I know he'll have a handle on this case. He's a millionaire, builds things all the time. He digs cows. You'll get along famously."

18

Like all refined cats, Cole was a gourmet. He dug nothing more than pizza topped with rat peelings. He could eat three in one go; his perfect physique required plenty of fuel.

The pizzas were supplemented with regular helpings of spring chicks, pasta, and juicy insects. A source in the local zoo smuggled out exotic specimens for a hefty fee. The keepers knew nothing about it. Cole found it amusing that their precious wards were being removed right from under their noses. Cole could afford any delicacy he desired.

Cole cooked up a repast for a very special guest.

"Bix!" he feigned happiness as he ushered the inspector into his house. He'd given his butler the night off. "This *is* a surprise." Nut followed the mouse to Cole's drawing room. "This is even more of a surprise," said the tycoon as a bovine aroma permeated his home.

"I hope this is okay," said Bix, self-consciously rubbing his nose. "I'm expecting a friend," Cole replied conspiratorially. "I'm cooking for her."

"Then she must be really special." Bix had gratefully received tipoffs and solutions from Cole in the past; he was the rich cat's contact in the prowler force. They'd met at some press conference. Bix was a media darling because of his unique status although he eschewed publicity whenever possible. "I'll make this quick." The mouse explained Nut's part in his investigation, asking Cole for assistance.

"An intriguing case," mused the tycoon coldly.

"Case nothing. This is my life in peril here!" Nut spluttered. "Cats are dead. I was abducted! We need your help."

"No need to get hot under the horns. There's nothing I can do. I haven't heard anything; I don't know anything. Now it's time I saw you out; my guest'll be here soon, and the dinner demands my attention."

"Of course," said the inspector with a curt nod. "Sorry to come unannounced."

Once Bix and Nut had left the mansion, the mouse lost his cool. "Nice one, you silly moo! That chap could've been very helpful to us. Now I'll have to creep back to him and eat crow."

"I didn't know he'd get upset," the cow simpered. "I don't understand cats. How can they be so cruel?"

Tim's workdays felt different now that he was a part of something bigger than his crew, bigger than the Public Works department, bigger than EGG. He was in the enticing loop of CREAM's charity work for hairless cats, donating robes and earmuffs to the poor unfortunates, its lobbying for stronger Prohibition, with a campaign to include hamsters in the forbidden fruit bowl, and fundraising for a groundbreaking, hush hush social research project codenamed the Big Experiment. Tim was living in an exciting new world full of potential progress and, more importantly to him, friendship.

Tim's day-to-day work was far less enthralling. Luckily, he made more friends outside of CREAM. Toiling along his garbage route, he spent a lot of time with Mandi, a Balinese cat with a dark head of fur, and Ralph, a Tonkinese fond of tomfoolery.

Even with the help of this close-knit crew, Tim's uphill struggle did not get easier. The sloping streets of Totterdown all needed to be cleared, and his four-cat crew was expected to do four times more work than a rookie. The Ithacats moved quickly, if not efficiently; trash bags were left behind, recycling skipped. A few rats escaped their clutches since the crew didn't have time to turn and give chase.

Little Tim did stop to help an elderly female moggy on Peregrine Circle. Once a week she took it upon herself to take all the bins in the street out to the curb, dragging them from their respective houses whether the residents liked it or not. Tim's crew assumed she did it for the exercise, although a cat taking unnecessary exercise was anathema to them. Tim and Mandi always waved to her when they saw her, helping her get the garbage in place for pickup. Ralph liked to perform a mean impression of her, stooped over her stinky black bags, trying not to catch her long, snaggled claws in the plastic. She wasn't the only cat who smiled when the Ithacats arrived; they were well-liked, and much needed, in their trash-stained section of the city.

Despite the friendly neighbors, the job was still a Sisyphean chore, and Lincoln didn't help the situation. He took pains to keep his pantaloons clean, although whenever he found a dry, unsullied patch of sidewalk he liked to lie down, flip on his side, show his belly to all and sundry, then hiss at anyone who came too close. In trashier areas he found the high ground, leaping onto ledges or scaffolding and mewing words of encouragement to his colleagues.

"Hustle up, guys! We're running behind! We got three more streets this morning and I can see from here they're bogging."

With two cats pushing the cart and Lincoln supervising, Tim was left to do most of the fetching and collecting. It was tiring, honest, fulfilling work, and he got to spend time with his closest friend.

At the top of the hill was Catty Corner, the oldest part of the neighborhood, with many nooks and crannies for trash to gather. No garbage cat looked forward to cleaning it because it was a dusty, cluttered side street always needing renovation. Domestic, business, and construction waste commingled to make Tim's crew miserable.

Lincoln didn't want any dust on his paws. He sprang effortlessly onto a fire escape, lording it over the crew as usual.

"You should get down from there," said Tim, watching the metal steps wobble. Reaching up to help his friend. Lincoln swiped at him and ignored his advice, pacing back and forth, bossing Ralph and Mandi around.

"There's a bolt loose—"

Lincoln wouldn't listen to Tim, who turned to Ralph and told him, "There's a bolt coming loose from the wall."

"He's right!" Ralph called to Lincoln. "You'd best get offa there."

Lincoln shook his mane, sniffed the air, and struggled to maintain his balance as the ancient fire escape collapsed under him. He jumped free of the debris, landing heavily on all fours. The iron mass crashed onto the sidewalk, kicking up dust and mussing up Lincoln's do.

"Mandi!" Ralph cried out. Mandi was caught under the metal, paws reaching out. Tim held them, but the claws were out in distress. He pulled back, Ralph and Lincoln behind him.

"Help me get her out!" Tim implored.

"We can't," Lincoln replied, gesturing at the cart. "Ralph will have to push alone; I'll make sure the incident report is taken care of."

Slowly, Mandi's claws retracted, and she stopped moving. Tim tugged his broom from the cart and used it as a lever to lift the metal scrap, but the handle snapped. He looked at Lincoln with plaintive, sorrowful eyes.

"She's not making any sound," said Tim.

"Let's move on," Lincoln told him, his voice as soft as velvet. "Work will take our minds off this regrettable incident."

"She's still warm, Linc!" Tim could hold Mandi's paws now, soft as Lincoln's tone, immobile under the rubble. "I need a moment."

Lincoln nodded. "We'll move on. Catch up with us when you're ready."

Tim curled up beside Mandi, wiping tears from his face with the back of his paw. He had trusted Lincoln to be considerate and wise. He could understand why the longhair was sticking to the schedule, to make their quota and distract them from the accident. But he couldn't subscribe to Lincoln's callousness, and that made him question his involvement with the union and CREAM. If Lincoln couldn't spare a second glance at a worker he'd known for years, how would he treat Tim when the chips were down?

This dichotomy, more than anything else in Tim's life, made him feel confused.

By the time Tim caught up with Ralph and Lincoln, they had cleared the rest of Catty Corner and were ready to move back down the hill. To Tim's disbelief, Ralph was pushing the cart and picking up cans like a rookie; Lincoln watched, idly scratching himself and picking his teeth with his claws.

Tim watched Lincoln closely from then on, frowning as the longhair made his workmates laugh back at the dump with jokes about Mandi, saying she'd lost a lot of weight, and she was the best kind of female—silent.

"Whose fault is it she's dead?" Tim blurted out, clamping a paw over his mouth. He didn't want to upset his friend, who surely felt terrible about the accident. Cats grieved in strange and different ways.

"Aw, don't listen to him," Lincoln said to the other garbage cats. "He was soft on Mandi."

This was the last straw for Tim. He didn't confront Lincoln—that was not his nature—but he decided to leave EGG, CREAM, and any other abbreviated food group that cared to have him as a member. From now on, he would isolate himself; no more family, no more abysmal meetings.

Once he stopped going to the meetings, he felt relieved. He had made the right choice.

The last cat the jobless Bug wanted to see was Tiger Straight. She fetched a saucer of milk for him all the same; he had a way about him that convinced people to do things for him. Bug knew she was being used, even when her old partner told her she could start work the next day.

"When I told you I needed a job—"

"This wasn't what you had in mind."

"I was thinking you'd hire me again. As your assistant, instead of getting me to do it for free and putting me to work in a bank."

"Take a sniff at these." Tiger waved a sheaf of printouts under her nose.

"Accounts. Dead people's accounts."

"It's amazing how easy it is to get hold of the deceased's credit records. There are anomalies in every one of these accounts. Some of these folk have been murdered in very nasty circumstances—the Hant brothers, Joel Venet, Farmer Scrumpy. Some of them suffered an accidental death, so the authorities reckoned. They all had sums going to a secret bank account. The only way I can find out who owns the account—"

"Get a bank teller to look it up. An insider job. Me."

"You said you could do with the income."

Bug threw up her paws in frustration. "This is the most boring job on the planet! Answering phones, totting up profits, assessing interest rates, mortgage advice, lines of tail-twitching customers so irate you need a Perspex screen to protect you from them—or is it to stop the staff running away?"

Tiger tried to reassure her. "Think about your paycheck at the end of the month."

"The *month!*"

"We have to make it look above-board, get you ensconced, friendly with your colleagues before we even think of snooping."

"Looks like you've been doing plenty of that already," mewed Bug, brandishing the printouts. "What did you have to do to get these? Sucker some other poor gal?"

"Not at all. I stole them from the prowlers. Bix Mortis, to be exact."

"Great."

"They're on the trail, too. Losing this should slow them down a bit." Tiger seemed intent on obstructing prowler procedure.

"You got something against mice?"

"No way. I just have to sort things out at my own pace."

"Sounds anti-mouse to me. And selfish. You were the one giving me all that 'lives at stake' spiel."

"The villains could win this one, Natasha. One wrong move and they'll cover their tracks completely. That's why we have to tread softly."

"Control freak."

"Your new job starts in the morning, 9 a.m.," said Tiger. "You mustn't be late."

"I miss my grasshoppers."

"Bug, if we pull this off, you'll be a hero. The zoo will welcome you back with open paws. If that's what you want."

19

This was it. On the trail at last. Cole had followed the one-eyed figure down back lanes, alleys, and main streets, maintaining a fair distance from his quarry. The cultist never looked back, single-minded, moving rapidly. Cole was starting to enjoy himself.

He'd been ready to give up when the break came. Uncomfortable about giving in to blackmailers, he had reassured himself by pursuing Connie. She was responsive up to a point, but he knew that it would be impossible to truly win her affection until he brought her brothers' killers to justice. He'd watched *Wonder Cat* as a cub, knew the form: the hero defeats the bad guys and gets the gal—at the very end of the episode.

With no end in sight, Cole had despaired of ever finding a lead. Young Lona's funeral had given him the key. He'd dismiss the parents as typical trailer trash tabbies; the father didn't even have a necktie. He'd discounted the robed, hooded, one-eyed cat watching from a discreet distance, supposing that he was one of the holy yahoos. The next day had proved him wrong.

ed calm, thinking the problem through,
to miss a detail. He couldn't stand up
n all fours, his tail probing upward,
eiling to touch the tip. There was no
or banging on the walls; he wouldn't
e machinery. He couldn't get out the
he bones were too broken and brittle
d slow the descent. The tip of his tail
e ceiling. He lay flat on his stomach,
nking cogs that turned the grinding

he nick of time, of course. He always
ld stop the crusher for a brief, evil
ld overpower him. Or agree to join
he tables. Or blow everything up.
verything up, though as a result,
s bonus long ago.
here was no escape this time, no
lause. No happy ending. As the
hed from his body, he felt like
lops had been the bait; he was
is eyes and thought of Connie.

On a routine inspection of the Duncan Hotel, he'd noticed the same galoot in the same Gothic get-up, joining a CREAM convention.

CREAM? Despite his wealth and connections, he'd never heard of such a thing.

No one at reception could tell Cole what the initials stood for, so he poked his intrigued nose through the doors of Conference Room E. It was full of males in capes and cowls, all sitting in silence, waiting for the meeting to start. Cole took a seat at the back, aware of the eerie silence. A furless bambino had handed him a glass of warm milk, and he'd lapped at it gratefully.

Finally, the boss had arrived, a creature Cole couldn't possibly have expected. Yet the cats sat rapt, hanging on this animal's every word.

"Cults have been getting a bad name in recent years," squeaked the leader. "I should know. I've been handling this organization's PR for years. You got sex-crazed cults, suicide cults, and vegetarian cucumber cults. We ain't like that. We don't do orgies, and we sure as Hecate don't abstain from eatin' meat." The audience members nodded their heads in unanimous approval.

"Why are we here?" the leader continued. "We're here because a great wrong has been committed. It's been going on for far too long, and it's about time it stopped. Cats have subjugated other species since the world began turning. They ain't the master race. Such a thing don't exist. It's time to right the wrong." The spokesanimal's words were welcomed with polite applause. "To do that, we must fight tooth and claw. Decimate traditional ideology. I educate citizens everywhere, show them that our way is best. Only then can we start afresh."

"When do we start?" asked a sealpoint in the front row.

"Soon, my brother," said the boss. "As soon as our recruitment drive is complete."

"What does CREAM stand for?" interjected Cole.

"Now here's someone worth recruiting. We have the hotel owner in our midst!" said the leader, his eyes widening. "Say hello, my brothers."

Some of the cultists turned and waggled their paws in greeting. The leader gave a nod to the one-eyed cat, who left the room in a hurry. When the meeting collapsed into a drone of administrative details—funding, accommodation arrangements, identity badges—Cole loped off to see if he could catch up with the cyclops. He'd be back to question the leader later; with any luck, he'd discover a lot more during a personal interview.

The shady character was easy to find in a crowd of cats in lounge dress. He'd hovered in reception for a while as if waiting for the clock to strike, then left the hotel as quite a lick.

Cole reached a part of the neighborhood he didn't recognize. It became harder to stay hidden with fewer pedestrians to shroud him. A church dominated the skyline on his left, strip lights struggling through the stained-glass windows. Scaffolding was propped against the spire; no doubt the local priest would be fleecing his flock for contributions. The bell tower had seen better days, and it would take more than a prayer to fix it.

On the right, apartment blocks stood like sentries on duty, surrounded by fences and patches of grubby grass. The fences had once been white; now they were mucked with soot and most of the paint had flaked away.

20

No one would talk to Little Tim. At first, he thought it was because he reminded them of Mandi's accident. He was a bad luck charm, a failure in a crisis.

Then he noticed the camaraderie between his fellow workers and Lincoln, who always seemed to smile and lark about.

Tim was surprised to find that he missed the meetings and the charity work. He didn't reach out to his former brothers, though, and he went out of his way to avoid Lincoln. Since they were no longer on the same crew, that wasn't too hard. Tim couldn't understand how CREAM's gospel of helping life in all its forms married up with Lincoln's heartless disregard for Mandi. Neither was Lincoln a sole exception; Anatolios was equally cold when Tim mentioned Mandi's family, and what should be done to commemorate her life. Anatolios said he was there to work, period. So Tim remained alone.

"Mandi's unfortunate death hit you hard, I understand that," Lincoln said to him, approaching him on break one day. "I know how you felt about her. But that's no excuse for letting your work ethic slide. You missed half your route this morning."

Tim didn't appreciate the longhair invading his space.

"I'll do better," Tim muttered. "If you promise not to talk to me like this again. Talk to me at all, if possible."

This angered Lincoln more than Tim could have predicted. He bared his teeth at Tim, letting out a high-pitched, frustrated yowl. Tim backed away, ears tilted back in distress.

"You never appreciate what you have," said Lincoln, taking an aggressive step toward Tim. "So many cats need a job. So many would give their right whiskers to be a part of our brotherhood. We gave everything to you on a silver saucer. That's the problem. You've never had to fight for the life you enjoy."

"Enjoy?" Tim hissed. "You really think I enjoy picking up garbage... scrabbling for rats... sitting in tiresome meetings... being blindfolded and pushed around? You think I like having no control over my life, no family, in a trailer park where the only neighbor I thought I could trust disappears? You think I appreciate a friend who treats my workmates like junk?"

Tim's words made Lincoln hesitate. The longhair spat at Tim, turned, and left the break area, leaving Tim shaking with anxiety.

By the end of the day, Tim found himself in Anatolios's office. The boss had bad news for his former Best in Show.

"There are times when I love my job," said Anatolios. "Barbecue days, when I put an apron on and pass bug-burgers out to all the staff. You haven't been here long enough for that. Days with extra-long shifts, when the garbage is piled high, and everyone's exhausted and Public Works achieves something greater than any one cat could accomplish. But there are other times, like now, when I would rather anyone but me was perched on this desk, telling you what I'm about to tell you."

"I'm sorry," said Tim, unsure of what was going on.

"I'm the one who is sorry," said Anatolios. "Little Tim... Mr. Tierney, we're going to have to let you go."

"Let me go where?" Tim asked, although he knew the answer.

"I can fire you, or you can resign."

Tim giggled. For once in his lives, he had stood up to another cat, and this was the result. "I don't want to get fired," he said. "I'll resign."

"Very well."

"Can you tell me why I'm resigning? So I know what I did wrong, for the future?"

Anatolios clamped his mouth shut, though for a moment. "To be candid, your background is part of it. We're looking for ... a higher caste of worker. Cats who are less rough around the tongue."

"Okay," said Tim with a look of utter confusion.

"There's also the questionable circumstance of Mandi's accident. The report I received does not place you in a favorable light."

"But—"

"Oh, I apologize; since you are no longer an employee of the Public Works Department, you must return the garments you borrowed from the career closet."

Borrowed? Thought Tim. "I'm wearing them."

"You can bring them in tomorrow," said Anatolios generously. "Can't you?"

Tim's head slumped. "I can," he said, turning to leave the office. "I will." He had one last question for his former boss. "Are you okay?"

"Yes," Anatolios answered with confidence.

"Thank you for everything you did for me. My life is different now because of you."

"You're welcome," said the boss, pointing a paw at the exit. "If you'll excuse me..."

With a nod and a droop of his tail, Tim left the office for good.

Cats prefer not to wait. Nub City Bank was full of waiting customers, all wandering around, sniffing at the potted plants, gazing at their reflections in the polished Perspex. Anything other than look like they were waiting in line. There was still a system: the biggest tom in the bank got served first. Some of the small ones waited half the day because larger cats always cut in. Any protests were met with a growl or a paw swipe.

Tellers were presented with bloody bird and chipmunk corpses, a proud grin on the customer's face. A chit was exchanged for the prize, endorsed with an inky paw print. Checks were easier to handle than rotten birds or voles, and for a small fee, the banks handled the messy bullion. Sometimes the deposits would live on, flapping about, causing a kerfuffle; the Perspex existed to contain the flying feathers, not the staff as Natasha had suspected.

The rarer the species of bird, the greater the value. Some genera were almost extinct because of this; mice were the gold standard, no longer used as day-to-day currency by the common cat. Poorer cats spent a lot of their time dreaming of a winged windfall, sky gazing, twitching, wondering how they could catch the creatures that wheeled so high above. They envied the taunting birds as they envied the upper classes, who could easily snatch a pigeon from the window ledge of their penthouse suite.

Bug didn't want to be rich. She *did* want to be in the black and pay off some of the debts she'd racked up while immersed in her studies. Her new boss Miss Angold wore bifocals, each lens like the bottom of a milk bottle. Despite her poor sight, she constantly watched over her employees—especially Natasha. The bug lover was too intelligent for her own good; Miss Angold didn't expect her to last long in the job.

After a week or so, Bug began to impress her, working overtime through lunch hours and evenings, asking questions about procedures, and taking an interest in the blandest of tasks.

Bug wasn't all that excited about banking; she was itching to get back to her fleas. She also wanted to impress Tiger and prove she was his equal. That meant taking risks, chasing up clues herself. Once Miss Angold trusted her enough to leave her in the office alone, she would act.

Tiger was concerned for Connie. Far as he knew she was fending for herself, still in mourning for her brothers. She was a prime target for the killer, and the detective had left her unprotected. He didn't count Cole; the selfish tycoon would be too preoccupied with his own life to care about Ms. Hant's. Tiger visited her apartment to deliver a progress report and check that she was safe. He hoped that she'd forgive his earlier outburst and allow him to keep an eye on her.

The devastated Connie had other things on her mind. She'd received an envelope that morning containing her lover's ground remains.

"I was supposed to meet him last night," she explained, snuffling on Tiger's shoulder. "A grubby pub he liked. He enjoyed slumming it every so often. I thought he'd stood me up. Then I got this."

Tiger pored over the envelope's crushed contents. "How do you know it's him...?" he asked as tactfully as possible.

"I can smell him. Bits of him. I sense he's not out there anymore, Tiger. I've lost him. I'm jinxed."

"No, you're not." The envelope bore no postmark or return address. The detective felt no satisfaction at the loss of his rival.

Connie's eyes were devoid of peace or hope.

"You've got to find his murderer. Murderers. Singular or plural, I don't care. Catch 'em and rip off their balls."

"Sure, sure. Ears, balls, anything. I need something to go on."

"He was well known." Connie sighed. "Respected. Had lots of friends and acquaintances. Someone must have seen him the day he disappeared."

"Did he say anything? Mention anything, the last time you saw him?"

Connie pursed her lips.

"Most of the time, he gabbed about his new hotel. Showing off, I suppose."

"I'd show off if I had what he had," Tiger blurted.

"His hotel was full of strange guests. He was going to throw them out, have any undesirables thrown out. Doesn't have anything to do with my brothers, does it?"

"I suppose not."

"You think the auld enemy might be involved?" asked Connie abruptly.

"I don't. Dogs are nasty, brutish and subtlety isn't their point. Whoever's behind this has cunning, guile, intelligence."

"Got to be female."

"I was thinking in more general terms," said Tiger. "I smell a cat."

"That's impossible. We may squabble, claw at each other for personal space, act with spite and greed. We wouldn't cull members of our own race. We're not stupid."

"Anyone can make foolish mistakes; even a cat." Tiger knew this from harsh experience.

"Come on. We can stumble or get caught off guard, but we always regain our balance. We wouldn't have conquered the Wild Lands otherwise."

"I want you to stay with a friend until this case is solved—until I find out what happened to Cole."

"Who'd put me up? I'll hex them before the week's over."

"A very nice lady who works in a bank. Temporarily, at least. Her name's Natasha. She likes insects."

"Quite a resume. Must be fun at parties."

"Nobody goes hungry at 'em, that's for sure. She can take care of herself and everyone else in her presence. Let's pay her a visit."

After he'd dropped Connie off, Tiger returned to Jo's house. He'd be able to relax, put his paws up, and examine the case in a peaceful environment. Certain things were bound to happen during the course of the investigation. There would be another corpse along any minute and that unlucky soul would likely disappear. Tiger would get sapped, struggle with some ugly customers, and make some smart remarks. He'd tell the prowlers little and drink a lot. His brain would turn hard, getting nowhere until a clue fell into place and inspiration struck. These were the rules of the job, with few exceptions.

Tiger was determined to play it cool. Why struggle to solve the mystery before all votes were in? He'd be methodical, ask lots of questions, take a long nap... by the time he woke up, the case would have solved itself.

His plans for a quiet evening were shattered when Jo invited him in; she had something to tell him.

"You'd better sit down for this," said Jo.

"My second favorite position," Tiger replied, perching on a windowsill.

Jo stared at Tiger.

"Out with it," said Tiger. "Make it snappy."

"I'm having kittens."

"I know. Calm down a bit, don't get yourself in a tizz."

"I don't mean that. I'm not upset. I *am* worried about what's going to happen to my children."

"I didn't know you were a parent."

"I'm not," Jo sighed. "Not yet. Gonna be soon."

"Does the father know?" asked Tiger bashfully.

"Not yet. I'm scared. Don't know how he'll react."

"Do you want to tell me who it is?" Tiger wasn't sure whether he wanted to know. He was too young to be a dad—any time before he reached pensionable age would be too soon for him.

"Cole Tiddle. Cole's the father. We only slept together once. He made me dinner. That was enough."

"How can you be sure?" asked Tiger, aghast.

"The timing's right. The vet gave a rough date. Plus, Cole's the only guy I've ever slept with." Tiger found that hard to believe. The night he'd spent with her came flooding back, a night of cuddles and nuzzling, a caring embrace. Nothing more.

"I see," said Tiger, to fill an awkward silence.

"Do you think he'd be alright? How would he take the news?"

"He never will," Tiger answered brusquely. "You've lost your opportunity to tell him. He's dead."

Jo slumped to the floor, her whiskers drooping. The detective felt terrible, hopped down from the window-sill, and tried to help Jo up.

"Leave me," she said. "Just need to sit down for a moment. It happens when you're pregnant. You lose your footing."

"How're you going to raise them, Jo?" Tiger asked, his voice tender now.

"They could still have a dad." Jo's eyes shone. "I need help, darling."

"You certainly do. You expect me to give it to you?"

"I don't expect anything. I do a lotta hoping. We could be together—if you still want that."

"I don't want anything." Tiger's tail flicked from side to side. "I need to solve this case. Beyond that..."

"Beyond that, nothing."

"So, we're both lonely," said Tiger. "But you're the one who acquainted herself with the local stud. Why didn't you tell me before?"

"I didn't know before. Not for sure. When I did, I ... waited. To talk things over with you."

"To frighten me. You succeeded."

"So I *am* good at something," Jo purred.

"Yeah. Good at turnin' me into a bag of jangling nerves."

21

The receptionist was a louche
Norwegian forest cat with big dimples. He knew
that the ladies went gaga for his face craters, so he
creased his cheeks whenever he could. His bushy
tail was always upright, and he treated guests in the
manner that suited their social standing. Business
executives staying for a night got top-star service;
low-rent families on a city trip, excited at visiting Nub,
weren't encouraged to return—they got the bum's
rush. It was obvious that Tiger, who'd been wearing
the same clothes for days, was penniless. The receptionist ignored him for as long as he was able, making
sure that everyone else in the foyer was served before
the detective got his turn.

"It's about the owner. Mr. Tiddle."

"I'm sure that any business of his would be
none of yours," the receptionist replied in his thick
Scandinavian accent, looking down his nose at the
investigator.

"This was the last place he was seen before he disappeared. Friday. The last place I know of, anyway.
Did you see him?"

The receptionist warmed to Tiger's tone. The snooty cat cast his mind back.

"Difficult. There was a big convention here last week. CREAM, don't ask me what it stands for. Lots of conspicuous ginks in robes. One crumb in particular had one eye. Hung round here forever, it seemed."

"What was this convention about?"

"Some kind of animal rights movement. *Jeg vet ikke.*" The receptionist pressed his dimples into service. "I administrate. I don't eavesdrop."

Tiger nodded. "That's commendable."

"Mind you," the snob continued, "I did hear a couple of them arguing over something. One was going to make a killing. The other advised caution. I assume they were discussing the stock market."

"Probably. What happened to the one-eyed guy?"

"That's just it. I wouldn't have mentioned him, but there he was, loitering without intent until Mr. Tiddle arrived in the foyer. As soon as One Eye clocked the boss, he barged out of the hotel and was followed."

"By Cole?"

"*Ja.* Must've forgotten something, eh? A wallet, a watch. I'm always doing that. Leaving things lying around, losing them. Mr. Tiddle always finds them for me. A first-class detective."

"You don't say. Thank you. You've been excellent."

The concierge squashed his mouth into a smile. "Don't mention it. Anytime you need a room..."

"I'll ask a friend. Can't afford this place. Ciao."

The concierge sniffed as the riffraff left the building. He hoped that Mr. Tiddle would turn up soon. It was almost payday.

Tiger placed his battered tan case on Jo's coffee table. He took a sniff around, making himself at home. He scrunched his paws on salmon-red carpet flecked with white and breathed an opaque fog by her bay windows, which were half-dressed in net curtains.

He warmed himself at a fire with fake coals, the mantelpiece holding a candelabra and plastic flowers. A mahogany bookcase opposite held dictionaries and reference books. As the light from the window faded, he lit an oil lamp with a long-stemmed taper. Its shade had trees stenciled on it.

Two pairs of frayed argyle socks sagged over a white radiator. Tiger wondered whom they belonged to. The lampshade bounced its patterns off the cream walls, peppered with black and white photographs in dark brown frames. He tried out both of Jo's sofas—one leather, one upholstered with saggy cloth. Each would accommodate two or three cats, more if they were prepared to get cozy and pinch up together. Tiger lay on his back, gazing up at the white-tiled ceiling. Water ripples had been carved into the plaster. Outside, a set of streetlights fizzed into life. Jo lived on a junction, and Tiger could see them through the net curtains.

Jo was prepared to put him up indefinitely although the situation made Tiger feel like a leech. He had been considering her proposition, wondering whether he could do the right thing. She had always been kind to him.

Bug was deep undercover and had her paws full looking after Connie, so Tiger had no recourse but to accept Jo's offer of a place to stay. He planned to sleep on the floor that night; it seemed right.

At least until their wedding night, if he decided to take the plunge. It did seem right. He'd bumped into Jo for a reason; she made him happy. Except when she sprang unusual surprises on him. If the babies had been his own ... it didn't matter. He was going to be a father! Jo could rely on him to look after her when she was tired and help her cope as she gained strength. He couldn't shower her or the kittens with gifts, but she had his full attention. She was stunning, took his mewl away; the thought of her made him want to purr. Thank the Holy One for landing him the catch of nine lifetimes.

They would solve the case of the mysterious CREAM. They just had to look at it from the right angle.

When Jo returned from her visit to the TV studio, she was fuming. Tiger tried to play it cool, asking her what was wrong. She explained that the makers of *Wonder Cat* had let her go, along with most of the production crew. The channel bosses couldn't afford to pay purr diem while their ratings-grabbing show "rested," and they couldn't count on more work when shooting recommenced. There were many hungry cats in the city desperate for a job in glamorous TV Land. Plenty of them could hold a boom, heft a light, or paint a face. They'd work for next to nothing, leaving skilled artists like Jo on the dole.

"You'll find something," said Tiger, trying to believe it.

"I'm pregnant. I've got no employer, no friends. I've got nothing to get up in the mornings for. I want my kittens to live well, have everything they need. I'm not having no schemie kittens."

"Let's get married," said Tiger. "Right now."

"What are you talking about?"

"The way we feel about each other... the way the world doesn't seem to matter so much when we're together—"

"You're crazy as a bedbug."

"Oh dear. You're supposed to say, 'Yes, darling, where's the ribbon?'"

"What ribbon?"

"I was wondering when you were going to ask." He delved into his trench coat pocket and pulled out a slender ribbon. "Here. Will you wear it for me?"

Jo reached out to touch the soft material. It featured Tiger's family colors, red with a gold hem. She held it to her cheek and her heart melted.

"When?" she asked.

"Is that a yes, then?"

Jo handed the cloth back to Tiger. "It's a question. If we were going to get married, when would it happen?"

"I was thinking right away. Less hoo-ha that way."

"Less ... hoo-ha?"

"Yeah." Tiger nodded. "Hoo-ha."

"What about our friends? Your dad, that bug lady?"

"They won't mind. Let's do it now."

"Next week," Jo decided. "That'll give us time to notify our finest and dearest. Nothing fancy."

"Definitely sounds like a yes to me." Tiger couldn't stop himself from chuckling.

"Let's have another look at that ribbon."

Bug pulled a sheaf of papers from her jacket pocket. She'd finally been left alone long enough to compare the figures Tiger had given her with the bank records. She could see that several customers were making payments into a particular account. All fine and dandy, except the customers were dead. Someone at the bank was pulling a fast one, and that made Bug wary.

Shivering in the dingy records room, she listened for the sound of another cat. She used her peripheral vision to scan 280 degrees, her muscles poised for flight. Miss Angold hadn't seemed suspicious—that didn't stop Bug being careful. She'd been shown the vault that morning, a vast tomb sealed with a thick steel hatch. The bank staff had begun to trust her. She felt almost guilty for betraying them.

The payments weren't being siphoned into one secret account; they were going into several with a series of digits that didn't match the other customer numbers. Bug printed them out and stuffed them in her breast pocket along with Tiger's information. Rushing from the records room, she bumped into Miss Angold.

"Good to see you working late," the boss purred. "We reward diligence at this bank. And we penalize those who disappoint us."

"I was boning up on some of your regulations. Finding things out…"

"I know, I know." Miss Angold let Bug pass.

There were plenty of sight-impaired cats in Nub City; not so many of them wore hooded vestments. Tiger visited contacts in the church and the theater, two professional bodies with a lot in common. They were both obsessed with getting bums on seats, giving their customers a rollicking good show, and using guilt and guile to extort every penny from the punters.

The manager of the Totterdown Pavilion was preparing for opening night. Although the theater had been graced by the work of many great playwrights and actors, winter was a slow time of year. Most theatergoers chose to spend the season in bed, sleeping even more than usual in a state of quasi-hibernation. This week the theater was host to the excesses of a local amateur group, Dramatic Paws. Their tales were tawdry, their acting execrable, but all their friends and relatives paid to see them and packed the house. After a seven-day run, the audience realized how bad the play was, and receipts fell. Ronald Appleby called it community support. The amateurs thought of it as a "spectacular showcase" for their talents. There was no hint of this when Tiger popped in to see his friend.

A dress rehearsal was in full swing, with the director in the wings. He seemed content as a troupe of dancers bumped into each other; he knew that criticism this late in the day would only upset his cast. Some would leave in a huff; others would get emotional. Better to encourage their antics—a laugh from the audience was guaranteed. "Don't they realize we open tonight?" Ronald asked the detective. Didn't expect a reply. "They haven't learned their lines, the choreographer's got his legwarmers in a twist, and the lead's still dry behind the ears. Thank goodness they're only here for a week."

"What's next?"

"Didn't you smell the posters on your way in, Straighty? Pantomime! *Cat and the Beanstalk.* The cubs love it, though most of the gags are aimed at the grown-ups. The performers enjoy themselves more that way."

"Your reputation ain't tarnished yet. Not with the great stuff you've had on over the years. That tragic thing with the Swampy McMahon soliloquy last summer..."

"*Wall Story.*"

"That's right. And that show with the monks?" Ronald's eyes widened.

"*Monk Story* was a lot more than a mere show, my lad. It was pure theater. The unabridged version of the play performed as it would have been when first written, generations ago. If only we could have changed the audience."

"What happened to the costumes? Did they get ditched or what?"

"They were purchased from us by a national organization. Can't recall the name." The Amateur Dramatics heroine was singing her solo. She would have had a beautiful voice if not for the stage fright that cracked every note.

"Would you have records?"

"Some sort of anagram."

"CREAM?"

"That was it. How did you know? CREAM LLC. Before you ask, there was no delivery address. A one-eyed gentlecat collected the costumes. Bit of a sour puss."

"Didn't it strike you as strange? This organization taking a honking great load of monks' robes from you."

Ronald patted a wall affectionately. "This old dear's seen better days. Her makeup may seem impeccable but take a closer look at it, and you'll see cracks." He pointed upward. Tiger saw that the ceiling was flaking. "The foundations are weak. The upkeep's expensive. People think we take their money, pay off the producers, and spend the profits on milk and honey. I put my faith and wages into the Pavilion. I didn't ask any questions of CREAM LLC. I kept my mouth shut and got the roof retiled."

"Anything I should look out for in the future?" asked Tiger as Ronald led him out of the auditorium. Scenery crashed down around the starlet.

"We have a prestigious production lined up," blinked the manager. "Once the panto's done its business. A gung-ho play by Julius Kyle. It's the story of a brick-layer called—"

"*Bricklayer's Story*?" Tiger guessed.

"How did you know? That was the title we were going to go with, yes. What do you think? Too literal?"

"Not at all," Tiger bade his farewells. "It's up to your usual standards."

Tiger and Jo organized the wedding together—that way, they could keep an eye on each other. While *Wonder Cat* was out of production and facing the axe, Tiger wangled his fiancée a post at the Pavilion. The theater didn't pay as well as the TV company; Jo still had enough to feed them both until she got a meatier job. Between the arrangement of the wedding cere-mony and providing makeup for a horde of luvvies, she was kept busy. More than that, Tiger had friends at the theater who promised to protect her.

It wasn't long before the couple had their first tiff. Tiger wanted to invite some unsavory guests to the reception because "they didn't get out much." Not a good enough reason for the bride-to-be. She was cagey about her family—long after the majority of invites had gone out, she still hadn't informed any relatives of her relationship with the detective. He thought she was embarrassed about him, his lack of money or social status.

After a day's bickering, they agreed to allow each other to invite who they liked. It was a special day that they wanted to share with friends and acquaintances.

"I won't let you down in front of your folks," Tiger assured his fiancée. "I ain't a well-bred pedigree animal. I wouldn't win any fancy club prizes. I *do* love you. If your mother and father have a problem with that, we can talk it over before the wedding. Please let 'em know what's going on. I want to meet them."

"It's not you I'm worried about." Jo sighed. "Or their reaction to you. I'm worried that you'll get one look at them and run a mile."

"They can't be all that bad," Tiger soothed.

"They're old, strict, gruff, respectable, well mannered... They'd pay for the wedding like a shot. I won't let them."

Jo was determined to pay for the event. Tiger didn't ask how or where she was going to get the money from; he offered to remunerate her as soon as he solved his case. Then he planned to knuckle down and get a proper job ready to provide for the kittens who were on their way. If it was a full litter, they would have several new mouths to feed. He'd always fancied a career in advertising, writing copy for wealthy corporations. Advertising was so ineffective that it seemed like a scam to him; if the seller was lucky, a third of consumers would sniff the ad. The number of cats who actually picked up a product was indefinable. He could be an officially backed grifter.

All his life, he'd been screwed. Clients had forgotten to pay. He'd labored for free in the hope of follow-up jobs and "exposure." He'd been exploited and abused. He'd always chalked it up to poor business acumen. He didn't have the drive or the mean streak to succeed in commerce. He could spot a pickpocket at a thousand yards, but corporate fraudsters fooled him every time. He'd hoped to learn something from their dirty deals; he'd fallen foul of them instead.

Tiger had set up his detective agency with nothing. The office, the filing cabinet, even the suit had been on short-term lease. Still young, he'd fooled clients into thinking he knew what he was doing.

From such lowly beginnings, the business had grown, expanded enough for him to keep himself in fresh litter, hire a secretary (Natasha), buy a telephone, have some calling cards printed. For a short while, he'd been a cat about time with pigeons in his pocket and a down payment for his Drove Loan apartment.

It hadn't taken him long, however, to realize that his work life ran in peaks and troughs. He could be wealthy one year and close to bankruptcy the next. This year he'd pushed things too far, lost it all. Usually, he would have been ready to build things up again from scratch; now it was too late for that. The unemployable would have to become an employee.

He could feel himself growing older by the hour, by the minute. Each morning, he would check his face in the bathroom mirror, find a new white hair or a wrinkle on one of his pads. He was middle-aged in cat years; he could kick the bucket at any time. His brother had dropped dead at the age of ten. Tiger wondered why cats bothered to build anything when their lives were so short. It wasn't fair.

Father Frank would have told him that after death, all true believers joined the goddess Bastet up in the heavens. The bad ones weren't so lucky. No scientist or priest had ever proved the deity's existence; she was something people could or couldn't accept.

Everyone needed something to believe in. Tiger had believed in himself. He thought he could still fight his way out of a wet paper hag, solve a mystery, and save a life. The case that Connie had brought to him would prove him right or wreck his world.

The Church of the Benign Bastet was a cold, slate-gray building. Tiger hadn't prayed there since his salad days, putting in overtime as an altar cub. He'd formed a strong bond with Father Frank. If anyone knew where the cyclops had gotten his robes, it would be Frank. The locals confessed everything to him, and he was a terrible gossip. A few cats kneeled in pews, purring softly as they communed with their goddess. The high-vaulted ceiling, richly frescoed with gold and white, gave the impression that you were in a train station.

A female sat at the back of the church breastfeeding her six kittens. Each newborn could home in on its own individually scented nipple. Brother Barry, the acolyte, stood and stared at the mother until she felt uncomfortable and moved away.

"Still not getting any, brother?" Tiger made Barry jump.

"Any what, Mr. Straight?" Barry was a young wire-hair, his face untarnished by strife or stress. His eyes were like two ripe slices of cucumber, glistening in the half-light of the church.

"Female companionship," said Tiger, sounding all concerned. "Sex. Making the beast with two tails."

"Don't mock the constricted, Mr. Straight. You know I've sworn an oath of celibacy. I haven't seen a naked female since—"

"Since that time the prowlers caught you with that round-heeled chippy."

"All charges were dropped." Barry's eyes were downcast; an uncommon moment of carnal weakness had led him to the nearest cathouse. On the pretext of saving souls, he'd sampled the specialty of the house—a talkative trollop named Claire with tattooed unmentionables. He'd tried to spread the Good Word in a clinch on a sack of kitty litter. The only convert that day had been him, and his antics had ended ignominiously in a scandal hushed up by the bishop.

"You got friends in high places." Tiger waved a paw skyward.

"They don't come much higher than that."

"Is Father Frank around?"

"He won't talk to you…"

"Since I had one of his flock rounded up. I know. I need you to be extra persuasive. Unless you want your prowler file reopened. The six o'clock news would love it; so would the parish magazine." Barry scurried to the vestry.

Tiger took a look at the altar, swept away by memories of youthful innocence. His parents had sent him to the church to keep him out of mischief, give him something to do on weekends, give them a break. Frank had been like a second abusive father to him, and he'd betrayed the old cat's trust. A year ago, a local parishioner had confessed a murder to the priest. Tiger had inveigled the information out of him and made his report to the prowlers. Tiger had been unable to let a killer wander free, and neither could Frank. There was still bad blood between them.

He heard mewling from the vestry. Barry was doing his weaselly best to convince Frank to greet his old friend. The priest refused in a gruff monotone. The churchgoers cocked their ears, eavesdropping on their shepherd.

"I'm not going out there. I'm not dressed." Two old dears in the pews shared a titter. Tiger sniffed at a ceremonial cup brimming with clear, cool water. He lapped at it thoughtfully.

"You can't do that." A voice resounded down the nave.

Tiger swung round, drops of water suspended from his whiskers. "Do what?"

Tiger was confronted by a gray-striped ocelot verger, who said, "Drink the holy water. It's been blessed."

"I ain't drank nothing." Tiger shook his head, and the ocelot was showered in droplets. "Besides, anythin' blessed by that charlatan ain't in the least bit holy."

"How can you say that?" The parishioner was shocked. "Father Frank went to priest school. Right now, he's in communion with the goddess."

"He's in his room having a cig. While you simpletons kill your hind legs kneeling on the floor, he's sitting on a plush cushion laughing his asterisk off."

"Blasphemy!" Father Frank exclaimed, bursting into the nave. Barry shadowed him. "Don't listen to this disciple of Hecate, my brother." The high priest landed a placatory paw on the verger's shoulder. "He plays devil's advocate, sews the sequins of doubt on all our shirts. Block your ears when he opens his mouth. Go back to your pew." Frank's words were rewarded with a purr; the ocelot left the church. The priest reassured the rest of his flock. "More prayer, my brethren. Remember to practice humility and discipline. An eternity of damnation awaits if you mess up." To Tiger, he said, "It's against their nature, all this piety. They'd rather be independent. Nevertheless, it gives them something to believe in. It fills a void in their lives."

"I don't know how they find room for praying, with all that eating and sleeping."

"You can't spend your whole life mucking about. We all need to be constructive from time to time."

"I wouldn't call this nonsense constructive. Destructive, if anything. It stops these fellers thinking for themselves."

"Individual thought is highly overrated," said Barry. "Better to switch off, lie back, and trust in a higher force."

Frank nodded vigorously in agreement. "You ever been in a lake, my son?"

"Not on your nelly."

"Swim out into the water and it buoys you. Lie on its surface and you can float. That is what my faith is like, although I use my tail for a rudder while swimming. Here my heart is my rudder."

"Why do you pious types always speak in metaphors?" asked Tiger, slumping against a pew. "Can't you speak plain for once?"

"Yeah," said Frank. "Bit boring though, don't you think?"

"Father Frank is a storyteller, a jokeswapper, a well of information," Barry explained. "We draw from that well whenever our faith is lacking."

"Must do a lot of drawing, eh, Brother Barry?" Tiger nudged the acolyte in the ribs. "Any faith in there? I don't see none, do you, Frank?"

"Don't you have devotions or duties to attend to?" Frank waved Barry away. The acolyte shuffled out of sight, leaving Frank to pat Tiger paternally on the head.

"Don't worry about the water. I drink it all the time. It's not very holy—unless the local tap water is sacred."

"I doubt that." Tiger wiped his chin dry, anyway.

"So, if you aren't born again, what're you doing here?"

"I came to wind you up—doesn't seem to be working—and pick your brains."

Frank sank to the floor with a sigh. "I've changed since you shopped that polecat, Tiger. My fur may be smooth, but I'm not a soft touch anymore. Saving souls is a big deal. You've got to keep an open heart and mind if you want to keep the faith."

"I tried having an open mind," Tiger scoffed. "Faith doesn't fill your belly or keep a roof over your head."

"I never said it did." Frank squinted. "I don't exist to provide excuses for you to be sassy, young sir. I don't throw people out of my church very often; I can make an exception for you. Barry may look and act daft. He can also be a hard nut if he has to be. I trained him myself."

"I wouldn't mess with you or your weans, Frank."

Frank frowned at Tiger, sizing him up. "You're a city cat, aren't you?"

"Bored and bred."

"Used to city life, hemmed in. No sense of perspective. No tranquility. Leads to spiritual corruption. I've been doing this all my life. I'm incapable of doing anything else. Can you imagine me delivering mail?"

"Not in that frock. Too windy out."

Frank touched his cheek with a hind paw in a graceful prayer to his antecedents. His head swayed from side to side. He had an inkling of the origins of the ritual; it had been passed down through generations. He took a deep breath and lapped at the holy drink. *Slurp, slurp*.

Tiger grew impatient. "I thought you might know something about a local group," he said. "A society. Its members wear robes, hoods. Like an order of monks."

"No robed folk in my parish, my son." Frank completed his ritual and scratched his head. "There haven't been any monks in Nub City since—well, since the city was founded. They all got pussed off and moved to the coast. They didn't go for the whole civilized progress shebang. They're extinct now although occasional sightings are made. Folk chalk the apparitions down to a trick of the light or a bellyful of sour milk."

"Ever seen a one-eyed lummox hereabouts?"

"There was a poor fellow who lost an eyeball. Sucked out by a psychotic Selkirk Rex—at least that's what I heard. He was a regular churchgoer for quite a while until he went and joined a cult. Don't know what it was called, but they're up to some dodgy stuff. Would that be the group you were asking about? Sorry, I can't be more help."

"You can. Where do I find One Eye?"

"Hangs out in a cafe. A greasy spoon in the Craigs. Think he owns part of it."

"Know his name?"

"Sorry, son. I'm not omniscient. Only one entity knows everything." Frank raised his eyes heavenward. "And she ain't telling."

"I don't know why you waste your time with all this religion." Tiger sniffed.

Frank smiled knowingly. "Ask yourself this question—it's the only one that keeps my beliefs alive. There are so many different breeds of cat in this city. A variety of colors, shapes, and temperaments. More than mere nature could possibly need. Surely someone created all these forms of life for a reason?"

"It'd have to be a damn good one."

"Yes, yes, that's right. We all have a purpose. I'm not sure what yours is; that's for you to discover."

"Gee, thanks, Father. You've reminded me why I stopped worshipping here." Tiger blinked at the priest and loped toward the exit. "Cheers for the info."

"Don't thank me," said Frank, following Tiger down the nave. "Thank my gossipy flock."

Tiger chuckled, stopped in his tracks, and said, "Oh, one other thing—"

"Yes, my son?" Frank always made time for heathens, and especially cats who had strayed from his congregation. He had six days' vacation a week; it didn't hurt too much to be patient on the seventh day.

Tiger took a deep breath. "Will you marry me?"

22

Was this the afterworld?

When Cole opened his eyes, it took him a long fuzzy moment to remember who he was, where he was, and what had happened. He lay on the arm of a couch, legs dangling off the edge, tail drooping to match his whiskers. If this was the afterworld, why did his bones ache? Why were patches of his fur missing from his legs and tail? Where were the clouds and the kitten cherubs floating around his head?

I survived, he realized. *I made it*. He had to figure out how and why.

He was out in the street, the stench of the abattoir hitting him before he saw it. The light had changed; he'd been lying in the gutter for a lot of hours, no one batting an eyelid checking on his tattered form. The cats passing him must have assumed he was just another derelict, curled up outside the slaughterhouse waiting for scraps. Or taking a very long nap.

Cole hauled himself upright and checked himself for damage. Aside from the missing fur, he was intact. He got a fright when he noticed red streaks on his forepaws, but when he licked them clean, they had an acrylic paint taste. He wasn't bleeding; he wasn't crushed; he was still the same height as ever.

I was right. I did escape, Cole told himself. Some instinct had helped him drag himself out of the trap in the nick of time. *With a little help—from whom?*

He couldn't recall. Either the trauma of his near-death was too great to retain, or he had been too out of it to register what was happening. He didn't dare go back into the abattoir in his dazed condition, lest One Eye was waiting for him. So, he loped home to clean himself up and clear his head.

Back at his mansion, Cole caught up on the city's business news. He was astounded to discover that he'd been gone for days. He was more surprised to learn that his company was running smoothly in his absence. The cheek of those old duffers on the board, doing fine without him! Apparently, they were used to operating without him, thanks to his sideline as a detective. He wasn't as indispensable as he'd always assumed.

Cole tried to figure out why he had slept for so long. Had he been drugged as well as trapped? One Eye hadn't got close enough to slip him a Mickey Finn. Unless he'd been doped before he reached the abattoir... he'd enjoyed the glass of warm, sweet milk at the hotel. Although he'd never been sick—illness was for chumps—he knew cats slept longer when they were distressed or hurt, to recover and boost their immune systems. Older cats slept longer, too.

He was getting old.

Cole looked on the bright side. He'd evaded a death trap, and he had a perpetrator to punish. Best of all, the only cat he really cared about would be waiting for him. The one cat who challenged him, shared his thoughts, and was a joy to spend time with: Connie.

The City Zoo was the only place in Nub where birds felt truly safe. An aviary took up a large corner of the park, split into grasslands, an aquatic habitat, a cypress grove imported from the swamp, and treetop perches. Netting separated the birds from the cats below, who paid an extra fee to enter the aviary and watch the colorful specimens flutter and flaunt their tails at the hunters. The visitors—the most obsessed of whom were nicknamed flappers—spent hours listening to the musical feast above, mentally stimulated, drooling onto park-branded bibs. Some would leap and reach up with their paws, instinct taking over from common sense. All cats were fascinated with the unreachable, the prey they could never catch; a life of ease led to tedium, a ghastly life sentence for natural predators.

Connie stood alone and very still in the center of the aviary, not daring to move lest she disturbed the birds. She wore a calf-length blue swing coat with wide lapels and a mink around her neck. The mink stayed very still as well, petrified of Connie.

High in the air, a sparrow hovered over the netting, plucking away loose strands for its nest. A woodcock zigzagged by. Starlings and common grackles twittered together in a birdbath.

If the sparrow keeps picking at the nylon fibers, Connie thought, *it might make a big enough hole to let it through, into the lower half of the aviary,* into her hungry mouth... Connie craned her neck up, shivering with excitement... then the bird flew up and away from sight. Connie sighed at her pipe dream. There were other birds to watch, but none so entertaining as the plucky sparrow.

It wasn't the same without Cole beside her, sharing the fun. Connie would never find a cat like him. She missed him and her brothers, too. Everyone she loved was gone, leaving her pining for company. Yearning for the unreachable.

Connie broke down, her sobs echoing around the vast chamber.

"Are those plaintive mews for me?"

"Cole?" He was standing, impossibly, a few steps behind her, looking tired but as debonair as ever.

"In my fur, doll."

"It can't be."

"It is!" As Cole outstretched his paws toward her, Connie looked toward the exit, moving to maintain the distance between them, her tail pointed straight down. "What's wrong?" Cole asked. "I wasn't gone that long."

"Where were you gone?"

"I was on a case."

"Where, in a cemetery?" Connie batted Cole's chest, making her mink tighten its grip on her shoulders. "You were dead, Cole." Her furry cheeks glistened with tears. "I saw your damned ashes."

"You saw my what?"

"They were sent to me, addressee unknown, I was sure that..."

"I'm fine, doll. That one-eyed magilla tried to ice me, but I got away."

Connie was still stunned. "Where is he now?"

"Took a powder. No sign of him. I have to dig deeper, find out what dog bed he's hiding under."

"No, Cole. I couldn't stand losing you... for real, I mean."

"I have to see this through. For your safety, as well as mine."

Connie nodded. She knew how stubborn Cole could be.

"Who else thinks I'm pushing up petunias?"

"Everybody. Tiger, Bug, Jo, Inspector Mortis, your cousin Felix..."

"We've got to keep it that way for a little while until I find out who sent you those ashes."

"Who wanted me to think you were dead?"

"Someone with ash to grind. I'll find out when I get to the bottom of CREAM."

"If playing possum means the two of us get time together, I'm all in." Connie held Cole tight, kneading his back in happiness. Birds sang high above, mirroring her relief.

When Tiger's dad found him, a fan dancer was heating him up.

She was already down to her essentials, ostrich feathers loose in her paws, dressed only in a G-string and six tinseled tassels. Tiger was backing away as she pawed him; he didn't want her to think he was a beast. A few pals had joined him in the after-hours bar—detectives, snouts, and half the Pavilion Theater Company.

"Put that animal down!" bellowed Ike Straight, who was a mackerel tabby like his son. Ike's gray fur was faded to off-white, his frame skinny with age.

"You mean me or her?" asked Tiger.

Ike ordered a pint from the bar. He was late for his son's stag do, just off the 4S from the East End. "Who's responsible for this orgy?"

"I am," admitted Father Frank. He was worse for drink, waggling his bottom to the distorted calypso beat that emanated from a wall speaker.

"Dad!" Tiger shouted, not sure where to put his paws.

"Make the most of her fan dance, son. This is yer last night of freedom before..." The hoofer gave Ike a wink.

"What kept you?" Tiger slurred.

"Got held up. I overslept. I was taking a nap and... well, you know how it goes. 15 hours later..." Every cat in the bar nodded. As Tiger rubbed against the fan dancer's leg, Ike muscled in. "Don't you have any respect for yer fiancée? Get yer paws off this poor young lady. She's not interested in a palooka like you."

"What about all that 'last night of freedom' garbage?"

"Must be getting old. It's a parent's prerogative to change his mind." Ike took the fan dancer to a discreet corner and whispered sweet somethings in her ear. Tiger watched her chuckle. His father still had the knack; a grizzled old prune with matted fur, his legs were bandy, and his breath could have been better. He was only a year older than his son, yet he seemed as ancient as a peat bog. The poor young hoofer didn't seem to mind.

Father Frank was enjoying himself, anonymous in the city center, getting friendly with a bottle of hooch. He was still a priest, though, celebrating his goddess with gusto as he drank, sang, and pranced. He'd insisted on tagging along with Tiger, curious about the tired and tested male tradition of the bachelor party.

Some of the cats from the theater sat at a table near the exit. They weren't impressed with the fan dancer, deciding they could do better. Tiger spent most of the night nattering with Ronald Appleby, the manager of the Pavilion. By the time the bar was ready to close, Ronald had convinced his friend to audition for pantomime dame at the end of the year. Ike was long gone, taking the hoofer with him.

Across the city, Jo was letting her fur down. She was accompanied by a few select friends from the TV production company that had employed her for several years. Her entourage included a couple of actresses, drawing drop-jaw reactions from passing clubbers. Sibyl Silvers, Whisker award-winning actress and star of *Wonder Cat,* had heard about an exclusive new club called La Chat. They had to go.

The posse had no trouble getting in, taking seats at the crescent-shaped bar, and ordering a round of curdled milkshakes. *Oh no I shouldn't, I'm watching my figure. I suppose one won't hurt, if everyone else is having one... go on then.*

It took the sassy cats a while to catch up on the latest gossip.

"Where'd this surprise spring from, sister?" asked Sibyl. "I never saw you as a blissful bride."

"Me neither. It's gonna happen though. You can make it to the reception?"

"Wouldn't miss it if I was dead." The conversation was brought to a halt as a bunch of half-naked furry hunks hopped onto a raised dais, tails erect, full of themselves. Patrons gave mewls of approval as the hunks began to boogie.

Only Jo frowned. There was something not quite right about the show. Her doubts were confirmed as more toms stepped onto the dais. Some were wearing studded collars; others were led around on leashes.

"This is disgusting!" she spluttered as the tethered males were yanked across the club.

"Outrageous," Sibyl agreed, savoring every moment.

"Trust you to bring us to a collar club," said Jo, shaking her head. "Cats on leashes. It's shameful."

"I didn't force you to come, sister." Jo knocked back her milkshake and headed out of the club. Sibyl shrugged, took one look at the hunky dancers, and followed her friends to a more traditional bar.

Tiger's dad was of mixed lineage and proud of it. He was the algae in the gene pool, the swine among pearls, the throwback of the family. He was old and sincere, still fit, gaining girth, eating all the right food the wrong way. He looked at his son with suspicion and high expectation. Ike had spent a lot of dough on the lad's education, had helped set him up, and raised him as a freethinker. Sometimes the effort seemed wasted. Right now, Ike had yet to give his approval of his son's nuptials.

He had made the following observations and informed suppositions:

1. Tiger was desperate.

2. He'd lost his home and belongings, needed a place to stay.

3. A wife provided instant security with a place to roost.

4. His son had always been a loner. Maybe he'd seen other couples happily united, wanted a slice of the wedding cake. Both tasted good but staled fast. Ike knew this the hard way; his son did not. Yet.

5. The bride and groom were embroiled in a case. During a murder investigation, senses were heightened, situations pressurized; in the heat of an adventure, it was a doddle for things to get romantic.

6. Tiger had always been possessive. If Jo was as cute a ball of fluff as the detective had suggested, he wouldn't want her to fall into enemy paws. Marriage wasn't just a declaration of love—it was a demarcation of territory. That went for proprietary females as well as males.

7. Ike was a wee bit jealous, seeing Tiger so happy.

8. He didn't see enough of Tiger, but after the wedding, he would see a lot less of him. Tiger would be busy nesting with Jo.

9. Ike missed his son.

The wedding was a good excuse for a party, getting together with old mates, catching up on unsolved cases. Ike couldn't wait to see an old flame of his named Sheba, a Somali darling with an impressively bushy tail.

There would also be pomp, punch, and mucho food: a big spread always put a smile on a cat's face. A wedding was never a bad idea, unless the groom forgot to turn up or the couple divorced within the month, in which case the feast was mainly remembered for its depressing aftertaste. It was considered bad manners to gossip with one's mouth full. Ike always cried at divorce proceedings...

Tiger had never been fickle as a kitten, seeing games through to their end, determined to win, chasing the bullies and snatching tuck shop thieves. As the wee lad had grown into a tenacious, hard-clawed detective, he'd stuck to his suspects' trails with shoes of gum. If he was as devoted in his relationships as he was to the mysteries he solved, the match would last a century.

Jo looked impressive in white, a veil failing to dowse her beauty, ears stuffed behind a tiara, tail waggling from a slit in her train. She looked like an empress, a distant diva, a pregnant Pavlova. Nobody said any-thing about her condition; some assumed she'd been overeating. Pre-wedding nerves or depression. It didn't hamper her style or dampen Tiger's Day.

They'd wanted a swift marriage. Corners had been cut, a ceremony swiftly booked. However, the wedding was still considered a notable social event by Nub City standards, the guest list a whodunnit of crime-busting cats. It began with a procession through Stenmuir, Tiger in the lead, followed by friends and relatives in their brightest regalia. Traversing half the district, the groom reached Father Frank's church. The veiled bride and maid of honor (Sibyl) were there. Persian kittens carried Jo's train, mewing a wedding march.

Tiger and Jo brushed their heads together lovingly, then led their brethren around the back of the building. A feast awaited them, meat and fish laid out on the ground like offerings to some ravenous god. Although there was more than enough to go around, the cats ate every bite. By the time the wedding ceremony itself began, they were bloated with eats and ready to burst.

Father Frank donned his best cassock for the job. He had no qualms about Tiger's lack of faith; Jo would be a sound influence on the sap, dragging him to church and getting into theological arguments as all good Nub citizens should. Bickering never hurt a couple in Frank's book; it strengthened their bond. Survive the strife, add an extra year to your anniversary expectancy.

Frank encouraged his acolytes to beat each other over the head with their hymnbooks to settle a disagreement. This prevented their lives from becoming too sheltered and prepared them for the rigors of the violent world beyond his church. The acolytes he sent to spread the word were also tough nuts. Refuse one of their pamphlets and you'd be given one anyway, stuffed down your craw. When they paid a visit to a house, it would be to collect protection money.

Their tactics had proved highly popular, making the congregation swell. They guarded Tiger and Jo's wedding, stalking the outskirts, hissing at curious onlookers. None of Tiger's enemies would spoil this day.

Aunt Farl wore a black knee-length skirt and floral pink bedsocks. A crimson pullover complemented her rusting gold earrings. Her pads were washing-up wrinkled and whiskers sprouted from places they shouldn't have. She liked to act dithery, trying to entertain the family, forgot names, came out with crazy sayings, and asked inane questions. Her folks found her scatterbrained antics annoying. They hoped she was assuming her idiotic airs, blaming her religious upbringing. They wouldn't tell her the truth, of course; instead, they smiled and tried not to stay in the same room with her for too long. They didn't get a chance on the day of the wedding.

Aunt Farl had been invaluable in the run-up to the ceremony arranging Jo's train, flicking crumbs from Father Frank's cassock, ensuring that everyone sat in the right place—her family on the left side of the church, Jo's entourage on the draughty side. They looked awkward in their formal suits and gowns, yanking at their collars and rubbing their corseted tummies. They were also impatient, with attention spans as short as an unfinished jingle.

The rival factions glared at each other, ready to jostle for territorial space. Tails lashed and eyelids batted. Frank's acolytes glowered at them; the congregation spoke in hushed mews. Two kittens sang choral chords as the bride and groom walked to the altar. Two witnesses were ready to sign the marriage certificate—Sibyl and Bug, who was disguised with a wig.

Frank proceeded with a warm smile.

"Do you, Tiger Straight, take Jo Madrigal as your clawfully wedded wife?"

"I do," Tiger purred.

"Will you share sun patches with her, hunt for her, and leave a little bit of food in your bowl when you've finished eating in case she wants a bite?"

"I'll try."

Ike sidled up to the desk and told Frank that Aunt Farl was supposed to be a witness. Jo didn't hear him; she saw a tinseled tassel stuck to his tail. She started to giggle.

Father Frank continued, "Do you, Jo Madrigal, take Tiger Straight as your clawfully wedded husband?"

"Teehee!"

Frank took that as a yes.

"Will you at least pretend to show interest in everything he says, laugh at his jokes, and refrain from flicking your tail in an agitated fashion when his habits annoy you?"

There were tears in Jo's eyes by now. She couldn't see to wrap the strip of cloth around Tiger's wrist. He helped her and added his own colors. "I'm sorry," she managed at last. She used the ribbon to blow her nose.

"This happens a lot," the priest reassured her. The bride and groom recited their pledge.

- When your tongue is tired, I will wash your fur.

- When you are hungry, I will fill your dish.

- When you itch, I will scratch your scruff.

- When you feel lonely, I will remind you what you mean to me.

As the couple put their paw marks on their marriage certificate, countersigned by Sibyl and Bug, Jo tried to explain why she found it all so funny. Tiger brushed it off as mild hysteria. He didn't blame her.

By the time the ceremony ended, the light was fading. The guests sat on stalls sheltered by canvas canopies, sucking on hookahs, and singing a sour cats' chorus. Old ladies gave the groom sloppy kisses. The males nuzzled the bride, and she bopped them with a playful paw. As the stars came out to take a gander, the conversation grew ruder and more raucous. The cubs were taken home to bed and the mouthiest members of the family performed limericks in the round. The guest list included a who's who of criminal investigation: Wilton Pirie, the genius jailer; John Hood, the brainstorming barkeep; Inspector Mortis and his talkative witness, Nut; Marlon Wakely, the bulimic boffin; Carol Griffin, the deductive dinner lady; Alex Van de Weyer, the crime-solving coach. Stan Spayed was one of the best and brightest, who made herringbone jackets in his spare time. They all understood that no matter how rife theft and murder were, they should have something to fall back on. All except Bix, who had a one-track mind, as Nut was beginning to learn.

"I'm not invited to weddings very often," Nut mooed.

"Can't imagine why not," Bix whispered.

"I *am* sure it ain't polite to give the groom suspicious looks all through the ceremony." Nut waggled a hoof in the inspector's face. "I was surprised when you accepted the invite."

"You know why we came here," Bix snapped.

"The free nosh?" Nut's stomach was full of freshly cut grass with buttercup seasoning.

"No, not the nosh. I'm still sure Straight's keeping something from us. A clue, a piece of evidence. Perhaps he and the makeup artist are colluding. I was hoping he'd let something slip, being his wedding day and all. I want you to keep your ears open and your mouth shut."

"Great!" Nut nudged one of the guests. "I'm going to be a spy." She turned back to Bix, who was pretending that he didn't know her. "I think you're very courageous, Inspector."

"How so?" the rodent replied resignedly.

"You're the most edible thing here, apart from the cucumber sandwiches. For cats, I mean—you're safe with me. I like cud. But in this place, you could end up covered in icing and carved into tender bite-sized slices."

"I'm an officer of the law," Bix railed. "And the eating of my kind is strictly prohibited. If one of these fatties eats me, they'll do time."

"If a cat's hungry enough, I don't think he cares about repercussions," warned Nut sadly. "Take care, Inspector. I'll watch your back." Her words were a small comfort to the small cop.

"Pirie! I see you're visiting from Bast." John Hood accosted his colleague.

"How d'you deduce that?" asked Carol Griffin. "The scents on his fur, the mud on his paws, the stains on his coat?"

"No," Hood replied coolly. "I saw him getting off the train."

Tiger had invited some of his old foes to the reception, rogues he'd sent to the caboose long ago: Flax Draxar, the crazed inventor; Kisselda, the korat with poison-tipped claws; Tanktop, the flat-headed ginger tom obsessed with deadly devices; and a couple of serial scratchers. With the acolytes helping to keep the peace, the heroes and villains got on famously, with a common point of discussion to start from. The villains' minds were all cesspits of death, corruption, treason, and plot. Some of the bad guys were surprised by how much their nemeses had to think like them to beat them; others saw it as a long-time goal to convert the detectives to their way of thinking. Using unorthodox methods to catch their prey, they would eventually become just as bad. All the guests agreed the get-together had been a fab idea and asked to be invited to the first anniversary party if the marriage lasted that long; crime fighters' relationships were notoriously short-lived.

Tiger got a kick out of seeing old alley pals that he thought he'd never see again: the half-dead, the wanted, the watched, and the hunted, all ready for a merry reception. All he had to do was ensure they weren't disappointed. To do that, he had Doctor Phat imported from Club Wu Wu, ready to serenade the couple under the moonlight. He also had his tan case ready for action once Phat had finished strutting his stuff.

Within the case sat Tiger's joy, his muse and mouthpiece, a shining collection of brass tubes and keys. The sax was all that mattered when a crime seemed insoluble, or the blues tapped his veins. When he played, the instrument became an extension of himself, a parping extra limb, warm metal and reed between his lips, the puck of soft padded keys clamping over hungry holes. Steam left his ears, and his hind paws tapped. His eyes rolled; his elbows twitched. It didn't pay the rent (not that he had rent to pay), bring him fame, or a fan base full of chicks. It brought him peace, even if the audience couldn't get any until he stopped.

Each detective had brought a sidekick, not all of whom were as intelligent as Bug. Some of them asked stupid questions all the time—wondering where they were, what was going on. Others moaned about the tedium of tagging after their partners. The younger ones didn't know any better, itching for a new adventure. "I don't know why I put up with him," moaned Bug. Nut agreed with her.

"They treat you like an object, not a living, breathing bovine, or other animal. We're all adults here. Why do you put up with him?"

"Reminds me of the old times. At least I have that excuse. When last I saw him, I was younger, more optimistic. Hanging around with him brings back those days."

"I don't know about that, but attending prowler investigations makes a change from standing in a shed."

"I know exactly what you mean." Bug nodded, brushing cake crumbs from her dress. "I'm sick of working in the same place every day, seeing the same people. Tiger takes me to new places. Admittedly grotty places with dead bodies and violent anti-social types, but it still spices my life up with a bit of variety.

I'm invaluable to him. Without me, he wouldn't have an inquiry. How come he acts as if I'm not there sometimes?"

"I don't know." Nut shrugged. "It's not as if the inspector misses me. I'm so bloomin' big. Always getting in the way, or so he says. I've only trod on his tail once. As far as I know. He can be awful quiet when he's thinking, never shares anything with me."

Bug bored Nut with stories of past glories long into the evening, until the lights dimmed, and a cleaner swept them away with a hard-bristled broom. Bug headed home and Nut went back to the prowler station. Bix wasn't in his office; she waited patiently for his return. Getting distraught would not get her home.

"This place is getting demolished next week. Did you know that?"

Ike dabbed orts from his paper plate. "Whole street'll be gone before your cubs arrive. A business park instead, with the central office slap bang where the church is."

"I'm sorry to hear that, Pop." Tiger and Ike sat on a step outside the church, staring up at the stars. While Tiger believed in progress, he felt bad for Father Frank. Urban renewal was transforming the city, brightening buildings, and gentrifying the slums. No more flophouses or dirty litter trays in the public conveniences. The future looked remorseless and fair for his kittens.

"Too right you should be sorry!" his father harangued. "You won't be able to take your sons and daughters out to show them where you got married."

"You never showed us nothing like that," Tiger grumbled.

"Me and your ma never got hitched. You're the peculiar one, tying the knot. Most cats're happy livin' day-to-day, not fussin' over consequences or makin' long-term plans." Ike licked his lips with a rasp. "Less complicated that way. Life shouldn't be all complex, son. It should be simple and plain; ephemeral. You look for puzzles where there ain't none."

"I like to use my brain."

"You think too much," Ike spluttered. "When you were born, I got a steady job. Earned enough to feed my scattered family and pay the mortgage every month. Saved up a nest egg for you and your ma. So what if I lost it all in a blaze o' drugs and carousing? That was after you left home. Where's your job? Where's your mortgage?"

"Ain't got one." Tiger was glum. "There're things I have to sort out first—before I rejoin the cat race."

"You're a quitter. Your business failed; life got too hard for you. Oh, you've changed your personal life. Now you gotta change the rest. Give up this detective stuff, son. Pull yourself together."

"How's Aunt Farl doing?" asked Tiger, trying to change the subject.

"Collapsed under a table. She was laughing at some joke, got too much for her. Don't worry, she's okay. Your Great Uncle Baff is with her. They're having a wheeze on the floor together."

"Aunt Farl's looking awful frail these days." Tiger felt guilty. He hardly ever visited his relatives, though they lived in the same alley. Stubborn pride had prevented him from asking them for help when he'd lost his possessions. At least a few of them had deigned to attend his wedding.

"Mebbe on the outside. Inside, she's stronger than I've ever known her. She's found something to believe in—joined a group. It's called CREAM, but I guess that's a gag, a play on words. Y'know, cats love cream."

"It's a rare delicacy, at least until this Depression ends."

"A lot of the old folks are members. You need something to laugh about when you're on your last legs, I suppose."

"Pretty sick for a joke. Where's this cult based?"

"The Beggars' Temple on Dempster Street. Got a dome like a lemon squeezer, you can't miss it. They dress up in red robes, with hoods and everything. A load of baloney, if you ask me."

Trust his dad to blunder into answers Tiger had sought for so long. "What do you believe in, Pop?" Tiger asked.

"I believe in you, Tiger." Ike coughed. "I know you can be a much better father than I ever was."

Tiger opened his mouth to thank his dad, but there wasn't time to say all the things he wanted to say. So he stood up and explained, "I've got to find Aunt Farl."

One of the good guys started it. Made an ill-advised comment to an old lag about his failed attempts to take over the world. After 29 fiendish plans (and several years in prison), wasn't it about time the evil genius retired? That was enough to start a brawl.

The church resounded with the sound of claws popping, ready for trouble. The lag's bottom quivered, his shoulders hunched, launching himself at the big-mouthed hero. His colleagues rushed to his defense— all except Stan Spayed, who hadn't been very active since his surgery, and Tiger. Aunt Farl had been carried home to rest; the day's excitement had proved too much for her and Great Uncle Boff had insisted on accompanying her. Now Tiger was busy dancing with his bride. It was the first chance they'd had to talk with each other that day.

"How did last night go?" Jo asked, swept off her paws.

"Dad stole the show and the entertainment. He's good at that. You?"

"We went to about three different clubs looking for something that wasn't bizarre and out of the ordinary. Stuffed ourselves stooped with shrimp cocktails. It went fine."

Jo couldn't dance for long. Not because of the excess weight in her belly; she'd kept herself fit throughout her pregnancy with repetitive pouncing exercises. She was famished, twirling the groom past the buffet table as often as possible. Despite the feast she'd enjoyed earlier, the little parasites inside her wanted more. So, more was what she gave them at every opportunity.

The scrap escalated as the thugs and lowlifes that Tiger had invited joined in. Flax Draxar bit Wilton Pirie's ear, tearing the tip. Tanktop raked a hind claw down Marlon Wakely's back. Kisselda spat in Alex Van de Weyer's eye, disorienting him. Heroes fought by the book, parry and thrust. The villains fought dirty, moving in for the kill.

A wedding fishcake arrived, and the greedy cats stopped squabbling to queue up for a slice. The cake lasted about four minutes. Ike decided to prevent any further fights by giving a boring speech.

"Now we've kind of settled our differences, a few words about why we're all here. Love." The guests nursed their black and bloody heads. "The love that's brought these two together." He raised his saucer in the bride and groom's direction.

"It ain't love that brought 'em together," came a cat-call from one of the less tactful guests. Maybe inviting the baddies hadn't been a good plan, although Tiger's intentions had been pure—to treat everyone in his life as a cat worthy of his attention. Jo instinctively covered her belly with her forepaws. Surely it didn't show yet?

Ike continued. "I've seen Tiger here grow into a fine specimen of an old has-been. He's grabbed this gal quick afore she realized how pug ugly he is. His new missus—my daughter-in-law—works in the movies, I'm told. No doubt you can find them on the top shelf of yer local video store. We know what you see in her, son." Tiger gave a wry grin. "He's intending to retire from the detection business," Ike went on. "To become a full-time hen-pecked hubby. This is one open-and-shut case that's well and truly solved. Good luck to you, lad. I wish the two of ye all the happiness ye can muster."

Tiger dragged himself upright to deliver a few words of his own. "I haven't known the love of my life long." Whoops from the crowd. "Long enough to find out what an open, genuine person she is. We didn't meet in the sexiest of circumstances..."

"Over my producer's dead body," interjected Jo. The villains let rip with their best cackling laughs.

"When our eyes met... I knew I'd have to question her," said Tiger. "In private. With the lights out."

Embarrassed silence.

"It's not gonna be easy providing for Jo, raising a family. We're gonna do it. With your support, we'll make a damn good start. Dames have always made a whole lot of trouble for me in the past. Always been after something—the goods, revenge, a place to hide.

Jo's different. I know she is. I'll do fine by her. She's beautiful, unique ... my wife. I'm confident we'll live happily ever after."

The guests supped more milk before Jo stood to say her piece. "Guys have always caused a lot of trouble for me," she smiled.

The comment raised a titter. "Including this one beside me. I've never known such a daft, doting, gentle soul. I've never wanted to marry anyone either. Here I am. Sorry for the waterworks earlier. Can't wait for the wedding video. Don't know if we'll live happily ever after. I'd like to think so." She bowed her head, enjoying the applause, then seated herself and drained her glass.

The guests were getting restless again, so Ike suggested his son give them a tune. Tiger unpacked his saxophone and played a soulful, yet totally toneless solo. Everybody left. Jo took him home and showed off a new nightie she'd bought for the wedding night. He'd drunk too much milk and felt sick, collapsing on the bed before insisting that he sleep on the floor. Jo let him sleep, wondering how she could scrap his sax and get away with it. Feed it to a goat, drop it under a tram, or leave it out for the garbage cats. Whatever measure she took would have to be permanent; he'd offer a reward for its return. She'd managed to trash the instrument he'd taken from Club Wu Wu only to find another one in the case he defended so readily. The mouthpiece was shaped to his lips, he'd told her; the sax wouldn't play for anyone else. Jo had decided that even if she did manage to destroy the instrument, there was always the possibility that he'd go out and buy another—once he'd got over the tragic loss—maybe take up the trombone. She couldn't win.

23

It was a leap of faith.

Cole said the water was warm and clean and felt like smooth soup. Connie chose to believe him and dipped her paw into the bay. She was glad to find that Cole was right—the water was delightful.

"I come here for peace, to think, to take a break from business or solve a crime amongst these little gray shells." Cole gazed along the shore. "And for the fish, of course."

"Of course," Connie purred, enjoying the sensation of water on her paws. She could get used to this feeling; once she'd gotten over her inherent dislike of getting wet, she felt relaxed.

"I don't need to ask what crime you're solving right now," said Connie.

"How do you know I'm not just here to spend time with you?" Cole said with a raised eyebrow.

"Because that's not you. At least, not you with unfinished business."

"Almost being murdered by the agent of an elite organization does count as unfinished business, I suppose."

"What else do you do around here, apart from play with the shells?"

"I mess around on boats." Cole shrugged.

"Who with?"

"I'll show you." Cole pointed a paw out to sea. A small fishing vessel approached, piloted by a sphynx in a red robe, large ears blown back by the open wind, wide blue eyes staring at Cole and Connie. As Gerry moored his boat, Cole introduced him.

"This is Gerry Igoe," said Cole. "I don't always get to sail with him, but when I do, I always catch plenty of fish."

"I know where they gather," said Gerry. Although Connie was perturbed by the mercat's lack of fur and wrinkled flesh, she followed Cole onto the boat, and they set out onto the water.

"How long have you two been fishing together?" Connie asked, flinching at the salt water on her whiskers.

"Not long," said Gerry, drawing out his vowels like deep-cast nets. "Mr. Tiddle hired me on his last visit here, didn't you, sir?"

"About that..." Cole lowered his voice. "I'm keeping a low profile, if you know what I mean." He glanced at Connie, and, as planned, Gerry got the wrong idea.

"I see, sir. You're just two cats enjoying a romantic getaway. I can mind my own business."

"Those robes look toasty," Cole said casually. "Glad you're keeping warm."

"It's not easy being furless."

"Seeing as how I'm missing a clump or two, I can tumble." Cole chewed on his itchy thigh. "Where can I get fancy duds like that?"

"Your fur will grow back," the sphynx said sadly. "I got mine from some religious souls. The Church of the Benign Bastet, I believe."

"So do they," Connie punned. She looked out at the sea, which was fearfully empty. No walls to scratch, no gravel to walk on. Nothing but water ahead and the harbor behind.

"Can we go back?" she asked quietly.

Gerry was too busy fish-spotting. "There's a bass!" he meowed. Connie sensed the same excitement she felt when she saw birds fly low.

"We won't stay out long," Cole reassured her. "Long enough to catch a mackerel, right Captain?"

"Aye!" Gerry chuckled, pulling his hood up over his frozen ears. "One for you, one for me, and one for the pot."

Connie rolled her eyes and rubbed them with the back of her paw. She'd gotten too used to spending time alone with Cole. Even an hour with this barefaced gooseberry would be too much. She wanted to be back in the city, in Cole's mansion. But she understood he wanted to play detective first and if that led to naming her brothers' killers...

Lona Dash had died out here, in the unyielding sea. Cole was scouring each crime scene for clues, connections, a pattern, or a trail. Gerry's red robe was a link, no matter how tenuous. Lona's background had also yielded helpful new hints, courtesy of the company she'd kept while alive

After they returned to the harbor, before they visited the church and settled back into the city, they had another stop to make: Lona's old address.

Nut could handle the funny looks she got from the clerks. She didn't belong there, mixing with civilized cats. She got in the way, took up too much room, had eaten every blade of grass on the back lawn of prowler headquarters, and all the shrubbery too. She spent six hours a day eating all the greenery in sight. The cats didn't understand why she was still hanging around. Neither did she.

If it was for her protection, there were safer places to be than the station. Cutthroats and scoundrels with more guts than a violin wandered in every day, and that was just the cops. Bix had left her in his office several times as he followed up lines of inquiry—a drowned kitten, a missing surgeon. She saw how wary he was around cats, scampering past them, nose atwitch. It took big mouse balls to work for the prowlers, whatever species you were. The paperwork was terrifying to behold, mounting up fast.

Despite her ordeal a week before, Nut felt strangely homesick. She missed her workmates, the shed, even her boorish husband. She spent many of the daylight hours wondering who'd replaced Scrumpy. Someone equally cantankerous, she hoped. A farmer who could adequately fill her old boss's galoshes.

This particular morning, she felt bloated, not sure why. Her partner or protector or whatever he was hadn't been in his office for 24 hours. Nut went walkabout, a hefty country lass absorbing the sights and scents of a municipal cop shop.

Activity throughout the building was frenetic pushing for chaotic. The harsh winter weather meant burst water pipes, citizens slipping on ice, longer nights for burglars to do their dirty work. All accidents, incidents, and complaints were logged in triplicate by the desk sergeant. He wasn't happy about it.

"Get that cow out of here!" he yelled. He was a round-faced Manx with bushy cheeks.

"It's the inspector's witness, Sarge," a beat cop piped up. "The one who didn't witness nothing." The sergeant grumbled to himself and let Nut pass. Reaching the main office, she could hardly move through the throng of frazzled druggies, booked hookers, and jaded pigs.

Someone had broken into a marshmallow factory and licked the coating off a whole batch. A suspect had been found puking in an alley not far away. A nest of nip addicts had been uncovered in the heart of the city; now a dozen junkies were going cold turkey in the jug. A militant leader calling himself TC was believed to be organizing a gang of alley strays to carry out scams. The only known fact about him was that he spoke with the commanding tones of an army officer. A shopkeeper was charged with selling smutty magazines.

When Nut spied the shopkeeper, she took a step backward, banging her rump against a white-collar criminal. Making her apologies, she approached the retailer who was being interviewed by a short-haired sergeant.

"I sell those things to holy guys, psychiatrists, all sorts of respectable gentlemen," the shopkeeper was explaining. He wore a tie-dye sweatshirt and flared dralons. "I didn't know it was illegal."

"Puss In Boots. Toms Only. Tail Action. Stiff Whiskers." The sergeant flapped the mags on his desk. The accused took a look around, embarrassed. No one was looking at him except a cow. What was a cow doing in a prowler station?

"You can get it in bottles, you know." The sergeant waggled a paw in Nut's direction.

"Can we help you, miss?" the prowler asked.

"I'm looking for Inspector Mortis."

"You see him at my desk? I don't think so. I'm trying to charge a bad guy here." To the hippie: "You could do some serious time for this filth. When you get out, your fur will be gray and your kidneys mush."

"He did it, Officer," cried Nut. "He definitely did it!"

The sergeant ignored her.

"I'm providing a service," the hippie cat whined. "These priests, they don't get no loving. They need magazines to help them contemplate and stuff. If you want to lock anyone up, lock up the readers. The publishers. Anyone but me. I can't go back in pokey."

"You've done time before, Mr. Sunray?"

Seedpod "Sonny" Sunray's parents had run a commune until their child had reached puberty. Now they were publishers, but Sonny had kept his remarkable name. He was too laid back to change it by deed poll. Too big a hassle.

"It was a long time ago," Sonny mewed. "When I was a student. We were protesting about the use of rodents in medical experiments. I got cold-cocked with a baton. Next thing I know, I'm working on a chain gang. It was a major bummer. I was a martyr."

"You're gonna get the chance to martyr yourself again. This time, I don't think the judge will be so lenient." The sergeant commanded an officer to lead Sonny to the holding cells.

"Hey! What about my stock?" the hippie yelled above the hubbub. "Confiscated," replied the sergeant, placing the magazines in his desk drawer. "As evidence."

"I know him," Nut mumbled.

"That third rate scumbag. Doubt if he gets out of his neighborhood much. Only reason he'd have to visit the countryside would be to pick mushrooms." The officer offered Nut a gentle smile. "I'll take you back to the inspector's office. He's due back any second."

Jo was always getting into trouble. As a kitten, her first step had led her into danger in the form of a hot pie left lying carelessly beside her. She'd burned her paw and learned a lesson. Her first trip to the ice-skating rink saw her pads caught under a boot blade and a severed claw. It hadn't stopped her skating. Her first date had been a disaster too, a mad fling with a special effects artist with a thing for foam latex. She'd learned a lot about the opposite sex, or a minority group of them at least.

Now she'd lost her head and her freedom to a tom she barely knew. His power and passion had overwhelmed her for an instant that would change her life. Or had she slept with Cole to spite Tiger, make him jealous, get him to notice her? A strange way to draw attention to herself; now everyone pointed and smiled at her swollen belly. The ladies turned to goo, and the males found her condition attractive. She was no threat to them, unless she had a notion to roll over them and squash them in the street.

She'd had pregnant pals before and as their weight increased, their public appearances diminished. Feeling frumpy, they spent lots of time indoors. Jo wasn't that kind of girl. She strutted her stuff until she was all strutted out—around the block was the furthest she could go. She enjoyed the sunlight, the cool breeze on her cheeks, the halloos from her neighbors who got used to seeing her out on the town, out of puff. Her solution was to curl up on the sidewalk, lick the sweat from her fur, even take a nap if the fancy took her. Any complaints? Take 'em to the gods of conception and pregnancy. If anyone stepped on her tail, they'd face the wrath of a famished female.

Her tail stayed untrampled.

A frustrated Bix entered the station. His leads had brought him no closer to solving his case; he wasn't even sure if the murders he'd investigated were connected, the *modus operandi* was always different. A kitten had drowned in a small fishing village; what motive could there be for taking a young life in such a sadistic fashion?

The Hant brothers, poisoned with their own killer chemical. Another sick act. The TV producer, Joel Venet—at least he had enemies. But as far as Bix could discern, none of the production team hated Venet enough to fry his brains to soot. That would require a whole heap of hate.

He found Nut in his office, delivering a steaming cowpat in his wastepaper basket. It wasn't her first deposit of the day.

"I'm sorry," she said demurely. "I didn't know where to put it."

"It's okay. Stay downwind of me. Do you want to open the windows?"

"They are open."

Bix couldn't see properly. Either Nut's stench was overpowering, or he'd been working too hard. He was unable to reach the windows. Many other things in his office constantly reminded him of his titchy stature. He used a miniature stepladder to reach the sill behind his desk.

"There was a cat in the main office," said Nut.

"Really? Oh my. I'd better run and hide. It might eat me!" Bix was a font of sarcastic wit. "Of course there was a cat outside! There's bloody hundreds of them."

"Yes, but I recognized this one. A citizen. The officer with him said he lived in the city. The only way I'd recognize him—"

"Is if he visited your farm. Do a lot of cats pop into your shed?"

"The only one I ever saw was Scrumpy—until he died. Then I didn't see him no more."

"So the only way you'd recognize this cat..."

"Is if he was there when my boss was murdered, or when I was kidnapped."

Bix's beady eyes gleamed.

"I'm sure he wasn't one of Scrump's temporary replacements," Nut continued. "I'd remember, I'm sure, if you could do something for me." The tag on her ear rattled.

"Anything," said Bix. "What would help?"

"Milk me."

"I don't think so."

"Oh, go on. I haven't been milked in ages. I'm sure a good yank'd really clear the cobwebs."

"I'm a prowler," Bix tutted. "Not a dairymaid."

"How badly do you want to catch this murderer?"

The cop didn't reply. Instead, he left his seat and positioned his tiny stepladder beside Nut's udders. Clambering up, he teased one of her teats.

"Moo." The cow closed her eyes tight. "That feels good."

"Anything yet?" Bix wanted answers.

"Keep going," giggled Nut. "Harder." She squirted five gallons of milk from her udders, drenching the inspector. "He was there! The shopkeeper, I'm sure. He wasn't alone—I didn't see the other fellow. I saw him. He didn't really want to be there."

"Of course, it would take two to lift you," muttered Bix as he hurriedly cleaned his whiskers.

"He distracted me; the other one battered me over the head. Never saw him again until now."

"Let's go pay him a visit."

Sonny, the miniscule Singapura, languished in a holding tank. He'd sniffed a large quantity of valerian on arrest—it had been on his person for medicinal purposes. Now he was high as a kite and twice as giddy. He greeted Bix and Nut with a lazy cheer. He declined to comment on the milk that dripped from Bix's coat.

"Why did you do it?" asked the horrified cow. She gazed through thick black bars at the hopped-up hippie.

"The money, lady. I make more offa jazz mags than a windowful of gift shop tack. I got a mouth to feed. It needs constant attention."

"We're not interested in your tawdry wares," Bix snapped.

He'd whipped Sonny's rap sheet from the sergeant's desk on his way down.

"I'm startin' to feel hungry now, Mr. Mouse," the shopkeeper drooled. "Anyone ever tried to smoke a rodent?"

"Why did you try to kill me?" asked Nut.

"I had nothing against you, lady. I was doing a favor for a friend. If I'd known his intentions were... I mean, I thought he was playing a prank."

At Bix's instruction, a guard released Sonny and slapped a pair of cuffs on him. The guard escorted Bix, Nut, and a floating Sonny to the hippie's high street store, Feline Groovy.

"I don't know what you're hoping to find here, dude. The prowler who arrested me, he took all my dodgy gear. Hey, does that mean I'm off his bum charge?"

"You won't go to prison for trading in black market literature," Bix squeaked, scouring the floor for evidence. "You'll be booked with kidnapping and attempted murder."

Scuttling through the shop, Bix tripped over a tail. Its owner apologized and helped the inspector up; this made him angrier.

"What are you doing here?"

Tiger and Bug tried to look innocent. It wasn't easy, as they'd already turned the shop outside in. Stock was scattered over shelves and counters. The bead curtain that concealed a back room swayed noisily.

"The shop was left open. We were browsing."

"Don't give me that. You're in cahoots with this gent, aren't you?" said Bix, staring up at Tiger. Sonny offered the detectives the peace sign with two of his claws. Bix asked, "What are you really here for?"

"We're not allowed to shop? It's a fundamental right, you know, to bear armfuls of consumer items. There'd be something in the constitution about it if we had a constitution. I don't know this guy."

"We know of him, though," Bug admitted. "Got a tip-off that he might know something about a—"

"A cheap lava lite," Tiger interrupted, stamping on Bug's tail to shut her up. "Here's one, purrfect! That's what I need for the office."

"You don't have an office," Bix squeaked.

"I will have. Soon. Need to furnish it. Who's the cow?"

Nut introduced herself, explaining that Sonny had apparently tried to kill her. Everyone admitted that this was a mean thing to do and that she was the best-looking cow they'd ever seen on the high street.

Bix ordered the guard to take Nut, the detectives, and the suspect back to the station. The inspector remained to check the stock room beyond the bead curtain. The room was mostly filled with empty cartons and cardboard boxes, although he made a small, unsettling discovery with the potential to put a whole new spin on his investigation.

"How are things, Bix? Everything running to course, I trust?" Back at the station, Chief Inspector Bowyer was making one of his rare appearances. A large seat had been brought into Bix's office for the chief. He leaned on the desk, which sagged under his great weight.

"Making headway at last, sir. We have a suspect under lock and chain downstairs. He hasn't confessed to everything yet, though we're close to breaking him. He had an accomplice—I have my suspicions about who that might be." Tiger and Bug were being detained in the corridor beyond his office.

"Wonderful," Bowyer crowed.

"Have you seen a cow around here, sir?"

"A cow? Well, bless my soul, I thought she was lunch. Sent her to the kitchens. Nice with some barbecue sauce."

"She's a witness. Might need her if this thing goes to trial."

"There won't be a trial. In these kinds of matters, justice must be swift, Bix. Any hesitation and the public could start to worry, or your suspect could escape."

"Whatever you say, sir." Bix frowned, always a stickler for legal procedure. "I'll go and rescue the cow."

"Sure. Rustle up another one for me, will you, Inspector? I'm famished."

"I'll see that the chef's made aware of your pangs," Bix replied tartly. He didn't like to be treated like a waiter, and prowler headquarters had no chef, only a vending machine and an AGA stove. He left the office without another word.

Chief Inspector Bowyer sat back on his padded cushion and noted the pool of milk souring on the carpet. Various animals running around made for a disorderly station, and he liked nothing less. He wanted everything to run smoothly. In his eyes, that meant maintaining a harsh reputation and an iron rule. He had no friends; those who did offer him a kind word wanted something (like Cole) or rubbished him behind his back. He had many peers and acquaintances, all helping each other to stay teetering on the top rung of the social ladder. The position was precarious, but he was party to riches, conspiracies, and political and religious maneuvers. He possessed vast quantities of information, which helped him to hold his position as the chief of the prowlers in Nub City.

Bix had climbed as high as he could in the prowler hierarchy. It was only his stunning intellect and perfect record that had allowed him to reach the rank of inspector. Bowyer would make sure that he got no far-ther. Bad for feline morale, for the grunts to be bossed around by a buck-toothed pipsqueak. He would move Bix to another division—litter patrol, TV licensing, a spot on the Bureau of Prohibition, or something equally, inherently pointless. He was sure the inspector would understand; perhaps Bix would be glad of a less dan-gerous post. All these murders could have an effect on the rodent's heart, and mice were ever so weak in the ticker department.

"Excuse me. You seen a mouse about? We're waiting for him." Tiger had nosed into the office, interrupting Bowyer's ruminations. "We do have other things to do, my friend and I." Bug was curled up patiently in the corridor. "Besides being at the beck and call of that little hairball. "

"I take it you are referring to Inspector Mortis?" Bowyer asked.

"Yeah. Has he got lost?"

"Carrying out an order for me. He is efficient. You are...?"

"Tiger Straight, private investigator. Mortis thinks I'm getting in his way."

"I see. You're privately investigating a murder or two. In so doing, you've crossed paths with the inspector."

"Been questioned by him," said Tiger with an ounce of pride. "We had nowt to spill."

Bowyer fondled his tail thoughtfully. "The inspector always gets his cat. Doesn't let anyone stand in his way. He can't afford to."

"Sure." Tiger looked bored and examined the impressive insignia shaved into Bowyer's jowls. "How's he getting on?"

"I'm sure he'll let you know all about it during your next interrogation." The chief provided his most diplomatic smile. "Isn't that right, Inspector?"

Bix entered the office, brushing past Tiger.

"I can't *wait* for the interrogation," said Bix.

"I'm going to do a little questioning of my own with our friend downstairs." Bowyer stood up slowly. "Fill in some blanks for myself, okey dokey?"

"Very well, sir. If you really think it necessary."

"I do. Goodbye, Mr. Straight. I'm sure you'll be a big help to us."

Bowyer passed Nut and Bug in the corridor. They shared a bunch of grass, Bug nibbling idly on a blade, Nut chewing heavily. Nut spent eight hours a day chewing. When she wasn't eating or chewing, she was usually asleep. It didn't leave her a lot of time to assist the inspector.

The two sidekicks sat for a while, watching a busy stream of feline traffic pass by: a cop barking like a vicious dog, a mean margay with mangy eyes, chained up and heavily guarded, a plump orange cat eating lasagna, and a captain bawling out two hapless rookies. A tough-looking cat in a scruffy suit sneered at Nut as he stumbled drunkenly to the gents. Bug decided he was an attorney.

"My partner hasn't exactly taken a shine to yours, has he?" Bug gave Nut a friendly sniff.

"I hadn't really noticed," the cow lowed. "To be honest, I'm trying to get home to my farm, that's all."

"A mouse and a cow," said Bug thoughtfully. "How did that happen?"

"Oh, no special reason. Extraordinary circumstances throwing two lonely souls together, forging a bond between them."

"They say the inspector is very efficient."

"Who says?"

"His head honcho. The bell cow. Chief Inspector Bowyer."

Nut said, "Bix does have a certain air of authority about him, especially for someone with his disadvantages. Do you think a mouse could feel anything for...?"

"Insects don't have this problem." Bug sighed. "No love pangs or peer pressure. The females shag anything that isn't disguised as a twig, then bite their partner's head off afterward."

"Sounds efficient." Nut rubbed her sore hooves. "He's dragged me halfway across the city looking for clues. Finally, I give him the goods, and he acts like I'm invisible. As if my usefulness is at an end. I almost landed up in the cafeteria, you know."

"Doesn't sound so bad." Bug licked her lips. It was a while since she'd last had a square meal.

"As the main attraction in the mixed grill? I don't think so."

"What about these goods you gave him?"

"Some hippie implicated in all this. He could have killed me! I don't think the inspector has even questioned him properly yet. I've a good mind to go down and talk to him myself. Maybe that'll speed things up."

"Let's do it then," said Bug, urging Nut into an upright position and leading her down a flight of stairs. A lot of time and thought had been spent on the holding tanks. The cells had been given a lick of mint green paint, fancy lanterns suspended from the ceilings. The aisle lights cast dull beams onto the prisoners. One cell was open, allowing Bug and Nut into a small area furnished with cushions and a bowl of gray water. The place smelled of rosehip and disinfectant.

"We're looking for the hippie," said Nut, barely able to squeeze into the cubicle. The chief faced her, shaking his head.

"Ain't down here," he belched. "Think he's done a runner." Sonny wasn't present, though his flares lay on the floor and the heady smell of valerian lingered in the air. Bug peered through a set of bars at the perp in the adjacent cell.

"You see him?"

"Not a thing," said a scared-looking cat. "I was working, minding my own business. Like you should, darlin'."

"You think he's escaped?" Nut asked the chief.

"I don't doubt it." Bowyer left the cell, rubbing his copious belly. "He's on the lam with no pants?" Bug sniffed at the flares, her nose wrinkling.

"In disguise," Bowyer explained. He tried to usher the two females upstairs. "This is no place for you."

"He'll probably get himself arrested again," Nut mused. "For decent exposure. We'd better get after him, eh, Chief?"

"I'll sort all that out. There're papers to fill in, APBs to bulletin. I don't want you two getting in the way—only slow things down."

"We understand," said Bug as she led Nut up the steps.

Deciding that the chief was embarrassed by the incident, Bug decided not to mention what had happened.

The residents of the Straylite Rest Trailer Park did not like strangers. They liked Cole and Connie even less. The couple was dressed in fine clothes and smelled like a flower as they gingerly stepped over broken toys and patches of crabgrass. When Cole and Connie visited Lona's trailer, her mother ignored them. Cole and Connie could see her in the window, staring into the distance, tail whipping from side to side. But she would not come when they called her.

"She won't answer," said the cat next door. It was Little Tim, now a total chonker with a swollen belly supported by short, stubby legs and his broad paws. He had kibble in his folds of fur, and seeds on his back where he couldn't reach to groom.

"We're not selling, we're buying," said Cole. "Information."

"We have questions we hope to get answered here," said Connie, allowing Tim to sniff her forehead. "Did you know the young cat who used to live here, Lona Dash?"

"We were friends."

"Friends?" Cole asked.

Tim nodded. "We grew up together. I cared about her, more than she cared about me."

"I'm sorry," said Connie.

"Lona's mom doesn't go out much. I bring her treats when I can afford it. Times have been hard for me, since..."

"Since when?" Connie asked with concern.

"Since I lost my job at the Public Works. Can't find another for the lives of me. I've even been turned down for volunteer work." Tim stopped talking, ashamed by the impression he was making.

"Times are so tough," said Connie. "But they'll come around."

"They always do," Cole joined in. "And you're hanging in there."

"I know what it looks like," said Tim, licking his chubby chest and finding a sizable crumb. "I got really good at catching rats when I was a garbage cat. Before I resigned. And my metabolism's all out of whack with anxiety. The less I eat, the more I gain weight."

"I know the feeling." Connie sighed as she and Cole left Little Tim.

"I'm famished," Cole grumbled.

"He looked so depressed," said Connie. "Can't you ... make a donation?"

"Never mind that, doll," Cole hushed her. "Did you see his paws?"

Cole was desperate for swank.

After the low-rent ravages of Straylite Rest, Cole needed to clean his palate. Despite Connie's warning about blowing his cover, Cole insisted on attending the Munchkin Salon, a spa where small cats pampered the large and important, offering intricate pictures and scalp shiatsus, belly rubs, and whisker licks.

Connie soon relaxed alongside Cole, reassured that they would receive total privacy and satisfaction.

"When you see cats in need like Lona's mom and her neighbor," Connie purred as her jowls got massaged. She was tucked up in a sack, its inside lined with warm saliva, secured loosely around her neck. It felt divine. "Don't you want to help them?"

"I sympathize with their plight." An ivory munchkin balanced its tiny paws on his back, kneading him softly. "I contribute to several non-profit concerns. But I need to safeguard my resources in case the Depression gets worse." The munchkin pressed harder, claws out, but they were so puny Cole hardly noticed. "I have friends who've lost everything," Cole murmured. "So I keep my moolah under the mattress."

"I thought that rustling was made by your cat's pajamas."

Cole laughed at the quip.

Flash! A camera bulb popped from the corner of the beauty salon.

Cole jumped up, sending the munchkin flying through the air and landing suspended on a tasteful drapery panel. A reporter, complete with press pass tucked in his hatband, stood brazenly staring at Cole and Connie.

"How did he get in here?" Connie asked her masseur, who held up his mink mittens in innocence.

"You're Cole Tiddle!" the reporter yowled. "The rumors are true."

"No, I'm not," said Cole.

"You sound like him!"

"So I do," Cole preened. "Well, tickle me pink."

As the reporter ran out of the salon with his scoop, Connie gave her mate a told-you-so look and climbed out of her sack, briskly washing herself. The cat was out of the bag.

Cole and Connie hurried back to the mansion, Cole fuming at the intrusion in the salon.

"Unbelievable," he scowled. "I was promised anonymity."

"It's hard to be anonymous when you're strutting your scruff all over town," Connie reasoned. "You said it yourself. We're in a Depression. Right now, cats will do anything for a kickback."

"I was just about to infiltrate CREAM," said Cole as they passed a long line of cats waiting for loaves of fly bread. "How can I do that if I'm alive?"

"It's for the best. You'd be risking your life, messing with CREAM. You almost died once already. This is no game, Cole."

"Oh, it is a game, doll." Cole stopped in the street and rounded on Connie. "With extremely high stakes. Now I'm in, I have to play until the end."

"Your end?" Connie sighed. "There are other ways to play. A tip to the prowlers, for example."

"A tip-off about an elite organization? What are they going to arrest CREAM for, throwing loud parties? I need more evidence before I accuse them of murder."

"Start smaller, then."

"Or real small."

Jo took up knitting, purling, and darning with her needly claws. It wasn't too physically demanding, something she could focus on for hours at a time. She also tried dressmaking; it was impossible to find decent maternity wear for cats, the high street efforts resembling spud sacks. She designed crosswords for the local school magazine, sniffed at kitten books. She wore a sports bra with six hefty cups.

Jo hadn't left the apartment in days, and that epic voyage had consisted of a trip to the neighborhood diner, the Greasy Hide, to get the chocolate chipmunk muffin she craved.

Tiger was aghast; this wasn't the adventurous femme he'd married. No more hunting, fishing, or love-making. She was likely to turn on him and give him a scratch when he wanted a cuddle. He hoped that life would get back to normal after the births, that his wife would revert to her old self as if nothing had happened.

"How was your muffin?" asked Tiger, trying not to sound jealous.

"It would have been better with a dollop of cream on top," Jo replied, resting on the back of her Chesterfield.

"I can get you another one," Tiger said, thinking he could get one for himself in the process.

"You don't understand."

"I rarely do." The detective smiled.

"When I mentioned cream to the Cheshire behind the counter, he had a hissy fit. Acted like I'd asked for my muffin to be drizzled with the blood of his firstborn. Ranted about all the good work he did, keeping the streets clean and thinking of others. Well, he wasn't thinking of me!" Jo panted a little to cool herself down.

"Bizarre."

"Then I thought, maybe he thinks I'm asking about CREAM—the shady organization you were investigating."

"That would explain his strange behavior," Tiger considered. "I'm sorry he was rude to you."

"It could be a lead."

It could be an excuse for me to buy more muffins, thought Tiger. "I'm taking a break. To keep you company."

"Why not have an unbreak? Just to get fresh air, and..."

"And more provisions." Tiger nodded. "I'm always ready to pop a topping on your pastry."

"Get your furry toosh out of here, you big galoot." Jo threw a pillow playfully at Tiger.

Night had fallen, and the sky was grim with clouds. Tiger donned his hat and trench coat, buttoning it up tight.

"You're not gonna be too long, are you? In case … anything happens."

"Nothing will," Tiger purred. "You're not ready to pop yet." Jo was seven weeks pregnant. She still had a fortnight to endure.

"You never know," the newlywed cried as Tiger left the room. "The kittens could be immature."

He worried every day that he wouldn't be there when the time came to help her to the hospital. After the attempt on her life, Jo had seemed *blasé* about the experience, rarely raising the subject. But Tiger kept his wits keen—he wasn't just guarding the lady he loved. He was guarding her unborn cubs as well.

It didn't take Tiger long to reach the diner, tucked at the end of West Street as if hiding from customers; another gray building in a row of drab shops and terraced houses, blinds closed, lights dimmed. A canvas canopy shaded the establishment like the peak on a cap and even the streetlights couldn't illuminate its aging sign. The canopy had been unrolled to keep the sun off; the proprietor hadn't bothered to put it away again. It jutted, gathering dust and city grime, losing its blue and white stripes.

Tiger's eyes prowled around the diner, following food as it scuttled along the counter. With its menu of bugs and small, sharp-toothed, unwashed rodents, the Greasy Hide was the only place in town where the food ate you.

Jo had become a regular customer during her pregnancy, and Tiger had nipped in a few times over the past couple of weeks to pick up treats for his wife. He found it hard to believe the proprietor was a member of CREAM.

The Cheshire at the register smiled at his clientele, serving them without complaint. Nothing to arouse Tiger's suspicions. Judging by Jo's instinct and her strange, uncomfortable encounter, however, every night at ten the Cheshire would close the diner, nip around the corner, bone up on his rites and chants, go enjoy a sacrifice or two with his buddies, and back to the missus before she knew any better. Tiger doubted the Cheshire's wife would be able to shed any light on his activities; many of the females in these parts turn a blinkered eye to the shenanigans of the males. So he stuck to good, old-fashioned gumshoeing.

Tiger was not the last customer out of the diner. He was far too wily for that, waiting in a shadowed doorway across the street. His trench coat collar was turned up against the cold. When the Cheshire finally placed a CLOSED sign in his window and trudged past the detective, Tiger followed ten yards behind. He was grateful for the dirty mist. He knew it was going to rain. It always did on nights like this; the heat rose and congested to form dark clouds that matched his mood.

Tiger followed the suspect through streets shining with the slick damp of old rain, stopping as the Cheshire entered a run-down apartment block. The detective crouched in a bundle of trashcans. His green eyes were mirrored in a front window as he looked inside. He could see a group of cats, dressed casually, trading greetings and rubbing against one another, checking out their individual scents.

There was a smack of lightning as a member of the group turned to face him: a gray-faced ghoul with one eye scarred shut. Tiger didn't duck, didn't move—the motion might clue the cult to his presence. Instead, he squeezed his eyes tight shut and hoped the light didn't give him away.

Nothing happened. One Eye turned back to the others. They weren't breaking any laws, but Tiger wanted to hear what they were saying. After a rapid snoop around the back of the building, he found a small flap leading to the cellar. He squeezed through and crept on all fours toward the front room, ears cocked.

Padding through a hallway, following his nose, he judged that the door opposite would lead to the front room. He placed his head against the door and listened. Silence. He stared through the keyhole; no one was there. Perhaps he had the wrong room. Perhaps his prey had gone.

A screen croaked open with a slight push, and he stepped forward, eyes adjusting to the darkness. Instead of rich carpet, his paws trod thin air, and he fell into a deep rectangular pit.

"You must be the private dick." One Eye had been waiting for his grand entrance.

"Astute." Tiger brushed down his coat with the fedora. "I've been hired to—"

"To mess up my life. It's not gonna happen. We're turnin' this place into a bathroom, buddy. You're at the bottom of a deep, deep sand tray."

For the first time, Tiger noticed four vents at the top of his pit. They began to spew fresh litter, spilling onto him. The pit slowly began to fill—he would be buried alive in a giant litter trap.

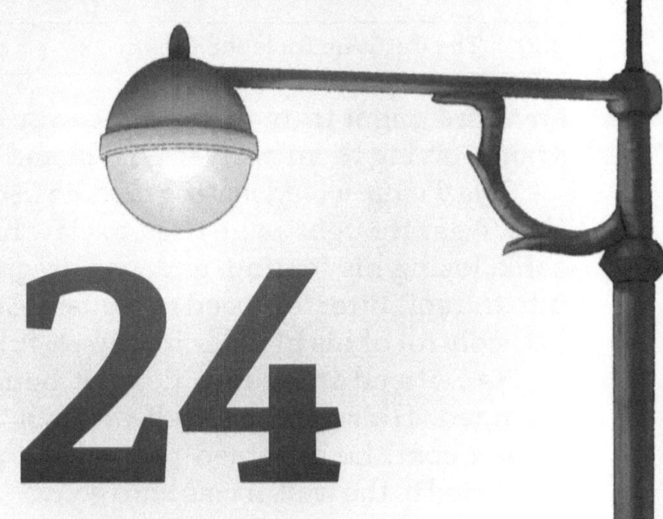

24

One Eye's laughter faded into the distance as Tiger was left to his fate. The detective gained purchase on a pipe that lined the wall and tried leaping for one of the vents, hoping to block it with his trench coat. Too high. He landed on the sand-strewn floor, grains jamming between his pads. He was already up to his knees in litter, and there was no way to climb back onto the ledge he'd dropped from.

Instinctively, he began to wash the back of his paw with his tongue. He swallowed more grit, his throat dust-dry, annoyed that he'd fallen into the trap so easily. Like a sticky old sucker.

The sand was up to his waist now, and he hacked and coughed to clear his throat. His eyes streamed, lids blinking to clear his sight. He'd learned nothing. One Eye hadn't stopped to gloat or reveal his plans; he'd vamoosed, left Tiger to die alone. The detective didn't want to go out that way—he wanted a fair death, a glorious one even, preferably with Jo weeping and eulogizing about how wonderful he was.

There was a roar in his ears, the sand rushing past him, stifling his breath. He couldn't see the vents anymore. Light from the entranceway danced on the grains, giving them a silver-gold luster.

Cole Tiddle would never get stuck in a situation like this, Tiger thought as he tried to claw his way out. He sank, losing his footing, and was dragged downward into the soft litter. He peed copiously. Even a hero can lose control of his bladder in a stressful situation.

He noticed the damp deposit beneath him had clumped. He raised himself an inch. Shucking his trench coat, he grappled toward the pipe that was bracketed to the wall. It was hard going—Julius couldn't see, and sediment slowed his movement. Reaching the pipe, he popped a claw and rammed it into the tubing. Water jetted from the puncture, soaking the sand around him. It toughened up and he clambered over the hard clumps, hopping onto the ledge.

No cat likes to take a shower. He had a score to settle with One Eye.

The kittens danced inside Jo's womb. At first, it had been a soft shoe shuffle, barely more than a flutter; now they'd discovered the stomp, the mash potato, and the black bottom. She felt focused, angry, tranquil, and listless by turns, as if each of her offspring had an effect on her, depending on the day of the week. Some were rowdier than others; she couldn't name them until she knew their sex, so she numbered them One to Four instead. One had the largest paws, Three the sharpest claws, Four was the docile one.

She developed a craving for marshmallows. As Tiger loved them anyway, he kept her well supplied.

Determined not to become a baby bore, she picked up no more than one related item per week. Nevertheless, she'd soon collected a pram, cots, sleep suits, diapers, and a papoose for Tiger to carry the infants.

She was fat as a barn and moody as a storm cloud. Her kittens wouldn't listen to her! She'd place her paws on her stomach, telling them to quiet down, yet they never responded. If this was what motherhood was like, she'd be visiting the orphanage.

Tiger had quite a story to tell when he got home. She didn't believe a word of it; she was used to toms telling tales. Film and theater types made a career of exaggerating their parts in life. So when her husband told her he'd faced death mere hours before in a giant kitty litter box, she told him that was nice; could he get her a saucer of milk before he went to bed?

As Tiger trudged upstairs to the bedroom, leaving a trail of sand behind him, she shifted her burgeoning belly across the sofa. It was a major effort to reach over and switch on the radio. She twiddled the knobs on the little red transistor until she found the only channel worth listening to. Her favorite show was about to come on. The show featured a good-natured mouse who was always getting into scrapes and a hobo cat who helped rescue him from his own folly. Every listener was aware that the cat was the real hero of the piece. However, the mouse would occasionally shine, performing kindly acts that improved public relations for mice in the real world. The show was called *Bless this Mouse.*

Tiger returned from the bedroom. He'd given himself a perfunctory bath and taken a fresh trench coat and hat from the wardrobe.

"Where you off to now, then?" she asked idly, listening to her favorite radio show.

"I'm going to see a dame."

"You can't," said Mrs. Straight.

Tiger's heart beat harder in his chest. He was about to find out who wore the pants in Jo's home. A chance to put his paw down.

"No can't about it, darling."

"You can't because you got a message. You've got to meet your assistant. She's got some info for you."

"Already?"

Jo hadn't been chastising her husband after all. Wasn't she the least bit jealous or curious? Didn't she care? "Outside the Beggar's Temple. Dawn. Sounds frightfully shady. You'll dig it."

"Thanks. I still have to meet this dame first. She's a real looker. I hope I can control myself."

No reaction.

"She might know something about the jackanapes who tried to kill me," Tiger went on. "Take it easy while I'm away."

"I intend to." Jo was missing her show. She was glad when her husband left the house. Peace at last.

Behind the Duncan Hotel stood a large yellow structure, triangular with a curved sidewall. Portals dotted around the building led in to a network of offices. The central conference suite formed the nerve center of CREAM.

The suite adjoined a smaller room, plush and skillfully decorated. Its color scheme consisted of relaxing browns and mustard, giving the office a rustic air.

Both rooms enjoyed the latest forms of entertainment—meowling pictures, long-playing records, and live broadcasts from Radio Kitty Music Hall. A partition could be removed to turn the two rooms into one. Behind a heavy black desk, surrounded by memos and calendars, perched on a swivel chair, was Musculus. He plotted and schemed for a living, and he was the best conspirator in the city.

Musculus wore a pinstripe suit with an austere silk tie. His round ears cast a heavy shadow against the wall behind him. His tiny eyes flitted about constantly, bloodshot with paranoia. Since he was colluding against others, they could be colluding against him. He controlled the city. He hadn't invaded the country, marched in with troops, or pulled off a political coup. He dominated Nub through the children, the media, and the products citizens consumed. He told them what to think and feel.

The takeover hadn't happened overnight. Musculus had spent years building theme parks, setting up clubs, and financing movies and radio shows. The people loved the movies—*The Aft Aglay Gang, Scratch 'n' Sniff, Inspector Repuss*. Ads for the shows, their memorabilia, associated merchandise, and fairground rides were everywhere.

Controlling the city wasn't enough. His domination had begun as a philanthropic venture; now he was bitter and vengeful. It was almost time for CREAM to rise up.

Wendy was always ready to receive visitors, even when they turned up in the middle of the night. She was a lonely cat with a dull life. The highlight of Wendy's day was a trip to her husband's diner; if customers were present, she'd nag him about the house chores he'd neglected or the promises he'd broken, just to shame him up in front of them. If the place was empty, she'd flex her claws and start a full-on argument. The Cheshire couple never bickered over anything consequential, and they'd never done time in prison for breaching the peace. They fought in private. They'd recently celebrated their silver wedding anniversary.

When Tiger visited Wendy, he found her too hospitable for comfort. She fussed around him as she entered her home and offered to rustle up some vole for him. The house was a two up, two down that smelled of rabbit droppings. It had been scrubbed so hard it sparkled. The living room was an obstacle course of furniture that was twenty years out of date. Tiger banged a shin on a glass coffee table, almost knocking the glass from its chrome housing. Wendy said nothing. She was far too magnanimous a host to scold him. Didn't hurt to give him a *do that again and you die* look, though.

Such a look was beloved by mothers throughout the city. Although Wendy had never had kittens—that would have required multiple trysts with her idiot husband—she was convinced that all males were little kittens on the inside, brash and mischievous. They needed guidance.

"Watcha lookin' for, Mr. Steak?"

"Straight. Tiger Straight. I'm a regular at your husband's diner, lent some money to a one-eyed cove. He's always there."

"Yup. Owns half the business. My husband reckons he's got the better half. Danny, his name is. Danny Faithful."

"So it is." Tiger tapped his head. "I've got a brain like a dog, sorry. Like I say, I lent him money. A lot. I need it back in a hurry. Thought you might know where he's at."

"I don't get around a heck of a lot." Wendy flapped her housecoat as a burp escaped from her ample mouth. "I don't know everyone's address."

"That's a shame. It would've been a big help if you could... if you'd known where Danny could be." Tiger left the living room, the cabbage smell lingering in his nostrils.

"I didn't say I don't know where he is," Wendy shouted after him. "Not sure about his address. I know where he hangs out."

"Yeah, the cafe. I already know that." Tiger didn't want to be rude. Neither did he want to waste any more time than he had to with his belching host.

"You must be good friends with him, to borrow him all that cash." Wendy stopped the detective in the hallway.

"He's good for it."

"He spent all his dough on the cafe. Buyin' his share. These days he hangs out with his old work buddies."

"Where did he used to work?"

The Cheshire cat belched again. "Apologies. Got a bad stomach. The neighbors call me Windy Wendy. That's why I spend a lotta my time indoors, with the windows open. I don't have to hang my washing in the backyard. Just open my cakehole, aim it at the laundry, and thar she blows."

"I wish I could remember where Danny worked," Tiger muttered, trying not to inhale. The Cheshire was crowding him now.

"The abattoir, Mr. Snake. That's where he'll be. Chewin' the fat at the slaughterhouse."

Night was almost over by the time Tiger had escaped the hugs and smells of Windy Wendy. The rain had stopped, rapidly replaced by a shower of sleet. He tugged his fedora down over his ears, suppressing a shiver. He needed a sunbath.

The rendezvous point was a narrow lane on the outskirts of the city, where only the rats and lowlifes bred. Tiger was on his guard as he approached. He knew not all the rats around here were little guys with twitchy noses and pink feet. Some of them were big cats willing to do anything for a fast buck, as long as it wasn't anything pleasant. Others bided their time, waiting for a sap to take a wrong turn and become easy pickings for moggy muggers.

A lantern died overhead, forcing him to move on to the next lamppost. He'd be a sitting target if anyone decided to take a potshot at him, but he didn't want to miss Bug. She'd promised information, and Bug was a lady who always delivered. While he waited, Tiger unbuttoned his coat and blew a few baleful notes from his tarnished sax, the sounds rising into the starless sky like angels looking for their boss.

"You were right," said Bug, still shrouded in darkness.

"Ain't I always?" The detective tucked the sax back under his coat.

"How's married life cheating you?" Bug showed herself. She looked attractive in a business suit, her tail wrapped over her left forepaw. She had a name badge tagged to her lapel. "That wasn't so bad."

"My playing?" Tiger asked hopefully.

"Getting here. Nobody saw me. Everything's cool at the bank."

"There's no chance you'll blow your cover," Tiger assured her. "Not if you're careful."

"Ain't I always?" Bug slicked up to her partner, rubbing her forehead against the brim of his hat. "Got some interesting folk connected with CREAM."

"That's not being careful. I told you—no snooping until you're settled into the job."

"I don't want to be settled into the job! They trust me. They're all pussycats, especially my boss, Miss Angold. She's getting so blind, she can hardly see the files. She wouldn't be able to tell if I took 'em all."

"You didn't!" Tiger gasped.

"No. I accessed the relevant databases and memorized some names. That's all. Check these out: Doctor Mopp. Hant Bros. Cole Tiddle."

"They all got money coming out of their accounts?"

"Going straight to CREAM," Bug nodded.

Tiger's whiskered quivered at the audacity of the scam. "CREAM is siphoning large sums from a lot of dead cats."

"Cole isn't dead," Bug reminded him. "It says so in the papers."

"No surprise to me," said Tiger. "He's been leaving his trail all over town. He's so wealthy, he probably hasn't noticed the drained funds."

"Like I said, these sums are big. Big enough for the fattest cat to notice ... and for us to trace."

"You know where it's going?" Tiger wanted to hug his assistant.

"I will," she said. "When I get the chance to get sneaky again. Won't be long. I refuse to spend a month in that creepy place."

"No one ever said anything about a month." Tiger gave Bug a winning smile, and it did its trick.

"Aw, don't go soft on me, Boss. I'll stay as long as it takes."

"If you get made…"

"I won't. If I don't pinch nothing, I'll be fine."

Tiger rubbed his cheek against Bug's. "Don't pinch anything."

"You worry too much." Bug giggled, tickled by Tiger's whiskers.

"I worry just enough. Get home and stay safe, y'hear?"

"Safe as birds in the bank," Bug replied dryly, watching Tiger slink into the distance.

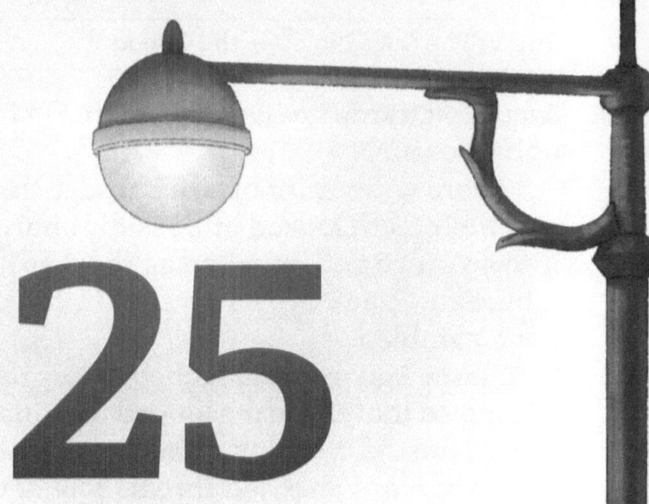

25

The Chop Chop Abattoir was deadly quiet when Tiger found it. The large rectangular building was solid concrete, with a wide opening on the side locked up with vertical and horizontal bars. Inside, there were signs of recent occupation: carcasses swinging gently from side to side, box lunches open with their contents still fresh. He couldn't understand how anyone could eat with raw flesh rotting beside them. He licked his nose, something he always did when he was close to iffy food.

Red lights helped add to the building's macabre character. Tiger tried a couple of rooms, finding nothing to guide him in the dark empty chambers. He reached a corridor, also drenched in scarlet light. He stopped suddenly, his back arched. The hairs on his back stood up like cornstalks.

Half a dozen cats led by a tall, silent wraith of a tom, waited at the end of the corridor. They wore red robes with hems that brushed the floor, long sleeves that covered their paws, and hoods that shielded their faces. They looked like demons, spike-topped goblins, circling him. They were the most forbidding security guards he had ever seen. He felt cold in their ugly presence.

There was a glint of white under their long sleeves, and their teeth looked impossibly sharp. Tiger ducked into an office and hunched as short as he could behind a bureau. Black eyes swiveled in his direction. He'd been rumbled.

The tall guard approached, paws together, sleeves joining so that the arms looked like one flowing silken tube. He said nothing. The silence shook Tiger far more than any mewled threat. The detective stepped into the open, chin up, defiant.

"You can't kill me," he said. "I'm cute."

The guard did not reply. Slowly, he opened his arms, and the sleeves fell open, revealing a set of glistening claws as long as bread knives. Ten daggers clattered together as the guard opened and closed his paws in a languorous stretching motion.

Tiger backed away. The other guards shucked their robes, displaying their own cruel talons. They moved in and out of vision like dancing tongues of bright red flame and extended their arms to block Tiger's exit. There was only one way out and he didn't want to end up on those claws, which were long enough to skewer a mule.

"He's right." The guards turned in unison to find Bug dressed in an orange trouser suit, a cheeky grin on her face. "He's cute as a button and twice as dangerous."

Tiger piled past the guards, scattering them like fleas off a dead dog's back. He raced for the exit, dragging Bug with him. In the old days, he would have stopped and fought the guards alongside his partner. Now he was struggling simply to survive.

The swish of their robes on the well-waxed floor was close behind. One of the goblins sank glass-sharp teeth into his shoulder, knocking him to the floor. Tiger and Bug were surrounded, the exit blocked.

"Excuse me!" Bug hollered, struggling to avoid their stiletto claws. "Lady in need of assistance over here!" Tiger hauled himself free of his attacker, who'd lost a tooth in the private eye's shoulder. Tiger drove him away with a vicious backswing, ripping open the cat's throat.

The detective maintained his claws for such an emergency. He would file them carefully, each claw serving a different purpose. He used a snub-nosed claw to attract the lead cat's attention, drawing him away from Bug. The other two felines lined up behind their vanguard.

"I ain't so cuddly when you get to know me." Tiger grinned, swiping at the cat. He put all his body strength into the blow, which knocked the attackers off balance. Before they could right themselves, the two investigators raced out of the abattoir, along the derelict streets, pelting away from the upriver slum, back to Connie's apartment.

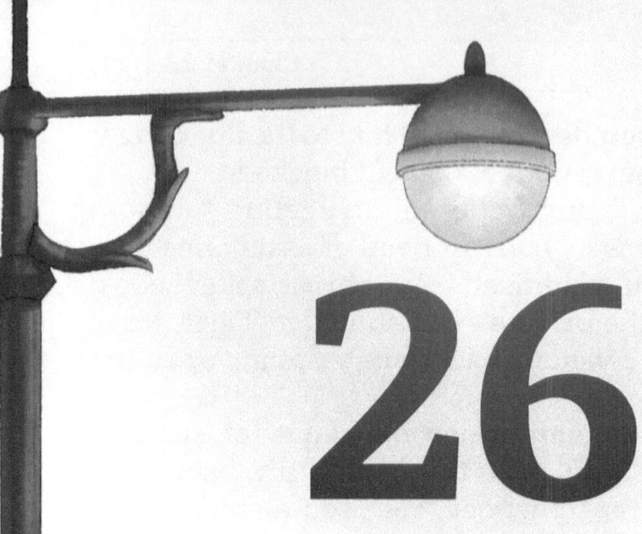

26

Tiger Straight slumped at the dining table, too exhausted to shovel food into his mouth. Straight's faithful companion, Bug, nudged a bowl of meat nearer to him. Tiger arched back in his seat; the smell of the food seemed to offend him.

"Lost your appetite, Tiger?" asked Bug, mussed fur shrouding her rounded face. "Nice of Connie to put me up, isn't it?"

They sat in Connie's apartment, framed pictures of Beast, Cammy, Grass, and Skead on a *memento mori* sideboard.

"Where is she?" Tiger mumbled.

"Out looking for work. She's had more interviews than you've had hot kippers. Heroes have got to eat too, you know."

"I'm no hero."

"Oh yeah, sure. Like all felines spend their mornings rescuing a maiden in distress from six crazies."

"More like you rescued me." Tiger sighed. "I don't wanna talk about it."

"You got three of 'em with one punch! It was incredible... darnedest thing I ever saw."

"Enough!" Tiger slammed the food across the table, bolting from his chair. A tear dribbled down his left cheek. "I didn't mean to hurt them."

"But they deserved it!" Bug insisted.

"Did they?" Her partner was already heading for the study. "I don't want to be disturbed."

Speechless, Bug watched as Tiger made his dramatic exit. She shook her head; maybe he was getting too old for the crime-fighting business. He certainly needed to brush up on his social skills. She was clearing up the spilled food when the phone rang.

"Yes, he is," Bug told the caller, then dropped the receiver. It swayed from side to side on its cord, daring Bug to swat it.

"Tiger!"

"What is it?" the PI snapped.

"The hospital. You've got to get the hospital, now."

Back in the dawn of medical history, the feline authorities had realized that if they put sick people in a building, they'd only infect each other. The Nub City Infirmary had been split up into a number of skinny edifices dotted around the center. One of these was devoted to newborn kittens and expectant mothers.

There were signs for the hospital everywhere, all pointing in different directions. Fine if you had a septic dewclaw or a flea problem but this was an emergency. Tiger and Jo finally reached a building flanked by pacing tomcats, puffing nervously on Gauloises. Tiger squeezed his wife inside, scratching at the reception desk until someone appeared.

"Take these," said the receptionist.

"What are they?" Tiger grabbed a sheaf of blue papers.

"Mrs. Straight's medical notes. Hang onto them." A chubby nurse helped Jo along a narrow corridor and puffed up a steep flight of stairs. The father-to-be brought up the rear, helpless. He tried to retain a dominant air. Impossible—he reached for Jo's paw to remind her he was there. Before they could connect, she was hustled into a cubicle with a gurney and a small cupboard. Tiger placed his wife's belongings in the cupboard and curled up beside her, scanning a breastfeeding poster on the wall.

A pair of porters lifted Jo onto the gurney and wheeled her into a lift. Tiger followed, making small talk with the midwife as they were shown the delivery room on the floor below.

"How long until they arrive?" Tiger wondered.

"When they're ready," the midwife explained. As if on cue, a series of contractions wracked the pregnant cat. "Your wife's insisted on a natural birth. We can't induce—" The midwife turned to one of the porters. "Where are Mrs. Straight's notes? They should be right here."

"Must still be in her room," said Tiger. He raced up the stairs, not daring to wait for the lift. In the maternity ward, he was accosted by the corpulent nurse.

"A little early, aren't you?" she snooted, pointing at the visiting times.

"Need notes," he wheezed, trying to get by. "Cat in theater needs medical notes. Now." The nurse gave a *humph* until the anxious cat popped his claws. She let him pass.

In Jo's cubicle, Tiger piled through the clothes and scrunched linen to find the blue forms. Holding them tight to his chest, he transported them back down-stairs to the—

Where was the theater? All the corridors looked alike. This place was alien to him and the disinfected smells confused him. This was a nightmare! He'd chased and scrapped with feral cats, saved the lives of strangers, but he couldn't help the cat he loved.

Tiger took a gamble, eenie-meenie-minie-moed his way down an eastward passage, hunting for a helpful sign. He recognized a gray room and saw a familiar pair of hind paws drooping off a gurney—Jo!

"Got... got notes," he panted. The midwife grinned as a high-pitched squeal assailed Tiger's ears.

"You have a son, Mr. Straight. He's perfect, got all his bits." The midwife took the sheets from him.

"Already?" he asked.

"Yes. Next one's due in about thirty minutes." She made the births sound like a tram timetable. He didn't mind; he was engrossed in his bawling child. Its large forehead was creased into a frown, its mouth pouting, paws curling and uncurling. The midwife helped Jo wash the newborn, warming and cleaning it, giving its circulation a boost.

The vet sterilized his claws, sharp enough to make a caesarean incision, dainty enough to deliver a kitten. Jo made a meal of the firstborn's placenta, building her strength for the coming ordeal.

Tiger put a paw on Jo's back, clenching and unclenching to soothe her. He watched as the second kitten appeared, squealing red, white, and blue murder. Jo washed its nose and mouth, ensuring that it could breathe properly. She gnawed through its umbilical cord and ate that as well. One male, one female. What sex would the next one be?

Half an hour later, the third newborn appeared, another male. His mother broke away the amniotic sac, and the tiny creature entered the world. He mewed softly, stirring Tiger's stoic heart.

The final birth was more difficult—a breach. Staying calm to soothe his wife, Tiger purred slowly. The sound relaxed Jo enough for the vet to perform a cesarean, bringing a second female into the world.

"They all okay?" asked Jo, feeling weary. She'd been in delivery for two hours.

"No. No, lover. The last one didn't make it."

For a moment, Tiger and Jo shared a common pang. Then the mother was wheeled away with her three surviving kittens, leaving her husband with the stillborn cub.

Bug knew where the regular debits were headed. She'd worked out the bank's code for particular accounts and traced the secret party that was benefiting from the arrangement. There were no lights on in the records room; she didn't dare announce her presence. Bug used her eyes to pierce the gloom, checking that her calculations were correct, removing a file from a dusty filing cabinet. Enough proof to expose CREAM.

Bug wore a mask that obscured the top half of her head. She figured that any security camera would show a disguised figure lurking round the bank, rather than an itinerant clerk. It was dark blue with antennae on top. She'd made it herself.

Neither the mask nor the darkness could prevent Bug's boss from finding her. "What do you think you're doing there?"

"Doing, Miss Angold?" Bug replied with a start. "I'm not doing anything. Lazy, that's me. Please don't take umbrage with that. Whatever umbrage is. Do you know? What an umbrage is? I don't think I've got one, whatever it might be..."

"Stop your gibbering, lassie. I know full well what you're up to. You want my job, don't you?" Miss Angold snatched the file from Bug's hot paws. "I think we're going to have to take you to see the manager."

"What's this 'we' business? You ain't royalty. Let me go." Angold had her in a taut grip, a claw poking into the small of her back. She nudged Bug toward the vault, ignoring the snooper's protestations.

At the vault, Angold dialed a combination, and the massive hatch swung open. Bug expected to be shoved into the vault; instead, her boss operated a small lever jutting from the wall. A panel in the hatch frame slid upward, leading to a narrow corridor. Urged into the passageway, Bug had to walk on the tips of her pads to squeeze through. There was no way to turn back if she'd wanted to; she was more interested in finding out where the corridor led and confronting the manager. Angold was close behind, nudging her bifocals up her nose. The panel and hatch closed behind them. "I've had a hard day," Bug whined. "I'm ready for bed. This ain't gonna take too long, is it?"

Angold silenced her with a nip on the tail. The skinny corridor wound left and right for half a mile, leading to an archway so small that the two cats had to squeeze through on their bellies. The other side was a different matter, however—an opulent, wide-open dining room lit with a chandelier.

"Thought you'd never get here," said its owner, offering Bug a seat. "Had a good day's snoop?"

"I don't get it," Bug stuttered.

"What's there to get?" The host took a seat beside her, taking care to remain out of her reach. "Your credentials were a little too impeccable, my dear. We didn't know what you were after, though."

"Give a mouse enough cheese and it'll trap itself," offered Angold. The host glowered at her.

"What are you going to do with me?"

"Same thing we did to Lona Dash. The Hant Brothers. There's no way to break it to you softly, my dear—you're nobbled. I would kill you myself, but someone else has requested the pleasure." Clearing his throat, the host announced the killer's presence. Appearing from the next room was the last face Bug expected to see.

27

Offspring are a mystery, a misery, and a miracle. They bring fulfillment and tragedy. They age you and rejuvenate you all at once.

Tiger had never sought fatherhood; it had found him. In his crime-fighting days, he would act as an idol for cats everywhere, a good (if violent) example to them. When they saw him hogging headlines or accepting awards, they knew what a good guy was. The closest Straight had got to cubs was a school talk or a treetop rescue. Now he was more likely to be found changing a diaper than making the world a better place.

He'd been amazed when his wife had given birth. It had been the most otherworldly, disgusting sight of his life. She'd asked for some privacy, but Tiger had stuck with her 'til the last cub had emerged. He hated to see his wife go through such discomfort, with a half-hour's wait between each birth.

The female kitten was named Fliss. White with a gray tail, she mewed constantly and let nothing get between her and her regular feed. Bello was also assertive, pushing past his brother to get to his favorite nipple. The last surviving member of the litter, Martin, was quiet and sleepy. He required the most attention, and Jo spent a lot of time nurturing him. The birth had changed her; there was a sadness in her heart as she mourned the lost kitten. She would never be close to her husband again.

Danny Faithful needed a cup of milk. He was thirsty and only a swallow of that white dairy nectar could quench his need. He tried to press a button on the drinks machine, missed. His depth of vision had been sadly lacking since he'd lost his eye.

Before the accident he'd been another furface in the crowd, Mr. Invisible, getting away with all sorts of cheap pranks. He'd stolen tinned food from the supermarket, chased protected bird species, eaten in restaurants and fled without paying the bill. He'd bullied prowler officers and kidnapped kittens. He'd never been selected during an identity parade; his mugshot had not graced the Sunday papers.

His last job as a professional criminal had been a doozy. Hang around a casino, wait until some big winner came out, swat him on the head and bail. The lucky guy would be drunk on his success. The job would be hassle-free, and his plan was simple enough to be foolproof.

Danny had wandered round the establishment for a time, played a couple of low-stakes games. Bash the Rat, Tails It Is, Rodent Roulette. Kept his eyes (*his eyes!*) on a gambler who lost a lot and won even more. Some doll was limpeted to him, fawning like a trouper. That wouldn't stop Danny. She'd run screaming as soon as he pounced.

The night had grown old, and Danny kept yawning. The casino overfed its patrons with kippers to keep them content. Following the gambler out of the building—Danny had always been a sneaky stalker—he had clocked his quarry with a hefty wallop. Instead of running for help, the limpet had turned feral. Before Danny had a chance to think, she'd knocked him flat on his back and bitten a chunk from his face. When the prowlers came looking for him, he was easy to find. He was the cat with only one eye. Now everyone looked at him: passersby, victims, and villains.

He'd done six months in the jug for his attempted robbery—the lady who'd attacked him had received a pat on the back. *Damn, I would never pass unnoticed again.* He'd become a victim, and it wasn't an easy feeling.

In prison, he'd learned to appreciate the sanctity of all living things. He'd been drafted into a cult dedicated to the preservation of that sanctity thanks to Callum, a sand-colored caracal doing time for breach of the peace.

Caracals were larger and stronger than average, with long ears that tufted at the tip. They made excellent predators and a sojourn in jail was especially frustrating for them. Callum could leap higher, faster than his fellow inmates. He took digitalis to strengthen his heart, giving him great stamina when necessary. He never tried to escape, patiently waiting out his sentence. Nobody ever wrote to him or came to visit him, and he wouldn't have had time to spare with them if they had. He was busy spreading the word amongst the prisoners. A lot of them preferred to see sense rather than offend the big cat.

Callum hadn't been incarcerated because of his breed or his color. White, blue, ginger, and tortoiseshell cats shared a cell with him. He was there because he'd dared to suggest that eating other intelligent animals was barbaric, that it bordered on cannibalism. He dared to say it out loud, on street corners and in city hall. The Governing Council of Cats had decided to let him stew for a while, hoping that a harsh sentence would cool his fervor. It hadn't.

"Life is sacred, my one-eyed friend," Callum would say. *"Nature forms subtle chains, a pattern for all creatures to follow. A mouse dies when nature intends it to die, when it's exhausted its usefulness in the world. Not when we get hungry for a snashter."* The black cat was quite happy to kill in order to protect himself or preserve his own life. Some of the toughest crims on the cellblock took a crack at him, aiming to prove their mettle against a caracal. They failed; Callum told Danny that Mother Nature had a higher purpose all ready for him. The black cat was indomitable.

Completing his sentence, Danny had gone to an address given to him by his guru. There, a group of cultists had given him succor. Today he was a fully-fledged member of CREAM, and the boss wanted to see him.

Danny was full of beans when he visited the West End mansion. The manner in which he'd bumped off the trench-coated detective still made him giggle. A fittingly gritty demise for the hard-boiled snoop. Callum greeted him as he entered the mansion, pointing him toward a study full of vegetarian cookery books.

The boss greeted him, and he hastened to make his report. "Tiger Straight's finished, sir. He don't tick no more. He's one dead dick."

"Funny." The boss wasn't laughing. He wasn't doing much of anything, sitting in an armchair with his legs crossed.

"How so, sir?"

"I have it on extremely good authority that Mr. Straight still lives. Callum?"

The caracal appeared behind Danny. "We've drained the sandpit," the black cat boomed. "No sign of a corpse. He got out."

"I can tell you're disappointed, boss," Danny whined. "This guy can't do any damage. He don't know anything. He's asking questions, but he ain't getting many answers. I'll knock him off if you gimme another chance."

The boss said nothing, shaking his head slowly.

"Before you give this job to someone else... let me try. I'm not going to fail you twice, am I?"

The boss smiled. Danny stared warily at his gnarled teeth. "Time to go, pal." Callum wrapped a forelimb round Danny's neck. "You've taken up enough of the boss's life."

"I don't have to put up with this from someone like you!" Danny shouted at his leader. He was scared now. With his paw locked around Danny's neck, Callum led him out of the study and into an unlit hallway. He continued to apply pressure on the smaller cat's windpipe.

"I thought you believed in the sanctity of life?" Danny gasped.

"Scum don't count." Callum squeezed the life from his friend and returned to the study.

Hairy Bancroft's career wasn't going to plan. Despite his assumed rule of the airwaves, the death of Joel Venet had cast a dark pall over his TV show. If Hairy had been in charge, he would have replaced the producer and continued making episodes without a hiatus. Those programs would, of course, be perfectly crafted as a tribute to the murdered cat. Viewers would understand; they'd realize how upset Joel's colleagues were about the death. They'd enjoy the stories and mourn Joel's passing. They'd also understand that the TV channel had to make money, and episodes of *Wonder Cat* always did that.

Instead, the lily-spleened executives had decided that there would be a respite. An indefinite one. They'd axed the program, believing that audiences would see further production as a callous moneymaking venture. Besides, it was time for fresh product; *Wonder Cat* had been running for long enough. It was getting tired and self-referential. Whoever had killed Joel had also killed the series, and Hairy's livelihood along with it.

There's a fine line between reality and TV fantasy. People in the streets had often mistaken Hairy for the crime-busting hero; offered him a friendly sniff as they passed by, gave him money. He'd been gratified by the attention, enjoyed being a hero instead of a poor actor. The children were especially ready to suspend their disbelief, giving him their pocket money (which he spent on drinks for himself at the local bar), and asking for his autograph. One flick of an executive switch had stopped all that.

When all had seemed lost, his agent had called with a job opportunity. It wasn't a prime-time series or a part in the Totterdown Pavilion's new production, *Bricklayer's Story.* Nevertheless, he took the regular work hungrily, afraid that he'd been out of the limelight for too long.

Now his face was everywhere, on billboards, in magazines, on the sides of trams, all marked with his personal scent. He was the figurehead for the largest advertising campaign the city had ever seen. His likeness was used to sell something that every citizen craved—it wasn't a useless gadget they didn't require or a pecuniary policy with no dividend. Every cat needed it and ate it almost every day. All Hairy had to do was pose for a few photos, stand in front of a video camera for a day, and spray his scent on a lot of posters. The messages were all along similar lines:

FISH! BUY FISH! EAT OUR FISH! OUR FISH IS BEST! IT'S BETTER THAN THE SCABBY FISH YOU USUALLY BUY! ALL DEBONED WITH ALL THE TASTE! FROM THE CLEAN GREEN WATERS OF DUNBAR BAY! PROTEIN! HAIRY EATS IT ALL THE TIME, HE CAN'T GET ENOUGH OF IT! FISH! FISH! FISH!

There was a subliminal theme in the ads if you read between the lines. It would seep into a consumer's subconscious with the subtlety of a late-night dream. For no obvious reason, the consumers would find themselves eating a lot, and when they ate, they were tucking into fish.

Hairy didn't really eat that particular brand every day. He had eaten it once in front of the cameras, an ad that would be broadcast citywide. It had tasted okay, nothing to get hyperbolic about. He enjoyed his recharged bout of fame, but his ego had landed. Success was no longer a given; he would have to plan for future slumps, look to his physical and spiritual health in order to survive.

Fortunately, his current employers had covered the spiritual aspect. They'd invited him to join a cult that worshiped at the Beggar's Temple. Hairy had always been suspicious of religious organizations, so he'd asked a detective to accompany him. He wanted nothing to do with the prowlers after his interrogation at the factory; he called Tiger Straight instead.

28

Tiger jumped at the chance to watch Hairy's back, sure that the cult had abducted Bug. She hadn't been in touch since he'd spurned her cooking, and he didn't consider her the sulking type. He agreed to trail the actor at a discreet distance, following him into the Beggar's Temple.

Hairy gave the temple guard two voles, an offering to the spirits of long-gone beggars. The guard asked the same of Tiger, who produced a juicy hare. It had been a wedding gift, but the guard insisted on taking it. Hairy had already flounced up a flight of stone steps. The guard put the hare in his mouth, clamped down his molars, and smiled.

Hairy had vanished by the time Tiger got inside. A tall cat stooped under the canted ceiling. He showed Tiger a veiled entranceway. The detective doubled up to descend into a tunnel; it was poorly lit. Ancient tools and weapons shone above his head. They had been bronzed onto the tunnel roof.

He reached an antechamber, tiled brown. On the tiles were obscure scent-messages and hieroglyphs.

He looked at the symbols and attempted to translate them. For the first time—

He understood.

He hadn't rumbled a Cadre of Ravenous, Evil Attacking Mammals or a Cult of Resentful Enraged Advocated Mousers. CREAM had a more sinister agenda, and he was in their domain.

Tiger passed through a rounded entranceway and found a second tunnel that had been carved into the rock. A slab ground into place behind him, sealing him in. The tunnel descended at a steep gradient, Tiger using his whiskers to find his way in the unlit passage. The smell from the charnel house above began to fade. The hairs on the back of his neck went cornstalk-erect.

He needed to pee.

His legs had grown tired by the time he heard chanting. He was unable to make out the words. A flicker of torchlight led him out of the tunnel into a vast crypt, cobwebbed with archways and helical supports. A group of cloaked cats formed a circle around a mandala, chanting and raising their forepaws in zeal. On the mandala stood Hairy, entranced.

Tiger kept in the shadows near the tunnel's mouth. On the opposite side of the crypt was a spiral staircase that wound upward, out of danger. The cats stood between him and freedom.

He recognized one of them. The big guy, he'd seen him at the cop shop. The chief of the prowlers, big, bold, and heading for his nook.

"I smell a cat." The chief blinked, his emerald eyes penetrating the gloom. "A snooper. A nosy parker. A fly off the wall. An inter—" reaching a giant paw into the alcove, he scooped Tiger out, "—loper." The desperate detective began to struggle. One of the brethren snuck behind him, grabbing the scruff of his neck between jagged teeth. Tiger was immobilized.

"I know you."

His belly was exposed and vulnerable. He tried to shake his head, couldn't. He managed to mutter, "I don't think so."

"The gumshoe. Mortis wanted you locked up. You wanted to eat him." The chief chuckled, then punched Tiger in the stomach. "How did you get in here?"

"I'm looking for my friend. Maybe she wanted to join your group."

"We select our members. This isn't a health club."

"Shame. I could do with losing a few pounds. What is it then?" Tiger winced as the teeth in the back of his neck sank deeper.

"Get rid of him. And his friend."

"Hairy! Help me!"

The actor was lying down now, breathing heavily. He'd been drugged. As Tiger moved to see if he was alright, the pain in his neck grew, and he joined Hairy in the realm of unconsciousness.

29

iger was a lone hunter, a primitive seeking prey. Trees stretched into clouds draped with swaying vines. Drops of rain dribbled down the bark, glistening occasionally as light fought through the forest roof. He saw a figure dart behind a tree—a small blur, enough to send him in pursuit.

He padded carefully through sparse undergrowth, noiseless. The hunted animal was not aware of his presence or had discounted him as a harmless neighbor. Tiger was hungry; he needed to retrieve supper for his family. He sniffed at the air, making his stealthy way toward the animal, closing the gap using scent and sound. It wouldn't suspect a threat until it met its fate.

The blur stopped at a concave rock, stooped over and defenseless. The raindrops had collected in a hollow; Tiger's prey was thirsty. The hunter tensed, his ears tilted, ready to warn of potential interruption. His whiskers twitched. His back end swayed from side to side, his tail a charmed snake dancing a slow waltz. He could taste his last meal bloody on his lips, hear the hunted's heartbeat quick and strong. The creature was still in shadow, but he felt like he knew every inch of its furry *little form. Tiger leaped forward, pincering his forepaws around his supper.*

It dragged itself clear of the razor-sharp claws, fleeing for cover. Recovering from his momentary surprise, Tiger gave chase, weaving past trees and thorn bushes, every step bringing him closer to the terrified animal. He reached out a paw, took a swipe. The flora took on strange shapes, characters of their own; faces laughed at the hunter, legs tried to trip him. Running out of breath, he had time for one more attack. This time he brought all four paws to bear, wrapping his limbs round the catch, digging his teeth into its skull. The animal collapsed under his weight.

The game was over. Craning his head forward, Tiger snapped the animal's neck with a savage bite. The little heart stopped beating, and the hunter stood clear, allowing his catch to flop onto its back.

It was Martin. Tiger had murdered his favorite son.

Whatever sunshine had penetrated the rainforest gave up; he was left in darkness. The dead body disappeared and the plants around him oozed together. Sick colors left the leaves and creepers, entering his head through his nose and ears. He tried to cry, couldn't. Let out a slow mewl. Woke up.

Tiger lay flat on his stomach, face pressed against black marble, legs akimbo. He blinked twice, shaking the ugly dream from his head. Checking himself over, he didn't seem too badly damaged. The back of his neck was gory where a pair of jaws had been.

He'd been dumped in the open air, a quiet lane that wasn't all that far from Jo's house. Trees arched over the lane, blocking any light from the moon. A row of lanterns hung from branches at long intervals, casting pools of scarlet onto the ground.

Following the lane, Tiger saw something lying not far ahead. At first, it looked like a sack or black bin liner. The artificial light made it difficult for him to tell. He closed in on the drab object.

A small, crumpled body lay in the last pool of light. Its limbs were outstretched like a bather doing the backstroke. Tiger kneeled down beside the stiff, his brow furrowed, his mind puzzled. Who would want to kill Bug? Knock her down, razor her throat, rip off her orange-red mask? It had been tossed aside, screwed up, its two antennae limp and ragged. That didn't seem right.

Tiger looked at the dead eyes of Natasha, the secretary with the pretensions of being a heroine. He'd been too blind to see it, to protect her before she got herself killed. Some detective.

Her tiny paw gripped a piece of cloth, green-checked and grubby. He picked it up, recognizing it immediately.

"Bless you, Bug." An invaluable asset right up to the end. With the help of her pathetic scrap of evidence, he'd be able to catch a killer. It would be the most difficult bust he'd ever make.

Tiger's wife was waiting for him when he got home. She was wearing a green checked dress, slightly torn at the hem.

"I wondered how long it would take you," she said as he unsheathed his claws.

"You made me so happy."

"I don't want to stop. Think about tomorrow, Tiger. Can you live without me to wash and cook and clean for you? Keep the kittens happy? Care for you all when someone falls ill? Do you love me?"

"Yes. Doesn't mean I'm not going to kill you."

"She deserved to die. She wanted you too much, and you didn't ever realize it. She was never going to be happy."

"Why did you take off her mask?"

"I did it before she died. I wasn't there to kill Bug. I'm not one of those damned arch villains you're always chasing. I wanted to kill Natasha. She was the one who deserved it. Your mud-slinging love slut, not your crime-fighting companion."

"That attempt on your life...?"

"There was no gas. I made a groove in the carpet with my paws. Fooled you, Mr. Great Detective." She unbuttoned her blouse, exposing her soft-furred throat. Tiger raised a deadly claw, and he touched the point against her fur. The slightest jab and justice would be done. She didn't dare swallow, ready for him. She stared into his eyes, silently imploring. She wanted him to get it over with.

Life would not be over for her for another decade, which she spent in a municipal jail after being frog-marched to the local cops by her husband. Bix was there, cow in tow.

"Case closed." Tiger sighed. "She's the killer."

"The lads at Headquarters have a sweepstake," said Bix with a wry grimace. "Betting on how long it would take me to solve the murders. Guess nobody won."

"Yeah." Tiger watched as Jo was led down to the holding cells.

"I didn't really want to eat you, you know." He stooped down to whisper to the mouse. "I have a lot of respect for authority. I always knew cops couldn't read or write. I'll help you with your report. He gave Bix a wink. His evidence put Jo in the slammer for good.

Despite the strict penal system, she made the best of her last years. Studied, wove sweetgrass baskets, and sang in the choir. She didn't talk much. She lived in the past, imagining she was still tucked up warm with her family. She seemed almost oblivious to her incarceration but did as she was told and served her sentence. By the time she was due for parole, she fell ill. Passed away in her sleep.

Tiger still mourns.

30

Little Tim lived off his savings. He'd be alright, he convinced himself; he'd brought home so many rats and treats and trinkets that his neighbors would remember and help him in a pinch while he looked for another job.

They didn't remember. Or if they did, there was no acknowledgment of his offerings. There were no words at all from the neighbors, except when he crossed their path and they made the effort to say, "Get out of my way."

This is what pushed Lona away, he thought. *Cold, inconsiderate treatment. This is what led to her death.*

Hunger and paranoia became his bedfellows. His neighbors were ignoring him because he'd quit CREAM. He'd lost his job for the same reason. After all, Anatolios was a prime mover in the organization. Tim was a pariah, and he'd caused his own downfall. He would move to another city, start a second life. But how would he fund a drastic move like that during the Depression?

A rap on his trailer hull reminded him of Lona. He rushed out to see which of his neighbors had broken down and was ready to help him and give him some company.

It wasn't a neighbor at all.

It was Lieutenant Butterscotch, Nub City's finest, serving and protecting with tooth and claw against suspected murderers like Little Tim.

"You've got the wrong cat," Tim told Bix, who was giving the chonker his best interrogative stare.

"Don't lick your lips at me, sonny," said Bix.

"I wasn't! I mean, I didn't." Tim felt lost and insecure. Was this another example of those Machiavellian cats in red robes conspiring against him?

The neighbors had watched in silence as the prowlers led Tim away. The bullies and old cats had scrubbed themselves as if washing away the stench of his memory. He wanted to go back, though. He wanted to go home.

"Where were you on the night of November 12th?"

"At home, watching a squirrel out the window."

"You have a good memory for a cat."

Great. Just Tim's luck to get grilled by a prejudiced mouse.

"Can anyone corroborate your whereabouts?" Bix asked.

These were big words, but Tim wasn't going to admit that to Bix. He creased his brow and took his best shot at the answer.

"Dunno."

Bix scribbled in his notepad. "It took us a while to track you down. Almost as if you were hiding."

"I'm living my best life," Tim joked.

Bix didn't laugh. "We found paw prints, Mr. Tierney. Unusual ones, on more than one crime scene."

"I was a garbage cat." Tim shrugged. "My job took me all over the city."

"And to the harbor."

"No," Tim protested. "I don't like water." He stood up. "But thanks anyway. I like a bit of company."

"Sit down," Bix squeaked. He slapped four photographs on the desk. "You know these cats."

"That one looks familiar." Tim poked a paw at an 8x10 of Selwyn Mopp.

"When did you last see him?"

"Two months ago, on the telly."

Bix slammed a minuscule fist on the desk, barely making a sound. "We know Lona Dash was your neighbor." A picture of Lona was set on the desk beside the others. "Don't play with me."

I don't play with food, Tim thought, but kept his mouth shut.

"What about the stash of cream we found in your trailer, eh? Must have been hard, buying that with no wages."

"I didn't buy it..."

"Aha!"

"I mean, I don't know anything about no cream."

Bix squeaked with excitement. "You're going to the chair, Mr. Tierney."

"Oh good," said Tim with an exasperating lack of scorn. "This stool is so uncomfortable."

"I mean the electric chair, for murder."

"I'm not trying to be rude, but you've totally got the wrong cat."

"Oh, yes?" Bix held up a paw print. "The evidence shows otherwise." It was a paw with an extra digit. The cat who had left the mark was a polydactyl.

As always, Bix had caught his cat.

With the case wrapped up, Bix took Nut back to her farm. A new cat named Chips had taken over from Scrumpy, equally gruff and indifferent. However, he knew his stuff about herbicides, silage, hydroponics, and low crop yields.

As Nut returned to her old stall, she felt sad. She missed the naked city, the bustling prowler station, and her reluctant counterpart. The barn was so quiet, so lifeless. Not for long.

Bix bade his farewells to Nut and passed the time of day with two cats dressed in blood-red robes. *He's forgotten about me already,* the cow sniffled. Her ears perked up as the robed pair snatched the mouse and shoved him in a sack.

"Oi! That's my partner you've got there!" Nut yelled. The other cows ignored her, used to her nonsense. Before Nut could free herself from her stall, the kidnappers were gone.

The kittens continued to explore and develop. Fliss was a bitch, a prima donna in full soap opera mode. She walked with shoulder pads foremost, dominating the other kittens in the neighborhood. Martin was cool, laid back, a drooper, draping himself over things. Bello, the larger of the two males, led his siblings on expeditions around the block, scent-marking their territory.

Tiger didn't like to leave them alone for too long. He always recalled the first time they'd been allowed in the back garden; it had been a disaster. He'd been checking through the account details that Bug had brought him. He still didn't know why the cultists had let him go, left him to suffer. There were disparities in the accounts that he couldn't explain. He was loath to close the case for good. He'd heard a yell from out back, excited mews, then—

Rushing out to help his offspring, he'd found them relaxing on a back yard battlefield. There was carnage all round them—a sparrow, three pigeons, a headless vole, two enormous magpies. All dead. Their kittens were terminators. Tiger had congratulated them on their culling spree and kept a close eye on them after that.

"Someone's asking for you, by name."

"A lot of cats ask for me. I was famous, once."

"This cat's insistent. A repetitious and frankly annoyingly wheedled request. The meowing tom gets the most meat, as they say."

"I've got my paws full with the little ones."

"I can see that. But this request..."

"Yes?"

"It's his last one. Before he's executed."

A strange, deep howl reverberated down the prison corridor, through the bars, escaping from a ginger cat's swarthy throat. The tabby made the sound for anyone who came near him, a warning to keep their distance or suffer the sharp consequences of his teeth.

On his way in, Tiger had kept to the other side of the corridor, way out of reach of the growling beast. He intended to take the same path on his way out. There was something mournful about the sound, though, and Tiger wanted to help. He couldn't. He was a father. Putting himself at risk was no longer an option, for his kittens' sake.

He did not feel safe. He was surrounded by feline felons, bank robbers, dog botherers, Bowery banditti, and prohibition-flaunting hoodlums. They were all locked up, thank Bastet, and Tiger couldn't ignore the request that had led him here, to the toughest prison in Nub, known to its reluctant residents as the Shelter.

Little Tim's cell was too small. Scant light shone through a small vertical slat, too narrow for a bendy cat to squeeze through, let alone a chonker like Tim. Not that he dreamed of escape—he was a model prisoner, following the rules, and staying quiet amid the chaotic sounds of the other prisoners.

"I can't do much for you."

"I've always been lonely, Mr. Straight. A solitary cat. I called it being independent. That changed, though."

"It did?"

"Yep. When I joined the Public Works Department."

"That's supposed to be one of the best jobs a cat can have. The perks!"

"The perks," Tim said sadly. "Nothing comes for free, Mr. Straight. When I learned what really goes on there, behind the trashcans, under the discarded, torn-up cat trees, in the darkest corners of this litter tray we call a city... I didn't do anything. Because, for once, I belonged to a fraternity. I didn't want to be lonely again."

"I understand," said Tiger.

"By the time I did do something—nothing brave, mind; I quit—it was only because I had no other option. My conscience won out. You know the funny thing?"

"What's that?"

"Part of me was glad when I got arrested. Living by myself, isolated, no one to talk to... It's rough as a mother's tongue in here, don't get me wrong, but I've made friends. They've got my back. The guards are good to me."

"I'm glad to hear that."

"I called for you because I don't want to be lonely again. In my single cell on death row, waiting to be put to sleep. And after, in the final darkness... help me, Mr. Straight."

"I'm sorry, I can't. but I know someone who might be able to." Tiger expected Tim to explode with rage. Instead, the convict's shoulders sagged in defeat.

"I don't mean to be harsh," Tiger went on. "You're treading a hard path. I'm not equipped to help you right now. I'm the single parent of—"

"Young kittens. I know, I get the paper in here and your life is steady news column fodder. I've had a chance to do some book learning since they sent me here, Mr. Straight. Sniffed a lot of books. All the inmates agree, crime may not pay, but increasing your vocabulary does. That way I know what my court-appointed lawyer's talking about when he opens his mouth. I know what corroborate means. I even know what an indigent is." Tim gave a wry smile. "Me. Thank you for visiting me, Mr. Straight. You've made it very clear how busy you are." There wasn't a hint of bitterness in Tim's voice. That made Tiger feel worse than any barb could.

"I..."

"Who's the lucky cat who gets all your cast-off cases?" Tim asked.

"I don't recommend him to many would-be clients."

"He's busy too." Tim nodded.

"He'll make time for you." *One look at those sad eyes,* Tiger thought, *and he'll take the case.*

"Who is this soft touch?"

"Someone who owes me an enormous favor. Cole Tiddle."

Cole jumped at the chance to hear Little Tim's case. Tiger was impatient with the dilatant, emphasizing Tim's dwindling lifespan.

"I'll get this done," Cole told the PI when Tiger visited his mansion. "I owe you, and I owe that poor polydactyl, too."

"Really?" Lapping at a cocktail, Tiger looked up at Cole, his eyes intense.

"I've never seen you and I as competitors, but we're not that different. I'll get that con out of lockup just as soon as you could."

"I use my brain." Tiger grimaced. "You're like a dog at a gate! Look at what happened to Little Tim."

"That was the cops," said Cole. "They needed a perp."

"Tipped by you! And don't tell me he bought all that cream in his trailer or stole it. He's not the stealing type."

"Like I said... I owe him."

"It's obvious to me that you planted that evidence to wrap up this case and impress Connie. Nothing got wrapped! You throw money at a problem instead of considering all the angles."

"That's your slant." Cole was embarrassed, but he kept listening. He revered Tiger.

"And that fake patter of yours…"

"What in the Sam Hill are you talking about?"

"Nobody talks like that. You say you're here to help. Stop play-acting and help Little Tim!"

The death row inmate didn't have much collateral. Once Cole heard his story, though, the amateur detective's curiosity was piqued. When Tim told him about the society he'd belonged to, Cole was all in. He could help a cat in trouble, and he could scratch away at the respectable veneer presented by CREAM. He needed to know who was behind it, and why one of its representatives had tried to murder him.

Cole hired his own attorney, Akim Koshkin, Esq., to take on Tim's case and push for better conditions for the inmate. No death row cell came with cushions, but Koshkin was able to get Tim a larger cell, gourmet sachets, and even plush toys for him to play with. Best of all, Tim had company. He gave Cole a detailed account of the inner workings of EGG, CREAM, and the Public Works—enough for Cole to decide how he would get close to the villains who'd got Tim in the hot seat.

Cole reveled in the art of disguise. Since his brush with death had made all the papers and he couldn't reply to reports of his demise to hide his identity, this case would push his masquerading skills to the limit. He smeared theatrical makeup in his fur, dulling his markings, and darkening the area around his eyes, making him look haggard. He put his oldest clothes—three weeks max—on the floor, popped out his claws, and dragged his garments around, scruffing them up until they were soiled and ragged. He wore these on his first day of training at the Public Works Department, where he had bribed his way into a position with the Ithacats.

Cole's first day as a garbage cat was a surreal experience for him. Usually, he never worked more than two hours without a snooze. He was rushed through instructions without time to wipe his whiskers or take a meal break. When he did eat, he was given leftovers by his fellow workers, cold, oily fish that he gobbled down like a starving dog.

The fish wasn't the only thing that was cold. Cole shivered as he stood in the open break area, making a mental note to bring warmer clothes the next day, clean or dirty, he didn't care. His trainer, a promoted Ralph, told him he would have to look more presentable when he cleaned the streets—if he was fortunate enough to make the grade.

Cole laughed. "This is total hogwash," he said. "I want to see the manager."

Anatolios was curled up on his paperwork, which was piled twice as high as in Tim's time. He was resting his eyes when Ralph showed Cole into his office, popped one eye open, then both, sizing up this shabby new hire.

"This ain't fair," Cole said in his best country bumpkin accent, jabbing a paw at Ralph. "This sap tells me I gotta clean up to do your dirty work. Where's the sense in that?"

"It's all about public perception," Anatolios explained slowly, washing his haunches with his tongue. "You will be seen out on the street, representing Public Works. If you look untidy, you make us look untidy. The citizens will lose their trust in us. Our whole system will collapse. You don't want that to happen, do you?"

"Seems like you think the cats around here are chumps," said Cole. "They ain't. They can see past surface appearances."

"Yes." Anatolios stared at Cole, who worried that he'd said the wrong thing. Could Anatolios see through *his* surface appearance? He turned to look at Ralph, standing stoic behind him.

"Nevertheless," Anatolios said waspishly, "we do require you to wear neat overalls or a work shirt without quite so many ... loose threads. They are too distracting for your colleagues, considering the meticulous, fast-paced work they have to perform. No cat can resist a dangly thread."

"You're doing a pretty good job of it right now," said Cole.

Anatolios stopped washing and cleared his throat. "Clean yourself up if you want to keep your job."

"I do," said Cole repentantly. "I can't afford no new clothes, though."

"Really? I'm sorry to hear that." Anatolios cocked his head, thought for a moment, still staring at Cole. "We do have a union that could help you. They have a 'career closet' to help those less fortunate, who are allowed to take three work garments per year."

A year? Thought Cole. *Back home, I wear three a day.* Yet he nodded, his eyes bright with excitement. Anatolios had fallen for his ruse.

"You'd have to join the union," said Ralph, gruff as sandpaper.

"Rest assured," said Anatolios. "No dues are, ahem, due up front; they are taken out of your paycheck."

"You run this union then, do you?" Cole asked.

"Bastet, no. I'm familiar with its existence because of my position here. If you want to join, you will have to meet with the union representative, Lincoln."

Cole met the rep, heard the spiel, joined EGG, and by day's end, found himself dressed in a denim boiler suit, warm and baggy. His plan was working perfectly. He had gained the trust of his workmates, met Anatolios and Lincoln, and infiltrated EGG. The downside was the manual labor he undertook as he got through boot camp and graduated to rookie status. He had never picked up trash before in his lives; he typically hired other cats to do it for him. He did not want to touch nasty trash with a broom, let alone his paws. The idea of using his tail as a duster made his stomach heave. Only the looks he got from passers-by, ones of respect and envy, kept him going.

Working alone, the thought occurred to him to pay a couple of ringers to clean the streets for him, but he didn't want to blow his cover, and good, honest hard work was a novelty for him. Plus, the perks kept him going, satisfying his appetite as he trudged through the day. Why pay others to snatch up the rats he could have for himself?

There were so many cats who would have been willing to do his work for him. As he cleaned the streets, he had to step over multiple destitute moggies or ask them politely to move along. He wanted to break his cover and break his oath, give them a handout, but he stuck to his subterfuge and gave them nothing. He felt incredibly lucky to have a place to live and rich, meaty chunks in his belly.

Cole liked working with his crew. The Ithacats he cleaned with were kind, thoughtful, and far more generous than the wealthy elite he normally hobnobbed with. Just as the garbage cats had shared their lunch with him when he started, they spread the workload, helping him when he struggled with heavy refuse, or pushing a cart up the steep hill to Catty Corner. They helped him catch rats, too, giving him tips on how to salt and preserve them so he could save some for supper. Little did they know that his supper at home was wild salmon and caviar.

He dropped his pretense while he was with his regular crewmates, Dougal, Max, and JD. When he stopped making up his fur and dropped his accent, they didn't care or judge; the change was gradual enough to avoid any shock. Cole only used his hayseed dialect when Lincoln aided the crew, pointing out spots they'd missed, coaxing them to work faster.

On Catty Corner, a small shrine of ribbons marked the site of Mandi's demise.

"What happened here, exactly?" Cole asked Lincoln, although he'd already heard the full, tragic story from Little Tim.

"A careless worker caused an accident. She walked under an unstable fire escape, and it fell on her. The only consolation was, we were with her 'til the last mew. We miss her."

"I can see that," said Cole, watching the ribbons twist in the wind.

Within weeks, Cole's charm had woven its magic on his workmates, the residents who waved to him as he cleaned their streets, and Anatolios. Cole was ushered into the boss's office again; this time Ralph left him alone with the Aegean.

"You really have cleaned yourself up, as requested," said Anatolios, eyes locked on Cole. "I'm impressed. It takes a lot to impress me."

"I'm not known for my smarts," Cole replied. "But I'm smart enough to listen to my boss when he tells me to do somethin'."

Anatolios sat behind his desk. His papers piled so high that Cole could only see his nose, eyes, and ears. He could tell the boss was smiling, though, his eyes gleaming with appreciation.

"You've already proven yourself a valuable workforce asset," said Anatolios. "And you're a smash at EGG. You've brought more new members into the fold in a month than Lincoln has all year."

"The more cats join, the stronger we are." Cole shrugged. "Shame you can't be a part of it. Might do you some good."

"How so?"

"Look at all your files there. You're swamped."

Anatolios had to admit that was true.

"If you were a part of the union," said Cole, "you could demand more help—get more help—and you'd have the support of hundreds of brothers and sisters.

One big paw to sweep away your papers." Cole stood up tall and swiped a paw through the air.

"You really recognize EGG's strength."

This was it. Cole held his breath, waiting for the offer to join CREAM.

"However," Anatolios continued. "As an elected local government official, it would not be proper for me to join you. Furthermore, EGG does not exist to make life easy for employees or bully the city into compromise. Your brothers are there to support you, not disrupt the system. Please return to work."

Cole felt his tail bushing, let himself breathe, and calmed it down. He would bide his time and penetrate CREAM, no matter how many hurdles he faced. Until then, he had garbage to collect.

Someone had to do the dirtiest job in the city. It was Cole's turn to do it.

The Grand Central Restroom was an art déco marvel of combined function and aesthetics, a massive, hollow concrete edifice. Frescoes were framed with angled borders and golden trim on the corners that sparkled in the sunlight. The gold was chipped with pieces missing, the frescoes scratched and faded, but the mighty bathroom still inspired awe with its size and its obscene original price tag.

The building was filled with litter, for all-gender use whenever the fancy took cats to dig their claws in white clay clumps, do their business, and move on. The litter filtered into dumpsters on each flank of the landmark. The Ithacats had to scoop out the dumpsters. Cole did not appreciate this task.

Cole's broom was converted for this gig, his brush replaced with a rusty metal scoop. It felt unwieldy in his blistered paws. Worse than the loose litter, the grit in his eyes, and the pungent upwind smells, was the assistance he received from Lincoln. While other cats would have helped him scoop, Lincoln sat back instead, counting down the minutes until they were due to finish. Cole reminded himself why he was there; it was good to spend time with Lincoln, earning his trust, getting closer to CREAM.

"You dropped some," said Lincoln.

"I know I dropped some." Cole forgot his plan, bristled up, and hissed at Lincoln, who hissed back.

"Pick it up."

"You pick it up." Cole instantly regretted his action, glancing at the spilled grit. His ears twitched in surprise when Lincoln rolled onto his back, showing his belly in submission.

Speechless, Cole passed the scoop to Lincoln. The longhair cleaned up the spillage and emptied the rest of the dumpster. Cole helped; he felt compelled to show that he was better than Lincoln.

Cole's invitation to CREAM came from an unexpected source. Ralph asked him if he remembered the old female moggy who lived on Peregrine Circle.

"Of course," Cole chuckled. He was working a shift with Ralph, who had a higher opinion of him after hearing about his run-in with Lincoln.

"Stubbornest cat I ever saw," said Ralph.

"She insists on bringing out everyone's garbage," said Cole. "Whether they like it or not."

"I've only seen two other cats lift a paw to help her. One, sweet Mandi, is dead. The other, Little Tim Tierney, is an outcast."

Do you know he's in the Shelter, on death row? Cole wanted to ask Ralph. His garbage cat yokel persona wouldn't have that kind of knowledge, though, so he worked in silence.

"We need your kind of cat in a very special organization."

Cole's eyes lit up, but he kept his mouth shut.

Cole wasn't impressed with the hydroelectric power plant. His mansion was almost as big, with more historical value. Nevertheless, he allowed Ralph to lead him into the cavernous lair, acting like a cat who cared, looking up and around at the ornately carved cornices and dusty gathered valances.

"I shall have to blindfold you," said Ralph apologetically.

"That's okay," Cole replied. "Anything for a friend." He pulled a silk scarf out of his pocket. "Do you mind...?"

Ralph shook his furry head and wrapped the scarf over Cole's eyes, tying it too tight at the back. Cole made his stumbling way deeper into the building, using his sense of smell, touch, and sight.

Even with Cole's scarf folded into two layers, he could see through the chiffon. He watched as a modest clowder of cats encircled him, recognizing a tall, imperious Khmer with a thick ruff around its neck, a caracal, and Lincoln before they covered their faces with their hoods.

Once the blindfold was removed and returned to Cole's coat pocket, he was given his own set of red robes and the litany to recite.

All lives are important to me and essential to the future of my city. CREAM'S spiel made sense to Cole. He wanted to take charge; it would be easy to control these dumb animals. He could be the cat who stole the CREAM.

Cole thought of Mandi, Lona, and all the others. CREAM was too corrupt, too murderous to fix with a bull-headed board meeting or a hasty power play. Even if he led the organization, there were too many dark components. Maybe he would create something similar but better, a foundation for all creatures, starting with the escaped mice.

"Welcome to Cats Rallied for the Equality of All Mammals," Ralph said with pride.

That's it? thought Cole. *I was expecting something more sinister.* He smiled at Ralph as they left the power plant. "My pleasure," Cole purred. "I can't wait to get to work."

The local zoological park had developed a machine that emitted a high-pitched signal. It was designed to deter visitors from killing and eating the resident birds. Tiger had made the mistake of taking his little ones to the park. The bleeping machine had provided them with some initial interest. When they got bored with the sound, they strutted past the machine and nobbled three doves. They hadn't visited the zoo again.

At five months old, they'd shed their milk teeth and were almost ready to fend for themselves. Their father didn't want to let them go; they were all he had to remind him of Jo.

A particular account number bothered Tiger, and he ran it by Connie when she offered to babysit. She had been alone since Bug's death, her apartment cold and empty. She'd thrown herself into her first job, a designer with a top firm of interior decorators. Her garish ideas had proved very popular with local citizens.

"This is where all the money was being siphoned off to," Tiger explained. "It's what Bug died for. To find this out for me. I can't do anything with it—there's no name, no sequence to the account numbers."

"What if these numbers don't denote the accounts? There's a pattern to them, Tige." The figures were split into blocks and rows:

132474222
132482252
132499794
132475222
132485252
132499794

132476222
132483252
132495794
132477222
132474222
132482252
132492794

132487252
132498794

132474222

132486252
132491796
132474222
132489252
132498796
132478222

132491796
132473222
132481252
132497796
132479222
132494796
132496796
132482252
132493792
132488252
132493722
132488252
132493796

"They could be safety deposit boxes," Tiger surmised. "Lockers, house numbers..."

"Or zip codes."

Tiger thanked Connie breathlessly, launching into a furious bout of postal decoding:

13247-4222
13248-2252
13249-9794

13247-5222
13248-5252
13249-9794
13247-6222

13248-3252
13249-5794
13247-7222
13248-2252
13249-2794

13247-4222
13248-7252
13249-8794
13247-4222
13248-6252
13249-1796
13247-4222
13247-8222
13247-3222
13247-9222

13248-9252
13248-4252
13248-1252

13249-8796
13249-1796
13249-7796
13249-4796
13249-4796

13249-6796
13248-2252
13248-8252
13248-8252

The zip codes corresponded to some certain well-known byways: Dempster Street, where the Beggar's Temple could be found and Burdock Road, which

Tiger and Bug had visited, seeking Danny Faithful. The most prevalent zip code referred to a street in a swanky part of town; one house dominated all its neighbors. It was an expensive townhouse owned by a corporate bigwig. Tiger decided to try there first.

"If I'm not back this time tomorrow, come a-looking. Take care, though."

Connie nodded anxiously, watching her friend from the window as he raced away. Martin, Fliss, and Bello required attention. She would have to settle them down before she headed after Tiger.

"Our organization is founded on trust," Lincoln and Ralph explained as they took Cole for a drink after work. So far, they'd hit two watering holes: the Burmilla Bar and Sokoke Karaoke, where Lincoln had sung a cat scat version of Cab Calico's "Minnie the Mouser."

"I get it," said Cole, pretending to be tipsier than he really was, encouraging his friends to get drunk and spill their guts, figuratively, of course. "You don't want me going around telling people you dress in evening gowns with extra tails."

"We do not," said Ralph with a dour expression, already three sour milks into inebriation.

"That's not what I mean." Lincoln led Cole to one of the oldest drinking establishments in town, the Blind Tiger. "By joining us, you have opened many doors. Including this one."

The Blind Tiger was quiet, with moody music playing on a dilapidated gramaphone. In a dark corner of the bar, Lincoln knocked on a small wood panel. A board slid to one side, revealing a hole large enough for a cat to peep through. Cole saw a bloodshot green eye on the other side.

"Password?" the peeper hissed.

"Gorgonzola," said Lincoln. The entire panel opened up, letting Lincoln, Cole, and Ralph into a den of illegality, permissiveness, and loose mice.

Cole's jaw dropped. He saw gambling and nip abuse, cats with silicone collars and velvet harnesses, mice in cages or trapped by their tails, corralled like pint-sized cattle. Cole had never seen so many *mus musculi* in one place, on one menu. All of them were hot now, melt-in-the-mouth, ready to eat.

At the height of Prohibition, undercover, flanked by killers, Cole was in the last place he wanted to be—a squeakeasy.

"What about the sanctity of all life?" Cole spluttered as Lincoln gobbled down a terrified field mouse.

"They're part of the food chain," Ralph drooled. "They sustain our lives. What could be more inviolable?"

Cole's cool investigative veneer fell away in an instant of panic. He couldn't stand to watch the mice getting tenderized, minced, or eaten raw. He reached for a trap and unlatched it with one claw, his eyes glinting as he watched the freed mouse scurry out of the squeakeasy. Ralph and Lincoln rounded on him.

"He's gone mouse happy," said Callum, emerging from a low-lit booth. "Happens all the time in here... the sight of all these morsels."

Cole scooped up a couple of cages, heading for the exit. Lincoln and Ralph blocked his way.

"Hey, what's the big idea?" asked Ralph, nose to nose with Cole. "Is that ... makeup on your face?"

Cole shook his head. There was no way he could free all these mice; he had to get out of the Blind Tiger and fetch a prowler.

Ralph dragged a paw across Cole's face and looked at his pads. They were covered in greasepaint. "Who are you, really?" Ralph asked.

Cole swung a cage at Ralph, the mouse within shrieking with fear. Ralph ducked, but the cage struck Lincoln's head, knocking him off balance. Lincoln hit his head hard on a table and didn't get back up.

"You killed him!" Ralph shouted. "Over a mouse! What kind of cat are you?"

Part of the food chain, thought Cole as he barged past Ralph. He was close to the secret exit now, a cage in each forepaw.

Callum sprang at Cole, shoving him against a wall. Before Cole could make another move, Callum lifted a massive paw and knocked him out cold.

The townhouse wasn't all that far from the bank, Tiger noted as he strode up the front drive. Lead-lined windows didn't give much away, and the gray facade gave the building an imposing air. He nosed round the side and found a trades entrance, open and inviting.

The house was gloomy, but Tiger's way was lit by a flickering amber light emanating from one of the many back rooms. He headed for the light, found the room in question, and was immediately mesmerized by a large glowing box fixed to the wall.

Red and orange colors danced, generating a heat that soothed him and made him feel sleepy. He drew closer, enjoying the sensation that smothered his body. His fur smelled of autumn leaves, his pads began to sweat. Still he moved closer, trying to absorb as much heat as possible before he scorched his nose. It was gorgeous; he was in paradise.

He couldn't help but lie down in front of the box, stretching himself out as long as he could, letting the heat brush his belly. All thoughts of fear or hunger left him as his stomach was filled with ersatz sunshine. He wriggled a little bit closer, getting drowsy. As he curled up for a quick nap, the aperture swallowed him up. There was nothing left of him in the hall except a few stray strands of fluff.

Tiger couldn't move his legs. He felt cooked to a turn, his head numb and his paws raw. The ground slid by beneath him, uneven. He wanted to throw up, though there was nothing in his stomach. His eyes were gummed together; strands of mucus obscured his vision. Snapping his lids wide open, he watched adaze as a baseboard passed him. The floor was tiled, dirty yellow squares bordered by red and gray rectangles. Each square grated against his cheek. Looking up, he worked out that he was being dragged. A big black cat was hauling him by the tail.

Tiger was dumped in an air-conditioned office, left to recover his senses. A cork notice board hung on one wall, surrounded by red rectangles similar to the ones beneath him. A few notes were pinned on the board, announcing a ceilidh, a conference, and a convention at the Duncan Hotel. He was in the headquarters of CREAM.

Tiger used a leg to hoist himself into a sitting position. It wasn't his leg. Too cold, too stiff. It belonged to a coffee-colored desk with a black plastic trim and four black seats. The seats were bolted on, covered in ink and crumbs. They looked unfeasibly comfortable to Tiger.

Plumping into one of the seats he decided that the floor was better.

He wasn't ready to defend himself when the big cat returned. "Callum." The heavy cat gave a bow. "Pleased to meet you."

"Do I know you?" asked the detective groggily.

"Kind of. We've met before. I was behind you and wearing a hooded outfit. Down in the crypt." Callum chattered his teeth together. "I didn't get the chance to introduce myself before, had a mouth fulla scruff. Thought I'd better do it now since we'll be working together."

"I don't see that happening. There ain't nothing would convince me to work for you."

"Never said anything 'bout you working *for* me." Callum's tail fanned slowly from side to side. Tiger's was standing straight. "You'll be workin' *with* me."

The detective pursed his lips together. He didn't have dimples. He didn't know what to say either.

"Still need convincin'?" Callum asked at last. Tiger said nothing but allowed himself to be led down a corridor to a gym.

"You going to exercise me to death?" Tiger broke his silence. The caracal shook his head and moved on to the next room. It housed a grand swimming pool. A mouse languished on a sun lounger, nibbling on a dinky slice of edam. It was the same mouse that had greeted Bug in a house not far away. The same mouse that employed Callum, Miss Angold, and Danny. Musculus.

Tiger wasn't looking at the big cheese. A net had been suspended over the pool, spinning and writhing as its prisoners tried to chew their way out. They were small yet feisty. The poor beggars. What had they done to deserve such treatment? Tiger moved closer to the pool and realized why Callum was holding him so tight. The net held three little kittens—Fliss, Martin, and Bello. Although they squirmed, they were wrapped too tight, the netting was too strong, and every movement they made entwined them farther. Tiger struggled more than ever; Callum bit hard, drawing blood. The stricken father forced himself to relax, turning back to Musculus. His throat felt dry.

"I didn't think. As soon as I found mouse droppings in that hippie's shop, I suspected. I didn't think a rodent would have the gall, but I'm wrong about practically everything these days. Why are you doing this to me?"

"It's the only way to make you see, Mr. Straight. See how my people have suffered. You didn't realize, did you? Didn't know what was going on. Oh, the sacrifices I've had to make to inveigle the guilty. The cult of CREAM ... squeakeasies ... murder! All to convince catkind to trust and obey me."

"A cat's facing execution for those murders." Tiger scowled.

"More proof that your species is too foolish to rule," said Musculus. "Callum?"

Callum held up a massive forepaw.

"A pair of misshapen gloves were all it took to throw the prowlers off the scent. That and some help from inside the department..."

"Bowyer."

Musculus nodded with a smug expression.

"Little Tim doesn't deserve to die." Tiger looked toward the pool. "And those kittens are innocent."

"Shouldn't have left them home alone, dear fellow. That's illegal, you know."

As Callum relaxed his grip on Tiger's nape, the detective broke free. Instead of attacking, the caracal backed off. He stood between Tiger and the pool.

"They've done nothing to you," the detective snarled at the lounging mouse.

"And what are mice so guilty of?" Cheese's whiskers quivered with excitement. "Are they the fallen? This is their hell, they're the damned. You still don't see, do you?"

"See what?"

"I want you to help Callum here with a small task he has to perform."

"No way."

"Do it or your cubs will suffer."

As Callum approached, Tiger addressed the big cat. "Why are you taking orders from a mouse? There something wrong with you? He got something on you, too?"

"We're going to do as we're told," Callum replied. "Unless you want those kittens drowned."

"You'd do it as well, wouldn't you?" Tiger's eyes were locked with Callum's, trying to see past the cold stare.

"Too right." Callum glanced at Musculus, who looked impatient. "No more dawdling." The black cat led Tiger outside and onto a train. They were the only passengers on board; the detective couldn't even see a driver. Still, the train set off at full steam.

"Where is it we're going exactly?"

"You'll see in due course." Callum yanked a map from his combats, sniffed at it intently. Tiger stole a glance at it and made out a vast complex with a perimeter fence. Callum folded it away before Tiger could get a better look.

"I can't wait," said Tiger sarcastically. "Anything to eat?"

"Nothing for you. Except this." The muscular cat handed Tiger a pouch full of black powder. The detective sniffed at it carefully.

"Not to eat."

"What is it?" Tiger wrapped the powder up again. "It's a mixture of potassium nitrate, charcoal, and sulfur," Callum grunted. "Musculus put it together."

"What does it do?" Tiger asked.

"Don't ask me. The boss said to set fire to it if and when we need to. It'll distract the enemy."

"Who are the enemy?"

Callum ignored the detective, taking digitalis to set his heart thumping. It beat like a piston; he was ready for a fight.

The train bumped over a set of points. There would be only one stop on this journey.

***

Connie had been lingering outside the townhouse for hours. She'd seen no one go in or leave; the whole street was still. She headed to Jo's house to check on the kittens.

No kittens. At first, Connie thought that they'd run away and gotten lost on some childish investigation. It took her a few minutes to realize the truth. The cultists who had used Jo so efficiently had abducted Martin, Fliss, and Bello. Connie decided to try one of the other addresses on Tiger's list—Collier Heights in the service sector. She would check every office on the block if necessary. She wasn't going to let her friend down again.

Musculus's private train followed the coast, choppy water on one side, green fields on the other. Tiger tried to gain his bearings as the world rushed by beyond his window. He rarely left the city; the sea unsettled him, too big, too deep. Too many mysteries beneath the surface.

The rusty tracks beneath his paws were used mainly for hoppers transporting seafood and minerals. The train passed through an abandoned coastal ward, a short swing gate leading to the village green. Soon it was a blurred memory, the train racing south. Callum said nothing, his eyes hard, steeped in thought.

After an hour's travel, they reached a grotty station as lifeless as the village. The train gave a sigh as it came to rest, steam escaping from its sides. Callum climbed out, followed by a watchful Tiger.

"Not much of a holiday destination," said the detective sourly.

"Keep it down," Callum growled. "We gotta be quiet about this."

"I've never been to the seaside before," Tiger whispered this time.

"Coast is a mile that way." Callum pointed with his tail. "Follow me and stay shtum."

They went up a flight of steps, onto a bridge that arced over the train tracks, and the cats could see how the land lay. The large cat continued to boss Tiger about, telling him to stoop low. Most of the surrounding area was scrubland and brown earth. A hunch of silos and warehouses were Callum's target. A high wire fence surrounded them, too high for even an accomplished jumper like Callum to scale. Tiger could swear that he heard a dog howl. He trembled, hunching his shoulders against the wind.

"They got guard dogs in there?" Tiger shuddered as they approached the fence.

"Naw. Some good impressionists though." The few floodlights dotted around the facility pointed inward, so the two cats got good and close to the wire under cover of darkness. The ground was frosty, and Tiger clenched his teeth as iced grass crunched under his paws.

"What are we doing here?" he begged.

"You'll see, little cat. You'll see." Callum gripped a section of mesh between his mighty teeth, clamping his jaws down on the cold metal. He gnawed at the wire until it started to rend. Tiger was astounded; he stood back, mouth agape.

"I thought you caracals were great at leaping?"

"I don't fancy getting barbed wire balls. You gonna help me here?" the big cat asked, taking a break from his meal. Nodding, the detective grasped some of the broken wire strands and pulled them clear, enlarging the hole that Callum had made. After more nibbling and pulling, the gap became large enough for Callum to fit his head through.

"Not big enough for all of me," he spat. "But I reckon a titchy thing like you'll be able to get in. Then you can run to the gate and open it up. We need to get the gate unlocked." He yanked his head from the hole and urged Tiger onward. Obliging, the smaller cat used his whiskers to judge the size of the gap, then pushed forward with his paws. Grasping the wire, he pulled his head and shoulders through. "Stop!" Callum cried. "Get out of there! Guards!"

Tiger couldn't see anything. He was halfway through, and it was a lot easier going forward than backward. Cocking an ear, he heard a hefty cat approaching. The guard had a small flashlight attached to his helmet, enhancing his excellent night vision. As he turned his head from side to side, the beam swept along the fence, dangerously close to Tiger's nose. He tried to reverse, but he was stuck with his hind legs and tail waggling in the air. Callum tried to yank him free as the security cat approached, shining his flashlight up the wall of a red-roofed building. Tiger panicked, scrabbling at the wire. The guard was mere feet away.

As the beam swung in his direction once more, he was plucked clear by Callum. The big cat clamped a paw over Tiger's mouth, keeping him low as the sentry passed. When the coast was crystal, Callum let the detective up.

"I think the hole needs to be bigger," Callum admitted.

"Really?" Tiger replied hoarsely. "You can climb through this time."

Callum nodded, wrenching at the broken mesh. By the time he'd made a cat-sized gap, the guard had completed a lap of the complex, and the two trespassers had to lie low again. By chance or negligence, the hole wasn't discovered; as soon as he was able, Callum dived through the fence and opened the gate for Tiger. No alarms sounded and no staff came running to investigate. "What next?" asked Tiger.

"Not far to go," the big cat replied, leading his accomplice to the red-roofed building. There were no windows to break or signs to guide them; they broke the lock on a corrugated iron shutter, stepping into a dark chamber.

Tiger wished he'd attacked the guard on patrol outside, if only to steal his helmet. He hated being disoriented in the gloom. He stood still for a moment so that he could listen out for company. Straw rustled across the chamber; cogs cranked and spun in a distant housing. He opened his mouth to ask a question that was never formed. A switch flicked behind them, and bright lights blinded their vision. The shutter was dragged closed with an angry bray.

As their eyes became accustomed to the light, the two cats found themselves surrounded by a band of wee, menacing rodent beasties. The mice sniffed at the interlopers, their noses twitching excitedly. Some sat on bunk beds, dressed in tiny white T-shirts and shorts. Others stood as if to attention, arms folded behind their backs, chiseled chins raised. They wore blue slacks and gray cardigans. The livelier ones were ready for trouble, paws clenched, teeth bared. The biggest mouse wore a navy-blue tunic with medals pinned to the right breast. A cap made him seem even taller than he really was.

"Looks like you've caught us red pawed," he squeaked.

"Who might you be?" challenged Callum.

"Fieldmouse Marshall Monty Montague. That's all you'll get out of me." Monty turned to the mice perched on their bunks. They were digging into white dishes laden with sunflower seeds. "May as well give it up, lads. Show them what we've been up to." The mice put down their dishes, shifted their bunks around, and revealed a tunnel leading out of the building. "Another feather in your cat chaps' caps, I suppose. At least we had a jolly good try."

Tiger shook his head. "We don't care about your tunnel."

"You don't?" a red-faced mouse named Shuggie piped up. "You have tae! We spent weeks diggin' that flaming thing."

"We're not guards. We're on your side. Here to help you escape."

Monty gave the two cats a blank look, trying to digest the news. "Impossible, I'm afraid."

"You like it here or something?" asked Tiger.

"We've tried to get out so many times, all to no avail."

"No Avail ain't much of a place, so we came back here," joked Shuggie. One look from Monty shut him up. The leader showed the cats an anteroom full of junk.

"Past disgraces," he admitted, pointing to a trap built out of balsa. "This one we called the trap attack. A cat-sized mousetrap with us as the bait. A guard comes along and SLAM! He's caught. That was the theory. Lost a lot of good mice to a lot of hungry cats with that one."

Monty showed Tiger and Callum a Shuggie-shaped coffin.

"This seemed like a good idea at the time. One of the lads would feign death, be taken out of the compound to the cemetery, run away while the pallbearers weren't looking. But they weren't taken out in a coffin. They were flushed down the latrine."

Tiger unearthed a half-eaten turnip. Whiskers had been painted on with a splayed brush.

"That went really well in the planning stages. As our chaps escaped, we disguised some turnips to resemble them. So they wouldn't be missed if there was a head count or what have you. Once the escapees got over the fence, they would hide out disguised as turnips. No suspicion aroused, you see."

"Were these disguises good?" huffed Callum.

"Too good," sighed Monty. "Unbeknownst to us, the camp commandant has a thing for turnips. Not only did he gobble up the escapees, he ate their substitutes as well. Gave him the runs for a week, though. Meagre consolation. This was a much better idea." Monty showed the cats several strips of cloth, split into sections by wooden splints.

"What're these? Camouflage?" The triangular cloth shapes were black or marsh green.

"Wings," Shuggie explained proudly. "We got the idea from our mutant friend over there." Chocolate was a quiet creature who was suspended from the roof by his feet, fast asleep. Webbed flaps grew from his forelimbs. "He could glide out of here anytime if he could see where he was going. He's as blind as a—well, a very blind mouse."

"Where did he get the wings?" Tiger asked, amazed.

"They did it to him. The scientists. Messing with nature. A month ago, he was a normal mouse. Now he's a freak." Chocolate opened his eyes sleepily, swinging slightly from his rafter. Then he went back to sleep.

"Why didn't you use the wings you made, then?" snapped Callum.

"Our intention was to glide over the fence to freedom. We'd have to start from a high place—a roof—and we don't think the wings would keep us aloft for long enough. We'd probably land on this side of the fence, right in the lap of a sentry."

"We're too heavy," Shuggie sighed. "There's not enough wind... we'd be reliant on air currents, y'see. Too risky."

Callum was exasperated. "Why build the things in the first place?"

"Hope, my feline friend, is the only thing that keeps us ticking. Besides, mice are experts with needle and thread. We have a whole division working on disguises and clothes. It didn't take them long to knock up some cloth, attach a few matchstick splints."

"Why are you prepared to risk so much to leave?" asked Tiger. "You've got food, warmth, a place to sleep."

"You don't know what they do to us here?" Monty, surprised, turned to Callum.

"He doesn't know," the big cat explained with a yawn. His mouth was big enough to engulf Monty in one snap.

"Then we'd better show you," grumbled Monty. Ordering a bunch of the prisoners to open the shutter, he led the cats to an adjacent building. "Take a look at this, old bean."

Tiger clenched a window ledge and hoisted himself up so that he could peek through a lead-lined pane, taking care not to be seen by whoever was inside.

Cats in lab coats wandered around the whitewashed interior, making notes on wadded clipboards. Much of the area was split into cubicles, partitioned with heavy glass and plastic. The technicians passed one compartment after another, back and forth, checking the conditions of the inhabitants.

In the first cubicle, a mouse was breakdancing. The floor was plated with heated metal, and the rodent was forced to keep moving in order to avoid serious burns. Next to him, a shabby-looking mouse had been treading a short conveyor belt for hours. Occasionally, a technician would throw a lever, increasing the pace of the conveyor belt. The creature within was being jogged to death.

Other mice had been coerced into equally infernal experiments.

One poor soul climbed up and down a set of steps. Others had electrodes connected to their brains, were fed toxic chemicals, or swam desperately in tanks of freezing water. Some of the prisoners had eyes or ears growing out of places they shouldn't have been. Tiger strained to get a better look, sickened yet mesmerized by the goings-on. His world was beginning to make more sense, even though the technicians' work seemed so senseless.

The worst was yet to come. Craning his neck, Tiger saw strange activity in a cell near his window. A group in Stetsons was being taught a series of steps to a repetitive country tune. The sorry souls looked like they were enjoying themselves. One of the indoctrinated captives was Inspector Bix Mortis.

"We have to get him out of there!" Tiger whispered down to Callum.

"We already have a plan that incorporates your presence," said Monty happily. Taking the cats back to the red-roofed building, he introduced them to Chocolate, the winged freak.

"Cool name," said Tiger, weary from the atrocities he'd seen.

"Thanks. My sight may be failing, but I'm still the best there is at nabbing the commandant's candy. Would you like a bite?" Chocolate offered them a bar, a hairy flap of skin tucked around his forelimb.

"No thanks," Callum interjected. He preferred mice for his supper, but that particular species was off the menu for the moment. "We don't have time. We *do* have time for your plan."

"Oh yes. You can get two of us out if the guards believe you're part of the staff. I don't think you can sneak out as easily as you snuck in. You can get two of us out by placing us between your nose and upper lip. One per cat. What do you think?"

"Mousetaches?" Tiger replied, incredulous. He knew why the captives were desperate to escape, but their plans left something to be desired. Perhaps their scaled-down brains had something to do with it—too small to deal with such a big problem.

"I have a better idea. It's simpler, and it's been thunk up by Musculus himself."

"Muscu-what?"

"Head honcho of CREAM. Devoted to giving mice what they deserve—and cats their just desserts."

"Let's hear it," Chocolate squeaked.

"We've unlocked the main gate. We walk out. If the guards give us any crap, we knock seven shades of sick out of them."

"Simple and direct," Shuggie admitted. "Let's do it."

"Who goes?" asked Monty.

"Your lot," Callum replied, leading the mice out of their building toward the fence. They moved in single file, shadowing each other closely, eyes skittering on the lookout for sentries. Despite their urge to escape, the lads were scared—if caught mid-flight they would be killed on the spot or sent to the cooler, the camp commandant's personal fridge, all Tupperwared up for his supper.

The caracal crept to the gate, easing it open, gritting his teeth as the hinges squealed. Once there was room for a mouse to get through, he beckoned the first volunteer.

Brett, a square-headed mouse in a flying jacket, pushed Chocolate to the fore, helping the shortsighted candy smuggler to the gate. Chocolate bumped his nose against the wire, edged through the gate, and ran for the cover of the undergrowth beyond.

"Choc's away!" Monty announced excitedly. Tiger shushed him, passing the next mouse to Callum.

One by one, the prisoners disappeared into the darkness on the other side of the fence. About half of them had reached sanctuary before a patrolling guard spotted the remaining creatures.

The massive guard took in the trembling mice and the two cats. Holstering his flashlight, he pounced on Shuggie, snapping the rodent's back with a bite. Two paws swept up a couple of stragglers, still in their underwear. Monty led an honorable retreat, scattering his gang across the compound.

Callum attacked the guard, who let out a dismayed howl. The caracal dug his hind claws into the sentry, splitting his soft belly. "Get out of here!" Callum shouted to Tiger, who was heading the wrong way. Somewhere on the other side of the complex, an alarm sounded, and the spotlights began to shift in their direction.

"I've got to rescue Inspector Mortis and the others," Tiger yelled. "I can't leave them in that torture chamber."

"Of course you can! This is your last chance!" The guard bit a chunk out of Callum's shoulder, but his strength was fading fast. Tiger had disappeared into the maze-like lanes of the compound. The caracal finished his opponent quickly with a hefty headbutt. Brushing through the gate, he slammed it shut behind him. The detective could rot.

As Callum and the escaped mice got all the attention, Tiger hid in a dark alcove. This hideaway smelled bad, as if lazy staff occasionally used it as a latrine. He'd always known that scientific experiments were performed on some dumb species—better than testing intelligent cats—but the research he'd seen appeared pointless and painful. After meeting Inspector Mortis and Musculus, he found it difficult to think of rodents as nothing more than food. His fellow dicks all had gimmicks; perhaps he'd found his. Tiger Straight, the card-carrying vegetarian cat detective.

Two females in Day-Glo orange jackets rushed past, flashlights held out before them. They were headed for the main gate and missed Tiger completely. After a suitable interval, he left his hidey-hole and made for the labs. He planned to muscle his way in, release as many of the test subjects as he could before he was questioned, then head for the hole in the fence. The guards would surely have spotted it by now, but they'd be looking outside the compound; they didn't know that he was still in their midst. Surprise was the only element worth using; he hoped it would serve him well.

He breezed into the labs, opening panels on each glass cell he passed. Mice ran from their traps, nipping to and fro around the building, looking for the exit. Tiger reached Inspector Mortis's cubicle, shared with five other rodents. They continued to repeat their pattern of steps, dancing to a dirge about lost love. The detective slid back a panel, allowing Mortis's five companions to flee. The inspector, however, was happy in his cage.

"I wanna dance! I wanna dance!" he cried, under the influence of potent drugs. Tiger dragged him toward the exit. The sozzled inspector was bound to draw unwelcome attention. A technician challenged them as they were about to leave the building.

"It's all part of the Big Experiment," Tiger explained, offensively charming. "Commandant's orders."

"That's alright then." The technician nodded, allowing the entourage to pass. They weren't so lucky with the second cat they bumped into—Tiger tried the same ploy with him, a Khmer in tight black leather.

"I am the camp commandant," said the Khmer with a swagger.

"I wanna dance," Bix told him.

"Round up these pipsqueaks," the commandant bellowed, bringing a squad of guards rushing to his assistance. Tiger was dragged to the Khmer's office, a drab brown room with angular, functional furnishings.

"Who was the other cat with you?" asked the Khmer, chewing on a turnip. One whiff of his breath was enough to make Tiger wince.

"Just a guy. Said he wanted to show me something. He got the gate open, let me in."

"That gate can only be unbolted from the inside," purred the commandant.

"Then some of your staff must have helped. How do you hire your guards? It's not the sort of thing you'd place in the recruitment section of the local rag. Is there an agency for louts and blockheads?"

"This facility is run by highly trained individuals," replied the commandant. "I train them myself. Apart from the scientists. They do their own thing."

"What good are these experiments gonna do anybody?" asked Tiger.

"Oh yes. You're one of these animal liberators. The technicians test the endurance, the mental and physical dexterity of the mice. The more we learn about them, the more we learn about ourselves."

"You got a point there. What are you going to do with me?"

"It's not often that we get the chance to experiment on our own kind. You'll make an excellent specimen."

31

Callum ran through the undergrowth, making for the old station. The digitalis was wearing off, and he needed a rest. He could hear a jet of steam leaving his train, the only sign to guide him. Tagging along was a large group of mice, led by Chocolate and Brett, his square-headed helper. Close behind was a crack squad of security guards, growling for blood. To be tracked by a cat is no laughing matter. Natural hunters, they are swift and silent. Even the laziest of their brethren is capable of stealth and cunning. Their night sight is exemplary, and once they have the scent, they will follow it for hours. Only once they have filled their bellies will they cease their pursuit. The mice were petrified; Callum was weary. If the guards caught up with them, he would have to face them alone. With the odds so heavily against him, his size and strength meant very little. At last, the station could be made out in the ashen moonlight.

The old building seemed to sag in the middle, ready to collapse through neglect. Callum sent the prisoners on ahead of him.

"Make for that little station. There's a train on the other side. We're leaving in that."

"What are you gonna do?" asked Brett.

"Give you a head start. Hurry up! We're on a strict timetable." Looking back, they could see flashes of green closing fast. Beady, hungry eyes and bright flashlights. With the mice heading for the train, Callum ducked behind a bush.

A whistle blew impatiently. The guards reached the bush and halted, wary. Callum's thick tail lashed from side to side, and he let out a long hiss, doing his best to imitate a snake. The guards took a couple of steps backward. They shone flashlights in the caracal's direction, watching the hypnotic swish of his tail.

The train left the station with a full complement of passengers. Callum chanced a look back at his escape vehicle and a beam of light met his face. Bristling, he puffed himself up as large as possible, arched his back, and bared his teeth. By the time the guards were upon him, the train was long gone.

First, the commandant ordered his guards to pluck out a couple of Tiger's whiskers in order to deter any attempted escape. Without his sensitive vibrissae, he was crippled and in agony. He still kicked and spat as he was dragged into a cold, mirrored room. He was strapped to a padded bench, his exposed stomach pinned down with a metal bar. Beside him he saw Cole Tiddle, lying on his side on a parallel bench, unconscious, with his tongue lolling out.

"What have you done to Cole?" Tiger bawled as the commandant gloated over him.

"Our experiments can be quite draining," the Khmer explained softly. "Especially this apparatus. We call it the weight machine. We gradually apply lead weights to this metal bar." He tapped the chrome with a ragged claw.

"You expect me to diet?"

"No. We expect you to talk. You give us the identity of your accomplice, and we stop adding the weights."

"I told you. My 'accomplice' was just some random cat."

"We will continue to add pound after pound until you give us a satisfactory answer," the commandant bellowed. "Or the breath is crushed out of you for good."

A puff-cheeked orderly placed a weight on one side of the bar. Tiger was already finding it difficult to breathe. He began to squirm for all he was worth.

"Give us a name. That's all I need."

"Do they call you the camp commandant because you're flamboyant?" Tiger gasped. "Did your mom dress you up in frocks when you were a kitten? Do you like comic opera and fearless self-expression?"

The orderly added more weights as the detective yanked his paws from the straps that bound him. Heaving his forelimbs against the metal bar, he held it up long enough to leave the bench and throw the weights to the floor, where they slammed down on the Khmer's tail.

Unlatching his claws, Tiger scratched the orderly's nose. The cat collapsed, holding his face to staunch the flow. Tiger shook Cole awake, dragging him off his bench. The commandant couldn't follow his prisoners out of the room; his tail was trapped and squashed pancake flat. He watched Tiger in dismay, ordering the bleeding cat to give chase.

"What's going on?" Cole asked, rubbing sleep from his eyes.

"That's another mystery for you to solve," said Tiger. The detectives didn't aim for the gate—still too busy with guards. Instead, they re-entered Monty's building and found the leader debriefing Inspector Mortis. The prowler apologized for messing up Tiger's escape attempt.

"No use crying over moldy cheese," Monty soothed.

"I'd eat it anyway," said a stocky mouse named Grant. "Where is it?"

"It's an idiom," Monty explained. "Don't mind him," he told Tiger. "Big belly, small brain. At least some of us got out." The Fieldmouse Marshall looked to Tiger for the next move.

"The rest of you are going to get out an' all," Tiger assured them. "I have a scheme. It's as barmy as one of Shuggie's master plans..."

"Anything's worth a try," said Bix.

"So your dancing days are over, are they, Inspector?" Tiger asked cheekily.

"Get us out of here, you furry old fart."

"Certainly." Tiger smiled at the snippy Bix, then turned to Monty. "We'll need those canvas wings you made. I take it we can get onto the roof?"

"No probs," replied Monty cheerfully. "We've been collecting stringy cheese, wrapping it together so it hardens like a rope. Pongs a bit. But needs must, and all that."

"Fine."

"Bring me a mirror!" the commandant screamed, sending a hireling scuttling. He soon returned with a flat silver tray, passing it to the Khmer and backing off fast. Trying to angle it at waist level, the commandant watched lamplight sparkle off the ornate tray.

He continued to tilt it until he caught sight of his stub of a tail.

Trapped by his own weight machine, he'd had to coil around and chew off his precious appendage. Flakes of bone and fur were still stuck between his teeth. He tried to swish the stump from side to side; it quivered, pathetic. He wanted revenge.

Throwing the tray to his second-in-command, he summoned his best guards and demanded Tiger's head.

"There's plenty of places he could've secreted himself, Sir. A lot of nooks where they could be prepping an escape, or tunneling out..." The second swallowed hard. "This facility was built to keep its test subjects in. Beyond that—"

"I know. Send in the goons."

Art and Walter Mirk had been taking it easy for a while. The last full-on search of the IE Institute had lasted days, with the nosy team unearthing several hidden rodents. The mice would do anything to avoid being experimented upon: build cat traps, wrap themselves in blankets, hide in cardboard boxes, disguise their scent with garlic. Escape attempts were rife despite the penalties—better to die running than to be dissected in a lab.

The goons prided themselves on their efficiency and application. They knew every inch of their territory, every scent and signpost. They could scoot through with their eyes closed in the dead of night. Art was one of those fortunate creatures who loved what he did and made a good living out of it. He didn't cling to his bed covers every morning, groggy and unwilling to go to work. He was up and at 'em, looking forward to a day's searching and destroying. If combining your job with your hobby was truly the key to happiness, Art was in paradise. His hobby was tracking down and killing furry animals.

Walter was more sadistic. When he saw a mouse hole, he was hard-pressed to prevent himself from breaking into it. He would not satisfy himself with trapping and killing an escaped prisoner—he would toy with it first. Once it was too scared to move, he'd give it the chance to run away. It couldn't take it—too petrified. With a moment's pause, to allow realization to filter in, Walter would finish them off.

Art had never been impressed by his partner's antics. They were pals, so he didn't get in Walter's way when he played his cruel game.

Art hoped that his friend would come around eventually and realize that their prey had feelings, too. The sadist's actions were immature and unproductive. Art got his job done as quickly and professionally as possible, and it was he who had earned them their reputations as stone-cold ferrets.

Today's search would be easy, especially after their long period of rest. Usually, they hunted mice, diminutive and difficult to find, so timorous that they'd find a hiding place and stick to it until they were unearthed. Their latest target was a smelly old cat, already worn out and wounded. There were only so many places for him to hide, and lazy guards used most of those as pissoirs. A sentry with a full bladder would be as likely to smoke Tiger out as the goons. Once he was in the open, he'd be easy meat.

Walter was particularly looking forward to catching the cat, an animal that he was seldom lucky enough to fight. There was more to tear into, more intelligence and fear in the eyes. Walter's game would last longer that day.

***

Grant squeezed past dirt walls and groaning supports, scurrying toward the end of the tunnel. He used his paws to dig upward, frightened yet excited, hoping that he didn't pop up in front of a sentry. It would take some time to gouge the hard earth away, and there was always the possibility that the tunnelers' calculations had been wrong—he could end up on the wrong side of the fence, still in the compound. Then, Tiger's diversion would be for naught, and they'd all end up in the labs.

Grant missed his wife and fifteen children. When last he'd seen them, they'd been pink and new, sniffing sleepily, infinitely curious. He'd been working on commission, cold calling potential customers. It wasn't easy; not many mice feel the need for double-glazing. But the thought of his hungry family had driven him on. So many small mouths to feed. He'd worked hard until the day when he'd found an enticing piece of cheese on a side street. It had been a large, bright yellow slab. His mother had always warned him not to eat strange food off the sidewalk, but here he'd made an exception. It had been a trap, of course. As he clamped his teeth onto the cheese, a taut metal spring had unleashed the snare.

Next thing he knew, he was being ordered around by Monty, organizing a tunnel out of the compound.

Grant wondered how his family was coping without him. They thought he was dead, without a doubt; he'd been gone too long. Perhaps his wife had remarried or taken a job. She'd always wanted to work, but he'd never let her. The babies would suffer. The earth overhead felt softer, damper. He was nearly there. He was showered in soil and a dim light hurt his eyes. He popped a paw, then his head, from the tunnel, ready to duck under cover at a second's notice. No guards, no sirens. He was out of the compound. The smart thing to do would have been to make a break there and then, return to his family, and get back to his job. Grant had never been the smartest jacket on the rack. He couldn't leave his friends behind. Nipping back down into the burrow he'd spent months digging, he hollered for Monty to come have a look.

The leader was busy seeing Tiger and Cole off. They'd worked out a schedule for their plan—all actions would have to be well-timed to ensure everything went smoothly. By the time the moon had descended so that its circumference met the top of the fence, Tiger and Cole would be in position and ready to start their distraction. Monty and some of the lads would be on the roof, awaiting a signal. They'd volunteered to act as decoys while most of the mice scampered through the tunnel.

"Go! Take care!" he said to the departing cat.

"This isn't my idea of taking care," Tiger retorted. "Making a nuisance of myself. At least the commandant will be in too much pain to care about us." He sidled out into the stark shadows of the complex, relying on his keen eyesight to navigate. Cole, still groggy, followed behind him.

Tiger usually used his whiskers to detect air currents, enabling him to wander around in the dark without bumping into anything. Now he found it hard going; it was as if he'd lost an essential sense. He headed for the large gray warehouse, crouching for cover whenever a guard passed by, his ears flattening on top of his head. It was taking too long; the pale moon was plummeting behind him. Monty would be climbing onto the roof of his building by now, and if Tiger wasn't ready in time, the mice would be spotted. Images of what he'd seen in the laboratory troubled him once more. He had to get a shift on, risk being seen, get inside the warehouse.

No one challenged him as he passed the ENTRY FORBIDDEN sign and entered the depot. The barrels he'd glimpsed before were piled high—there were enough dangerous chemicals stacked up to choke every mouse in the city. Tiger took some of Callum's powder from the pouch he'd been given, sprinkled it in a circle around the barrels, and trailed it toward the exit. Still no guards—the chemicals were too toxic for anyone to stick close for long periods of time. He lit a cigarette, taking a quick drag. It eased the pain in his jowls. The commandant spoiled his reverie.

"Shouldn't have lit that thing," said the leather-clad Khmer through gritted teeth.

"So my doctor tells me."

"I might not have spotted you here, in the dark."

Tiger's fur stood on end, buffing him up for a fight. Cole stayed in the shadows, unseen.

"No entourage this time, Commandant?" Tiger asked.

"I don't need them to finish you. Besides, you've got them running around like headless hens looking for you and your friends. I didn't think you'd turn up so close to my quarters."

"Cheek's my middle name." Tiger took another suck on his Gauloise. "Speaking of cheeks, how's your rear?"

"You took my tail. I took your whiskers. An exchange of sorts, if not a fair one."

Thank Bastet for some action at last. Slim Rick had been on sentry duty for five nights on the trot, pulling the most boring detail in the compound. Although the camp was vast, he managed to make several circuits in a shift. His only consolation was his standard-issue flashlight, which he would waggle at anything he felt like. Although his eyesight was as good as any other cat's, the light penetrated the deepest of shadows. It made strange patterns as he flicked it against the fence. He would point it upward, watching the light dissipate amongst the clouds. Sometimes the shadows would play tricks on him. He would see phantom mice crawl along the fence, just beyond the harsh beam of the flashlight. They weren't real. All prisoners were locked up tight.

Slim made sure he knew as little as possible about what went on in the labs. He didn't want to know; he received food and lodging, he was up for promotion and that was enough to keep him content. The escape attempt that day had been on someone else's shift, so his job was secure. However, he stayed more alert than usual; the whole camp was on tenterhooks.

They hadn't expected anyone to be able to break into the installation. This was the first time that cats had caused them any trouble—most citizens minded their own business and weren't aware of the goings-on at the IE Institute. Slim was secretly pleased by the day's events. If any more mice tried to flee, he hoped that it would happen during his patrol. It would relieve the tedium of guard duty, and he would catch the offenders. That would get him promoted for sure.

Someone rattled the gate and Slim approached it cautiously. More troublemakers? A cat on the other side of the fence was shivering in the cold, his hind paws white with frost. He was dressed in a guard's uniform, so Slim unbolted the gate and bade him enter.

"Been hunting the escaped prisoners," the guard gasped. "Caught something much more interesting." Slim tensed as a big black cat was dragged through the gate, five guards pinning him down, staying well clear of his ragged teeth. All thoughts of bravery or promotion left Slim's lonely mind. Callum smelled of death.

"I think you're sick," Tiger scowled. "You've gotta be. Otherwise, you wouldn't be able to mess with these mice. It's amoral."

"Please!" To the detective's surprise, the Khmer burst out laughing. "Mice aren't important. They're fodder when clean, vermin when dirty, statistics at best. Morality doesn't come into it. You throw a pebble into a lake—do you care what happens to it? The ripples on the water are more important than that pebble. It's matter that doesn't matter. Dumb and senseless. We're doing good work here, watching the ripples. Learning."

"You're right," Tiger lied. "You're not such a bad cat. Leather suits you, y'know."

"I know," said the Khmer proudly. Tiger brushed past him, forepaws raised in surrender. Once he was clear of the warehouse, he flicked his dog end toward the barrels.

"Cole, run!" Tiger yowled. The commandant spun around, pricking his ears at a fizzling sound. Callum's powder was aspark, crackling toward the barrels. The Khmer went to have a closer sniff; Tiger ran in the opposite direction, ready to dive for cover once he'd put some distance between himself and the—

The commandant heard a hiss, as if the chemicals in the barrels were bubbling, and the sound of compressed air, containers struggling to hold it.

"Here, kitty, kitty!" Cole pounced on the Khmer, dragging him back into the depot. The Khmer pinned his ears back and snarled, a last expression of defiance before both cats were caught in a terrible explosion.

Tiger was thrown into the air by the force of the blast. He landed on all fours and rolled onto his back, watching an amber mushroom cloud rise into the sky. An unearthly smell reached his nostrils; he tried to hold his breath. The chemicals he'd unleashed made him choke, his eyes stream. He wanted to lick his fur clean.

The mice received their signal, almost knocked from their perch by the explosion. Monty let out a war cry, leaping from his perch with forelimbs outstretched. The others watched to see if he flew or fell— and cheered as he glided toward the fence. They didn't give themselves the chance to get scared, flinging themselves after their fearless leader.

Grant heard the barrels crack open even though he was deep underground. He led a second group of mice through the winding burrow, telling them to move slowly, breathe easily. It didn't take long to reach the exit. Once again, he peeked out into the open. Attention seemed to be centered on the gate fifty yards away, where Callum was using the explosion as an excuse to attack his startled captors. With a happy squeak, Grant left the hole and disappeared into the undergrowth. His group followed, glancing from side to side, ready for trouble. Nothing stopped them from following him to safety.

A guard held onto each of Callum's legs, another scratching at his tail. He'd had enough. He had caused enough chaos to give Tiger time to find out exactly what went on at the venerable Institute. The guards did a double take as the warehouse erupted, so he hefted a paw onto the nearest cat's head. Injecting his claws into the skull, he made the cat let go of him and fall to the ground with a howl. Slim raced toward the warehouse, ignoring the fluttering sounds above him.

The captors decided that it was better to knock Callum off than continue their tiring struggle. The frost-pawed guard opened his jaws wide and slavered over the caracal's throat.

Shuggie had been correct: the mice weren't aerodynamically sound enough to glide over the fence. Monty flew too low to pass it; in fact, he was approaching the wire at an alarming rate. Behind him a mouse shrieked, thrilled to be dozens of feet in the air, buoyed by a winter flurry. Monty looked down, watching the guards attack Callum. There was no such thing as a good cat as far as the mouse was concerned, not after the things he'd seen. Callum had his own motives for helping the prisoners, but he had put his life in peril on their behalf. Monty circled the melee, then swooped down toward the cat at Callum's throat. He landed on the guard's back, surprising him. The caracal broke free.

The guard spun round, twisting his head to nip at the mouse. The other cats looked up as a flock of mice sailed through the open gate. Callum joined them, barging past the security staff. Monty was thrown to the ground and stamped to a pulp, his cap in ribbons; his killers bolted the gate and collapsed, knocked senseless by the chemicals that now clouded the air.

Everyone was too busy worrying about the big bang to bother Tiger. He made it to the gate with his hide intact. The guards lay on their sides, unconscious. There wasn't much left of Monty. Tiger mumbled a quick prayer for the mouse and blundered back to the sleeping quarters. Stringy tendrils of cheese hung from the guttering, brushing against his face.

Inside, the bunk beds had been shifted with no attempt to disguise the tunnel mouth. Tiger made for the escape route, squeezing his way down the hole. Although it had been built for mice, there was enough room for him to wriggle through ·if he held his tummy in and stretched himself lengthways. The tunnel threatened to collapse behind him—every movement put a strain on the supports.

The air above was thick with toxic gas by now. Art and Walter were relieved to find the tunnel—it provided some cover, and it meant their search had ended. Diving into the darkness, they used their noses and whiskers to navigate the treacherous burrow. It was a tight fit for them and the tunnel mouth closed behind them. They could only move forward.

Tiger heard the digging behind him and knew that he was being followed. The pursuers were making a lot of noise, too clumsy to be mice. As far as he knew, Monty had successfully evacuated his lads. Tiger tried to speed up, breathing heavily. If some of the chemicals had reached the tunnel, he could suffocate where he lay.

He jolted as Walter bit his tail. Kicking the goon with a swipe of his hind paw, Tiger moved on. There was no light ahead, only the sound of trickling earth. The roof would give out at any time. The goons were blooded now. They would dig their way through the tunnel, chewing through the cat to get out if necessary.

There was no room for their quarry to turn and fight; he didn't stand a chance.

Tiger stopped moving, flattened himself into the cold soil, and listened closely. A shower of dirt and stone sounded up ahead. The roof was caving in. A support cracked; the earth came tumbling down in front of his nose. He was cornered.

He shoved his aching face forward, using his nose and forepaws to make a path. The soil was loose enough for him to push on, but his pace had slowed so much that the ferrets caught up, nipping at his pads. In a frenzy, Art and Walter muscled toward him, trying to climb through the tunnel side by side. Another support gave way, burying them together.

Unable to breathe, Tiger smashed his way through the burrow, dragging himself out into the open. He took a deep breath and promptly coughed it out again, spitting a metallic taste from his mouth. The chemical cloud was rising, but he wasn't clear of it yet. Holding a paw over his mouth and nose, he stumbled toward the train station. To his surprise, Callum was waiting there with the steam train, which had returned to pick up any stragglers. With the remaining mice already on board, Callum helped the detective into a carriage and the train whistled on its way.

32

"Now do you understand?"

"I think I can see where you're coming from." Tiger stood in the gym, disheveled and whiskerless, slouching with fatigue. Callum was slightly ruffled, while Musculus looked impeccable as ever, flanked by robed bodyguards. He invited the cats to sit down, with bowls of water close by to quench their thirst and platefuls of fish to replenish their strength. Callum tucked into his portion; Tiger abstained.

"Good." Musculus nodded. "Shall I tell you what isn't so good? That wasn't the only facility around here, you know. Last year, 457,292 mice were experimented on. A few survived. Murdered so that household appliances, food additives, cosmetics, toiletries, and tobacco could pass the safety test."

"What are you hoping to achieve?"

"I lost my brother to lewisite. They shaved his back, rubbed the poison into his skin. He was in agony for a month. They gassed my sister and electrocuted me, leaving me for dead. I rose again, Mr. Straight, to avenge my family and set up a kitty killer cult."

"That doesn't give you the right to destroy my family, too. Let 'em go, please. I'll help you."

"They stay where they are now. I'd like to say they're being looked after; I'm afraid they're in terror for their lives. You understand my motives. I don't think you're going to agree with my methods."

"How do you get cats to do your dirty work? Rig secret bank accounts? Murder their own kind?" Tiger stalled for time, watching Connie appear from a shadowy hallway.

"They disagree with the research experiments almost as much as I do. I have the mental wherewithal to convince them that killing certain community members will help the cause."

"That young cat, Lona. How could her death help?" spat Tiger.

"She deserved it. Selling cigarettes and checking hats at the Blind Tiger squeakeasy without a care for the mice who suffered there."

"Her life was just starting!"

"Her murder was nothing but a test of loyalty for my underlings, Mr. Straight. I told them she had to be destroyed, and they believed me. Those members of the cult who have qualms about killing—your wife, for example—well, I help them along a little." Musculus held up a tiny capsule. "Marlax. A mixture containing *valeriana officianalis* and acetylsalicylic acid, among other things. A small dose drives cats wild, almost psychotic; an overdose is fatal. A surgeon named Selwyn Mopp helped develop it before he died. From too much shopping, I understand."

"You're gonna poison all the cats in this city? That's a toxic brew you've got in your paw." Tiger signaled to Connie with his ears, waggling them in the direction of the swimming pool.

"You should try some of the fish," Musculus sneered. "It's quite delicious. Isn't it, Callum?"

The caracal didn't reply. Shaking his body from side to side, his eyes bloodshot, he was having a rabid reaction to the fish.

"Don't look like the fish agreed with him," said Tiger.

"He'll meet a destructive, painful death." Musculus shook his head slowly. "Got to hurt."

"But he's so loyal!"

"Really? This greedy puss steals cream wherever he finds it. Not just any kind, either. Mice cream. How can I trust him?"

"Your chemicals are in the fish everyone's eating?" Tiger asked.

"Call it an experiment." Musculus twitched. "A marketing project to see how gullible your race is."

"I don't get it," Tiger scowled. "Nub will be a dead city."

"Select members of my organization will be spared. The *crème de la CREAM*. You can survive as well, Mr. Straight. Pledge an oath to me and I'll let you live... I'll let your babies live." A bell rope dangled beside the mouse. He batted it with a free paw.

"Your brethren have already had a few goes at me. Killed my partner. They didn't sink low enough to attack my kittens." Tiger spared a glance at Callum. He was hunkered down, biting so hard on his lower lip that blood was beginning to flow.

"I changed my mind," said Musculus. "Saw your true potential. It took a while, but I saw it. I had to order the death of your assistant, however. A show of strength."

"Join you? I might as well join the commandant, help him with his experiments, if I could tell the difference between you both."

Musculus pulled on the bell rope. In the distance, the kittens squealed. The mouse addressed his henchcat. "Get rid of him, Callum."

The caracal wasn't the sanest animal in the room at that point. Frenzied and hungry, Callum loped for the closest food source in the room, a small, succulent mouse. Caught by surprise, Musculus let out a squeak as Callum devoured him.

Tiger ran for the poolroom, desperate to save his kittens; Connie joined him. The mouse's guards jumped onto Callum, ready to avenge their boss. They soon changed their minds. The big cat threw them against the dining table, emitting a deep-throated yowl. The guards backed off fast, running from the room.

Sniffing the air, his mind fuzzy, Callum followed Tiger and Connie in the direction of the swimming pool.

The kitlings fell into the water, mewing in unison. Connie fell into a crouch at the poolside, scanning the water for signs of life. The cubs struggled beneath the surface. Overcoming her fear, she rolled into the deep water, stretching out her limbs to scoop up the little ones.

Tiger snatched at the net, using it to fish for the kittens. They were getting weaker, running out of breath. Connie splashed and choked, blinded. Tiger yelled directions to her, watching her tail quiver as she descended.

The ripples ceased; Tiger couldn't see. He'd already lost his wife, the kittens' mother—would he lose the rest of his family as well?

A paw yanked at the net, almost unbalancing the detective. He hoisted a tiny figure from the depths. Tiger got as close to the water as he could, claws out, trying to gain a solid purchase. He pulled Bello clear; Fliss was wrapped around her brother's tail. Tiger dipped his forepaws into the pool and helped Martin free. There was no sign of Connie. Making sure that the kittens were breathing, Tiger held his nose and flopped into the pool, eyes stinging as he searched for his friend. By the time he found her, her lungs were full of water.

Placing Connie on her side, Tiger washed her rapidly. A shadow loomed over them. Callum still had his claws unsheathed, mouth bloody. The kittens were too weak to run; their father was too busy trying to revive Connie to care if Callum attacked him.

Callum bent down and placed a hefty paw on Tiger's shoulder. "She's dead," he said gently.

Tiger didn't listen, sniffing at Connie's face, desperate for signs of life. A sobered Callum was relieved to find the father weeping for joy over the spluttering form of Connie Hant.

I must be on my ninth life.

Cole washed himself again, desperate to get himself clean, the faint taste of Marlax on his tongue. Not enough to drive him crazy, but enough to make him gag and spit hairballs. He was curled up under a bridge that spanned the train tracks near the IE camp—or what was left of the camp, now that Tiger and the mice had wrecked it. Cole had stumbled from the ruins along with a few guards and scientists lucky enough to escape the toxic gas; making sure to stay upwind of the chemical, Cole had hunkered down to recover. He still had all his whiskers and nothing more than a lump on his head from Callum's attack in the squeak-easy. As usual, he was fortunate.

For how long? How many more risks can I take?

He had a company to run and a cat to love. He would find Connie and offer to take care of her—although she would be the one taking care of him, really.

We'll take care of each other.

He would take care of the less fortunate, as well, whether they were cats, mice, or cows. They all deserved his consideration.

Who was he kidding? He was a cat, selfish and greedy. He would keep most of his wealth for himself. Most of it.

It took Cole hours to reach a farmhouse with a phone. From there, he called his office and arranged to be picked up. Back at the mansion, he learned that Tiger had solved the case of the cat who stole the cream. Connie and the kittens had survived their very own brush with death, and the threat to the wellbeing of Nub City was over.

Cole hoped the information he'd shared with Tiger had helped.

Despite the near-death experiences and the bad taste in his mouth, he wasn't quite ready to give up his hobby. He needed someone to watch his back, an assistant to defend him in perilous situations, and ask him questions. Someone trustworthy and guileless who would make him seem smart. A cat with first-paw experience of the legal system and the worst acts villains could commit. A cat who needed a job. Little Tim.

Cole wondered what their first case together would be.

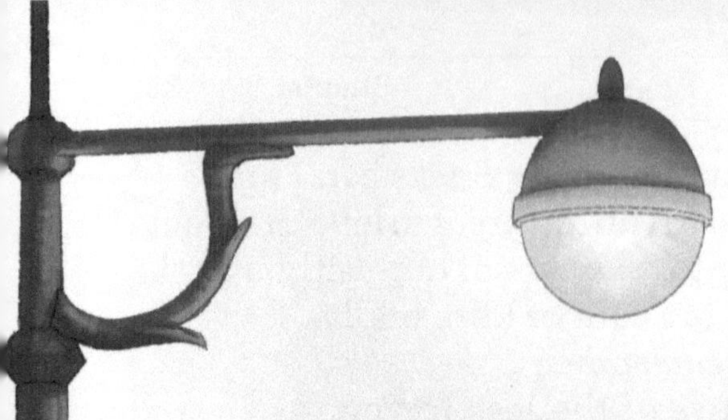

Epilogue

Soon after the case of the cat who stole the cream, Tiger retired to look after his kittens. He took small divorce or surveillance cases to supplement his welfare check, but stakeouts are tough with a pack of squealing weans in tow.

He loved to watch them grow, let them fend for themselves—yet he was always there for them. He'd amuse them with bedtime stories of old cases: battles with villains like Darius Gold, the serial kitten drowner, the Goat, or the serial tail puller of Serval Square, adventures with Bug, solving mysteries, and getting into scrapes.

Rain battered at the windows, begging to come into the house and smother him with damp drops. The panes rattled now and then, craving attention. No Bug to share a meal, no wife to hold him close. His kittens were his sole joy. Soon they'd be old enough to help with chores, if they didn't leave home in a quest for independence.

The house was colder without Jo. She'd kept him warm, held him close, her hot breath on his neck and lips. The bed was half full, the teapot half empty.

Nobody nagged him or wasted his time conjuring foolish chores to keep him busy. His spare time was flat and there was too much milk in the fridge. It went off, but Tiger still drank it. His tastebuds were numb and his stomach an unquenchable well.

The cubs would soon be old enough to visit their mother in prison, seek their misfortunes, and look for jobs and accommodation in Central Nub. He taught them as much as possible, using reverse psychology whenever he could. Preaching to them hadn't worked; he'd told them not to follow in his pawsteps and they'd already started playing detective. The other day he'd caught Bello looking for smugglers in the back garden. So he'd changed tack. Drink sour milk! Try smoking and eating vegetables! Take a dead-end job! They'd learn from their own mistakes instead of his. It would take a little longer, but they seemed to want it that way.

Occasionally, he'd hear a prowler whistle or a store alarm and grab his coat and hat. He didn't leave the house. He was getting too old, and worried that he'd get himself killed. He had aches and a buzzing in his ears. He felt slower, clumsier. Who would be around to welcome the cubs if he got his fool head knocked off? It was wiser to stay indoors. Read about crime in the papers. Give the authorities a few tips over the phone. That was all he needed to keep content for now.

Thanks to Bix, CREAM was disbanded and outlawed. The mouse had taken all the credit for exposing the conspiracy. He was now living with Nut in a coastal commune, where animals didn't judge each other according to their species. The effects of Musculus's marlax were mercifully short-lived; the Cambor fish were taken off the market and Gerry the mercat had to sell his red robes to make ends meet. The mice that Tiger had rescued from the research compound sold their story to a tabloid newspaper. With the money from their exclusive, they'd bought the camp and transformed it into a training center, teaching mice survival techniques with help from Callum and other ex-members of the cult, community service for their wrong-doings after pleading that they had been drugged by Musculus and were commensurately repentant. The center turned a tidy profit.

Chief Inspector Bowyer took early retirement, and no blame for the dastardly murders, despite eating a suspect. Miss Angold was now manager of the Nub City Municipal Bank—her predatory nature had proved highly useful in the financial world. Lincoln had survived a bloody concussion, but was out of work, joining the eternal bread lines of the Depression.

Little Tim had proved to be the perfect foil for Cole Tiddle, asking just the right obvious questions to get the amateur detective's deductive juices flowing. Together they had solved several baffling cases, keeping the streets cleaner than Public Works could ever manage.

Ike Straight wrote and published educational books.

Tiger had taken his sons and daughter to a business park in Stenmuir. He'd tried to explain to them that he'd married their mother there, that he missed her gravely. Martin, Fliss, and Bello were too busy playing around a fledgling willow tree.

As the rain withdrew its siege, Tiger drifted off to sleep. He dreamed of past glories on an underworld battlefield, his sidekick Bug looking up to him, waiting for him to save the day.

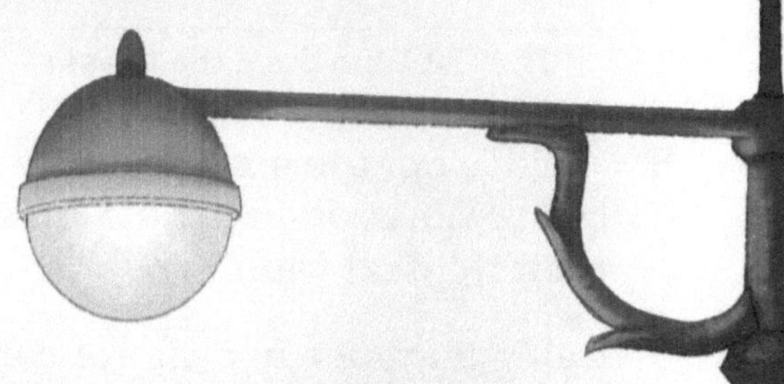

BOOK CLUB QUESTIONS

1. Bad kitty! How would you punish Lincoln the cat for causing an accident?

2. Is Cole right to play detective, or should he leave the sleuthing to the professionals?

3. Cats are instinctive mouse-catchers. What treat, if you couldn't have it anymore, would have you climbing the drapes?

4. Dr. Mopp loves to shop. What gift would you buy for a cat—or a cat-loving friend—to brighten their day and spend some silly money?

5. Cats are not fond of cucumbers. What do you think Scrumpy grew on his farm?

6. Cole Tiddle has unlimited funds and lives in a fancy mansion. If you were a millionaire moggy, where would you live?

7. Nut likes watching TV too. If you were a cow, what would be your favorite show?

8. Gold is not the most valuable commodity in Bug's bank. What do cats hold most dear, locked up in their tightest vault?

9. Being a mouse in a city of cats is no picnic. What is Bix Mortis's biggest concern, apart from potentially getting eaten?

10. Who is the cat who stole the cream?

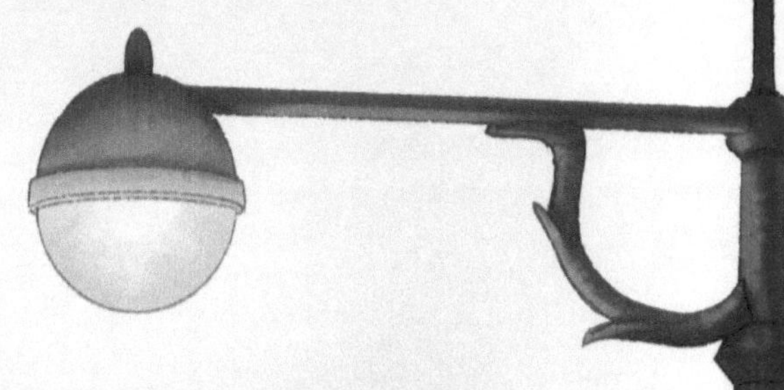

AUTHOR BIO

Nick Smith was born in Bristol, England. His books include *Eat Happy, The Secret Life of Teddy Bears, American Spirit,* and *Cloudwalking*. He is also a feature film director and producer, with 100 movies and TV credits, including the award-winning action movie *Cold Soldiers* and the supernatural adventure *Fears*, which he directed and co-wrote. He lives in New York, where he works as a film professor.

Other works by Nick Smith

Anthologies
Eat Happy
The Secret Life of Teddy Bears

Poetry
American Spirit
Cloudwalking
Songs for Persephone

Non-fiction
Fletcher Crossman: The Age of Endarkenment
Scriptwriting: The Secrets Unleashed

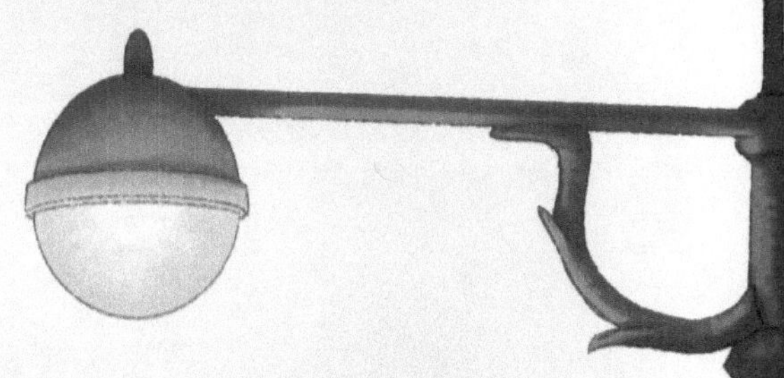

Discover more at
4HorsemenPublications.com

10% off using HORSEMEN10